Angel's Breath

by B. Michele

The contents of this work, including, but not limited to, the accuracy of events, people, and places depicted; opinions expressed; permission to use previously published materials included; and any advice given or actions advocated are solely the responsibility of the author, who assumes all liability for said work and indemnifies the publisher against any claims stemming from publication of the work.

All Rights Reserved
Copyright © 2024 by B. Michele

No part of this book may be reproduced or transmitted, downloaded, distributed, reverse engineered, or stored in or introduced into any information storage and retrieval system, in any form or by any means, including photocopying and recording, whether electronic or mechanical, now known or hereinafter invented without permission in writing from the publisher.

Dorrance Publishing Co
585 Alpha Drive
Suite 103
Pittsburgh, PA 15238
Visit our website at *www.dorrancebookstore.com*

ISBN: 979-8-8852-7180-6
eISBN: 979-8-8852-7636-8

Prologue

The fight for earth between Heaven and Hell heats up…two empires building. A seer prophesizes a female witch to be born in 1988 who will shift the powers towards good, giving Heaven the boost they need to win the battle for Earth. Thirty babies were born that year, three of them survived and where kept in hiding…only two were known. The prophecy changed once all of the surviving babies were hidden. It came to the seer after meditating for three days; a baby girl was given angels breath and survived. This was the one they needed to find. Not only was she a threat to evil, she held the key to the gates of Heaven. This would give Hell the advantage, allowing them an entrance into the heavens above.

Demons sought out help from the immortals, as did the Angels. The immortals split their allegiances. Vampires were sought out from the demons with promises of the Earth being ruled by vampires, and keeping humans as mere animals to be hunted, used, and fed upon. Not all vampires are bad and wanted this, so a war between vampires started. Many good vampires were killed, leaving a small group of hidden and endangered good vampires left. The witches were approached from Heaven; the witches pledged their love for the heavens and all the elemental powers of Earth. It was a given the witches would take on this great honor. Werewolves and shape shifters formed alliances with the witches, working with Angels for the protection of Earth and Heaven. The vampires who had lost their way aligned themselves with demons of all sorts.

The search for the baby starts… a plan is in place… a key is hidden and, through the tears of love from heaven, an angel's wings will be revealed.

1

At the end of a precious life, a frantic, blood gurgling scream ripped throughout the entire mansion. The stuttering sounds of a defeated young women pleading for her life echoed the stone lit halls.

"You ask me to spare your life, witch? And how is it that you could be of use to me?" Cyrus' evil voice filled her ears, but before the she could answer, she was silenced by the slice of a blade disconnecting her head from her body, making it the last voice she would ever hear as she once was on Earth. All was silent for a brief moment, which seemed to stop time, as the witch's body slowly fell to the floor like a single feather falling from the sky, disrupted by the thud of her body hitting the floor. Once again, she made the halls echo.

Caleb was outside the door with Ali and Jamahl, waiting for further instructions. They could hear everything going on inside of the room, and they listened in so they could get an idea of what they were in for. After they heard what they knew was a body hitting the floor, their father began to speak again.

"I need for you guys to leave right away and check out the first witch," Cyrus said loudly.

The door to the seer's room suddenly opened and out walked Aidan, Aiah, and Rory. "You're up, ladies." Aidan said with an evil grin as Aiah and Rory started to snicker, but before any of them could comment back, the halls of the mansion echoed once again with Cyrus blaring impatiently for them to enter.

The mansion looked more like a castle, damp and dark, lit by dim lights which aligned the long hallways and stairwells that fled through the mansion like veins. On the top floor of the dark castle was a large room blocked off by a heavy metal door. The walls were lined in shades of black stone, like something out of the middle ages. There was only one window, painted with dark colors that shed out the light in the daytime, but illuminated the intricate patterns in the moonlight. The room had one single bed, a large desk fit for a king, and two dark wooden chairs and was lit only by numerous candles. Along the wall behind the desk was a book shelf which took up the whole wall filled with olden text from a time where more was known about the supernatural. The room belonged to an ancient telepath they called the Seer. He was the only one left on Earth, and indebted to Cyrus, an ancient vampire who saw his opportunity for power and leadership by siding with the demons. In return he was granted enhanced powers, making him Head Vampire for those who had fallen.

Cyrus was now very powerful, he had been turned into a vampire over a thousand years ago. He was born an immortal; his father was a warlock and his mother was human. Once he had been bitten by a vampire, he still had the powers of a warlock, though he could not enter into the sunlight as his soul faded from his heart.

Caleb, Jamahl, and Ali entered the room on command. The head of the witch had rolled far away from its body. They all quietly stared at it for a brief moment, each fighting the bloodlust as they all felt a quiet, unexplained sadness for the deceased witch.

"Caleb, quit staring, grab the witches head, and bring it over here now!" Cyrus commanded.

Caleb strolled over to the head and gently picked it up. He saw the fear in the witch's face, though her soul was no longer connected to her body. He acted as if he was about to toss it across the room like a football to his father when Cyrus snapped at him.

"Enough Caleb, when will you learn to take this seriously, my son!" It was more of a statement than a question, but without any more hesitation, Caleb brought it over to his father, who grabbed the head with both hands and held it in front of the seer.

"What do you see?" He curiously asked the seer.

The seer pushed his thumbs into the eyes of the dead witch and soaked the tips of his talon like fingertips into the frontal lobe of her brain. "Hmmm…

" he groaned as he looked around for information. "Ahhh, yes that's it, the second girl she's still alive and beginning to come into her full powers…I can feel the location of the last one now…" He paused, taking his time to read through the information left over in her mind before the memory imprint faded.

"This is the oldest, she is being raised by a shape shifter and her birth father…I see green, lots of water, but it's beginning to snow… Ahhh, I can smell the air now…wet rain bringing in new life…Midwest, yes, somewhere in the Midwest." Seer held a few moments longer before talking again. "No, it's fading…I cannot see what is next…" He suddenly pulled his hands away from the head and grabbed his right wrist as if he had just broken it, his mouth twisted from the pain.

"Get me some water, now!" Cyrus yelled. Just like that, both Ali and Jamahl had water waiting for the seer. Caleb just stood off to the side with a smirk on his face; he always found the antics of the seer a bit dramatic, and took pleasure in the amusement of it all.

"Caleb…" The seer pointed to him and paused briefly, taking in a few deep breaths before beginning again. "Caleb, you will find her…this I saw."

Before Caleb could roll his eyes and make a smart-ass comment back to the seer, his father interrupted, "How will Caleb find her?"

After a few deep breaths, the seer slowly spoke. "Through the blessed tears of Heaven he will find his Angel as she whispers her wings will be revealed." The seer took another sip of water.

"So I am supposed to find some sort of angel witch and you guys are putting this all on me with nothing but a clue? Oh that's fair." Caleb said dispassionately.

"Caleb, I wasn't just referring to the riddle, I was referring to a thought I saw you have inside your head."

"I don't understand. If I am supposed to find her, then why are you sending Aidan out for the other girl?" Caleb said, hating to have to do any job alongside Aidan, even if countries separated them.

"Caleb, it's all about the timing, these questions won't help you. The seer senses the future, but the future can change at any moment. What I do know is that I need that girl! The seer didn't say you would find the right one, just that you would be able to find the other witch," Cyrus snapped.

"Yeah, that makes even more sense," Caleb said as he rolled his eyes.

"Caleb, trust your instincts," the seer said, sounding weaker now.

Caleb just thought he looked even more crazy than usual and started to roll his eyes again when all of a sudden he felt a sharp sting through his heart as the seer pointed at him. Angered, he snapped at the seer. "What the fuck are you talking about? You are crazy, old man!"

Startled by his son's reaction, Cyrus studied Caleb's face for a moment and said, "What is it, Caleb?"

Looking away from his father, not wanting anyone to know he felt a pain deep in his heart, not having ever known of pain, replied, "Nothing, I just wish Seer could spit what the fuck he was seeing out. I'm tired of his fucking puzzle pieces and poetry bullshit!"

After studying Caleb a bit further, Cyrus replied, "Caleb, the seer has great power and we need to have patience and respect for him. So, show some. That's not a request, Caleb, it's an order!"

Caleb looked at the seer a bit longer before carefully choosing his words. "So how am I supposed to find this girl, and what the hell are the Blessed Tears of Heaven?"

The seer looked right into Caleb's eyes. "We are still trying to figure that out. All we have so far is an ancient passage from this happening thousands of years before even our time, when an angel gave life force to a human who recorded what he remembered before his life was finally taken. The passage roughly translates: 'Whispered through the blessed tears from heaven's spirit, an angel's wings will be revealed. From a single corner, as the light shines truth from within, a mark will take its place. Upon death, the angel will resurface.'...but Caleb you must be careful. There seems to be something about her that you are drawn to, and I can't see what it is or why. But what I do know, Caleb, is that she could destroy you as you are."

No one spoke for what seemed like a few moments. Ali wanted to get Caleb off the hook. He, Caleb, and Jamahl were raised as brothers and he didn't like the look on Caleb's face, so he interrupted, "Ok well how do we find where in the Midwest?"

Jamahl was also angry Caleb had been aggravated. "We only have one of the locations from the witch, why did you kill her before knowing the second? What if she is the one?" He added

Cyrus moved directly in front of Jamahl with the quickness of lightning. He narrowed his eyes and spoke through his teeth. "Because, Jamahl, the witch's powers were no longer bound. Her power was too strong. She was one of the Seven Points of Light Council members, and we had only one single moment before she broke free because her blood kept regenerating with a quickness I hadn't expected. It's almost as if she had a protection spell of some sort. So you see, Jamahl, had that happened, they would have realized we were on to the information upon her escape and then we would be screwed. Or maybe you want that, Jamahl. To live under the radar while our food walks the Earth freely, making it us who has to hide and live with rules protecting them when it is us who are higher on the food chain! We are the lions, they are the lambs; yet, they are ruling our jungle. Make no mistakes about it, my son, I HAD NO CHOICE! Do not question my judgment again." Just like that, he was back at the side of the seer, putting an arm on his right, sunken shoulder. "Besides, the seer has another way now, don't you seer!"

The seer, still looking at Caleb, shook his head in agreement, but added, "Although I now have a better way." All of a sudden all eyes were on Caleb.

"Why are you looking at me?" Caleb said hesitantly.

"I saw that it was you who would find her, but not just that, you will be drawn to her. All we need to do is cast a polarizing spell that will pull you towards her. Jamahl and Ali can perform the spell as you concentrate and listen to where your heart pulls you. Warning of caution, Caleb. You already have a natural pull towards her, you must be careful around her. Do not let her sway you or you will be ruined."

Caleb couldn't help but be amused at the thought of anyone being capable of destroying him, except for his father who was granted enhanced powers from the demons as payment for being leader of the fallen immortals. Cyrus was currently leading vampires, dark wizards and warlocks, and any other creature which had fallen to the dark.

"Not worried, so let's do this so I can get it over with…this is really going to put a cramp in my social life, you know!" Caleb added with a smile. His brothers started to smirk, trying to hold back their laughs with not much luck.

"Caleb!" Cyrus snapped. He composed himself momentarily. "Son…take this seriously, please. Go clear your head and meet us back here in 30 minutes, we will be ready by then." His father said, looking at the seer for confirmation more time was not needed in order to perform the polarizing spell.

"Whatever," Caleb said, shrugging his shoulders. He then turned around to walk out the door, following the vein like hallways of the dark mansion to the front door, which then unleashed him into the night for a quick bite to eat.

With Caleb gone, the seer got out a diamond globe, something worth so much money, it could buy a small country, and a spell book which smelled of must, as the once white pages had aged to yellow and opened to the page containing the polarizing spell. Jamahl, Ali, and Caleb were all half vampire, half witches, born to witch mothers from vampire fathers, and the only known living besides the one girl Cyrus was unable to obtain. The mixing of the species was seldom ever heard of, and frowned upon by both good and bad for the fear of the amount of power these mixed species had. These three sons of Cyrus' were not blood brothers; however, Cyrus raised each of these as his own, though they never knew the truth behind why he became their father. They never had reason to question it, he was their father, and that was that.

Being raised by a powerful vampire with special powers only gave them some guidance with coming into their witch powers, but they still lacked the knowledge because they had no witches around to teach them. Cyrus still was in touch with his Warlock side, but Warlocks' didn't have as many powers as witches did. Witches' powers were centered from within. They could orb from place-to-place, they could make things happen by manipulating the elements, and could also talk to one another telepathically if they were near each other or closely connected. They also are able to perform spells, which is something they picked up in the middle ages from wizards.

Wizards could only use spells. They only had the power to make spells happen with potions and concoctions, but they could not make the elements move from within, and they had to have a conductor for the potions to work, which is why a wand is associated with wizards. They can't orb, nor can Warlocks.

Warlocks were from a darker place than witches. They cannot orb, but they can move the energy force from within. They tried to make potions and spells work, but they weren't granted that kind of power. Because all they could do was use the energy within, they became very good at channeling that energy and perfecting it's use as a weapon. They were very quick, because that is all they had, and they focused on it generation after generation. Warlocks could not manipulate the elements, however. This was why they often felt inferior to witches, and many hated them for it. They could, however, communicate telepathically to each other in a coven. It was once said a warlock was a witch whose powers were defective, and over time, after the breeding of defective witches took place, the warlock was officially a species. Much like the vampires, the warlocks and wizards were torn between good and bad. Those who sided with the darkness looked to Cyrus for leadership, which only made him that much more powerful. Those who sided with the light stood behind the Council of Light.

Because Caleb, Jamahl, and Ali were the only one's born into both witch blood and vampire blood, it gave them more freedom because they could walk in the daylight, as well as utilize magic on all levels, but they were alone, with no one to guide them except for Cyrus. For most big spells, they needed Cyrus and the seer for direction, having never had any training, with exception of Caleb. He was the only one out of the boys who seemed to have a knack for it. He also could tap into his energy faster, using the elements to make things happen quicker. His birth mother had been one of the most powerful witches ever known, and she died shortly after his birth. Her strength is what bled through Caleb, making his powers stronger, while giving him the ability to use it naturally.

It would take some work, Cyrus knew that, but he couldn't make spells and potions work, which was one of the reasons he needed the powers that Caleb, Jamahl, and Ali possessed. Caleb was the natural choice to perform the spell, since it was him who the seer said would be drawn to her. Cyrus needed this witch. With her having the energy force of an Angel, it gave her limitless powers, as well as the right to enter in and out of the heavens freely. If he could use her powers for himself, he would be unstoppable. Technically he should kill her to prevent the powers shifting towards good on Earth, but he felt he had a way to stop the prophecy while gaining even more power. Cyrus was power hungry. He was on top and intended on staying there, no matter what the cost. If others found out this information, then they would surely be after her for the same reasons, so he kept this quiet. Only the seer, Caleb, Jamahl, Ali, Aiah, Rory, Aidan, and himself alongside of the dead witch. They were all who knew what he was up to, and Cyrus intended on keeping it that way.

It had been 21 years since the prophecy showed back up again. When they first killed all baby witches after the seer's vision, the prophecy changed; something was added. At first it was a baby girl witch would be born during a certain year which would shift the powers towards good on Earth, giving the side of light an advantage. But when it surfaced again, twenty-one years later, a piece was added, she would now possess the life force of an Angel, which would give her unimaginable powers. At some point during the witch killings, an Angel had spared one of the babies by giving the baby her own life force to borrow so she could live. By doing so, the witch would be able to make things happen which defied the laws of nature, and Cyrus had just the plan for her.

2

The night was a perfect 72 degrees, with a clear night sky which allowed the stars to shine bright. Being a half-breed required Caleb to eat like a human during the day, but a vampire at night. He needed to keep the fuel balanced in his system; fuel for each side of him.

As he walked around the corner into a darkened parking lot, he spotted a tall young blonde in a short skirt fumbling with her purse in front of a yellow mustang as the broken street light flickered above. He waited briefly, deciding on whether he would kill her or just drain her a bit for a light meal. A part of his predatory side always debated on a kill, but as usual, it was more appealing to drain someone rather than kill them. Besides that, the pain in his heart the seer inflicted was still there, causing a curb in his violent thought.

"Are you having trouble getting into your car?" Caleb's dark, sexy voice asked the young blonde.

She looked up from her purse, immediately stunned from the beauty of Caleb. He was tanned, unlike a real vampire, with medium brown hair woven with some lighter brown streaks, which Caleb considered a gift from the sun. His eyes were the color of a Caribbean sea on a dark stormy day, with an exotic, almond shape. The perfectness of both his body and his face made her knees weak, and the fullness of his lips made her step closer to him.

"I'm just l-looking for my keys. I just can't see to…" she said, stumbling over her words as she continued to search her pocketbook for her keys with her hands.

Caleb stepped closer. Every ounce of her body told her to flee.

Slowly, he walked forward, staring at her as his eyes burned into hers, which put her in a slightly tranced state. He stopped directly in front of her, still focusing on her eyes. She couldn't move. Suddenly, with the speed of light, she was in his arms and completely at his mercy as he moved with quickness unseen to take hold of her. She tilted her head back freely, as if she were offering him what she knew he came for, but she was hoping he would take more. Humans were powerless against the mind control of vampires. Like a spider's venom temporarily paralyzing it's pray. Caleb put one hand on the small of her back and pulled her hair with the other, the girl let out a groan before he even touched her. He was aroused, and then without wasting any more time, Caleb sunk his teeth immediately into the pulsating vein on her bare neck.

The young woman moaned softly, as if she had never felt pleasure this intense before. If a vampire had never bitten her before, then she would be right. Every hair on her body stood up and her skin was flooded with goose bumps. She wanted him to go further, to take her right there and have his way with her, even if it meant killing her at the end. That wasn't even part of the hypnosis; she wanted him right there; a one night stand as the venom of a vampire caused intense pleasure for their victim. Caleb was controlled, however. Not that he thought it wouldn't be a good time using her for his pleasure, but the pain in his heart was still nagging at him. As if he just took a few sips from his juice box and set it down on the counter top, never to be finished, he was full enough and set her down.

He left her partially drained, with her memory erased of the incident. Having to then erase the physical evidence, he bent over and gently waved over her neck once, using his powers from within, and her bite disappeared. Still sitting up against her car, it looked as if she had drank one to many shots of whiskey, purse in one hand and keys in the other. Caleb smirked at the sight of her while he wiped the corner of his mouth with the back of his hand.

Just as he started having some second thoughts about letting her off the hook, as the blood flew through his veins like a power surge, he finished wiping his mouth and his watch caught his attention. He realized thirty minutes had passed and he was due back home. He strolled out of the parking lot, not caring if anyone had witnessed him, then he blended into the busy streets of L.A., back to his motorcycle.

Caleb had no real need for a moving vehicle, he had his own means of transportation. Transportation given to him by a bloodline which included extreme speed and ability to teleport as well as to fly. But Caleb loved motorcycles and cars. They were nothing more than mere toys to him, despite his father constantly getting on him for not making more use out of those powers. Caleb did whatever Caleb wanted, and Caleb wanted to ride his motorcycle fast and pick up a quick bite to eat, and so he did.

The veiny halls of the mansion were quiet this time as Caleb made his way back through them and up to the seer's room. He could smell the burning of the candles and caught the scent of some other smells which were unfamiliar. He knew it was from the potion concoctions and it was ready. It was time to perform the spell, find the girl, and get back to his normal life. A life of surfing, money, endless days and nights, feeding, partying, and fast vehicles and women, just to name of few.

He approached the door, but before he could open the door, he heard his father invite him in. "Caleb, it's ready."

"Glad to see the four of you are still useful!" Caleb joked, making both Jamahl and Ali chuckle as he made his way through the door.

His father and the seer didn't share in the humor. Caleb, with a half-cocked smile on his face, shook his head.

"Fine then, whatever. I'm ready," reluctantly Caleb obeyed.

"Alright, stand over here by the globe," Cyrus said, holding one of the Dowsing Rods in his hand. "Take this metal rod in your right hand and place the other hand on the globe," he added.

Caleb stepped over to the diamond globe. The globe was the size of a regular classroom globe, only it was made entirely out of diamonds. Ali and Jamahl were looking over a spell written on a piece of paper, each holding cups that had mist seductively seeping out of the tops.

Ali's cup had a dark green mist coming from his cup, making his olive skin seem even richer. Ali was of Middle Eastern descent. He was the same height as Caleb, a perfect 6 foot, with black almond shaped eyes, and a thick head of black wavy hair. Ali was so handsome, people often referred to him as being beautiful, yet there was nothing feminine about him.

Jamahl had a silver colored mist coming out of his cup. It looked like chrome dust seeping slowly up from the cup. Against his silky black skin, it crept up hypnotically looking as if the mist was trying to be as graceful and strong as he was. Unlike his brothers, Jamahl was four impressive inches taller, with every muscle in his body precisely defined. He wore his hair shaved bald to the scalp, which revealed his perfectly shaped head. His smile was just as perfect and his teeth sparkled a brilliant white. His eyes were a rich hazel color, making him look even more exotic than the depth of his skin.

"Bring the potions over here, sons!" Cyrus ordered.

Ali picked the piece of paper up with his free hand and headed towards Caleb as Jamahl followed.

"Form a triangle using Caleb as the top point," the seer started directing. As they formed a triangle around the globe, Caleb stood in front of it with his left hand placed over the midwestern part of the United States while he held onto the metal rod with his right hand.

"Ready," Caleb confirmed.

"It is important for you, Caleb, to concentrate on your heart and let it pull you in. You must filter everything else, trying to float into your head. This is the only thing you need to do. This is important Caleb; do not make this a joke," the seer said.

"I got it!" Caleb snapped again, feeling annoyed.

"Alright then, my sons, you may begin the spell!" Cyrus said, with his hands in the air as if he alone could move heaven and earth.

Ali began to chant under his breath. It was too quiet for Caleb to understand what it was he was saying. After a few minutes, he stopped to take a sip of the dark green mist. Then, as Ali started to sip the dark green mist, Jamahl began chanting under his breath in an even lower tone. Ali finished the last of the mist and slowly moved the cup away from his mouth. Caleb noticed Ali looked like a statue, not even a hint of movement was made as the green mist encompassed his body.

As soon as Jamahl stopped chanting, he followed Ali's lead and took the chrome mist into his mouth. He too became like stone as the chrome mist made its way through out his body. The two sat there like statues for a few minutes as the potions entered their veins and took over their bodies.

All of a sudden, their eyelids popped wide open. Noticeably, the mysterious mist had taken over. Ali's eyes looked like jewels; like dark green emeralds. Jamahl's eyes had turned the color of chrome that shined like metal. They began speaking in unison this time. It was another low chant, only this time their voices were not their own. The chanting started to sound like a couple of snakes hissing slowly as the words seeped out. Ali's lips released a slow, dark green mist which crept as he spoke his words. At the same time chrome mist was creeping from Jamahl. The mist seemed to be controlled by the words being spoken, each color staying within its own free form, yet intertwining like two snakes slithering around each other.

Eerily, the green mist started to slowly wrap itself around the chrome mist. Thickening like a heavy fog, the misty serpents inched their way methodically dancing towards Caleb. Once the fog came to the foot of the globe, they split off from their entangled slow dance forming one arm each, followed by a hand that had eyes of a snake. The two hands searched around the globe as if they were reading brail.

As they got closer to Caleb, the hands turned back into snakeheads as the eyes remained. They slithered around Caleb, lowly hissing as if they were reading him. But Caleb stayed steady, unable at this point to see what was going on because his eyes were closed. Caleb remained concentrated, but he could feel them wrapping around and taunting him as his heartbeat began to quicken. He stood over the globe breathing easy, fully concentrating on where he was being drawn as he held out the rod. The green snake stood over his right shoulder, looking at the globe. The chrome snake was over his left, also staring back at the globe. Each snake started to grow an arm with the same hand that surrounded the globe just minutes before.

The snakes arms slinked down each of Caleb's arms, wrapping around them. As the snakes hands made their way for Caleb's hands, the chanting grew faster and even more erratic. He couldn't be quite sure, but it felt as if every hair on his arms stood up like metal spikes.

The pounding in his chest started to get louder, and the beating became in sync with the chanting. *Boom, Boom, Boom,* like bass coming from a loud stereo from a car down the street heading your way. All of a sudden, just as he felt the car would surely be in front of his house by the sound of the bass beat of his heart, he felt two strong grips, one on each wrist. The strength of each took him by surprise as he tried to remain calm and concentrated. Caleb was unprepared for what happened next. He felt one of his hands be pinned down to the globe with such a force, he tried to pull it away but he couldn't break free and, before he knew it, the other snake forced the rod right through the meat of his hand.

"MOTHA FUCKER!" Caleb shouted as he opened his eyes, but was surprised from looking at his hand the pain he felt was not in his hand, but in his chest.

"Caleb, do you have the answer?" Cyrus asked, paying no attention to the rod sticking through Caleb's hand.

"She's in Michigan," Caleb answered, holding his bleeding hand, with the rod still sticking through it, as he cursed his father in his head so his father could not hear him.

His hand started to throb and he knew he needed to pull out the rod. Without hesitation, he grabbed the end of the rod and yanked it out. The rod left a whole in his hand and stung as the air from the room blew through the open space. Fortunately, his genetic makeup would heal the wound shortly.

Caleb noticed the room went silent. Caleb looked at his brothers, who were still in a trance with snake like fog creatures stirring around them as if they were looking for something to eat.

"How do we wake them?" Caleb scrambled as he wrapped a towel over the hole in his hand.

"Son, I'm not always going to be at your side. You must learn how to figure these things out yourself," Cyrus replied.

Caleb could feel his temper start to rise. He hated the games his father played. "Fucking shit, just snap them out of it so we can move to the next plan," he yelled back.

Cyrus just started to laugh as he guided the seer by his arm and out the door, leaving Caleb to deal with it on his own. He didn't have time to think about how evil his father was; right now he had to save the only family he really felt like he had, his two brothers.

"Ok, fog...snake like...two, one can't work without the other...energy drawn from life..." Caleb quickly said out loud as he tried to puzzle it together to retract the creatures. He thought about the colors, one earth colored, like the grass and the trees, the other the color of metal and cold.

Just then it came to him without having to read a spell or make a potion. He didn't even have to keep putting the puzzle pieces together. Caleb grinned slightly, and with his unwounded hand, pointed at Ali first and silently commanded the green serpent fog to him. The serpent screamed in resistance, but Caleb just pulled harder thinking about how payback really was a bitch, and like a magnet, the serpent was in his hand. Caleb squeezed the snake by the neck, the serpent started to scream a high pitch scream as it struggled to get free. Caleb squeezed a bit harder and suddenly the serpent started to quiet as it's form began to break up like the clouds moving above after a light rain dissipates and the sun starts to shine its way through, breaking up the clouds and removing the evidence it had ever rained. Ali's body fell to the floor.

He repeated it with Jamahl, only this serpent didn't fight. It was weak without its counterpart. Jamahl then fell on the floor.

"You guys going to sleep all day or are you coming to Michigan with me to nab a Witch?" Caleb stood over his brothers, grinning.

His brother's, both rubbing their heads, looked up at Caleb then looked at each other while shaking their heads. "Well I guess if we get to go to a football game I'm in!" Jamal said randomly.

"Yeah, I'll even buy you a hotdog!" Caleb replied. They all busted out in laughter as Caleb gave hands to his brothers, helping them to their feet.

Aidan had been standing outside of the door, listening in on the spell. He wanted to know where the other witch was, just in case the one he was supposed to check turned out not to be the one. When Cyrus came out of the room to find them standing there, he became angry.

"I told you to leave, you should have already been gone by now. Don't just stand here, GO!" He yelled.

Not wanting to aggravate Cyrus any further, Aidan just nodded his head in compliance and turned to head out through the veiny halls and towards the front door. Aidan turned back to watch as Cyrus then guided the seer down the opposite direction of the hall. Aidan turned his head as he reached a winding corner, following Aiah and Rory out.

"She and Rowan are in Michigan, make sure we keep in contact with the dynamic trio so we can keep tabs on where exactly they are, just in case we have the wrong girl. We'll see yet who has the most power." Aidan, while squinting his eyes, said as he thought of Cyrus. He was tired of Cyrus and his leadership, the last thing he wanted was Cyrus to become more powerful. After all Aiah, Rory, and Aidan were just like him; made by him.

They were all half warlock, half human who, at some point during history, seemed to become popular as the warlock population began to fade. The half breed population became more frequent, which diluted the power of the warlocks. A true warlock had much more power from within, half-breeds still possessed power, but it was diluted, as if their powers had been watered down. Again, because they were made not born, vampires and mixed with human blood, they could no longer walk amongst the day. Aidan had missed the sun desperately. He was born into the sun and worshiped its every essence, even more than he loved the extra strength, power, and immortality he gained from being a vampire. There was a time in which he relished at his newfound place on earth, but endless life was a long time and lately he didn't feel the freedom he once had. Aidan was not going to just accept a life full of existence. He wanted to live, and the prophecy was just what he had been waiting for, a chance for him to gain what he had lost so long ago.

3

Caleb wasn't being his usual cocky self. He was determined to make this a short trip. His father thought it may take a few weeks, depending on the situation, but Caleb intended on making it take a matter of days. As soon as they checked into their hotel, Caleb was ready to hit the city to look for Rowan.

"Come on guys, let's go," Caleb ordered.

"Calm down, little bro," Jamahl snapped back.

"Yeah, what's your problem? We just got here and you've been acting shady since we arrived," Ali chimed in as he pulled out his books, organizing them into their proper stacks.

"Nothing, I just want to get this done and I'm not sure exactly how we are going to find her…" Caleb answered, getting lost in thought.

He had felt uneasy since they landed in Detroit. He thought perhaps it was just the uncertainty of how they were to find Rowan. Certainly he was not afraid of a female witch, especially one who was just coming into her full powers. The thought of fear made him smirk. No, the uneasiness was something else, something he couldn't quite put his finger on. *That's it, this is all because I have no concrete plan to find her,* he tried to convince himself, but the seer's words were playing through his head like a puzzle.

"So, Caleb, you want us to leave right this minute. You're snapping and impatient because you have no idea how to find her, but you want us to leave immediately?" Ali said as more of a statement than a question, still organizing his stack of books.

"Come on man, let's just do another finding spell," Jamahl suggested.

"Not going to work, we don't know her so we have no energy to draw upon," Ali answered.

Caleb sat quietly for a moment as he went through the things the seer had said to him. *I would be drawn to her…she could destroy me…listen to where your heart pulls you…* and finally an idea dawned upon him.

"I got it!" Caleb shouted with a grin.

"What?" Jamahl asked as he raised his right eyebrow in leu of Caleb's grin.

"The seer said I would feel drawn to her and that I should listen to my heart." Caleb stopped.

"Ok, sooo…" Jamahl asked again with a confused look on his face now replacing his grin.

"Look, all I have to do is draw from the elements and just follow to where it is that I feel drawn to. And if what the seer says is right, to listen to my heart, then it should beat louder and faster as we are getting closer." Caleb said with somewhat of uncertainty.

"You sure this will work?" Ali questioned the simplicity of the plan.

"No, I'm not sure. But I don't think it would be a good idea to perform any experimental spells to find her. If this town has a lot of witches, then they probably have a magic filter that tells them when and where magic is being used. And if they know about her, they will be on the lookout for spells that could find her. We need to come in seemingly human. We need to find her and draw no attention to ourselves, and if she is not the one, then we need to wait for further instructions." Caleb explained.

"Exactly, we need to help find the other if Aiden is still having a difficult time getting to her. Which he probably will, considering he cannot walk into the daylight like we can." Ali added.

"He might have a hard time figuring out if she is the one, but once we have eliminated Rowan, then we won't need the holy water, since by process of elimination, she would be the one we are looking for." Jamahl followed.

"If that even works," Ali said, seriously questioning the method the seer had in mind of revealing her wings.

"That's it then, I will let my self be drawn and listen to my heart," Caleb said, half hoping it wouldn't work just so the seer would be wrong, but half hoping it would so he could get out of Michigan sooner.

"Let's do it princess!" Jamahl said with a half-cocked smile.

Caleb started to laugh at his brother's attempt at a joke, which implied he was girly for having to follow his heart. "That's very funny, coming from a guy who takes over an hour getting ready for the day!" Caleb quipped back.

Jamahl stood there for a moment with a smile still plastered on his face, and before Caleb could react, Jamahl had swarmed in with the quickness of a cheetah, pulled him over his head, and pinned him to the ceiling. They were both off of the ground and wrestling around on the ceiling. Caleb wrapped his legs around Jamahl and began to squeeze as they were laughing in their game of who is the strongest vampire-witch. They struggled, equally matched, when Ali looked up and noticed the ceiling begin to crack.

"Knock it off guys, the ceiling is starting to crack, and for people who were just talking about going in unnoticed this is not one of those things that go unnoticed," Ali quietly, but firmly, commanded. They both let go of their grip and dropped to the floor. "It's time, let's go," Ali added. They got up, dusted themselves off, and went out the door.

They walked out of the hotel and stood in the fading sunshine as the night filled the sky and there was a light breeze blowing. Caleb looked up into the sky and tried to clear his mind. It was strange to him how he immediately began to feel a pull.

"This way," Caleb said within only minutes of being outside. Ali and Jamahl looked at each other with dumbfounded looks on their face, but without question followed Caleb to the black Grand Cherokee they had rented. It was a good car to be incognito in due to its tinted windows.

They drove for ten minutes, taking a few quick turns as Caleb would feel another pull. Right, right, left, then right again, and soon they were in a very nice neighborhood. All of the houses looked well-kept and were made of neutral shades of brick and stone. The landscaping was rich with flowers and beautifully displayed plants accented with various size rocks and lighting. There was also a ton of trees in the neighborhood. Many were full grown trees that looked as if they had been there forever.

As they entered the neighborhood, Caleb slowed down again, taking a few turns. Right, then a left, followed by another right, pulling onto a street which had houses along only the left side of the street. On the right side was a large park with a large playground, four baseball diamonds, and some soccer fields amongst plenty of seating for bystanders to watch. There were also plenty of woods with what looked like walking and biking trails throughout it. He could smell a creek nearby. As he listened, he could hear the flow of the water running through the park. Far off to the right side of the park appeared to be a large pool which appeared to be alongside of a small water play area. Outside of the pool, he could see it was aligned with a couple of tennis courts. It was a beautiful park, from what Caleb could see, he thought to himself before shaking his head and wondering what the hell was wrong with him. He wasn't a suburb person, but this felt peaceful to him, almost as peaceful as the ocean felt to him. He decided it was due to the vastness of the park and shook it off.

Riding slowly down the street, with the park on his right and houses on his left, he started to feel his heart beat speed up. It started to get louder as they passed each house until, all of a sudden, he could hear and feel his heart beating into his eardrums. Closing his eyes for a second, he pulled to the right and put the car in park. He then opened his eyes and looked at a two-story stone and beige brick colored house with a large porch on the front donned with two large wooden double doors and beautiful, large pots filled with green plants and a few beautiful flowers.

Instinctively, he looked up at the window with white curtains backed by dark midnight blue curtains on the inside layer. A soft light was on and only the sheer white curtains were drawn all the way shut. The blue layer was still open creating a frame for the room and allowed Caleb to see a silhouette standing side profile in the window. She had long hair and looked thin and athletic, and he felt a curiosity burning deep inside of him. He wanted to go right in to see what it was he was so drawn to. She looked to be talking to someone and he was more interested in what she was saying than who she was talking to.

"Caleb!" Jamahl interrupted, bringing Caleb out of his quiet, obsessive state.

"Sorry, I think this is the house... I think that might be Rowan up there in the window." Caleb said, pointing out the window with the silhouette. Only now there seemed to be two silhouettes. *So that must be who she is talking to...* Caleb thought to himself as he watched the second silhouette, also female, wearing a pony tail and a couple of inches shorter with the same athletic thinness, pass by the girl with the long hair and sit down on what looked like it could be the bed.

They sat there for a moment, as Caleb got lost in the first girl's movements. At the way her hips shifted slowly, almost snake-like, as she was now facing away from him and toward the girl with the ponytail sitting on her bed. She must be telling her something she's angry about; he could almost sense she was angry. He looked at how much her hands moved as she was telling the story, as she would take a break and tuck her long hair behind her ears. He noticed the perfect outline of her backside when, all of a sudden, he felt something hard plunge into his shoulder.

Taking his eyes off the window, he looked at Jamahl, "What?" Caleb asked calmly, as if he hadn't just been slugged in the arm.

"Man, what are you looking at? Is that her?" Jamahl asked impatiently.

"Yeah, Caleb. Is it or not?" Ali added.

Caleb paused for a moment before speaking. "I think so, I'm not sure," he answered, turning back towards the window to find the light in the room was now off. Feeling agitated by this, he gripped the steering wheel tightly in his hands, forcing out all of the blood and making them ghostly white.

"What's wrong with you, Caleb?" Ali said observantly from the back seat.

"Nothing," was all he could manage to answer. He looked towards the house again and saw the front door was now opening.

"Someone's coming out," Jamahl took notice at the door opening, as well.

Without answering, he focused on the two girls in the doorway. The one with the ponytail was now leaving, and the girl with the long hair was bent over, picking up a tiny black dog who was trying to makes his way out. He couldn't see her face. He wanted to see her face and felt as if he needed to see her face. Just as he almost could no longer take the suspense, and was about to rush the door to cup her face in his hands to look at the thing taunting him, the girl looked up and yelled after her friend.

"Rowan, don't forget to bring the note cards tomorrow. I'll need to look over them one more time before our test during lunch." Mikayla shouted after her friend as she held her little black dog, Mocha, in her hands. Rowan waved her hand at Mikayla.

"You're still bringing us lunch so we don't have to wait in line, aren't you?" Rowan asked before getting into her car. She seemed more worried about her lunch then her test.

"Yes, I will pack us something good!" She replied.

"Well, I won't forget the note cards as long as you don't forget our lunch. Oh, and something to sit on! It's supposed to be sunny tomorrow and I could use some sunshine!" Rowan said, finalizing their plan. She then got into her car and shut the door.

Caleb paid no attention to what she had just said. Her beauty stunned him. She was slightly tanned with high cheekbones and full lips. Her nose was perfect and set between almond shaped eyes that looked Egyptian, filled in with the color of the ocean. A deep blue peace which made Caleb stir, panicking inside. Her hair was full and dark brown, with lighter shades of brown woven throughout, and it cascaded down to the middle of her back shaped by soft long layers all around. As she stood there in jeans and a soft blue tank top tightly fit to her body, he could see the perfection of her curves even better. He couldn't help it as his fangs came slightly out, and his mouth began to water.

Losing all grip on reality, he was about to get out of the car right there and rush right to her when she looked at their car. Startled, he snapped back into reality and his heartbeat sped up even faster, and then it stopped, as did everything for a brief moment. He stared quietly; his breath was now shallow as if he was now the prey hiding from his predator.

She held her gaze on the black jeep briefly, before moving on to the other cars parked along the park side of the street. She then looked over to the baseball diamonds, all lit up in the park and filled with ball players, before turning around to go back inside of her house.

As she looked at the car one more time, Caleb couldn't help but hold his breath, as if doing so she would not sense his presence. The car windows were tinted and it was now night, logically he knew she couldn't, but still he felt as if he could get caught. There were also other cars parked along the street from the ball players in the park. Although there were a few parking lots which surrounded the park, many people used this as extra parking since it was closer to the fields. This also would ensure their presence to be undetected.

As she made her way back into her house with the little dog in hand, Caleb let out a deep breath. "That was close," he said, not realizing he had said it out loud. Jamahl and Ali thought he was joking and started to laugh, so he played it off and laughed with them.

Rowan was already in her car, heading down the street. They waited a few seconds before following her. She took a left at the end of the street and went up two blocks, and hung another left before heading down a court another block down on the right hand side. Caleb didn't go down the court. Instead, he drove slowly past to see where she parked her car and watched her open the door before losing sight of her as they drove on past.

"That must be her house right there," Ali said.

"Well, what next? She might be under protection, so we can't just go in. Plus, she might not be the one we are looking for and cannot take the risk of stirring up alarm," Caleb added.

"What are we going to do then?" Ali asked, looking to Caleb for an answer. Caleb just shook his head. He was still a little dazed from the girl in the window.

The drive back towards their hotel was quiet as they all sat calculating the next best move. Caleb couldn't get focused. He kept seeing her face. His mind was racing as his heartbeat was finally stabilizing. *Grea,t first my heart is out of control and now my mind has decided to take place where my heart beat left off,* Caleb thought to himself as images of the girl whirled through his head.

4

The moon lit sky was filled with a subtle breeze. Aidan loved the smell of Italy. Caleb was off with his two brothers and Aidan was sent to check on the other girl with Aiah and Rory, who were like brothers to him the same way Caleb, Ali, and Jamahl were. Aidan, Aiah, and Rory were much older, over a few hundred years older than Caleb, Ali, and Jamahl.

The girl they were looking for was Layla Valenti. She was one of the two witches known to have escaped their death at birth, and possibly living off the energy of an angel called Arella, a female angel who was a messenger between Heaven and the supernatural on Earth working for good. The seer saw she had jumped into the lifeless baby to give her energy, so the baby could have life. Her energy was now a part of the witch, they just weren't sure which girl it was.

Arella would only be released upon the witch's death. Until then, she was just an energy source. Aidan laughed at the prospect Angels had no concept of time, for Arella it could be 300 years or more until she was awakened again. When she did, it would only seem like minutes.

Aidan and his crew weren't worried about uncovering the witch. They had a little help from a dark wizard named Ragnar. They knew Caleb and his brothers were going to try using holy water. It was the last thing Aidan heard while listening through the door back at the mansion. He knew it wasn't going to work, and had no intentions of telling Caleb this. Aidan had his own agenda, oneonly he, Aiah, and Rory knew about. It was better for them if Caleb and his brothers wasted time.

There was only one clue to the revealing of an Angel's wings, but Aidan had the help of the wizard's expertise. The wizard was old and well-read in the ancient texts. Aidan grinned in satisfaction, knowing tears through blood would need to be drawn from her and a mark of some sort would be revealed. He was surprised Ali hadn't thought of this yet, but he knew it was only a matter of time before Ali would.

Aidan and the wizard had been gently conspiring for months as they searched for the witch who was just beheaded in the mansion the night before. As weeks passed, Ragnar and Aidan passed more and more information with each other without making the mistake of saying anything that would incriminate either of them, admitting their hidden agendas. Both had grown tired of Cyrus.

As Aidan thought about Ali, he wondered just how long it would take him to put together the clues. Ali was younger, and didn't have the experience Aidan had, but he was smart and it would only be a matter of time until he sat down to decipher the puzzle. Aidan was hoping it would take Ali long enough to figure it out as they checked Layla. If she was not the one, then all he needed to do was show up were Rowan was, unsuspected, and execute his plan B.

Like a puma in the night, they needed to be sly about their approach with Layla, or the other girl would surely be taken into deep hiding if Layla wasn't the right witch, and that would ruin his plans. At least he had an exact location of where she was living. She was attending a culinary school in Calabria. It was beautiful. Aidan wished he could see what it looked like in the day. He hadn't stepped foot in the sun in well over a couple hundred years. He was hopeless of finding a way to change his fate, until now. The wizard told him of things a witch who was given angels breath could do. Her powers would have no bounds; limitless magic. With this, he knew he would see the sun again. For now, he needed to find the girl.

"Let's just cut her in an alley somewhere, if we take her purse, it may seem like just mugging," Aiah said.

"That's not going to work. What's the likely hood anyone would buy it? Plus, remember she is a witch and she is coming into her full powers soon. We don't know what she can do yet," Aidan said back as he looked out onto the Mediterranean, holding a finger up to his mouth as he thought.

"You guys are making this harder than it needs to be. We just wait till she is alone, surprise her from behind, bite her, and drain her powers. We then cut her and look for the marks. If she doesn't have them, then we erase the memory from her brain. Although it won't work long term on a witch, it may buy us enough time to grab the other girl," Rory said as if it was all so simple.

Aidan stared blankly at Rory for a moment as Aiah did the same. They turned to each other and looked with disbelief as they started busting out in laughter. Rory didn't get the joke, but chuckled along anyway.

"You are always so quiet Rory, and just when I forget you are even around, you come up with the simplest things that actually end up being good ideas." Rory wasn't sure if that was a compliment, but decided not to waste any time trying to figure it out. He was just glad they had a plan.

5

The alarm went off louder than Mikayla remembered setting it. She was so tired. It was the last day of finals and she had two left. The alarm was relentless, so she reached over to make the annoying beep stop. *Ok get up…just open your eyes…* she said to herself, dozing off again.

Kali are you up yet? She heard Rowan's thoughts come through her head.

Rowan, maybe we need to set some hours of telepathic operation, this being one of those no thought times, she thought grumpily back to her best friend. Rowan just laughed and asked if she wanted to get some breakfast first because she was in the mood for blueberry pancakes.

With one eye open, she looked at the clock and realized they still had three hours before class. She thought about sleeping for another hour before waking up until images of hot, fresh blueberry pancakes popped into her head and she realized she really was hungry.

She didn't eat a whole lot the day before because she was doing some serious studying. She had also left the dinner table early due to an ongoing argument she had with her parents. Her brother was home for dinner and only made the argument that much worse. She wasn't sure if it was the fact they had two different sets of rules, one made for her and the other nonexistent rules for her twin brother Romario, or if it was just his presence always siding with them. He also took it upon himself to try and make things worse, sounding as if his words were Dominick's, and not his own. It was if he was always trying to intimidate her into backing down.

Now she loved her brother very much, but she was getting older and still seemed to have all the rules placed on her as she had in high school. She felt there wasn't much she could do about it, after all, her parents were paying for her education. Perhaps if she had decided to go full-time into the family business like her brother, then she would be able to have all the freedom he had. Perhaps it was just the fact she was in school and they wanted to keep her on track. All the possible thoughts crossed her mind. But Mikayla knew she didn't want to work for the family business, she wanted something different, something she could do all on her own.

She also wanted to be respectful of her parents, so she would always back down and let the fights go and blow over, until lately, that is. Mikayla was now too restless to bite her tongue. One more year left of school and then they wouldn't have a choice, she thought to herself. Perhaps they would even be supportive of her moving out. She thought about it further and realized it would only start them trying to force her back with Dominick, which they only began to stop a year ago.

Tired of thinking about the moving out subject, she slammed her face into the pillow and held her breath. She was going to hold it for as long as she could, until Rowan interrupted. *So Kali, pancakes are awaiting. I am awake and today is the last day of school and then we are free for the summer!*

Mikayla's attention was now focused back on pancakes as her stomach gave a gentle growl telling her she better get up and get some of those pancakes. *Alright, we can get some pancakes. Are you coming to pick me up soon?* Mikayla, still with only one eye open, asked to Rowan from across the neighborhood.

I will be there in forty five minutes. Rowan said cheerfully back, having got her way.

The space inside Mikayla's head was finally silent again. She stared at the brilliance of her window and admired the sunshine coming in. In the warm sunny months, she would only close the white part of her curtains. They were shear and smooth. They flowed all the way to the ground, covering her large two paned window. The outer layer of curtains was made of a thick, heavier fabric in dark, midnight blue.

Her room had white walls with alternate stripes from matte white to shiny white all the way around the room. Her furniture was dark wood which matched her queen size bed. The covers on her bed were feather down white with dark midnight blue tribal flowers and beige accents. It was something she had designed herself and made with the help of her mother. Mikayla was very artistic. She had pillows with the same colors to match. She also had a plush, oversized midnight blue blanket for extra warmth she would fold and keep at the foot of her bed.

She had a night stand on either side of her bed which faced a beautiful large, dark wood armoire that housed her music player, CDs, and TV set. She had one long dresser with a mirror on it and another taller dresser, but not as long on the opposite side. She also had a dark wooden desk with a midnight blue chair, one they had to specially order to complete the look of her room. She also had an oversized midnight blue microsuede chair with matching ottoman, and a soft white throw she kept over the arm of the chair. Her bedroom was the second largest in the house next to her parent's master suite. It had a soft, thick shag carpet in a light beige she had tied into the décor of the bed set. She even had her own bathroom and walk in closet in her bedroom.

Not a day went by she didn't realize how lucky she was to have such a nice room and realized when she finally was a teacher, the things she would be able to buy were not going to be quite as extravagant. This didn't bother her in the least. She couldn't wait to make her own way.

She shut her eyes one more time before realizing she was falling back asleep and decided to get up, get ready, and wait for Rowan to pick her up. It was the last day of finals. They were going to study by the student center before their very last test, which looked like it was going to be a hard one.

The student center was brand new. It had tons of restaurants and study spaces. It even had game rooms and stores. It was a bright building, and had almost all windows on one side. Mikayla liked to study there in the winter time. It made her feel a part of something. It also made her feel independent, which currently she was not feeling. She knew she was capable, but her current situation didn't quite foster her need for independence. Soon it would change. Soon she would graduate.

Outside of the student center there was a pond that had tables around it and plush landscaping, making it a beautiful place to study when it was warm and a beautiful view from inside the student center when it was not. There was also a very large, open grass area that had tables on either side. It created a large space people used to play sports on while the onlookers took up tables to watch, hang out, or even study. The open space was just grass, but on either side of this space was a little bit larger, the size of a football field, where lots of pretty trees made for great shade during the warm, sunny days. It also made for a breath taking view in the fall when the leaves would change colors.

On the opposite side of the student center, across the large open field, was a long hill. That was another popular hangout spot. You would see more of the artsy crowd hanging out up there with their guitars and pads of sketch paper. Mikayla loved looking up there in wonder. It was where she even saw a couple of boys who caught her eye. She had a weakness for a boy with a good faux hawk who looked like he was trouble. Dominick chased a couple of those boys off, she remembered while she was finishing getting ready.

There was also a small hill by the student center itself. When her brother or any of his friends decided to take a class or just show up on campus to see Rowan or spy on her, it's where they would always be. She always thought it was funny even though none of them were full time students, not even close, they seemed to have staked out this one area and claimed it as their own. No one ever even thought about challenging them for the spot. Mikayla liked to think it was because people in college were much more mature, rather then it being because the boys were all so intimidating. It wasn't intentional; it was just how they naturally were.

Despite the fact they were a little scary, she knew they had good hearts and meant well. For as many times as she had seen them intimidate people , she had seen them use it for good, as well. They were always the first people there helping out when someone needed something, even if it was a stranger. Above and beyond was how they handled most things.

Just as Mikayla had finished brushing her teeth, she heard the honk of Rowan's car outside. She grabbed her bookbag and shoved her tiny brown purse inside, then ran down the stairs and out the door to grab the blueberry pancakes which were now making her mouth begin to water.

"Good idea on the pancakes!" She said to Rowan as she got in the car.

"That's all I got is good ideas, girlfriend! Oh, did you bring the lunches?" Rowan said back as she zipped quickly down the street.

"Yes, and we will have a good couple of hours of sun outside of the student center to help us study!" Mikayla replied.

"Well, don't forget the people watching and working on our tans!" Rowan said smiling and raising an eyebrow at Mikayla. With that, Mikayla just shook her head as they headed for their favorite little diner before school.

6

It was early the next morning. Finishing getting ready, Caleb thought about how when they arrived back at the hotel last night things seemed to unfold so easy and, within hours, they had already formed a plan. They had decided to go to the hotel bar and figure out a plan to get Rowan in a position to test whether or not she was the witch they were searching for.

They had gone back to the hotel the night before after locating Rowan. As soon as they walked in, they headed straight for the bar. They walked in and took a table in the back. The bar in the hotel had black walls with black lighting along with neon graffiti paint along the walls. The tables were dark wood with chairs to match and dark red cushions. Candles lit the tables. There was a stage there, although unoccupied of a band for the night. Instead, heavy metal music was being played by a stereo system stored behind the bar. There were a couple of pool tables, one being played, and three dart boards with high tables in each area for those playing darts to set their drinks on and have a seat as they awaited their turns.

"Hi, can I get you guys something to drink?" A cute waitress with short, dark hair and tattoos asked.

"Pitcher of beer and three glasses," Jamahl said, smiling at the waitress.

"What kind?" She smiled, in awe of Jamahls beautiful features.

"Whatever you like," he said, flirtingly back.

She smiled and headed to the bar to place their order.

Caleb and Ali spent the next few hours until closing discussing possible scenarios of how to get into the position of exposing Rowans wings, or whatever it was they were looking for, while Jamahl spent the better part of the night flirting with the waitress.

They were still unsure of how to use the holy water and came up with two ideas: ingestion or spraying water on her back. They couldn't fathom any other idea that would work.

They felt they had solved the mystery of the Heaven's Tears. They needed to collect rainwater and have it blessed by a priest. This would take some minor workings of glamour and a poor sucker to complete the task.

One problem solved, the collecting of Heaven's Tears and having it blessed. Another problem close to being solved was how to expose her wings. The last was a bit trickier, how would they get her in the position to test either theory? They threw around several scenarios, including one that was a drive by water gun shooting they laughed furiously at, but none which were actually applicable.

It was after last call and they were all a bit intoxicated, especially Jamahl. One of the results of them being half witch was alcohol had an effect on them, unlike a full blooded vampire who would never feel more then a slight weakness in the knees if feeding off of an extremely intoxicated human. That slight rush would last only minutes before disappearing. For Caleb and his brothers, it was different. They could get tipsy just like a witch or a human.

The cute waitress came over to collect her tip, with her purse slung comfortably over her well-structured shoulder.

"You guys, we are officially closed. I hate to kick you out, but we are about to lock the doors," she said apologetically.

Her short dark hair exposed her neckline. She was fair skinned, which only exposed her veins even more. It was nighttime and all three brothers' feeding instincts started to come out, especially under their intoxicated state. The tribal tattoos along the back of her neck and down her right arm only made her more tantalizing to them. Especially to Jamahl, who had a thing for girls who wore tattoos. Her eyes were large and dark, her nose looked slightly Mediterranean and still petite. Her lips were even and looked soft, as did her skin.

"Hey girl, I don't think I ever got your name," Jamahl stated a question.

"Mary, and you are?" She replied.

"Jamahl and this here is Ali, and Caleb," he answered. "Well, Mary, do you have a ride home tonight?" He then added, hoping she did not so they could be the ones to drive her home.

"Yes, my car is out back," she said.

"Out back? We will walk with you and keep you safe," Jamahl lied through his teeth.

They weren't thinking clearly, yet they were all thinking the same thing. Dinner. Jamahl was thinking more.

"Ok, then." Mary smiled and led the way through the door to the bar Jamahl held open.

The veins in her neck seemed to pulse louder and faster, drawing the three brothers in. The predators inside started to show themselves. All of their eyes lit up two shades and became brindled with slight dark shades throughout. It wasn't something someone would notice right away, but was obvious enough for anyone looking at them that something was off. A warning, of sorts, people could sense but not quite put their finger on. If you knew them you would wonder why you had never noticed their eyes were so light and cat like. You might even guess they had put in contacts, they had even used that excuse many times.

"I'm just over there," Mary said as her heart began to beat faster. An instinct inside her told her to be afraid, and her heart speeding up confirmed that. The three of them said nothing back. Jamahl smiled down at her without showing his teeth. His fangs had already come out at the rapidness of her heartbeat. Ali's and Caleb's were also out. They couldn't keep a clear head at the moment. All they wanted was blood.

As they approached the back of the four door silver sedan, Caleb instantly sobered up and his teeth retracted when he noticed a parking sticker of some sort hanging from her review mirror. "What's that sticker for?" He suddenly burst out, sobering his brothers.

"It's an Eastern Michigan parking sticker," She replied as her heartbeat began to slow at the simplicity of the conversation. and Jamahl looked at each other, confused, and then to Caleb.

"I know that. I'm sorry, I had a bit too much to drink. We go there as well…it's just that I haven't seen you in any of my classes or around campus," he lied through his teeth. Mary gave him a strange glance and finally accepted this as the truth, as both Ali and Jamahl confirmed together Caleb was telling the truth.

"So are you guys ready to take the last of your finals?" Mary asked.

"Piece of cake," Caleb said.

"Not really," Ali said truthfully.

"Girl, I will ace everything so I have more time to spend with you this summer and not on class work," Jamahl added.

"Well I am not and so I must go so I can get some sleep. I have a big study day tomorrow, followed by a big test," Mary informed them as she unlocked and opened her car door.

As she got in and shut the door, she wrestled around for a moment and rolled down her window. Without Jamahl having to even ask, she handed him a torn piece of paper with her phone number on it. "Call me some time. I mean, if you want," she said only to Jamahl, and he took her number and put it in his pocket without saying anything back. He just grinned a confirming grin that said for her to not worry about it, he would.

She put her car into reverse and backed out of the parking spot. Her window was stilled rolled down, and she paused a moment before driving off. "Hey, if you guys go to Eastern, why are you staying at a hotel?" She asked skeptically.

Ali and Jamahl looked at Caleb, unsure of his whole plan, but knowing he must have one. "Well, it's my fault really. We had an apartment and, well, let's just say we just got evicted. Not a story I'm proud of, so I will spare you the details. We are just staying here until our new apartment is ready," Caleb said convincingly.

"Well, that make's sense. Perhaps Jamahl will share the dirty details with me some day!" She answered, satisfyingly, back.

"Perhaps," Jamahl said, smiling back. He felt amused at how quick she was.

Mary finally rolled up her window and took off out of the parking lot and turned left onto the street before any of them said anything. Once her car was far into the distance, Ali and Jamahl looked at Caleb.

"Rowan had the same sticker hanging in her car. I think I have an idea," Caleb said, grinning ear to ear. "Back to our room, I will fill you guys in," he added, still staring after the silver four-door sedan no longer in sight.

Neither of his brothers said anything, they just headed back towards the room. They were to hungry to argue or demand an explanation on the spot.

Once in the room, Caleb had explained to them how the sticker in Rowan's car meant she, too, was a student at Eastern. "Listen, we go in to the office and get her information. Once we know where her classes are, we can devise a plan to meet her. We get in socially with her, or at least find out where she hangs out, show up, and then we will be on our way to finding out if she is the one. Simple," Caleb said to his brothers.

"Simple, huh?" Jamal said, disbelieving the word simple. Ali just started laughing and shook his head at the absurdity of it all.

"Come on, it may work. We have to meet her some way, and we need to do it undetected. If anyone even suspects what we are up to, it will ruin everything. Our best bet is to make things look just like chance," Caleb said encouragingly.

"Well, I don't really have anything else to do tomorrow, so I guess I'm on board," Jamal said, jokingly.

"Alright, let's at least try this way out. If it doesn't work. then I say let's just snag her, check, and then erase her memory with a spell," Ali said.

"Seriously, Ali, that would be a great plan if there weren't people close by watching out for things like that... Come on man, this is serious. We have to use something we aren't use to...patience. So, let's just try," Caleb said wisely.

Ali and Jamal looked at each other and started laughing. "Um, when did you two switch places?" Jamal said between giggles.

It was true, Ali was usually the level headed one, not Caleb but somehow, at this moment, Caleb was having some clarity as Ali was starting to lose his.

"Ok, ok I get it. I'm really thirsty. I'm on board, just do me a favor please and don't compare me to Caleb. That alone might kill me," Ali joined Jamahl as they laughed even harder.

For a moment, Caleb sat quietly just looking at the two of them, and then he, too, started to laugh at the irony of it all.

Caleb had just finished tying his shoes and was putting on a fresh clean tee-shirt as he finished going through all the details of the night before when he saw Jamahl come out of the bathroom already with his shorts on.

"I can't believe you're ready. Don't you still have to do a facial and paint your nails?" Caleb took a quick shot at his brother as a morning greet.

"Shut up, man," Jamahl said, sounding rather grouchy.

"Come on, don't be upset. I will make it up to you. How about I take you to the spa later today for a pedicure?" Caleb harassed his brother a little more.

Jamahl grinned, then took the bottle of lotion in his hands and threw it hard and fast at Caleb. With his quick reflexes, Caleb caught it perfectly with his right hand as he laughed at his brother's attempts to quiet him.

"Nice catch," Jamahl said as he pulled on a tight white tank over his shorts. Just then Ali walked through the door.

"Are you two ready yet?" He said, handing them each a coffee. Ali had already been up and about and getting things done, as usual.

They each took a coffee as they grabbed their things and headed out the door. It was potentially a long shot today, but a long shot that might actually work.

7

The day was bright and sunny. They were smart, and paid attention to details the night before which led them to being on a college campus dressed in shorts and gym shoes. Caleb just hoped his hunch was right. If it wasn't, nothing lost yet. After all, they really did just get to Michigan the day before. They had anticipated it taking a few days just to locate her, but they were able to locate her within hours of stepping off the plane.

He was trying not to think about the other girl, but the rush he felt inside was powerful. He knew he would see that girl again. The one from inside the house whose silhouette teased him as he sat out in the car staring up into the soft light, which made the window look like a peepshow, only she wasn't dancing or undressing. It was just the way she moved and the outline of her figure that had seduced him. He also remembered her eyes when she showed her face briefly at the door. He was far away, but to him it was as if he was looking at her right in front of his face.

Caleb pulled up to a parking spot in front of the student center. It was an old brick building surrounded by a lot of big trees and green bushes. They entered the building and went up to the administration office where they pulled a number. The place was busy for a day of finals.

They waited for only ten minutes, despite how busy it was, for their number to be called. A young woman with red hair and bright green eyes stood behind a desk. Caleb was already putting her into his trance as he locked eyes with her and made his way up. She didn't blink once.

"How can I assist you?" She asked quietly.

"I need to know the location of a student," he said even quieter, so no one around would hear them.

"Who?" She replied, matching the Caleb's quietness with her own.

Caleb said Rowan's name and within in just a few short seconds, a paper was printed up for them with Rowan's class schedule.

"Anything else?" She asked.

"Yes, where is the student center?" Caleb asked.

The girl said nothing. Instead, she made her way towards the copier and grabbed another print out. Before handing the printout to Caleb, she circled two items. She had circled where they were at, the administration offices, and then circled the building known as the student center. Caleb thanked her. All the girl could do was nod her head at him. They walked out of the office and Caleb looked back at the girl to make sure she was snapping out of it. She was holding her head, as if briefly confused, and then called the next number. Caleb smiled and made his way towards the stairwell with his brothers.

.That was easy... he said only to his brothers, without moving his lips. Jamahl smirked at how clever he thought they were. Ali looked a bit more reserved. His motto was always, "it ain't over until the fat lady sings."

"It's about time to get this whole thing wrapped up and back to California," Jamahl said, not being a big fan of the Midwest. Although the girl from the night before struck his curiosity, he was ready to get back to home. The couple days here had his little brother acting strange. He knew he'd see the girl again before he left because there was still a use for her yet, and he thought if he was lucky before they left, he would get to taste her, and then some. He didn't want to end her existence, he only wanted to taste her. But not until she got something for them they needed.

They had been tossing around the football for a while, fairly confident they would soon show up as they had overheard the girls confirming their plans the night before. Caleb was in the midst of throwing a pass to Jamahl when he noticed several male heads turning their attention to something behind him. He had let go of the football and left it spinning perfectly in the air towards Jamahl and turned around to see what the attention was for. Sure enough, his heart stopped quickly as he glanced her way and saw her in the sunlight. She was even more beautiful and alluring in the sun. He had hoped it was the mask of the night sky that had made her so alluring, but it wasn't. It truly was just her. There was just something about her, he thought to himself, before remembering he needed to keep playing his part for a bit.

Let them eat first or they may be too distracted to start up a conversation or keep one going. Hopefully these girls don't take all day to finish, it's getting hot out here, Ali thought to his brothers.

This caused Caleb to look over at the girls for a moment and watch Mikayla. Her skin tone was perfect. She had a slightly olive tan glow and long dark hair, but her eyes were a deep, dark blue shaped into large almonds, creating an exotic look that complimented her high cheek bones and full lips. She was the perfect build, 5'6 with the body of a cheerleader. It was hard for him to wrap his head around any human girl having that much beauty. He was used to the perfection of vampires, but humans no matter how good looking they were, didn't have the allure vampires had, and this girl had more allure than any vampire he had ever come across.

He watched as she unfolded the blanket they had brought to sit on. She was gentle, but efficient with it, and she even smoothed out all corners before placing their bags, along with themselves, on top. She took off her shoes and neatly put them next to each other on the corner of her side of the blanket. She took the head band off her head and shook out her hair before putting it back in place, which left her hair full and long but off of her face, creating even more of a slant to her dark blue eyes. Rowan started to take out their lunches and handed her a soda, she smiled, and Caleb noticed even her smile was perfect. Her teeth were as white as untouched snow as it first fell from the sky creating a blanket across the ground. He always got a kick out of people referring to beautiful girls as Angels, and although he had never seen one himself, he laughed at his own first instinct, this girl was an Angel.

He started to get lost in thought as he stared at Mikayla when he was suddenly interrupted by a hard blow to his upper chest by none other than Jamahls pass back to him. "Shit!" Caleb said, honestly startled, out loud.

Ali and Jamahl just started laughing. In the moment Caleb started laughing too, as he chased after them, hoping to tackle Jamahl. Ali wasn't much of a challenge for Caleb, but his larger, older brother was stronger than anyone Caleb knew and he loved a challenge.

He thought play fighting with his stronger, older brother was what had helped him to become so strong himself. Ali was more of the logical one. Though he was strong, his strength just couldn't compare to that of Jamahl.

The open grass area by the union was almost full. There were people doing everything from studying to playing catch. They were twenty minutes into their lunch study date when Mikayla looked at Rowan.

"Alright, ready or not we better go over this one more time." Rowan didn't reply, she just got up to throw out the unfinished lunch she and Mikayla had just ate and let out a big sigh.

When Rowan came back from throwing out their trash, she grabbed her book bag and reached inside for her note book. Rowan, as usual, didn't have her paper work put away securely, and as soon as she stood up, all of her papers fell onto the ground. She bent over to pick them up when Mikayla sensed something was coming. She looked in the direction her senses told her and saw a brown football heading for Rowan's head at the speed of light.

Mikayla worried someone would see what she was about to do, so she took a quick glance to check for onlookers. Not noticing anyone in particular looking their way, she quickly got in front of the ball and blocked it. She just as quickly pretended it hit her in the face, then paused briefly before remembering to drop to the ground. She played along, grabbing her face and letting out a loud "OUCH!"

"Oh my God! Kali, are you ok?" Rowan asked.

"Fine," Mikayla replied before starting to get up. She realized the ball still had not been claimed.

At this point, she figured she at least better wait long enough for the ball to be claimed before getting up. Mikayla thought it was important for dramatic effect, just in case anyone had seen what actually happened, it might trick them into thinking she really did get hit. Mikayla had actually stopped the ball before it even touched her. No one besides Rowan knew of her powers, who oddly enough had the same type of powers as Mikayla.

All her life, she could do tiny little things and never thought much of it until the week Marcus left. Oddly enough, a week of finals in high school, the week she still felt guilty for but always tried to tell herself she really had no idea what happened would or ever could even happen. That was the point where she realized, for some odd reason, she was able to do some things most people could not do. She never told anyone besides Rowan out of fear they would lock her up and throw away the key.

Mikalya, pretending to be in a bit of pain by holding her shoulder, sat on the ground for a moment. She heard someone running up. She could hear them breathing. "I'm so sorry, are you alright?" A male voice asked.

"I'm fine," Mikayla said as she took her hand away from her shoulder and tilted her face up to find the most beautiful eyes she had ever seen. For a brief moment, everything went silent and nothing seemed to move, not even her heart.

At a loss for words, she heard her heart start to beat. Slowly, at first. Eventually the rhythm started to beat faster and the pounding became louder. He seemed to be at a loss of words too, as he looked down at her and deep into her eyes. Everything around them was still. Everything around them was quiet.

Finally, the boy with tan skin, brown hair kissed by the sun, beautiful blue eyes, and a killer physique broke the silence.

"I'm so sorry," he said as he extended his hand to help her up.

The world started to move again as she found herself to her feet.

"Thanks," was all she could think to say.

As they stood staring at each other, their hands were still connected and the world around her, which had just started to breathe life again, began to speed up. Everything around her looked like a blur and she couldn't make sense out of anything around her except his face.

"I'm Mikayla, most people call me Kali," she said, trying hard to focus.

"Hi Mikayla, I'm Caleb," he said back, also at a loss of words and feeling the same way.

Mikayla and Caleb just stood there, with Caleb gripping her hand. She had been off the ground for a few minutes before the trance was broken.

"Hello, Earth to Kali and boy who almost took off her face," Rowan shouted, waving her hands like she was guiding a plane in for landing. They both looked away from each other and turned their attention to Rowan.

"Uh, you can let her hand go now, she has been standing for five minutes and hasn't fallen yet, so…" Rowan said in a sarcastic tone.

Caleb and Kali both squirmed a bit and let out a couple of nervous laughs at her joke.

"I must have been slightly dazed from the ball," Mikayla said, trying to play it off.

"That can happen when being hit in the face with a football," Caleb said, smiling at her, charmed by her charade. Caleb knew at that moment it wasn't true, he saw she had somehow blocked the ball before it even touched her. He knew at that moment there was more to her than what had seemed. He figured the block came from the help of Rowan. He was satisfied this was, indeed, the Rowan they were looking for.

Rowan looked at the both of them, staring at each other again, and decided to step in because she was either going to go to class or get Mikayla a date.

"So, are you finished with your finals?" She said, turning to Caleb while slightly nudging Mikayla in the shoulder.

"Um, yeah. Me and my brothers just finished this morning," he said as he pointed back to Ali and Jamal.

Rowan raised an eyebrow. "Brothers huh?" She said in a disbelieving way.

"Um yeah, we were raised by the same parents," Caleb told a half-truth of having parents rather than parent.

"Oh, that's cool," Rowan said, feeling a bit bad by her mistrustful gaze.

Rowan nudged Mikayla again, trying to get her to speak up. Mikayla felt as if the cat had literally just bit off her tongue and wouldn't give it back. She couldn't really form a sentence, let alone a thought. Her mind felt clouded and she was a bit dizzy.

Rowan turned towards Mikayla, and then to Caleb, and started to small talk again for a few moments before she devised a plan in her head to help Mikayla get a date.

"Do you guys ever go out to the Portage Lake chains?" Rowan directed her question at Caleb.

"Um, yes, actually we have been there a few times." Caleb lied through his teeth, which was something he was very good at.

"Well, Kali and me will be out there on Friday afternoon, if you're not busy, you could meet us out there. Do you have a boat?" Rowan asked with a smile.

"Oh, uh, yes we have one. We aren't busy, we could meet…um, there…" Caleb said, trailing off and looking back at his brothers.

Caleb's head was turned and Mikayla all of a sudden got an uneasy feeling. She started to examine Caleb and his brothers. She crossed her arms and tilted her head to the side while squinting her eyes.

"Hey, I have never seen any one of you on campus… What year are you?" She asked somewhat rudely.

"Seniors. Funny, I haven't seen you here either. What year are you?" Caleb all of a sudden was on his A game.

"Juniors. And what are you studying?" She shifted her weight from her right side to her left.

"Business. All of us are in the business school, and you?" Caleb asked back sharply, getting a bit annoyed at her sudden shift in attitude.

"Education. Both of us," she snapped back. "Funny, I have never seen you at the lake, or at school…" she added.

"Funny," was all Caleb could manage to say back.

Feeling like she had to defuse the situation, suddenly Rowan piped back in. "Well it's nice to meet you. The offer still stands, if you guys are around that day." Rowan went back to inviting them out to the lake Friday.

However, Mikayla was still on Caleb.

"So, where are you guys from?" She shot back real quick.

"California, and you?" Caleb shot back, just as fast.

"Here," she said quickly.

They stood there, half annoyed at each other and half taken back at what each had felt in the touch of their hands. Mikayla couldn't shake the feeling something was off. She also couldn't shake the feeling of wanting to stare at him. To stare at his eyes and his perfect face, with his bright white, even smile and the little dimples on either side of his full lips set into a chiseled facial structure. He was gorgeous. Currently he was shirtless, and he had a cut at every curve a man could possibly have a cut. He had an athletic body, muscular and lean. His body was slightly tanned from the sun and she was desperately trying to resist the urge to keep looking.

Stop it, Mikayla. You're being rude… He is really cute and seems polite! Don't blow it or you will forever be hanging on to Dominick, and never find someone you can fall in love with. I can see and feel that there is something there, so STOP IT!" Rowan sent a message to Mikayla telepathically.

It was something they had discovered they could do with each other. Again, no one knew about it but them. Mikayla knew Rowan was right, she didn't know why she was being so rude. She decided she was being stupid and backed down.

"Um, really, do you guys have a boat?" Mikayla looked at Caleb almost apologetically.

Caleb melted for a minute at that, he just wanted to touch her again, to grab her and hug her. *Hug her? What the fuck, I don't hug*, he reminded himself before answering.

"Yes, we do back home, and just to let you know, we were already planning a trip to the lake Friday to celebrate the official kick off of summer, and the fact that we are now finished with college. We will probably just rent one here," Caleb assured.

"Oh, well that's cool," was all Mikayla could manage to spit out.

What is wrong with you… Since when have you ever been at a loss for words… Come on Kali get back in there! Mikayla decided having Rowan in her head like this was going to get weird and gave her a look letting her know to stop it, she was only going to make things worse at this point.

Caleb noticed the look and his warning flags started to go off. First, he could have sworn this girl had stopped the ball from hitting her face without touching it. Now she was looking at Rowan as if she had said something, only she hadn't been speaking. Caleb was going to get down to the bottom of that, but for now he needed a reason for them to meet up.

"Do you wake board?" Caleb asked her, trying to engage her.

All of a sudden her eyes lit up.

"Yes Caleb, I do wake board. do you?" She asked.

"Hell yeah. There isn't many water sports that I don't do, the water is a natural place for me," Caleb found himself being well himself.

"I know exactly what you mean, I always have felt a connection to the water. Sometimes when I feel that there is too much noise around me, I go out to the lake and run to the end of our dock and jump in. I love the sudden silence of being under water and the feeling of weightlessness. I stay there until I can't hold my breath any further and make my way back up." Mikayla felt herself opening up and she could see in his eyes he knew exactly what she was talking about.

"I know exactly what you mean." Caleb said, repeating her, and now smiling and looking only at her.

They started talking and Rowan, for once, was made silent. She stood still, just smiling in satisfaction at the interaction between the two of them. They didn't seem to notice she was no longer in the conversation. They didn't seem to notice anything besides each other.

They talked more about the water, it's mystery and ability to produce calm and quiet. All along the way they each had a hard time looking directly into each other eyes. Caleb's eye would catch Mikayla's and her whole body would tingle, and his felt as if it were on fire. He felt exhilarated. It was some kind of unknown high, he thought to himself.

Twenty minutes had past and neither one of them noticed anything but each other. They had both forgot what it was they were supposed to be doing. He was supposed to be connecting with Rowan, to see if she were the witch who had been given angels breath, and she was supposed to be having a last minute study session before her last final.

As Mikayla looked into his eyes, she noticed the exotic shape of them, almost Egyptian, yet the color was like the Caribbean on a bright, clear day. She could see something behind his eyes, but couldn't pick up on what it was. It felt dark and lost. Those eyes were fixed on hers.

Looking down, back at Mikayla, Caleb was trying to read her thoughts. He couldn't read anything, all he could see was she had the most beautiful eyes he had ever seen. Her eyes were like a predator, he thought; sexy and seductive, yet behind them was a purity and he was drawn to her. He had never felt drawn to anything before. This was a new feeling and he lacked control. It made him want to run, but it wasn't running away from her, but to her; wanting to tear her apart until he could figure out what it was about her that was making him so intoxicated.

Caught up in the moment of looking into each other's eyes, they both fell silent and the world around them again faded away.

Caleb, what is taking so long? Ali said telepathically, who could see Caleb wasn't focused on Rowan and he needed to break the spell. Caleb looked away from Mikayla and realized where he was, and remembered again why he was there in the first place. He used all his strength to pull back from her spell and get back to his job.

"So, you guys going out on the water for sure?" Caleb asked.

"Of course, we wouldn't miss our opportunity to have the boat to ourselves!" Rowan said smiling. *The next three weeks you won't have Dominick and Mario stalking you constantly, and it may just give you enough time to actually get to know someone before those jerks chase another guy off. Please, don't be mad. I'm about to seal the deal.* Rowan sent a message of her own back to Mikayla, and then looked back at Caleb.

"So, Caleb, what's it gonna be? Are you going to meet us on the lake then? Say around one or two?" Rowan said before Mikayla could get a word in.

Before he could answer, he looked from one to the other. Mikayla gave her a warning look that she had given out too much information.

"Well, maybe we could meet up, that is if you all don't have other plans, or boyfriends that might get jealous?" Caleb asked, as if he had just read that line out of a handbook on pick up lines for dummies.

He added the last line mostly to find out about Mikayla, although he thought anyone with her was just a hurdle he would have to jump. *Why the hell would I care, anyways. I always take what I want anyway! Where the fuck is my head at?* He thought to himself, frustrated by the nature of his current thinking.

"Well, I have a boyfriend, but he won't be there. But Mikayla is single!" Rowan said, practically standing on her tip toes, grinning from ear to ear.

Stop it, Rowan. This guy's gonna think there is something wrong with me the way you keep throwing me at him. Besides, maybe I don't want to hang out with him! Mikayla sent a telepathic message to Rowan and looked at her with furious eyes.

Rowan looked away from Caleb and to Mikayla, still smiling. *Yeah right, Mikayla. You totally want to so shut up and take advantage of your up and coming freedom.*

He could swear they were communicating. He knew Rowan had the capability, being a witch and all, but he wasn't sure about this other girl. This perfect angel who deserved to be possessed by him, he thought to himself. Something wasn't right, and he knew it, but couldn't put his finger on it. But he knew he soon would. Perhaps Rowan conjured up some sort of spell for her friend to be able to speak to her telepathically. That made perfect sense to him, yet it didn't explain why she was able to stop the ball from hitting her face. His brain started to spin. She couldn't be a witch because of her age. They knew there were only two alive at this age. Not wanting to think about it any further, he decided he was seeing things and to drop it.

"Yeah, that sounds good. How will we find you?" Caleb joined back with the present.

"Just go to the sand bar," Rowan said, matter of fact.

"The sand bar?" Caleb said, trying to get more information. She said it was a chain of lakes and they could easily spend all day looking for them instead of being with them.

"I thought you were familiar with the chain? You said you've been there," Mikayla was back to feeling suspicious, partly because she was drawn to him and partly because she felt something dark behind those eyes.

"Of course I have. I just didn't know which sand bar you were talking about?" Caleb took a shot that if it was a chain of lakes, then it was likely there was more than one sand bar.

"Oh, uh yeah. I guess there is," Mikayla said, embarrassed by her current bi-polar behavior.

"We always go to baseline, were the college kids hang out," Rowan came in to try and salvage the rest of the conversation.

"Yeah, we've hung out there. I just never remember seeing either of you, so I assumed you might be talking about another one that I may not have known about. Remember, I'm not from here and I haven't lived a lifetime on the lake like you girls. We just get out there when we can and float around." Caleb said so convincingly, he smiled inside at his ability to manipulate and twist things and ate it up every time another person fell for his trickery.

He was definitely Coyote, both trickster and creator in his own mind. Someone definitely worth writing about, he thought to himself.

"Can't say I remember ever seeing you either," Rowan said genuinely, still smiling. Caleb smiled back because he knew he had gotten away with his lies, yet again.

He turned his attention back towards Mikayla, wanting to still talk to her. He wanted to see if she might be excited to see him, too, when he heard a deep voice call from a ways away.

"Mikayla!" The voice shouted.

8

"Oh great, here come the guard dogs," Mikayla said as she squinted her eyes watching her brother and Dominick walking over from the steps of the student center.

"Shit!" Rowan said as her smile dropped slightly. Then she turned towards Caleb.

"Whatever you do, don't say anything about meeting us on the water. You see that shorter boy with the shaved head, covered in black tribal tattoos? That is Romario, Kali's brother and my boyfriend. He is way overprotective of her and, well, of me. Dominick is a thousand times worse over Kali. It's not what you think, he's not her boyfriend anymore. I mean, it's been years but he acts like a mix between a jealous boyfriend, big brother, and overprotective father. Long story, perhaps you will hear it one day. But please, for now just be cool. Oh, and sorry for the treatment you are about to receive." Rowan added as the three of them watched Mario, with his olive skin covered in tribal tattoos and shaved head, which revealed black hair starting to grow in, walk over alongside of Dominick.

Mario moved steady, his arms swinging coolly at his sides as he walked, not taking his eyes off of Caleb for a moment. Caleb could see every muscle in his bare arms were well defined and the look in his dark eyes was familiar. Like another predator, but not one he had ever encountered.

Caleb smiled with the right corner of his mouth and glared back instinctively at them. It wasn't something made for a college campus. This was raw, not human. It was something that should be kept away from the civilized human population. Predator versus predator.

Dominick, the taller one, was even bigger, Caleb noticed. He also was draped in tattoos of fine art and ancient symbols, not just tribal work like Mario. Caleb had a few himself, but he thought these guys had excessive amounts and assumed it was a testosterone issue by the size of their muscles. By the definition in the taller one's arms, he assumed these guys had to be on steroids. The taller one had a slightly lighter shade of olive skin, and by the coloring in his eyebrows assumed he had dark brown hair, but he couldn't be sure because he had a white bandana covering the top of his head. He could see his green eyes shining and coming fiercely his way.

They watched in silence as the two overly muscular boys made their way over. Instantly, Mario grabbed Rowan and pressed tightly against her. Caleb smiled even bigger, amused at the display of possession and thought to himself the guy might as well have just lifted his leg and peed on her. This poor guy has instincts like a dog, he thought, further entertaining himself, and focused his attention back on Mikayla only to find Dominick in front of her with his arms crossed.

Caleb wanted to laugh, at first, at this display of overprotective steroid users gone dog, but he suddenly felt enraged at being blocked from Mikayla. It was like two animals fighting over the same carcass, only he had no want of feeding off of this girl. He didn't know exactly why, but he just knew he wanted her, whatever that meant, and right now this over grown ape was blocking his way.

Dominick stood in his way of Mikayla. Caleb, angered by this, started to tense up, his teeth started to ache and he could feel the sharpness of his canines starting to poke through his gums. He was going into fight mode instinctively. All reason was out, it was just nature. He had to get what was his and would kill this thing standing in his way. Just as he was ready to pounce, Jamahl entered into his head.

Be cool there, little brother. We are not here for them. If you blow this now, there will be no way for us to get close to them again. Back down. Now, little brother, back down. Play the innocent nice guy. Caleb, BACK DOWN... Jamahl saw the tightness in his jaw drop and then added, *That's it, little brother, focus.*

Caleb's muscles began to relax. His teeth began to retract and the coloring in his eyes that began to lighten started to even out again.

"What's up, man? I'm Caleb." He managed to say friendly, and stuck out his hand to shake Dominick's.

But Dominick just stood there, unmoved, with his arms folded in front of him and his chin tilted up, despite the fact he was a good 5 inches taller than Caleb. "That's nice, Caleb, but I think you better take your ball and get back to your game." Dominick said, not moving an inch.

"Get out of my way Dom!" Mikayla said as she tried with all her might to push him aside. He was like puddy in her hands and he let her move him a bit so she was now in front. "Sorry, these guys were absent on the day politeness was given out." She added as she glared back at Dominick.

Caleb smiled again, amused by her spirit.

"Mikayla, I think you need to get to class, now," Mario jumped in as if Caleb weren't even there.

"Mario!" Rowan snapped and pulled slightly away from him, but he was much stronger and kept a firm grip on her.

"Mario, if my watch breaks I will let you know, but mine is working just fine and it says I still have a half of an hour, but thanks for your concern." Mikayla snapped quickly at her brother.

Caleb tried to hold it in, but couldn't help but laugh a little. He was even more amused at her wit.

"What the fuck are you laughing at, bro?" Mario stared directly into Caleb's eyes. Caleb stopped laughing, but was still smiling.

He was about to say sorry to try and keep the peace, when all of a sudden he noticed a shift in Mario's eyes. His eyes were almost black, normally. Caleb could see that from far away. The shift happened as Mario's black iris suddenly collapsed inward and then exploded quickly outward, making the entire open eye black. Not an ounce of white shone anywhere, and just as quickly as it turned, the eye collapsed quickly inward again, returning to normal. All of a sudden, Caleb recognized the scent in the air, and it wasn't human.

Caleb just stood there for a moment, the smile had left his face. He was feeling as if he might be falling into some sort of trap. He knew now exactly why these guys muscles were so defined and why their testosterone levels were off the charts, and it had nothing to do with steroids.

"Mario, he's laughing at you being stupid!" Mikayla snapped.

Caleb stood there, still, and thought carefully before answering.

"Sorry man, it's just that my ball accidentally hit your sister and I was just apologizing," he said as if he were truly sorry for the inconvenience and didn't want any trouble.

"Well, apologize and move on, man." Dominick replied, looking down at Caleb with his arms still crossed. Mikayla whipped her head up at him. "He already did, so back off Dominick," she said, even more agitated now.

Caleb wanted to take these two out immediately. It took everything in him to contain his rage. The one thing that was helping him was her. She was full of life and apparently had no trouble speaking her mind. He could tell she was innocent, but timid she was not. He had a brief moment of imagining tearing out their throats, one-by-one with his teeth, exposing a bite so fierce it cut down to the bone until his eyes caught hers again.

"Thanks for saying you're sorry, but really I'm alright. Thanks for the school information, that could be useful and I will look into it," she said to him, winking.

She had made the last part up, and Caleb knew it was a code which meant she would see him Friday.

Smart little girl... he thought to himself.

"Hey, no problem. Maybe I will see you around," he played along back.

"Or maybe you won't," Mario added as Rowan's face went from mad to irate. But she didn't speak for fear of causing a scene at school. Besides, she knew it wouldn't do any good anyway.

She loved Mario with every ounce of her soul, and despite her outgoing personality and zest for life, he was the dominant in their relationship. He treated her like gold, but was overly possessive, which turned her on despite the annoying moments like these. She couldn't help it, she was defenseless against his charm. And he loved her fiercely.

"Why don't we just let fate decide," Mikayla said, staring directly into Caleb's eyes.

His smile came back and everyone disappeared again, and for a few moments it was just them again. Time seemed to stop for the third time during this sunny, warm day. Without taking his eyes away from hers, he replied. "Let's," was all he said.

The silence was broken when an overgrown, tattooed arm grabbed Mikayla and pushed her slightly behind his wall of a body.

This fucking guy... Caleb thought to himself, and to his brothers about Dominick.

Again, the anger started to surge within him at someone taking what Caleb already decided on was his.

Caleb, calm down. Come back and play catch. It will make them less suspicious of you. Remember, don't fucking blow this. When we are done with our mission we can take these fuckers out. For now, be cool. Ali reasoned back in his head.

Just like that Caleb smiled at Mikayla and winked. He turned with the football in his hands and started to jog towards his brothers.

"It was nice to meet you!" Rowan yelled after him as he headed back towards Jamahl and Ali. Mikayla just stared at him, admiring his athletic physique and slightly tanned body. His shirt was off and his skin wasn't just well defined and lean, it was smooth and completely perfect.

Mikayla's admiration of Caleb stopped when she heard her brother getting angry. "You need to stop being so friendly to strangers!" Mario barked at Rowan.

"Whatever, Mario. Not all of us feel the need to alienate the rest of the world," she said and tried harder to break free of his grip.

But again, he only held on tighter, and this time picked her up and acted as if he were going to slam her to the ground. She screamed and then they both started laughing. He then let her down gently and she playfully hit him, but he grabbed her again and planted a kiss on her.

"See, you can't stay mad at me!" He said, sure of himself as he began to place soft kisses on her neck that tickled her, causing her to giggle with pleasure as she didn't deny his claim.

Mikayla rolled her eyes, disgusted at her best friend's attraction for her brother, and then turned her attention to Dominick.

"What the fuck is your problem? I mean you guys always do this to me! You had no idea of what that guy was doing. He's nice! You two have got to stop this! Lately you guys have been a hundred times worse! What the fuck is going on? I want an honest answer," she demanded.

Dominick looked at her, confused.

"What do you mean?" He asked, playing stupid.

"FORGET IT!" She yelled back and began to walk away.

She took a couple of steps forward before feeling an oversized hand grab her upper arm.

"Mikayla…" Dominick said, sincerely this time. "Wait, I'm sorry," he finished as he turned her so they were facing each other. "I just don't want you to get hurt again," he added.

This hurt her heart. She knew exactly what he was talking about. Maybe that's all any of this jealous behavior ever was, just friendship. They were practically family and they hadn't been a couple in four years. He had even stopped trying to get back with her over the past year. Perhaps it was all just genuine concern coming from an overly testosterone filled twenty one-year-old man.

"Thanks, Dominick. I'm glad you are my friend and care about me, but at some point my heart will probably get broken again. It's all right, these are the things I have to go through in order for me to find the person who won't. Put a little more faith in me." she said, smiling up at him.

His heart melted right there and then. He had loved her since childhood, but he had screwed it up. He wasn't strong enough during the change to remain faithful. His hormones were running amuck and the surge of animal instinct he had developed made him unbearable. He was alpha. This he knew and he didn't blame her for never giving him a fourth chance. He struck out three times. She would never forgive him. He pushed his feelings for her deep down so they were manageable.

During the past four years, he had several girlfriends. A couple of them he even had strong feelings for, and in those times it seemed to help keep him from thinking about her. He hoped one day to find the girl that would break him free from her completely. He would never care about her any less. Again, they were like family, and despite the rocky times they went through, they were very good friends with an unbreakable bond. But he prayed one day a girl would come along who fit him so well, the spell Mikayla had over him would be broken and they could then just be friends, and family.

"I'm not going to apologize for trying to protect you, and I'm not going to make false promises that I can't keep. But know this, anything I do when it concerns you is out of the best possible place," Dominick said, looking down into her beautiful blue eyes.

She became a bit overwhelmed looking into his eyes, still a bit sad for her childhood sweetheart. How she used to love him. She still did, only now as just a friend – a close friend, and as family.

Looking up into his eyes, she swore she saw his eyes tear up and she knew right then he was still in some pain over her.

Rowan, this is killing me. I wish I could just forget everything that happened and fall back in love with him to stop this from hurting him. Or better yet, I hope a girl comes along that is so amazing that he will say, Kali who? She said telepathically over to Rowan, who looked at her and gave her a gentle smile.

When the time is right, a girl will come along. It's nature. Rowan replied.

You sound so sure? Mikayla thought back, surprised.

I will tell you how life works some other time, but now we really should be moving to class! Rowan replied in thought again.

Rowan grabbed her bag and turned to Mario to give him a kiss goodbye as Mikayla watched and waited. "Later," was all she could muster up for her brother. She was very irritated at his behavior.

"Stop talking to strangers," he yelled back at her, laughing and giving Dominick a high five. Dominick started laughing, too, although he did at least try to control it. Mikayla didn't feel the need to reply. Rowan just looped her arm through Mikayla's and led her towards class, supportively.

As they made their way through the large, grassy park area, she tilted her head to catch one more glance at Caleb, who was already back playing football with his friends. The minute she turned her head, he stopped and starred back at her, almost missing a ball coming right for his face. Without even looking at the ball, as his eyes burned through hers, he somehow managed to catch the ball. She should have found this strange, instead it just made her whole body tingle at his superman reflexes. Embarrassed by the tingling feeling, she turned quickly away from him, afraid he would be able to see what she was feeling. She kept her eyes forward, looking at the building across the way.

"He's still staring at you," Rowan whispered, as if Caleb could hear them despite the distance between.

"That's nice," Was all Mikayla said, and then the two of the began to laugh..

9

Caleb stood there for an extra moment admiring Mikayla's well-shaped backside. This girl had the body of a goddess, he thought. She was perfect in every way. He began to feel hungry, but not for blood. He felt a couple of eyes upon him and he looked to his brothers, who were flinging their arms in the air, trying to get him to throw back the ball, but that wasn't the eyes he was feeling.

He shifted and scanned his eyes instinctively back to where Mario and Dominick were standing, now joined with three other equally as defined boys. The pack was looking down at him. He wondered if they had sensed the vampire in him. Him being half witch should throw off any vampire sent, plus the walking in daylight thing surely wouldn't make them suspect something of him, he thought. But sure enough, they were there watching him carefully.

Fuck, you got to be kidding me! Werewolves? Ali thought to himself, but thought loud enough for his brothers to hear.

Yup. Caleb answered back.

Caleb decided he would give them a show. He began to play his heart out. He knew they weren't completely buying it when they started to pace on top of the hill as they watched down at them. Then he saw his opportunity to make himself seem legitimate.

A group of seven athletic looking boys were coming out of the union. Caleb tossed the ball to Jamahl. *Trust me...* he thought to his brothers to let them know he did, indeed, have a plan.

The boys were out of ear shot from Mario and the boys, as far as Caleb knew, but he also knew their hearing was better than the average human, so just in case, he put on a show from the beginning.

Caleb approached them with his arms raised to the sky, as if to ask what was taking them so long. The boys, at first, looked confused, until Caleb used hypnosis and a small spell to captivate them. All of a sudden, one boy responded. "Sorry man, we had to finish eating, but we are ready now." The boy with blonde hair replied.

There were three Caucasian boys in the group of seven, one of them with blonde hair and blue eyes, and the other two with brown hair and hazel eyes. Then there was a Korean kid with a shaggy cut that had some of the tips dyed red; he looked punk rock. One kid looked like he may have been of Persian descent, and another kid was Mediterranean of some sort. There was also an African American kid who was athletically built with a short fade and hazel eyes. Caleb admired, for a moment, the mix of the crowd, reminding him of his own brothers. It's the one good thing Caleb held on to: a sense of community. Even though he and his brothers were a different breed of being, they were descendants of different nationalities, he always found it odd when people took issue with skin color, race, or religion. At times he felt it was only one more reason humans were beneath him. Racism didn't exist amongst the immortal beings, and they all shared a common knowledge of belief, which was only divided between Good and Bad and allowing room for some to choose neutral. It also made him wonder, at times, if his father's idea of having humans live like animals out in the wild for them to pick each other off wasn't such a bad idea. After all, the way humans treated each other at times made them seem like the stupidest being of all.

As he stood facing the crowd, he planted a question in each of their heads for them to answer quietly, inside their own heads. *Give me your names…* Caleb commanded.

One by one, they each answered back. *Jackson, Ben, Paul, James, Carson, Nader, and Dino.* Caleb took their names in and sent them to his brothers.

I'm not going to remember these names, Caleb. Ali said, concerned this may raise suspicion from the group of, now, seven watching from the top of the hill.

Caleb thought a minute, and then closed his eyes and chanted under his breath. While chanting under his breath, he held up his hand and high fived each of the seven boys. When he opened his eyes, he saw each of the boy's names written in black on the inside of is palm. The writing was visible only to Caleb, Ali, and Jamahl.

This wasn't a trick Caleb had just learned. When he was younger and being put through home school, he would always get in trouble for not completing his work. So one day he went to the library and looked through spell book after spell book until he found something that would give him the best of both worlds. What he found were ways to get information out of one person's head, and have it printed upon his palm from contact with the other person's palm. He passed many a test that way. Caleb still giggled every time he thought about how his teacher would smile because she thought Caleb thought she was so cool, giving her all those high fives. Little did she know, he just needed the answers to the test he would fail to prepare for the night before.

Jamahl and Ali realized the trick he was pulling and looked at each other and immediately started laughing when they realized he had just pulled the old trick from their school days on the unsuspecting group of seven.

After Caleb had imprinted each of their names on the right palms of their hands, he began to laugh and talk with them as if they had been friends for years. The boys were being themselves, other than the fact they were under a spell which made them think these three guys were a part of their friend group.

They headed back over to where Jamahl and Ali were standing. Caleb stepped forward with the ball and high fived each of his brother's to transfer the list of names to them as well.

"Jackson, you can be a captain," Caleb pointed at the blonde haired boy he had first approached.

"Jamahl, you will be the other captain," Caleb then threw the ball at Jamahl.

The two captains stood facing the group and picked team members one-by-one until they were all picked. They didn't mess around with a lot of details and rules. Football was football. They just began to play as if they had done so every Sunday for the past four years.

Despite this being a smoke screen, Caleb was enjoying himself. He got a big kick out of these boys. They were funny, and a bunch of smart asses. They all seemed to lack the fear gene and played fiercely, unafraid of getting hit, even by Jamahl, despite his size.

During the game, Caleb was checking from time to time to see what Mario was doing. The last time he checked, two more boys had joined them, but Caleb only continued to play.

About an hour passed by. Caleb was laughing and breathing hard, all at the same time. It had been about twenty minutes since the last time he checked on Mario. All the pack of overly grown boys had gone, except for one.

They had left a scout behind. The scout sat on top of the hill watching the game. *Smart doggies...* Caleb thought to his brothers.

Jamahl glanced quickly up at the hill.

They are really confident, aren't they... it seems they can sense something, but technically we don't exist, so they don't know what it is they are sensing. Looks like their control issues may be of use to us... He sent a message back.

Ali just continued the game, not joining in. He decided to just play it cool. The group of boys they were playing with were having fun. Jamahl and Ali were also having fun. Caleb, especially, was having fun. He felt normal for once, not that he had ever wanted that, but had always wondered what it would feel like. Today he was getting his first lesson.

The day was getting late. It was time for them to wrap up the game. Caleb threw a pass to Carson, who made their team's winning touchdown. Caleb, who played on the opposite team as his brothers, jumped in the winner's pile up with Jackson, Nadar, Paul, and Carson. He was truly enjoying this moment of triumph façade. The opposing team was still in good spirits laughing and talking smack at the winner's pile up.

Things settled down and it was time to tell them good-bye. A few man hugs and fist pumps later, Jackson spoke to the three brothers. "Hey man, we all rent this house downtown and we are having a start of summer bash tonight, why don't you guys come by?" He said sincerely, hoping they would.

"We're there man!" Caleb said as he took out his cell phone.

Caleb quickly plugged in phone numbers from each of them, acting as if he were just texting as Ali and Jamahl carried on conversations in an attempt to mislead the scout on top of the hill. Ali and Jamahl also spent a little time hypnotizing the boys unsuspected, trying to gather bits and pieces of personal information about each of the seven boys while transmitting back bits of information about the three of them. All of this was just Caleb, Ali, and Jamahl being overly cautious. They needed the alibis if the wolves decided to check around.

Caleb was unsure what made Mario and friends so suspicious. He didn't know if they had been expecting something was going to happen, or if it was just the large amounts of testosterone pumping through their bodies. Caleb did know about the werewolf legends of power surges which would happen before they were in full use of their powers. One at seventeen and the other at twenty one, and those guys had to all be around the age of twenty one. Caleb hoped it was just that and they weren't expecting them.

Caleb finished putting the rest of Jackson's number in his phone, but before he closed it, he looked around them to make sure the hypnotizing spell had taken effect. He knew it had by the way Jamahl and Ali were interacting with the seven boys. It was done. They now had some alibis, just in case.

Perhaps this is being a bit paranoid, Caleb thought to his brothers.

No, we are leaving no room for error, Ali assured him this whole production was not a waste of their time.

Besides, we can't have only work and no play, Jamahl added and smiled at Caleb.

The group of seven headed back to wherever it was they were heading to in the first place as the boys remained on the open field. Caleb felt an air of relief as he turned his head back up to the top of the hill where the scout had been left to spy on them, to find he was no longer there. Suddenly he felt a pair of eyes on him, instantly he scanned the crowed to find out where they were coming from.

"The scout is gone, but I can feel someone watching," Caleb said calmly to his brothers.

"Easy Caleb, don't be too obvious that you feel it," Ali said and paused a moment to slowly scan the area to try and get a read before adding, "Funny, I can't feel it."

Jamahl was doing the same thing now as both of his brothers. "Caleb, I can't feel it either," Jamahl added.

"NO, I can still feel it! Someone's watching," Caleb said calmly, still scanning the crowed.

"No, Caleb. I don't sense or see anything out of the ordinary," Ali said, giving a last search. He couldn't feel anything, and neither could Jamahl, so they brushed it off and picked up their shirts and water bottles.

Caleb was still looking around. He could feel the eyes watching him, creating a tingling in his body that was getting more intense until it started to burn a little as he searched the crowd. Not a hot fire, more of a warm explosion in his body. A feeling he had never had before. Still, he saw nothing. Finally he decided to try and ignore it. He walked over to his brothers to pick up his t-shirt and take a few sips of water. Perhaps he was just hungry, he thought to himself.

"Caleb!" Caleb heard as he was taking a sip of water.

He didn't even need to turn around to know who it was. Every inch of his body stopped working for a split second, causing the flow in his veins to back up and then rush out twice as fast when they started to flow again, causing an electrical surge throughout his entire body. He quickly turned towards the voice.

"I just wanted to say that I am so sorry. Please don't let the boys bother you. They just get like that when they don't know someone. They are a bit on the overprotective side, but I assure you, harmless. No one has died... yet!" Mikayla said with a smile across her beautiful face.

"I wasn't worried," Caleb said as he put the same smile back across his face. Her knees became weak at his confidence, or was it his smile, she couldn't decide. Outside of her brother and his friends, especially Dominick, the only other guy she had known who exuded that much confidence was Marcus. She had hoped this wasn't a bad sign. The more confident the guy, the stronger her attraction was for them. But so far, she had two strikes and was hoping this would not be strike three, or she was seriously going to look into hypnosis to have them block the chemical in her brain attracted to these overly confident, cocky type of guys.

A slight wind started to blow through the air, causing Mikayla's long dark hair to fly in front of her face. The wind pushed the scent of oranges and vanilla over towards Caleb as he watched as she gently took her hand to tuck the flying pieces neatly behind her ear, exposing her neck. Caleb started to fixate on the veins in her neck while the creamy scent of fruit and vanilla intoxicated his senses. As if they were one, he could see the rhythm of her heart beat coming through her aorta.

He waited for the blood lust to start, when his jaw would start to ache and his eyes would have extreme clarity. Any minute now his senses would become even more heightened than they already were. Soon the feeling of being out of control and the strength it took to stay in control would take over. But oddly, none of that ever came. Caleb felt hungry, but not for blood or for food. The hunger was more of a need, a need to be close to her, to be alone with her. A hunger that he wanted to know her.

She stared at him, looking past the color of his eyes and beyond the beauty of his face. Mikayla now was looking through him and as she briefly glimpsed into what she thought must be the aura of his soul. She felt her knees buckle, unsteadying her as she felt a rush of excitement flutter throughout her veins.

As Mikayla looked deeply into him, for a moment Caleb could have sworn he felt something flying around inside of his stomach. He fought to brush off the strange feeling and composed himself as he reached deep inside and pulled himself out. "Your brother isn't going to stop me from going to the lake, Mikayla. I hope he isn't going to stop you," Caleb said, trying to give her a reason to make sure she showed up. He needed Rowan to be there, but his own needs felt more urgent at the moment, and he needed for Mikayla to be there more.

"Like he could," she said as she smiled, showing perfectly straight, white teeth. His confidence had helped snap Mikayla out of her slightly tranced state. The confidence he exuded she was already well accustomed to from her brother and all of his friends.

Caleb smiled back and they found themselves locked on each other's eyes for a moment before she looked away and led her eyes over to the top of the hill. Caleb guessed she was looking for her brother or any of his friends. He realized, at that point, this must be a normal occurrence in her life ,which was a good sign perhaps it wasn't that the wolves were on to them. Instead, this poor girl is trapped, he thought to himself and found he was feeling sorry for her the same way he felt when he saw any animal or bird caged.

"Well, I got to go," she said as she checked her watch. The day was getting away from her and she had a family dinner to attend. She really didn't want to go, but felt a little like the cat had stolen her tongue. Something about this guy made her nervous.

"Yeah," was all Caleb could manage to say back. He didn't feel the need to come up with a smooth line as he would have normally done. At that moment, he had a feeling of purity. He knew the feeling because it was the same feeling he had when he was surfing on the water. The water was his serenity, and his ego for that brief moment no longer existed.

He watched her walk away again. This time he wasn't admiring her beauty, this time he was watching her in pure curiosity. Why was he so drawn to her, he wondered. According to the seer, he was supposed to be drawn to Rowan. As he thought further about it, he realized the seer didn't say Rowan, specifically. Perhaps this was what the warning was for, something may cloud his judgement, he thought further.

Caleb looked away from her and up into the sky. *I will not let her get in the way of my job*, he commanded, trying to convince himself he wouldn't. He would use all his strength to make sure his job would get done.

He then glanced back at her. She was still in sight, and his stomach started to feel a bit uneasy again. He thought it was strange that while she made him feel at peace, she also made him feel a little bit like what he decided must be the feeling of motion sickness. Trying to put a finger on this new found feelings, he all of a sudden realized this was what having butterflies in the stomach felt like, motion sickness.

For a moment his brain raced. He had always been immune to these types of feelings, or at least so he thought. He felt a loss of control and was feeling uncomfortable. Angered by this, he looked away and towards his brothers. "We have a lot to do before Friday," he said authoritatively, trying to get back some of the control he felt he had lost.

"What do we need to do?" Jamahl asked, not because he didn't know himself what needed to be done, but because he could tell his brother was struggling internally with something. He wanted to give his brother a different focus, and if there was one thing Caleb loved to do, it was to be made to feel as if he were solving problems. It made him feel like a leader.

"We're going to need a boat, for starters," he said matter of fact. "We will also need to get the holy water and I don't think it would hurt to make quick friends with our football crew, just in case the pack decides to show up on the lake. My hunch says that they will, so the more alibis we have the better. We have to throw them off, not just until we can figure out if she is the one, but if she is not we don't want to raise any suspicion that we are looking for the witch with angels breath," Caleb said, finally feeling a bit more like himself, and even more in control as he went down the list, more to remind himself why it is they were there in the first place.

"Caleb, we don't even know if they know anything. They may just be over-protective because of their nature. Especially since Rowan's friend is one of them," Ali said, trying to put things into perspective.

Funny how she didn't smell like one, Caleb thought to himself and then shook it off. She wasn't his concern, and he had to figure out how to get her out of his mind.

The three brothers with their next few moves in tact headed back to the car. They had a few loose ends to tie up to get ready for Friday.

10

The sun was starting to make its way across the horizon as night time was on its tail, pushing it down as it was now his turn to shine. They had hoped to catch Mary back at the bar. Jamahl had remembered she said she was getting off early that night and thought it would be a perfect opportunity for him to get her to help them out. They didn't know for sure whether or not the holy water was, in fact, the way to reveal if Rowan was the witch who was given life from the sacrifice of an angel. The seer just had assumed from the direct quote of the legend that is what is used to reveal an angel's "wings." Whatever that meant, and as well as one more thing they didn't quite have the clue to.

Ali wasn't so convinced the holy water would work. To him, it didn't follow the laws in which he knew to be true. He was known as the smart one. One of his passions was myths and folklore, and he researched them all the time, both those known to the human world and those known only to the world of immortals and other magical creatures. Humans never had access to those myths. Anything written down they didn't have the means to decode, or the eyes to see what had been written. It was more for their protection than the protection of the magic world. For now it was what they had to go on, so they decided to try it.

In the meantime, Ali was doing a bit of research on his own to try and find if there was anything out there that would give him a key to decoding the riddle. Somehow it seemed much too simple to him all they would need to do is either spray her or make her drink holy water. It just seemed to obvious and simple. It also seemed to him as if it being made so simple was created to throw people off somehow because of the potential danger a person in that position could possess for themselves and the world. Havoc could wreak if it really were just that simple.

They walked into the bar as Mary, the waitress from inside, was on her way out. "Awe you're leaving? I was only coming in here to see you." Jamahl said as he flashed his beautiful white smile.

All she did was laugh, she wasn't falling for his pick-up line, but was amused at his efforts.

"So this is the part where you are supposed to ask me if I am busy tonight, because now that you are off of work, you are free." Jamahl gleamed down at her, determined not to glamour her; to see if he could pull her own his own.

He loved to do things like that. He was always much more proud of himself when he was able to get people to agree without having to charm them into it. It made him feel even if he didn't have all the powers, he would still be very powerful.

"Oh is that what I am supposed to say?" Mary said, now bordering flirtatious.

"Well, it's just a suggestion," Jamahl made his smile drop to a curious grin.

"Alright, I will bite. Are you free tonight, Jamahl?" She said, still smiling.

Ali and Caleb were in the background laughing at the "will bite" part.

She assumed they were just laughing at their friend trying to put the moves on her.

"No, actually I have plans. Maybe some other time," he joked as she slapped him in the arm and started to laugh. "No, really if you are not doing anything we, I mean, I would love to hang out with you. That is if you are indeed free," he then said ever so smoothly.

"Ok Jamahl, I will tell you what, some girlfriends and I are going to go bar hoping in downtown. If you can find me, then I will go out on a date with you," she smiled, looking into his eyes without blinking.

Jamahl was amused. Of course they could find her, they were predators. They were made to find prey. "Then we have a deal, as long as I can have my date tomorrow," Jamahl said back.

Mary chuckled at Jamahl's self-confidence. There were many more bars and restaurants downtown, you wouldn't be able to get to all of them in one night, even if you only stayed fifteen minutes or so. Then there was the difference between the Main Street area and South U, not to mention all of the bars and restaurants in between those two areas, that were a good couple of miles and a ton of streets a part. Although she did want to see him, there was a part of her that wanted to outsmart him so he would chase after her the next day, and she liked that thought. There was something about him which was different and alluring, and the thought of him chasing after her thrilled her.

"What do I get if you can't find me?" She asked.

"Oh, I will find you." Jamahl said and smiled down at her as he stared into her eyes.

Mary felt weak in the knees and started to reconsider her previous thought. Now she was starting to hope he would indeed find her, but she refused to give him any clues. She would leave it up to fate.

"We'll see," she said and brushed passed him as she headed out of the double doors, heading towards her car.

The brother's watched as she made her way across the parking lot and then got into her car.

"Game on," Jamahl said.

"Game on," Caleb agreed.

Ali said nothing and started heading up towards their room.

11

The sun was still shining bright as Mikayla was finally home after taking their last final. They were going out to dinner with their families, as per tradition on the last day of school. It was important for their families to celebrate those small little accomplishments. Tonight they were going to the restaurant Mikayla's family owned. It was an upscale Italian restaurant called Luna Piena, which translates to Full Moon. Mikayla had never worked in the family restaurant, and for that she was glad. She loved the atmosphere and the food, and knew working there would have ruined the allure.

It was six o'clock when Rowan caught her attention from across the neighborhood. *What are you wearing tonight, Miss Kali?* Rowan said as she was busy getting ready at her own house for the big dinner.

I'm not sure yet, I have a couple of things picked out. Perhaps it is the kind of night that is perfect to wear a dress…or jeans and a nice shirt and heals, or perhaps…hmmm, well what do you have? Mikayla posed the question back in Rowans court, hoping Rowan's very decisive ways would already have an outfit picked out.

I'm going with a short midnight blue sun dress, with a pair of short heeled sandals that I just got the other day. Just wanted to make sure I wasn't over doing it if you were just going in jeans. Remember, we are going out with the boys afterwards, Rowan said, reminding her of a night of bar hoping with all of her bodyguards.

Oh, joy, Mikayla said back.

She did have fun with them, but it still felt restrictive to her. It was hard not to be able to just reach out and talk to whoever without one of them lurking close by. It was so frustrating, lately she had been passing on nights out.

Tonight she wouldn't. It was the first summer they were all twenty-one and it felt like a rite of passage, like actually being an adult, and she wasn't going to miss out because she felt constricted. She reminded herself at any given time she could figure out a way to pay for school herself and move away to get freedom. After all, what could they really do? She was living in America; she was free, wasn't she? She often thought to herself.

Mikayla drifted off, thinking about Caleb, hoping he would show up on Friday. She was fixated on his eyes and the way she felt electric currents go throughout her body when he had helped her to her feet. She had a rush of butterflies when she thought about how brave he was around her brother and Dominick. That was unusual. The only other person she had ever known who wasn't afraid of him was…Marcus, she thought to herself. She quickly shook her head, snapping herself back into the task at hand of choosing an outfit for the night.

She glanced down at the few outfits she had laid out on her bed and started to put them back into her closet, leaving behind a long white sundress that tied behind the neck like a bikini top. The dress was light and made out of a light cotton blend. It accentuated her bust line and made her look angelic. She decided to wear it, so she wouldn't have to tramp around in heals all night; she could wear a pair of flip flops instead. She had bought a pair which went with the dress perfectly. Her hair was already down and brushed straight, so she didn't have much else to do. Just as she was putting the finishing touches of makeup on her face, she heard her brother calling.

"Are you ready? Come on it's time to go. I'm driving separate, so you can go with me," Mario said, knocking on her door.

"Yeah, I'm coming," she said, still looking into the mirror.

She often looked into the mirror and wondered why she was so ungrateful of everything she had and of her family. It was because she felt trapped, and she didn't like it. She could feel a meltdown coming on any minute. It would take her thinking about graduation to calm her down. She would then prove to her family she wasn't as helpless as they all seemed to think she was.

Turning off the light in the bathroom allowed herself to shut off the negative feelings and she grabbed her purse and breathed. She was determined to put all of that aside for the night and have some fun. All else she would figure out later, but for now she needed to enjoy these moments for what they were before she became one of those people who always complained about how everything in their life was so bad. Mikayla shuddered at the thought, and then put pleasant thoughts into her head. She walked out of her bedroom and into the hall where her brother was standing. He smiled at her and headed down the stairs in front of her. Her parents were already heading out of the door.

"We'll see you guys in a few minutes," They said as they walked through the door. Mario was behind her now, shutting and locking the door.

They had to pick up Rowan on the way. Mario had picked them up just to spend a little extra time with Rowan. What a beautiful couple they make, Mikaya thought as she watched Mario go up to the door to get her. They had been together forever, but he still treated her like she was a precious gift, never taking her for granted despite his overprotective nature. When they arrived back at the car, she noticed how he automatically opened the door for her as she waited. Mikayla smiled at the interaction as they headed towards downtown.

12

Caleb had just finished getting ready, Ali was already ready, and now they were just waiting for Jamahl to finish. Jamahl always took the most time getting ready, and they always thought it was funny because he didn't have any hair to style, and most people noticed him first because he was so beautiful. They were all striking, but Jamahl was beyond striking. He was completely perfect and structured. He also knew how to wear clothes, which hung upon his athletic physique like it was custom tailored to every inch of his body.

"Alright Jamahl, come on we need to leave," Ali said, trying to be punctual to the plan.

"I'm coming," he shouted from behind the bathroom door, just as he was opening it. As usual, Jamahl looked just a little bit better then Ali and Caleb did. Slightly nicer dark blue jeans with a few fade marks and an orange shirt neither Ali or Caleb could ever get away with wearing. Ali was wearing a simple green polo and dark jeans with sandals. He looked like a frat boy. Caleb was also wearing dark blue jeans, but the shirt he was wearing was white and laid back, as if he had just rolled over on the bed and grabbed whatever he felt first. Still, they were all more attractive than the average human being.

It was time for them to leave, so they could find Mary in order for Jamahl to have a date with her tomorrow so they could trick her into getting them holy water, since they weren't sure they would be able to enter a church without warning bells going off. Vampires weren't always banned from churches, but once a large group of vampires had renounced Heaven and sided with hell, a spell was put on churches, temples, mosques, and other places of worship as a way of giving people a safe haven on Earth, protecting them against evil.

They needed her to have the river water they collected, after leaving Eastern's campus earlier that day, blessed. Ali still thought it was a waste of time, but so far he couldn't find anything else in his research for them to go on. So, they would at least start there. They were hoping to get lucky, but if not, they were sure if anyone could find the way to reveal the angels wings, it would be Ali. They knew no other person who was quite as smart as he was.

Ali, the brain, Jamahl, the charmer, and Caleb, the powerful. This was how they were known, although Caleb had a sideline tagged to his name, which was loose cannon. He was sporadic, at times, and hard to read. Truly he was the one who danced to the beat of his own drums. It made him seem a bit unstable, but at the same time, his instincts were great and the power he had behind him was even greater.

The sun was still out, but it was getting ready to set. The sky was beautiful and Caleb had a good feeling about the night. He wasn't sure why, but he did. They headed to the car and drove it to downtown Ann Arbor. For sure Mary would be down there. It wasn't going to be hard for them to find her. Jamahl had taken in her smell and tapped into her brain. It wasn't going to be quite as easy as it would be if he had bitten her and made her drink from him, but it wouldn't be hard. He would just have to pay a bit more attention.

As they arrived downtown, they choose an open parking lot to park in. They stepped out of the car and Jamahl closed his eyes, took in a deep breath and smelled the air, trying to focus on that same brain he had tried to tap into earlier.

"She's not here yet. She is on her way, I can feel," Jamahl ,said and then paused with his eyes still closed. "mid...um, no...net...no...night..." Jamahl said as he was trying to find a name to where they were headed. "That's it!" He said, opening his eyes with a sinister smile plastered upon his face.

"Ok, man. You lead the way," Caleb said as he looked at Ali, letting Jamahl lead the way, which was unusual for Caleb. He usually kept himself in front.

They walked a block up Washington and made a right on Main street. They walked a couple more blocks past restaurants, bars, and shops, and then came across another large block of bars, clubs, restaurants, shops, and coffee houses. They aligned both sides of the street and it was busy. Caleb was taken back by how busy it actually was. If he didn't know better, he would have thought he was in a large city, like New York or L.A., by the way Main Street looked with its crowds, although it was also charming with its small city feel. He could see as they crossed streets which, down each side of the crossing streets, it was equally busy with people and places to go. This pleased him, as well, and he felt a little more at home.

Suddenly, Jamahl stopped at a place called Midnight. A large place which seemed to be more than a few stories tall, with what looked like condominiums on the upper floors by the way the windows and balconies looked. There were a lot of young people drinking out on the balconies, looking down on the crowds below. He saw a small sign that read, "No entrances to condominiums, please go around back." He wondered if there was actually a way to get into the condos from inside the club. The thought a busy night club would be a perfect place for him to slip quietly out of and up into a person's condo for a drink of blood.

Part of what made Caleb and his brothers so dangerous is they defied any known law to vampires. They did not need to be invited into people's homes; they could also walk amongst the day, which took away their vulnerability, and on top of those two things, they could actually survive without blood. The downside of not having the blood was it drained their powers, and if they went long enough without them, they could become vulnerable to a rare disease which could potentially harm them permanently, or even kill them if they weren't careful.

The amount of time they could survive before they were in danger of the disease wasn't an exact science, but from the research Ali did, it looked as if they were safest making sure they fed at least a few times of year. They fed more, however, because they liked the power surge it gave them on top of the insatiable yearning they felt towards human blood at night. It wasn't even a tenth of what a real vampire felt, but knowing that only made them feel glad they were only half.

Sometimes the bloodletting urge was more instinctual than anything else. The desire would take over and before they knew it, they had finished. They weren't in the practice of killing; they preferred to take what they needed and move on. Other vampires in their circle looked down on them for that, but although they were lethal and could kill, it wasn't the game they liked to play.

They came up to the large, tinted, double glass doors and walked in. The club was huge and they could see it had a few levels of seating areas, as well as bars. It all centered around one big dance floor. There was also comfort seating, with leather couches and ottomans for private use, separated by long, shear white, shear silver, and shear black curtains separating the sitting area's for different groups to sit in while obtaining some level of privacy. This was amongst normal, high silver and dark wood tables with silver and dark wood chairs with black leather cushions. The tables were by no means simple, they looked almost ancient, with dark black intertwined into the silver metal, which gave it a modern twist. The lights were dim, with hints of blue lights throughout the main floor, on the second floor, hints of a darker blue light with spots of pink and purple spread throughout. On the top floor, it was black lights with what looked like stars shining on the ceiling and a full moon shining down. It truly was amazing, and did indeed look like a midnight sky. There was also plenty of waterfalls and greenery around the walls, making it look like they were outside in a hidden forest. Caleb was impressed.

They were charged ten dollars apiece at the door, and Caleb noticed a sign that read, ***All entrance fees are donated to local charities.***

Caleb smiled as he shook his head, hoping they did carry beer and not Shirley Temples. They went up to the main bar on the first floor. The bar was made of glass, chrome, and some dark wood, and was beautifully highlighted in the same blue lights from the first floor. Mystical was an understatement to describe the inside of this bar.

The bartenders behind the counter wore all black outfits which were all different, yet still had continuity. The girls were pretty and the guys were handsome. "How can I help you boys?" A beautiful, blonde waitress asked.

"A pitcher of your beer on special and three glasses," Caleb replied.

"Also, three shots of tequila!" Jamahl added.

"Could I trouble you for some water, as well." Ali asked politely, and with that Caleb and Jamahl just started cracking up.

Once they had their drinks in hand, they looked for a high table around the dance floor so they could catch Mary as she walked in. They opted to not take hold of one of the private couch areas, for fear they may miss her walking in. They wanted to surprise her by being there first. Now they were in place, all they had to do was wait.

It didn't take long. They had already finished one round of beers and had just come back to the table with a second round when Mary and three friends walked in the door. They headed straight for the bar and Jamahl got up from the table and followed. He crept up behind her and willed her to turn around. Without knowing why she felt the need to turn around, she was completely surprised to find Jamahl standing there with a beer in his hand.

"What time did you want me to pick you up," he said with a grin plastered across his beautiful face. She couldn't say anything for a moment. She just stood there with her mouth wide open.

"Cat got your tongue?" he said, adding insult to injury. She started laughing and turned around to pay the bartender for her drink, but before she could reach into her purse, Jamahl had already handed the bartender a twenty and told the girl to keep the change.

"Alright, fine. Tomorrow you can pick me up around noon. I have to work at night so you will only have a few hours to entertain me," Mary finally said. "Oh, and thank you for the drink," she said, almost forgetting her manners, still in shock.

They stood talking at the bar for a good twenty minutes before she had introduced them to her friends. She got lost in him for a moment, and him with her. "Oh I am so sorry!" She said as she realized she had just been blabbing away without acknowledging her friends. "This is Sarah, Kim, and that's Lindsey," Mary made the rounds of introductions. "And this here is Jamahl," she finished with his introduction last. Jamahl took that as his cue and invited them back to the table.

It didn't take much coaxing when Mary's friends saw Caleb and Ali sitting at the table. The three were abnormally good looking, and Mary's friends were on top of it. They made a beeline straight for the table.

Looks like a swarm of bees, Caleb thought to both of his brothers. They both laughed under their breaths, thinking the same thing.

Too bad they are walking right into the Lion's den, Ali thought back. Caleb turned to him and laughed.

"Way to easy," Caleb said to Ali, just as Jamahl and the girls reached the table.

They made introductions around the table and allowed the girls to flirt with them so Jamahl could work his magic with Mary. They could tell Jamahl was actually getting a kick out of Mary. Jamahl often had girlfriends from time to time who were human. He loved how vulnerable they were and how emotional they became. It had an aphrodisiac effect for him, making him feel much more powerful. He was definitely digging her.

The girls started to dance, running back and forth from the table to the dance floor when a good song came on. They mixed in and kept the girls entertained so they would stay around while Jamahl worked his magic. He needed to get her onboard with blessing the holy water. He was going to tell her it was something he needed as part of a scavenger hunt his fraternity had him go through as a part of his graduation. The plan was he was going to tell her all the graduates of his fraternity had to do it, but the winner received a five hundred dollar visa gift card. They thought this would be a good plan.

This wasn't the only trick up their sleeves. They had a few more things to do before Friday, and going to the boys' house they played football with earlier that day was part of their plot, along with getting a boat. It was a bit of work, but they knew they would get everything done they needed. Worst case scenario, they would cheat a little to get things done. They just knew they were supposed to use minimal magic, in case there was some sort of feeler spell out there on the lookout for other immortals and people of the magic world the immortals and magical creatures of the area were unaware of. For now they needed to keep the girls entertained, so they ordered more drinks – beer for them and martinis for the girls, except for Mary, who was drinking beer. All was working out the way it was supposed to; easy.

13

Dinner was great. Mikayla had to admit to herself she loved the big family dinners. They had to put six, four top tables next to each other just to get everyone around. She ordered her favorite meal, a fettuccini, sausage and mushroom dish in a creamy alfredo sauce, and a cold coke to wash it down. Mikayla always cleaned her plate when she ate that dish. From time to time, her Mom would make it at home, and since the restaurant used her recipe, it was made to perfection. Desert was just being cleared away from the table when she heard the boys talking about what they were going to do next.

"Let's just go next door, I want to check out how the club is running tonight anyways before we go out of town for three weeks," Dominick said, making a strong suggestion to go to his family' club he currently managed.

The club was large, and could even be rented out for weddings for the right price. Most people couldn't afford the price of the club, but they did own a building next door attached to the club by the inner workings of the back of the club. The kitchen and storage room was shared between the two buildings, but from the front part (the only part customers had access to) there was no way to go from the club into the banquet hall. It was one of the most popular venues for weddings and other celebrations throughout the year. It was equally as beautiful as all the other clubs, bars, coffee houses, and restaurants on this part of Main Street. It had plenty of room and a huge dance floor. It even had an outdoor terrace on the second floor. The banquet hall was only two stories tall, unlike the club next door, but it, like all the buildings on the street, had condos and office suites above the buildings. Mikayla loved to watch the weddings, and would often volunteer to work a few of them in the summer time for extra cash. The food was out of this world, and they even had their own bakery, which was connected to the backside of the building, and Dominick's family also owned.

"Sounds good to me, bro," Mario said, in agreement, back.

Mikayla actually didn't mind. It was the best hangout spot downtown and, despite her constantly being watched, it had three floors, which meant plenty of room to get lost. With a decision made, all the boys got up from the table and headed to the bar in the restaurant to have a shot before the night's outing.

Rowan and Mikayla weren't big drinkers, so they stayed behind to finish their tea as people started to leave. They thought it was important to stay behind to say thank you to everyone for coming and celebrating their last day of school. This dinner was better than the past year's. Since her and Rowan only had a year left, everyone was focused on hearing their future plans. Mikayla loved sharing her plans for the future. Everyone also gushed all night at how proud they were of them, which was always a good thing to hear. For the moment, Mikayla felt a bit guilty for feeling so angry towards her family. For the moment, she felt grateful, and any other negative feelings she decided to push deep down inside. She was truly enjoying herself.

Rowan was finishing her cup of tea when she held up a finger at Mario. He was waving for her to come over to him. She got up from the table after excusing herself and walked towards the bar. Mikayla watched as Rowan took a shot with the boys.

"Kali, you want a shot?" Rowan called over to her. She just smiled and waved a no thank you back. Just as Mikayla went to take her last sip of tea, she saw Dominick coming over towards the table.

"Kali, are you ready to go?" He asked as he pulled out a chair next to her and turned it around to sit, so his chest was against the back of the chair.

"Yeah, I think I have had all the desert and tea that one can take," she said, thinking about just how full she really was.

She thought to herself how thankful she was she had chosen the long white sundress, because it was very forgiving after a big Italian meal. Unlike jeans, which would have had her in pain from the tightness on her belly after all the pasta and bread she ate, not to mention the desserts, to make matters even worse.

Mikayla, Rowan, and the boys stood around the dinner table saying thank you to all the adults who were still there, and all expressed what a great time it was. It was customary for them to not exit fast. It always took a good twenty minutes or so for them to exit gracefully amongst their elders. It was a show of respect. Mikayla, as usual, was the last to leave, and she did so with one more thank you and a beautiful smile which seemed to light everyone up. Then they all gathered at the door and, with Dominick leading the way, they left the restaurant and headed for the bar.

14

Across the street on a roof top, Aidan, Aiah, and Rory staked Layla out. They took careful observation over a couple of days. Her house was very busy. She was rarely alone at night. There were people coming and going, and she seemed to always be in a group. It wasn't going to be as easy as they had thought it would be to get her alone, not with them having the limitations of the sun.

It was Thursday and the house was finally quiet, but she wasn't there alone. She was on the terrace with her brother. They had hoped he would go back into the house, leaving her alone, but no such luck. Instead, they turned in early and shut all the lights off. Aidan thought this was strange and worried, but there wasn't anything they could do but to still wait.

They came back the next night to find the place still dark, as if they had never woke up from the night before. They needed to find out what was going on. It was time for Operation Information to ensue.

Aidan stood outside of Layla's apartment, and loudly yelled slurred, drunken words hoping one of the neighbors would get mad enough to open their door to tell him to shut up. It must have taken him a good ten minutes before he saw anyone. A dark haired young man, dressed for a night out, was just coming out of his apartment.

"Who are you looking for?" The young man said in English with a thick Italian accent, having heard Aidan speaking in English.

"My friend Layla said that she was having people over on Tuesday?" Aidan managed in his best-drunken speech.

The man giggled and said, "Tuesday? No, it is Friday! You are a few days late, my friend."

He said, still amused at what he thought was a really drunk Irishman.

"Oh, oops, maybe it's next Tuesday," Aidan said, even more sloppily than before, now rubbing the back of his neck for added belief.

"No, my friend. I can assure you that you are probably just confused. Layla and Ajay have gone away for a couple of weeks," the guy said, still chuckling.

"Away, I don't remember her saying anything about that…" he said, trailing off, hoping the neighbor would fill in the gap.

"They went to Lebanon to visit grandparents," he said, looking just as amused.

"Come back in a couple of weeks, they should be home then," the young man added.

"Good idea, thanks," Aidan said, and stumbled away from Layla's apartment.

He made his way across the street and scaled up the side of the building with the quickness of a cat.

"Shit, they are in Lebanon. We are just going to have to wait. It would be like tracking a ghost, since all we have is night to travel and all of Lebanon to explore. We are just going to have to come back." Aidan said to his brothers, who witnessed the drunken scene from across the street.

"What if Caleb, Jamahl, and Ali find out that Rowan is the one we are looking for in the meantime. Perhaps we should make our way that way, just in case." Aiah said.

Aidan took a few minutes to think about it.

"No, we can't take the chance of being seen. Besides, the hyenas have already arrived. I told them to find Caleb and stir up trouble. I promised them more power, and to set them free if they obeyed. For now, let's just hope they do as I told," Aidan brushed the back of his head with his hand.

"I still don't understand the hyenas?" Rory questioned.

"Michigan is a hot spot for Werewolves. I want the hyenas to be used as a distraction to throw them off the trail. If the werewolves in the area have anything to do with the witch's protection, then sending the wild hyenas will distract them. The action will also throw off Caleb and the boys, hopefully buying us some more time."

Rory nodded his head in comprehension.

"What should we do in the meantime?" Rory asked, wondering what the hell they were going to do for the next week or so.

"First thing we are going to do is make a visit to the wizard, but first we need to get a little bit of information out of the dynamic trio. Aiah, give Ali a call, see what information they have so far," Aidan ordered.

Aiah grabbed his cell phone out of his pocket and dialed Ali, walking a little ways away.

While Aiah was on the phone, Aidan took out his phone and dialed the number of the wizard. The wizard was well over three thousand years old. He was older then Cyrus, and had always practiced black magic. He was one of two wizards who were still alive from his time. The other wizard practiced good magic, and was the leader of the Glen Council for Wizardry, also a part of the council of light.

Aidan suspected he, too, was fed up with Cyrus, as well, as the wizard was giving him bits and pieces of information no one else seemed to have about the possible powers one given Angel's Breath could possess. Aidan became obsessed with the idea of tapping into that power to finally feel the sun upon his face after a couple hundred years of its absence.

The powers the wizard told Aidan of, he was sure somehow Cyrus had access to the same knowledge. Although Cyrus would never admit what it was he knew, or what his intended plans were. One thing was for sure, he was going to hoist her powers and use them to his advantage. The wizard said the witch who possesses Angel's Breath could bring some one back to life when on the verge of death, they could also create anything and grant other powers. Aidan knew that it would be the way for him to walk in the light again. He was desperate to find her first, before Cyrus, so he could accomplish the things he had on his agenda.

The wizard answered his phone.

"Hello, Aidan," he said.

"Hi, I need you to do me another favor concerning the hyenas," Aidan said, trying to feel out whether or not he thought the wizard would comply.

"Of course, dear boy, what do you need?" He said, seeming more than willing to help.

"I need a location for them, and I need you to help me get a hold of them," Aidan said, knowing it could be a dangerous move to include the wizard further, but his gut told him the old wizard had his own agenda. He had just hoped the wizard being fed up with Cyrus was enough for him to keep his mouth shut for a little while at least. The Rynard definitely had his own agenda, but it was a risk Aidan felt like he needed to take.

"Why of course, are you ready to tell me what this is all about?" The wizard asked, hoping to understand the details so he could watch the havoc unfold piece by piece.

"In due time, I promise. In due time. I owe you for this," Aidan said.

"You have my help, for now. I will call you back with the location and tell you how long you have to get there," the wizard said and hung up the phone.

Aidan closed his phone and walked over to Rory and Aiah, who was just getting off the phone with Ali.

"What did Ali say?" Aidan asked Aiah.

"Well, they have already located the girl," Aiah answered with a worried look in his eyes.

"That was fast." Aidan paused to think. "I expected it to take much longer. Perhaps it is true that Caleb was drawn to her. Maybe that really is possible," Aidan said, and trailed off again, lost in thought.

He was nervous they had already located her; he expected it would take them a bit longer. It was a good thing he had a plan B, he thought to himself.

"Well?" Aiah said, waiting for him to finish and breaking Aidan's thought.

"The wizard will be calling any minute with the location of the hyenas. We can add some things for them to do. That will be the first thing we do," Aidan said, looking down at his cell phone.

"What do we tell Cyrus?" Aiah was worried.

"We tell him we are working on it," Aidan said as his phone began to ring.

"Yeah," Aidan said as he picked up his phone.

"They are what?" Aidan's eyes shot wide open. "What does that mean?" He began to shake his head as he listened. He H"And you're sure?" The look on his face was fury. "Fuck!" He shouted as Rory and Aiah watched.

Again Aidan snapped his phone shut and looked at them.

"Alright, the hyenas are missing," Aidan said, aggravated and hoping they hadn't opened their mouths.

"What do you mean missing?" Rory said.

Aiah and Aidan just looked at Rory for a moment.

"Can't mean anything good," Aidan said as he put his phone back into his pocket.

"What now?" Rory asked.

Aidan said nothing as he turned to look out towards the darkened sea.

15

The music was getting louder and the crowds started to pour in. Caleb couldn't believe the amount of people that seemed to be lining up just to get into a bar in a town small in comparison to where they had been living in Los Angeles. The girls were pretty much drunk at this point. Ali was sober, and as for Jamahl and Caleb, they were feeling good. They each had one too many to be considered sober, and one too few to be drunk. They actually were having fun. Caleb thought all missions should be this fun as he poured another glass of beer from the sixth pitcher of the night.

As he sipped on his beer, he had a feeling in his gut. It was the same feeling he had felt when the seer had pointed at him, and the same feeling he had felt when he saw Mikayla from her window. His thoughts went out the window, and he went into instinctual mode and looked towards the door. They were walking through the door, Dominick and Mario, who was holding Rowan's hand. He saw the pack behind them, and then she walked in. His heart stopped a beat as he watched her enter the club in what seemed like slow motion. She was even more stunning than she was that afternoon. Her long hair draping down her back, and a long white dress tied at the back of her neck like a bikini top showed her cleavage and the structure of her collar bones. The dress flowed down to her feet. It wasn't a tight dress, but it was cut well enough to show the thinness of her waist, and as it flowed to the ground it lightly hugged her body. Caleb naturally thought to himself she looked like a fairy or an angel. He was lost in thoughts of wanting to rush over there and push her up against the wall and kiss her, every inch of her, taking in her soul. He wanted to bite her, but not feed on her. He just wanted to drink in her soul and make her drink his back so he could always know where she was. He wanted to possess her in every way.

Just as before, he almost lost his composure and he suddenly realized he needed to snap out of it. The boys were there and losing control could be a potential set back. If they were around Caleb and his brothers too long, they may start to get a sense of what it was they were, and possibly what they had come for. Caleb had to send thoughts out to his brothers so they could figure out what to do. *The Wolf pack is here*, he thought to both of his brothers.

Shit. Was all Jamahl could think to say.

Ali didn't say anything. He didn't even look towards the door, knowing if they had already been spotted, it may instigate them to come over. He knew at this point they needed to play cool.

They are with Rowan and her friend, Caleb added.

Well if we leave right now, it might be just as obvious to them that something is up than if we stay for a while before leaving. And Caleb, stay away from that girl, she makes you act weird, Jamahl said, thinking under pressure.

Oh right, if I say nothing to her then what if they don't meet us out on the lake Friday. Rowan only wants us out there for the sake of her friend, that much is obvious, but if I blow her off then she may not be for it, Caleb said back.

He wasn't trying at that point just to get to talk to her. He meant it, and he had a good point.

Alright, you do have a point. We need to just play cool. Didn't Jackson say to come over to their house tonight for a start of summer bash?" Jamahl said, thinking about another place they could go.

Yeah he did! Caleb said back, already taking his phone out of his pocket, knowing exactly what his brother was thinking.

Well, you might want to dial that number because in 5,4,3,2,1, yup they have spotted us. Dominick is whispering into Mario's ear... yup, Mario is looking our way. It's only a matter of minutes before they come over here to try and intimidate us, Jamahl said as he watched the boys discreetly.

Dominick bent over to Mario's ear to tell him who he had just spotted.

"We need to take the girls to the private area before they see those boys. Rowan will insist that Kali talks to that boy, and Kali herself will want to. She seems interested, but I have never seen them and something isn't setting right with me, but I can't get a sense of what it is. I could be paranoid, but something right now tells me that danger is close by," Dominick said in Mario's ear only.

"Are you sure that this isn't just to keep my sister from dating anyone else?" Mario asked respectfully, trying to decipher whether or not they needed to be on guard.

"Mario, close your eyes and breathe in," Dominick commanded gently. "Tell me what you sense," he then added.

Without a fight, Mario closed his eyes and labored his breathing. He blocked out the commotion of the bar and concentrated on using his sixth sense. Just as he was about to give up, he felt it. The hair on the back of his neck slightly rose. He could feel a danger nearby, as well.

"You think that is from them?" Mario asked Dominick quietly.

"Really, I don't know, but so far they are my first suspects," Dominick answered as he peered over towards the table they were sitting at.

"Alright, let's take them behind the bar so they won't see them," Mario said, and quickly rounded up everybody and their drinks to lead the way back to one of the secluded lounge areas.

They see us and are trying to avoid us, expect them to come up soon, Caleb. I am pretty sure they are trying to avoid the girls seeing us, Jamahl thought as he watched Mario lead everyone behind the bar to what he assumed was a back way around to the last secluded lounge area behind the bar on the main floor. From their table, they could see the area, though it was slightly privatized by the curtains hanging around the sides of it. He watched all follow, except for Dominick and the scout from earlier that day. *And here they come, Caleb. Make the call,*" Jamahl warned as Caleb hit send on his phone.

Caleb's back was to the bar, so he couldn't see Dominick coming towards them, but he could feel it. Jamahl didn't even look at them, he was putting all his efforts into Mary. Jamahl quickly looked into Mary's eyes and pulled her in close for a kiss. She put up no fight and kissed him back. Her friends were busy on the dance floor. Just before Dominick had reached the table, Jackson had answered his phone.

"Jello!" Jackson said, obviously having had one too many beers himself.

"Hey man, it's me," Caleb said, knowing Jackson would know who it was after having used hypnosis on them earlier to make them think they had been friends all along, and also recognize each of their voices.

"What's up for tonight?" Caleb added loudly so Dominick could hear him.

They thought if they had a legitimate place to go, they could throw off these wolves. No doubt they would be listening in on the phone conversation with their supersonic animal sense of hearing, and would without a doubt send a scout to make sure that is indeed where they were heading.

They had to throw off this pack so they wouldn't cancel their last initiation into full adult wolf-hood. It didn't take long for Ali to put together the cycle of the full moon, their ages, and the fact they were going away for three weeks to realize what it was that the wolf pack was up to. If they cancelled now, they would be stuck for another month until the next full moon. Caleb half thought it wouldn't be a bad idea, because he would get to spend more time with Mikayla, but then thought if the wolves were around they would make sure it didn't happen. The wolves had only four more months to do the initiation, from what Ali remembered about werewolves. So at some point, they would have to leave for three weeks over the summer.

"The party is just getting started, man. Where you guys at?" Jackson said back to him.

"Man, we are with Mary and some of her friends at the bar for a pre-party. We will be there in a few, we just have to polish off our drinks and pull the girls from the dance floor, and then we will head that way," Caleb said as natural as if he really believed this conversation was real.

"Alright man, hurry up! I am ready to school you in some beer pong!" Jackson said.

"In your dreams," Caleb said back with a chuckle, and looked up to find Dominick towering over him.

Caleb closed his phone and put it into his pocket, looking up at Dominick.

"What's up, man. Dominick, right?" he said as innocent as possible and extended his hand, knowing Dominick wouldn't shake it.

"Yeah, that's right. So what are you guys doing here?" Dominick asked, quite rudely.

"What do you mean? We are out having a few drinks before going to our buddy's party," Caleb said, trying to seem a bit confused.

"If that is all, then I think you all need to be moving on," Dominick said sharply.

"Well, Dominick, we will leave when we are ready, and we are not finished yet with our drinks. I don't know what your problem is, but if it's about your girlfriend I want you to know that I didn't know she had a boyfriend, and I am sorry if it looked like something else," Caleb said, again trying to sound as sincere as possible.

"Funny, I have never seen you before, and I find it odd that we show up in the same place twice in one day as her. So, know this. We all watch out for both her and Rowan. I don't know what it is about you, but something isn't setting right with me, so you just need to stay away," Dominick said, trying not to say too much just in case it really was a case of misidentification.

He had heard the boy on the other end of the phone. It seemed like a real conversation and he couldn't get a scent on Caleb, so he scaled his aggression down a bit. Just then, Caleb's phone rang.

"Hello?" Caleb answered as he held up a finger at Dominick.

"Hey man, I forgot to ask if you can bring another case of beer with you?" Jackson said on the other line, talking to Caleb as if they had been friends for years.

Dominick heard him on the other line and Caleb knew it.

Jackson could be my favorite person here yet, Jamahl thought to him, still sitting with Mary on his lap.

"Yeah man, no problem. See you in a minute, bro," Caleb said back, and then shut his phone, turning his attention back to Dominick.

"Man, I don't really know what you are talking about. I am just hanging out with my friends. I thought that Mikayla and Rowan were nice so I talked to them. Sorry if I have offended them, or you," Caleb said to Dominick.

Jamahls blood was starting to boil just then, as well as Caleb's.

You guys cool it, just keep looking confused about this guy's problem. Do not blow this. We have an out. I will let you know what on the way to Jackson's. For now, keep it cool, Ali thought to his brothers as his eyes were focused on a table three tables down from them, further away from the bar, at a group of four at a table. He knew soon the heat would be off of them when he recognized what he was looking at.

"Look, I am not trying to tell you guys what to do. All I am saying is that you need to leave Mikayla and Rowan alone. Did they tell you that they were coming here tonight?" Dominick asked as his guard was a bit dropped, trying to find out how they could have known where they were going to be, or if they knew.

"No man, I swear I had no idea, and even if I did, I still don't understand what the problem is. But I don't want any trouble, so we will just finish and leave," Caleb said, completely controlling the demon trying to rise up within him, ready to unleash on the alpha male and take him out for good by ripping out his spinal cord with his bare hands.

Dominick shifted his eyes around the room suddenly. The feeling he had when he walked through the door came on again, only it was more specific. Having sensed four people, three males and one female, at a table three tables down, he realized why his senses were on alert. He stiffened and breathed in deep. At that point he was distracted, and somehow Caleb and his friends no longer seemed like a threat.

"Just please stay away from her. Well, you boys have a good rest of your night," Dominick said, completely distracted at this point.

"We'll do," Caleb said, but Dominick had already left the table and headed back to the private lounge area his pack was at.

Caleb looked at Jamahl and started laughing.

"Apparently there is something in here much more interesting than us!" Caleb said to his brothers.

Hyena people... Ali thought to his brothers, unable to say it out loud in front of Mary, and for fear one of the wolves could still be listening. He then nodded to a table three tables down at a group of four. Both Caleb and Jamahl inconspicuously looked towards the table.

There was one girl and three guys. They didn't look like your average college students; instead, they looked ancient, yet youthful and very beautiful. They were well structured, and their clothing choice was definitely on the side of theatrical. As Caleb stared he saw the light shine in one of the males' eyes and saw the yellowness of a light shine quickly, and then disappear.

What the fuck are they doing here? Usually they sense an after party, Caleb thought to his brothers.

I am not sure, but I will find out, but later. We can use this to our advantage, the wolves will think that's what they were sensing and get off our backs. They will certainly run the hyena people off tonight and feel free to go to their initiation. Ali thought back and took another sip of his water. Ali had made it through the night on one shot, half of a beer, and 2 glasses of ice water.

Rowan was taking another shot, Mikayla thought Rowan was defiantly intoxicated at this point. Rowan was normally very funny, even the boys would laugh at her jokes as if she was just one of the guys, she had a way with them. Mikayla used to be the same, one of the guys and funny like Rowan, but somewhere along the way in the past few years she had lost touch with that side of herself. She was too busy feeling trapped and suffocated. Tonight she decided to try and put all that behind. She watched the boys laugh as Rowan was saying something else about a foot up some teacher's ass when Mario pulled her down on his lap. Mikayla thought it was the perfect opportunity to take a quick shot the way she used to.

"I think the only ass Mario would let you put a foot up in his!" Mikayla said out of left field.

Everyone got quiet, having not seen this side of her in years. After a brief silence, everyone burst into laughter. Rowan took the lemon wedge off her shot glass and threw it at Mikayla. She gracefully dodged the lemon wedge and reached for a shot herself.

"What the hell!" She said and she took a shot of tequila as everyone at the table cheered. She liked the words of encouragement and the laughter she brought, and reached for another shot as everyone looked on in disbelief. As she took her second shot, more cheers flowed amongst the table. In the back of her mind, a thought occurred; well if you can't beat them, then you might as well join them.

Dominick walked up just as Mikayla was throwing down shot number four.

"What the hell are you doing?" He looked down at her and grabbed the fifth shot out of her other hand.

"Whadda mean, I'm partying! Woohoo!" Mikayla exclaimed as the alcohol had already started to set in. Rowan laughed, but the boys tried hard to contain their laughter, having seen Dominick wasn't as thrilled as the rest of them at Mikayla's sudden urge to take shot after shot as if she were a machine gun unloading.

"Kayli, you don't drink! What is wrong with you?" Dominick said strictly, shoving away another shot she was reaching for on the black candlelit table.

"Hey!" Mikayla said, looking up at Dominick with a pout.

Dominick thought she looked so cute at that moment, and he wanted more than anything to kiss her, but there was danger close by and he needed her to be sharp, not drunk and careless. He wasn't as worried about Rowan because she would be attached at Mario's hip, and knowing the two of them, they would be upstairs in Dominick and Mario's condo within the hour.

"You just don't drink Kali, and you need to slow down," Dominick said, now bending over her talking close to her ear.

"Yes I do!" Mikayla said back, and reached again for another shot. Dominick pulled that one out of her hand and put it back on the table, but as his back was turned Rowan had slipped her another. When he turned back around, Mikayla had already taken the shot. He was furious and he grabbed the empty shot glass out of her hand.

"Don't be such a party pooper!" Mikayla said, smiling up at him, pointing in his face.

"I drink, I just usually drink one or maybe two spread out over a night, and tonight I had ummm, what did I have?" She said losing her train of thought, giggling as she looked towards Rowan, who was also giggling herself.

"You had a dirty martini and five shots! Whoa, Kali girl you're gonna feel that tomorrow!" Rowan shouted from Mario's lap.

"Yup, that's what I had. Want one?" She said to Dominick, reaching for another shot.

"No, I don't want one and you can't have any more either!" Dominick said, loudly this time, looking at the crew as he made the cut off signal with his hand to his throat.

The table got a bit quiet.

"Relax man, our place is right upstairs, she's alright. Besides, I haven't seen Kali in a silly mood like this in a long time. Maybe she has finally snapped out of her mood," Mario said, playing the big brother role.

"No man, it's not alright! No one give her anymore!" Dominick commanded as his eyes flashed all black.

This time Mikayla was looking at his face.

"Hey, what happened to your eyes," she said pointing up at him.

Dominick didn't acknowledge her question, he stared at Mario and Mario got up as if he was silently told to. He and Dominick went off to the side as Lucio followed.

Mikayla's eyes started to wonder around in their absence until it met a beautiful pair of blue eyes that seemed to be burning into hers. It was him. She couldn't help but smile, and all the butterflies started to fly furiously around inside of her. He motioned to his lips, "Shhh," then mouthed the words "top floor." Mikayla instantly understood and nodded once, quickly.

"I'll be right back. I have to use the restroom real quick," she whispered to Rowan.

"Want me to go with?" Rowan said, dizzily.

"No, cuz then they will have one of the boys follow the way Dom is worked up, and it isn't one of those trips you want a boy waiting for you outside," she said, in case any of the boys were listening; and somehow she knew they would be.

Don't say anything, Rowan. Caleb is here, he motioned for me to go to the third floor. Dom is on some sort of Dom trip and he will just ruin this. I don't know why, but I feel drawn to Caleb and I have to figure out why. Please cover me!" She thought to Rowan, letting her know the true reason she needed to leave the table for a while.

Rowan understood in her drunken state and nodded. The boys were still in the corner talking as the other boys looked on, not paying any attention to Rowan and Mikayla. With their attention focused on Dominick, Mikayla, slipped away undetected.

Dominick was still talking with all attention focused on him. They had completely missed Mikayla slipping away from the table. Right now, their focus was on something else. Dominick had seen what it was that was causing the feeling of danger in the air. "I want you guys to look over there," Dominick said, pointing to a table with three males and one female.

The female had a golden skin tone, a kind of yellowish brown; very exotic. Her eyes were black, but had a yellow light intertwined in them. It was mesmerizing. Her hair was long and thick and silky, and just as dark as the black in her eyes. It stood out against the gold of her brown skin. The three males had the same coloring, and were equally as beautiful. All of their cheekbones were high and they had perfect noses and full lips. Although they resembled each other in hair and eye color and skin tone, they all looked very different in their facial features; all beautiful, but the female stood out as the most beautiful to look at. She was flawless. They were all lean and muscular; it made it obvious to Dominick they were not human. The hyenas looked much too perfect, much too beautiful, like nature.

All of the boys' eyes focused on the table, and immediately they saw what it was they were sensing. Though they had never actually seen any in person, they waited for Dominick to speak for confirmation.

16

"Hyena people are here. There is a pack of four, three males one female. I think that is what we have been sensing," Dominick said.

"I don't know of anything that has happened, usually they show up around the time something happens, or shortly after, hoping to feed on the wreckage. It's by taking in human and immortal carcasses that they can keep their human form. It's not like them to show up too early, before something will happen. So either there is something going on right now, or something has already happened. Doesn't make sense that somehow we are unaware of what it is," Mario said back.

"Why would they be here otherwise, unless they started hunting humans breaking their oath?" Dominick said questioning, thinking of the stories they had been told about Hyenas.

Hyenas are a rare breed. Seemingly selfish, they are tied to the earth. The sole purpose for a hyena was to eat the hearts out of those who were killed in haste or war. Eating of the hearts allowed the sole of the murdered to be freed. When a heart is not taken, the spirit of the soul lingers, becoming a ghost. Hyenas, in turn, from eating the hearts have the ability to transform into a human form. Without the heart's consumption, a hyena would only be just that, and never have the ability to transform into human form.

They are a neutral breed. Killing is what allows them to change form, so they count on it. Yet they remain neutral from killing themselves and only do what it is they were intended to do. It was not always this way; however, in the 1700s in France, a demon manipulated the minds of a group of hyenas, turning them into killers. And kill they did, as the whites of their eyes became a putrid yellow. The people were unaware of hyenas existence, and blamed them on a mutated wolf – a werewolf. Werewolves, however, weren't killers of man, rather they were protectors of man.

Through the fight to get the Hyena's under control, an Angel came down and granted the werewolves hierarchy over all animals, including hyenas. From that day foreword, hyenas became werewolves' prey if a hyena became a murderer.

With all of the shifting of powers on earth, the wolves were on high alert a demon would soon try again to persuade the hyenas to submit to the dark powers at be. Unfortunately, it is a real curse the hyena's bare, because it is the killing which allows them to consume the hearts of men to become human themselves. Without the killings, they would only be animals, but if they killed they lost control over their humanity. Hyenas are always vulnerable to swaying. For the past couple of centuries, the council of light has tried to pursued them to join the powers of good, but they had refused, not fully accepting they truly had a place above as they felt tied to the earth.

To spot a hyena hanging around alerts a possible murder or war which has just happened, or is about to. They have a sixth sense if war or murder is brewing in the air. If one is spotted by a werewolf, the werewolf goes on alert immediately, as he is a protector and would want to prevent this from happening. Again, the werewolf and hyena butt heads, as they are on two sides of the agenda.

Mario was quiet, as he was deep in thought for a moment, before speaking again. "Perhaps they really are feeling something coming, I have to admit, for the last week I have been on high alert, but I thought that was from the moon and the last initiation coming forth," Mario said, still looking a bit confused at why this area would be of any use for the hyenas.

They had never encountered any; it was just through their training they had gained knowledge about them, and in their natural instincts they could sense them. It was more likely in countries going through turmoil to have a group around. Dominick had a bad look on his face as Mario looked to his alpha for his opinion. Mario didn't like the look on his face, it wasn't a look he had recognized before, and Mario felt Dominick might know a little more than he was leading on.

"I think we need to confront them and see if we can get any read on them. It is unlikely that they will give us any information, but with the right questions and using our instincts, we may be able to pick up something," Dominick said, scratching the back of his neck, which was starting to itch from the stress. "You know the other possibility is that a vampire is around, funny though, I haven't sensed any…" Dominick said, trailing off.

"A vampire hasn't been in this area for a couple hundred years, maybe our senses have adapted to not being able to pick that up?" Mario said as a possibility.

"Not likely. I was able to sense the hyenas just fine, and a vampire is even more easily sensed for us. Perhaps one is coming, and if that's the case, things could start getting very serious," Dominick said, still scratching the back of his neck.

"Off of one vampire? Doubt it," Mario said with a confident chuckle.

"Mario, there are some things that you don't know. I can't tell you right now, but I need to do some checking, so let's start with the hyenas and try and figure out why they are here," Dominick said as he turned his head back to the table, taking inventory of everyone. As he scanned the lounge area, he counted heads and noticed one missing.

"Where's Kali?" Dominick said fiercely as he turned his attention back to the table. Everyone was stunned at the tone in his voice and fell silent for a moment.

"Woops!' Mikayla said, tripping on the last stair to the top floor, to a couple of girls going down the same staircase. They giggled as Mikayla smiled at them.

She quickly recovered and scanned the room for Caleb. She didn't see him, but decided she should be looking over the railing on the other side of the room, it was in perfect view from downstairs on the first floor, where everyone was at. She thought it best to go around to the side so if she looked over the railing on the same side as Dominick and her brother, they wouldn't be able to see up.

She made her way quickly around and took another quick scan at the private booths for Caleb, but still, he wasn't there. She came up to the railing and looked down. The place was packed. She wondered if in a crowd this large she would be so easily spotted. The lights were so dim on this third floor, Mikayla thought it was the romantic area of the bar.

All of a sudden, a popular dance song came on. The base was booming and Mikayla felt a rush of freedom as she watched people swarm the dance floor. It was a loud tribal beat that pumped throughout her body. She closed her eyes briefly, feeling a moment of independence, when she felt two hands touch her waste. She didn't need to turn around to know it was Caleb, and the thought of knowing made the butterflies in her stomach fly furiously as her heart beat pounded into her ears.

"Don't turn around fast, meet me in the booth behind you," Caleb whispered into her ear.

She didn't say anything, she defied him and turned around as quick as she could to make a smart and flirty comment, and was in shock to find he wasn't even there. For a moment, she thought she had imagined it, and decided in her slightly drunken state she was hearing things, until she looked to the booth to find Caleb sitting there with a half-smile upon his gorgeous face. She was so excited, and a bit tipsy, she didn't have time to think about how fast he had left her side and got into the both.

She slowly began to walk over to him and thought to herself how he was even more handsome than she remembered. He was wearing a pair of dark blue denim jeans, slightly faded in the front of the thighs, with a button down black collar shirt that looked like it was tailor made to his body, and a pair of casual, black, soft leather shoes to complete the look. He looked clean cut, yet dangerous and edgy at the same time, sporting a few visible tattoos and an earring. His blue eyes pierced into hers, making her take in a double breath. It seemed like it took forever for her to reach the table just a couple feet in front of her. As she approached, he didn't take his eyes off of hers, not even a moment to blink. Finally, as if it all happened in slow motion, she reached the table.

"So, uh, you're pretty fast," was all Mikayla could think to say.

"No, you're just slow," Caleb said back, smiling. Mikayla, a bit embarrassed, just laughed and shrugged her shoulders.

"Crazy how I don't see you in the three years I've been at school, and now I see you twice in one day!" Mikayla said, trying to make small talk.

Right now she didn't know if it was the alcohol or the way he was looking at her, but she didn't want to talk, she wanted to kiss him. She had this strange feeling talking wouldn't be enough to satisfy this strange urge she couldn't explain inside of her.

"Perhaps its fate, and not crazy at all," Caleb said smoothly and smiled at her. Mikayla felt her cheeks flush with blood. Caleb could sense the rush of the blood, and still wanted to kiss her above wanting to bite her.

They sat at the table for a moment in silence before Mikayla broke the silence by sticking to a safe topic. She had told him about the family dinner they had just had, and how many shots she had and apologized for being a bit tipsy. Caleb laughed at her apology and assured her there was nothing wrong with walking on the wild side once in a while at their age. They started talking more about the water, which led them into a conversation about freedom again. Mikayla had said too much. She had told him how overprotective everyone was of her and Rowan, and how she was feeling the need to break free, but she was feeling ungrateful for thinking such things. Caleb knew what she was talking about and couldn't help but want to take her away from all of it. Perhaps when this whole thing was over, he would, he thought to himself.

Mikayla started to laugh and make jokes to lighten the mood, and was pleased Caleb was laughing right back. He watched the way her lips moved as she talked, and at the spirit in her eyes. She smelled sweeter than anything he had ever smelled before. It was a mix of her lotion and soap that started to make his mouth water; a mixture of sweet orange and creamy vanilla, with a hint of brown sugar. He was starting to feel a loss of control. He started tracing the line of her neck, he wanted to kiss every inch of it, tasting her, taking her in. The thought of biting into her made him feel aroused. This wasn't normal for Caleb. For him, it usually was the rush of power as the blood ran wildly through his veins that made him want to sink his teeth into someone's neck, but this was different. It was a mixture of feelings bouncing back and forth from wanting to kiss her to wanting to bite her, but bite her only a little. It took every bit of strength he had not to invade her space at that moment. He could tell she was sensing something, as she started to stir uncomfortably and began to fidget with her rings, but she still managed to continue the conversation.

Mikaya was babbling on and on about all the places she was going to travel during the summer months once she was a teacher. She started telling him how she was determined to learn how to surf, that she had tried some small waves off the coast of Florida, but she really had no knowledge of what she was doing. Mikayla began to stir some more as her whole body started to tingle, she knew he was listening, but something unspoken was happening. It was as if he was studying every part of her body. She felt like at any moment he was going to grab her, which both frightened and excited her at the same time.

"I'm sorry, I think the alcohol has me babbling," she said, trying to break whatever trance he was in. Mikayla feared the trance was boredom from her rambling.

"I'm not," Caleb said as he raised an eyebrow while moving his head slightly forward.

The two of them sat silently for a moment, looking into each other's eyes. The smile had left Caleb's face as he reached behind her neck with one hand, bringing his mouth to her ear. She was helpless and just let him. For a moment, the room went silent. She thought he was about to kiss her, but he didn't. Instead he started to whisper into her ear.

"They are coming to find you. I have to leave now. I promise I will see you Friday," he said so close to her ear, his lips brushed against it a couple of times, causing goose bumps all over her body.

She didn't move, she didn't say anything. All she could do was nod.

"Promise me, Mikayla. I need to know that I will see you Friday," Caleb said again, wanting a confirmation from her.

She turned her head so she was face-to-face with Caleb and looked into his eyes.

"I promise, Friday," she said so closely, he felt the heat radiating from her face. He knew at any moment he could lose control and this was not the time nor place. With every ounce of his being, he pulled free from her and stood up.

"Here they come," Caleb said as he stood up. He then turned to her and bent down, as if he was about to kiss her this time. She was surprised she actually was hoping he would, but then he paused instead and took a deep, long breath in, as if he were breathing her in quickly one more time to remember her. Just as Mikayla herself was about to lean in, feeling drawn to him, he was gone.

Caleb could see Dominick running up the stairs, so he decided to go around the opposite side, back to the staircase so he wouldn't run into him. Not once did Caleb take his eyes off of Mikayla or Dominick. Caleb could see Dominick was furious, which only made Caleb realize he was walking a fine line, and he could be potentially be putting their mission in danger with his obsession of this girl. This supposed werewolf of a girl who didn't smell or read of one whatsoever. This only intrigued him more. Maybe she is a wolf without wolf power, perhaps she was a dud and it made them think of her as being weak. Perhaps that's why she doesn't have the scent or senses of a wolf, and why they were so overly protective over her, Caleb thought to himself as he watched Dominick turn the corner, heading straight for Mikayla.

He watched as Dominick came to the table where Mikayla was sitting by herself, staring off into the realistic blue and black backdrop to the glittering night time stars on the ceiling of the club. Quickly he turned his head, looking around to make sure no other wolves had thought to circle around the other side to catch him. *Stupid dogs*, Caleb thought to himself as he realized he was in the clear, and then he turned his attention back on Mikayla.

"What are you doing, Kali?" Dominick said sternly, as if he was the father of a teenage girl out of control, and the teenager just happened to be Mikayla.

"What do you mean? I'm having fun drinking and socializing the way you guys do. What's the problem now?" She snapped back, sounding a little less composed than usual, and almost bordered on the attitude of the teenager he was treating her like. He then reached down and pulled her up by her arm.

"DOMINICK YOU ARE HURTING MY ARM!" Mikayla said venomously through clenched teeth.

Immediately, Caleb's blood began to boil. He wanted to go over there and take Dominick by the throat and squeeze until he turned blue and Caleb could hear the sound of his neck snapping for touching her, for being rough with her, for grabbing what he started to feel like belonged to him, and, most of all, for taking away her freedom. He couldn't understand why they were so protective over her, especially against humans, even if it was because somehow the wolf gene had skipped her. Again, he thought back to the fact her not having powers probably made them this way, but still something was nagging at the back of his mind.

Just as Caleb was about to lose it, he took a deep breath in and remembered why they were there, and knew if he did anything, he would not see her on Friday and that would be the end of any chance they would have to get close enough to Rowan to decipher whether or not she was the witch they were looking for. As he closed his eyes, he let the deep breath out to try and focus. Feeling centered, he opened his eyes again and watched Dominick quickly guide a drunken Mikayla back down the stairs. Caleb let them go down the stairs as he hid in the shadows before he made his way down, and thought it was best he let his brothers know now was a good time to exit.

Well I think the party is over, boys. We need to head over to Jackson's place, if I am right they will for certain send a scout, especially now that I have been up here with Mikayla for the past fifteen minutes, he thought to his brothers as he started to make his way down the stairs.

Back down on the main floor, Jamahl and Ali looked at each other as Ali just shook his head. "What is his fascination with that girl? He's going to make this harder on us then he needs to," Ali said to Jamahl, still shaking his head.

"Maybe he was just trying to make sure that they were going to show up on Friday," Jamahl said back, wanting to believe his little brother wasn't being side tracked, but his gut was telling him something else. "Besides, nothing makes a girl want to something more than when someone is telling her not to, and at this point, I think that they will put their foot down at the thought of her going anywhere with him. They obviously don't trust him," Jamahl added, holding hope Caleb wasn't on the verge of some vampire/witch breakdown.

"I hope your right because, by the way they look right now, something is about to go down. I'm hoping it's the hyenas that have them in a frenzy and not us," Ali said as he quickly glanced over to where the wolves were gathered around, no longer drinking and obviously waiting for their alpha to come in to take charge.

Jamahl shook his slightly at the sight. Never would he or his brothers ever wait around for some alpha to tell them what to do next. An image of Cyrus came into Jamahl's mind, making him take notice of the hypocrisy he had just stated. Unwilling to entertain that thought, he refocused his attention back onto the hyenas.

"You don't think the hyenas can sense that we are part vampire, do you?" Jamahl asked, suddenly having a thought they could possibly out them.

"Not possible. The witch side of us makes our vampire aura neutral. Hyenas can only sense vampires, murderers, war, and demons when they are trying to create havoc of killing. Their natural place is to release tormented souls killed innocently, in turn they are able to take on human form and live throughout life times. It wouldn't be in their best interest to out a vampire, even if they could sense one. They are addicted to the heart's adrenaline and need it to take on human form," Ali informed.

They watched as Dominick made it down the stairs with Mikayla and headed over to his pack. They could see he was angry and trying to keep it under control. Mikayla looked agitated, but seemed to be in a strong hold by Dominick's massive hand. Once he reached the table, he barked some orders for Mikayla and Rowan to grab their purses; he was ending their night out, that much was obvious.

Ali sent Jamahl a worried look.

Rowan and Mikayla both started to put up a fight about leaving when they noticed Caleb making his way back down from the top floor. They weren't the only ones who noticed. Dominick quickly turned to head Caleb off.

"What the fuck are you doing, man?" Dominick said, charging over towards Caleb as he held a pointing finger down as if he were holding a gun in a robbery, right in Caleb's face.

Play it cool little brother, Caleb heard Jamahl trying to calm him in his head.

"What do you mean, man? I just went to the bathroom," Caleb said, trying to sound innocent. Dominick responded back by throwing him up against a wall as a few people, too afraid of his size, looked on.

"Look man, this is my bar. I actually own it, which means I can look at all the cameras throughout the club, and I saw you sitting with her and you were sitting a little too close. What do you want with her? Why are you here?" Dominick said as he looked into Caleb's eyes, trying to get a sense of who he was and if he was more then he claimed to be.

Caleb took a minute to think. Just as he was about to speak, a small hand with black painted nails grabbed Dominick's arm.

"Why are you roughing up my cousin?" Mary said in a very firm voice.

"This guy is your cousin?" Dominick said, still not letting go. "Somehow I doubt that," he then added.

"Yes, this guy is my cousin, his mother is my mother's sister! Now can you please let him go, we have a party to attend to and I would be so pissed if you gave him a fat lip before we leave here." Mary said, lying through her teeth.

Caleb was really starting to like Mary. She was a natural.

"Well, tell your cousin then to leave my girl Mikayla alone if you don't want something bad to happen to him," Dominick said, still holding Caleb hostage against the wall without as much as blinking while he stared hard into Caleb's eyes, burning in warnings for Caleb to back off.

"Well if it's that girl my cousin met today, he hasn't been able to stop talking nice things all night. I think you misunderstand his intentions. He is interested in her in a purely respectful way. Besides, what is wrong with you to tell another person who he may or may not be friends with? I think that sounds evil, and if that's the way you are, your friend is probably that way too, so it's just as well that he not talk to her any more anyway. We don't want any problems with thugs like you,"sShe said.

Brilliant, Caleb thought back to his brothers, still with a subtlety fake fear plastered on his face. He tried hard not to let the smile slip from beneath his false sense of calm.

Dominick turned back to look down at Mary, he looked carefully into her eyes and sized her up as a non-threat.

"Look, I am sorry. I'm not a thug it's just that she is my ex-girlfriend and she doesn't always make good judgments, I just want her to be alright," Dominick said truthfully. "I may have over stepped my bounds, but it was coming from a good place. I hope that you can believe me," he then added, feeling bad for this beautiful, dark haired girl with big, dark eyes looking back up at him with urgency.

"Look man, I really don't mean any harm. I just think Mikayla is very pretty and funny. I kind of like talking to her, sorry man. We really don't want any problems," Caleb said even more innocently now.

Dominick said nothing as he let him go. "Well next time keep your distance. You talk to her in public, don't try anymore of that sneaky shit. It would be best if you just didn't talk to her at all. This town is crawling with women, why don't you just do everyone a favor and pick someone else to have a crush on," Dominick ordered before turning around and not waiting for a response back from Caleb.

This, Caleb felt, was a good thing, that way he didn't have to make a commitment to a wolf he had to break causing even more suspicion. For now, he was just glad the wolves were more concerned about the hyenas.

Caleb stayed by the wall Dominick had him pushed up against and waited with Mary for the others to meet them so they could leave and make it to Jackson's. Caleb glanced over to the wolf pack and noticed one pair of eyes upon him. It was the scout, and Caleb knew for sure now they were going to be followed. It was up to them to make a good case they were not a threat so they wouldn't cancel their initiation ceremony. This would be the only chance they would have and they didn't want to blow it. He also had another agenda, getting closer to Mikayla. Perhaps he would just take her with him, convince her a life with him would be one of freedom.

Caleb was lost in thought for a moment before being nudged by a small elbow in his side. He looked down to find Mary smiling up at him.

"You alright?" She asked.

"Yeah, I'm fine. Thank you, by the way. Good thought on the cousin bit," Caleb said sincerely as he flashed one of his devious smiles across his face, showing his perfect white teeth.

"No problem. I find that when people think of family they tend to back down. It seems to give them something to identify with. I am pretty quick on my feet when I want to be," she said and started laughing.

Caleb started laughing back at the way she was so proud of herself. He got a kick out of Mary and could see why his brother was a little more into her than he should be.

"Yeah, I'm starting to notice that!" Caleb finally said, admitting she was pretty quick. She was that way the night they met and hadn't disappointed them since. They both watched as Mary's friends followed Jamahl and Ali, walking towards them.

They are sending a scout, Caleb warned his brothers.

We know, Ali replied.

Better make a good case, then, Caleb added.

They all gathered together knowing the party must go on to convince the wolves nothing was going on.

"Let's hit Jackson's!" Jamahl yelled as everyone in the group cheered and out the door they went as the scout prepared to track them. Mostly Jamahl shouted for the wolves to hear, the same reason Ali managed to join in the cheering. Normal circumstances would have Ali the odd man out, remaining calm, quiet, and in control.

17

Dominick stood at the table as Rowan and Mikayla sat waiting for them to decide what they were going to do with them. They could already sense something was in motion. Rowan and Mikayla were both drunk, had way too much to drink, which was completely out of character for both of them. Especially Mikayla, who preferred to have a clear head. The fact Mikayla had taken shots had worried Dominick. He knew she was doing it out of frustration and he was sorry he was part of the cause.

She had no idea of the real reason he was so protective over her. Yes, he loved her still, but if things were different he would allow her the right to live her life. He knew he had hurt her and he had blown it with her long ago, and he was willing to take on a lifetime of consequences from that. But she had no idea of the danger to her. She didn't even know where she really came from. Nobody but a few people knew. Dominick found out just before prom, and it was almost too much for him to handle. He was still dealing with finding out who he really was, and then was thrown off when a year later he found his precious Kali wasn't even one of them. It was almost too much for him to take on, but he was the alpha and so he accepted the burden of full responsibility of her protection.

Rowan turned to whisper to Mikayla with a big smile plastered on her face. "So," was all she said.

"So what?" Mikayla said with a giggle.

What did he say? Rowan switched to telepathy now.

I don't know, we just talked, but he got so close and I felt like I couldn't breathe. It was kind of weird in a really good way, Mikayla thought back. *He said he was still going to see me on Friday. I just hope after Dominick's display of caveman, it doesn't make him give up, but somehow I believe that he might be braver then most. It's just the feeling I get,* she added as a smile melted across her face.

"You fell in love in a day," Rowan whispered playfully, switching to actual talk so the boys wouldn't start to wonder why they were just looking at each other. She then began giggling.

"Shut up, I am not. It's just that he is really cool and, well, smart and we have a lot in common," Mikayla, still smiling, whispered back.

"You forgot cute!" Rowan said, now laughing, which only made Mikayla give into the alcohol and laugh back.

"Trust me, I didn't forget. Do you think he is still here," Mikayla said and asked, now looking around to see if she could spot him.

She looked over to the table that they were at to find it was empty, then looked over to the bar to find they were not there either. Then she focused her attention over to the door to find them heading towards it. Just then, she felt a tug on her arm. It was Dominick lifting her up, as Mario did the same to Rowan.

"Come on guys, party is over, you're going upstairs," Dominick said as he guided Mikayla away from the table.

"Wait, it's only 11:30. I'm not done shaking things up," Mikayla said as she stumbled over a stool. Dominick turned to pick up the fallen stool and proceeded to pick her up with his other arm and sling her over his shoulder the same way Mario had Rowan, only Rowan was laughing and Mikayla was not.

"Dominick, put me down. You can't tell me what to do," Mikayla shouted in her intoxicated state.

Caleb heard her shout and turned around instinctively. His whole body became tense and his fists were clenched so tightly, all of the blood was forced into them. He quickly turned to walk back in towards Mikayla. He could feel his gums tingling as his teeth began to poke through and the color in his eyes started to change. Just then, Jamahl grabbed him and turned him around as Ali stood behind them and shoved him out the door.

"You have to let it go, man. He's not going to hurt her. She is alright with them, it's you she's not safe with," Ali reminded him.

When we are through you can do what you want with her, whatever that I,s but your obsession is going to blow our mission. Is that what you want, Ali added in thought, so the girls couldn't hear them. It was more of a statement than a question, asked to remind Caleb what they were there to do.

Caleb didn't say anything; he just walked out the door, remembering the scout was not far behind them. That seemed to be enough for him to contain his rage for the moment. Ali and Jamahl just kept laughing and joking with the girls all the way down the street to their car.

"What the fuck is your problem, Dominick? You are even weirder than usual," Mikayla said as she was riding over his shoulders up the stairs of the kitchen inside of the club to Dominick and Mario's condo, which was above the club.

"My problem? What is *your* problem? You don't drink and I turn around for two seconds and you have slammed shot after shot like an alcoholic. Then you run off with some guy who is just trying to get into your pants and, with the state you are in, probably figured you were game!" Dominick shouted back, half angry because she was in potential danger, and half angry he could tell she was interested in this other guy.

"I am so irritated with you right now," was all Mikayla could think to say back. She tried to wiggle, but it was no use. Besides, she knew the only place for her to go was down the stairs, and it was likely that her neck would break the fall.

They had reached their condo and the boys put the girls inside. Mario wasn't worried about Rowan staying put because she trusted him, and if he said, "please do this for me," she did. It was Mikayla, the wild card, they were afraid of, although Mario wasn't quite sure why such urgency was involved. He figured it was partly Dominick's fear of the hyenas and what they were there for, and partly the presence of Caleb. They were at least about to find out why the hyenas were around as soon as they could get the girls settled.

Dominick wasn't going to take any chances on Mikayla, so he put her into his bedroom and shouted at her. "Just please stay put, for once in your life, listen to me. This is for your own good. One day I will be able to explain, I just need you to be a team player. Please, Kali," Dominick shouted, half angry and half pleading.

"Whatever, I am not staying here. I am going to call a cab," Mikayla said defiantly, pulling out her phone to call a cab. Dominick grabbed the phone and put it in his pocket.

"Alright, have it your way, Kali. You want to play it this way, fine. I will play it this way," Dominick said, shoving her inside of his bedroom and locking it from the outside with his key.

All the boys had locks on their bedroom doors, both inside and out, which required a key, for when they had parties to keep people in the living room, rec room, and porch, out of their private domains. Dominick smiled at how easy it was to keep her locked and safe, and giggled when he realized how handy these locks really seemed to be.

"Hey, what are you doing, Dom!" Rowan said with a disturbed look on her face.

"Trust me, please. I am not doing this to hurt her, it's for her own protection," Dominick said, putting the key into his pocket as Mikayla sat on the other side of the door, banging and shouting at Dominick to let her out, and warning him of how sorry he was going to be later.

Dominick headed to the door and Mario turned around to plant a kiss on Rowan, who turned her head in disgust at the sudden drama of the night.

"Just be cool, you know Dom would never do anything to hurt her. Trust me," Mario said to Rowan after she had turned her head. Rowan said nothing back as Mario leaned forward one more time to kiss her on top of her head, but she still just stood there with her arms folded.

"Oh, and stay put!" Mario shouted as he turned around and flashed her a smile before he went out the front door.

Rowan waited to hear the lock turn before running over to Dominick's room.

"Kali, they are gone. Stop yelling for a second. Are you ok?" Rowan sobered up real fast to check on Mikayla.

"No, I feel even more agitated then I did earlier today. What is going on? Things are getting stranger and stranger. I know he means well, but pulling stunts like this isn't exactly wooing me back. I have got to put my foot down, Row. I just cannot live like this anymore. I don't think I can wait a whole year to have my freedom," Mikayla said back as tears streamed down her cheeks.

"Ok, well first, honey, let's break you out of there," Rowan said trying to calm her down and break her best friend out.

When either one was upset, the other one felt it, and right now she could tell how bad Mikayla was hurting. It was starting to concern Rowan how restless Mikayla was actually feeling.

"How am I supposed to get out of here? I am locked in and Dominick took the key. He is way too smart to have left a key inside," Mikayla said, and then paused for a few minutes. "Unless he was moving too quick to grab a spare," she then added, already rummaging through his things, trying to find a spare key through tear filled eyes.

She opened all of his drawers and looked through them, but found nothing. Then she looked through his closet. She had spent fifteen minutes looking fiercely through his things while Rowan talked to her from the other side of the door.

"I can't find anything, he doesn't have one laying around anywhere that I can see!" Mikayla said, ready to give up and lay down for the night.

Both girls sat down on the ground with a locked door between them. They started making small talk, trying to make the best out of the ridiculous situation they found themselves in. This led them into talking about Dominick and all of the things he had done over the years to prevent her from dating other guys, but neither of them could deny the way he loved her. Mikayla started to think about the times he had come through for her, and one time in particular which stood out was prom.

"I just don't get it, if he wants me back so bad, why doesn't he just say so? And if he loves me, why doesn't he understand that I don't like to be controlled. I'm telling you, Rowan, something is just not adding up. Things have been strange ever since prom. More than just with him. Look how we can talk to each other telepathically, it is strange. We are complete freaks! We know it! Yet we just accept this and never talk about why it is we can do it," Mikayla said, staring up at the white ceiling of Dominick's spotless bedroom.

Rowan didn't respond. She was lost in thought about what Mikayla had just said. She knew what Mikayla was saying was true; they had never addressed the oddity of their telepathic powers. Perhaps they were both just too scared, Rowan thought to herself, before she heard Mikayla talking again.

"Row, are you still there?" Mikayla said, wondering if Rowan had finally passed out for the night.

"No, I am here. I am listening but what you said just gave me an idea," Rowan said as she sat up. "Talking to each other telepathically isn't the only things that we have been able to do. We don't do things a lot and I think it's because it scares us when we do and I am not sure if we are both just crazy or something is different about us, but perhaps if we try," Rowan broke off for a moment, trying to figure out the how, when Mikayla sat up on the other side, understanding just where Rowan was going with it.

"Wait a minute, you are right. It's worth a try, and if I can get out of here, it might teach Dom a lesson in trying to contain this wild flower." Mikayla, now on the page, answered back in excitement as she wiped away the tears from her eyes. Rowan started giggling at Mikayla's comment about her being a wild flower, and teased her briefly as Mikayla laughed along, which helped to dry up the last of the water from her face.

"Ok, well what do you think it is that we are supposed to do for a lock?" Mikayla said, eyeballing the two-sided silver lock.

"Should we come up with a rhyme of some sort, like in the movies?" Rowan said, half giggling but half serious, not really sure of how to make something like this happen.

The other times things happened wasn't because they tried, it was just something that seemed to happen, so they weren't really sure what to do. They had almost seemed more like a coincidental miracle more than anything.

"Well, maybe if you try to say you wish like you did that one time in school, it will happen." Rowan stopped laughing and said seriously.

"Yeah, good idea!" Mikayla said, and quickly tried to center herself in front of the door.

She looked at the lock and tried to remember how she felt when she had wished for the answers to come way back in school. Feelings of desperation and last resorts first came to mind, somehow that didn't seem like it would be feelings of power, she thought to herself. The lock itself looked unbreakable, but she was willing to take a shot. She closed her eyes and placed her hand on the lock and breathed deeply in, letting her breath out slow and steady on the exhale. Rowan stood quietly at the door on the other side so as not to disturb her concentration. She knew it was a long shot, and at this point was more intrigued of whether or not she could do it rather than seeing her get out. She stood in complete silence and wonder. Mikayla stood with her hand on the lock, repeating the breathing pattern slow and steady until she could feel some sort of energy. She wasn't sure what the energy would be, but it felt like a sixth sense telling her what to look for, but nothing was happening yet. Rowan could feel Mikayla starting to give up.

"Don't give up, Kali. Keep going," Rowan whispered words of encouragement, which got Mikayla to refocus and concentrate harder.

Five minutes had passed by as time seemed to stand still to Mikayla. All of a sudden, she could sense a warm white light surrounding her face, much the same feeling as the rays in the early morning coming into her room to greet her for the day. It was warm like the sun, and shone like a glittering star. It reminded her mostly of the morning time in her bedroom during the warm summertime months.

The light began to spread down her neck and around her shoulders, and quickly draped down the rest of her body until she felt encompassed fully in the white light. She took that energy and forced it all to her hand touching the lock as she commanded the lock to open. As soon as she said the words, she felt the rest of the white light travel at what seemed like the speed of light to her hand and release out from her palm and fingertips at the lock. The feeling sent goose bumps throughout her whole body, yet she was not cold. She was actually hot, almost on fire, as she felt the energy release at the lock. With her eyes still closed, she heard a click and quickly opened her eyes. Rowan standing on the other side of the door, heard the click itself, and covered her dropped jaw with her hand in disbelief.

"Rowan, I think I heard a click," Mikayla said quietly, with her hand still touching the lock. Her heart beat began to race as if she had just been caught doing something she wasn't supposed to be doing.

"Kali, I heard one to," was all Rowan could think to softly say.

Mikayla took her hand slowly away from the lock. She was a bit freaked out from the flow of energy, and hoping this wasn't some sort of Wizard of

OZ scenario in which she would open the door and find herself in another land. It could be the land of the crazy people, at this point, and she wouldn't be surprised, she thought to herself. She took a deep breath and grabbed the door handle, turned the knob, and pushed. Sure enough, the door opened and Rowan was standing on the other side, looking like a deer caught in headlights. They were both in utter shock and said not one word to one another.

18

Dominick ran down the stairs as Mario followed. Mario was a bit disturbed by the way Dominick had flown off the handle. It wasn't his place to question the alpha, even if he was his right hand man, but he couldn't understand why he was treating his sister so harshly. Even for Dominick, it was a bit over the top. They were always protective over her and Rowan, but Mario felt this was beyond, and was beginning to think there was something more going on. He trusted his alpha and knew his behavior could only mean one thing, he was protecting her from something.

"So, are you going to tell me what is going on?" Mario said, following Dominick down the stairs.

Dominick felt relieved to hear Mario say that, he knew his behavior was a bit beyond, even for him, and had hoped Mario would pick up there truly was a good explanation for it all.

"When I can Mario, I promise I will. I'm just glad that you understand it's out of need, not want at this point," was all he could say at that point without saying too much.

Mario realized now was not the time to push things, as well as the fact he was good about following the lead of the alpha male. He thought twice, since it was his sister, but knew Dominick would always take care of all of them. Dominick was stronger than all of them, and more brave, but he was also very smart. Mario wished Mikayla could just get over the past and fall back in love with Dominick, but he was pretty sure that was not going to happen. The most he could hope for at this point was both of them would find people who suited them well, and eventually everyone could all get along. Somehow though, he just couldn't see them not ending up together.

As they made it down the last step, the rest of the pack, minus the scout, was waiting for them. No one made a move until Dominick made his way through them to lead as they followed, with Mario on his right side and Lucio on his left, as the rest of the crew followed right behind. They made their way calmly over to the table of hyenas, who were sitting around drinking and eyeing all the humans.

It was stranger than Dominick thought it would be to see them in person. There was something about the look in their eyes that reminded him of something he was told. Long ago, when a demonic force had manipulated them to take life, rather than to release life, he remembered the light in their eyes shone a dark yellow. He then remembered the color of light in their eyes should be a white light, which shone in their eyes when they were doing what they were supposed to and releasing light.

Dominick grew stiff as he noticed the color in this pack of hyenas eyes was shining yellow. He racked his brain, not hearing or feeling anything had happened close by that he had felt, so he was pretty sure whatever they had done hadn't happened in his area. However he knew by the look in their eyes someone had manipulated them yet again, and it was just a matter of time before something in his area would happen. Dominick was not going to let that happen.

The wolf pack finally reached the table and the hyenas didn't look surprised to see them. This worried Dominick.

"What are hyenas doing here in Michigan?" Dominick side-stepped the small talk and just came out with it.

"Why, whatever do you mean, dog?" The female hissed eerily.

"Cut to it, you're obviously not surprised to see us here, and you're only supposed to go where you feel a pull towards something happening, or if a vampire or demon is around, so come with it." Dominick said coolly.

"Wow, this little puppy has done his homework. You're a little more forth coming than your father or grandfather was," the female hyena said again, with a coy smile plastered across her face.

"Yes, you are bigger too, aren't you? But you haven't completed your last initiation… tsk tsk tsk…Looks like you don't have all of your powers yet, puppy," she then added, taunting Dominick.

Without saying a word, Dominick grabbed the back of her neck and slammed her face sideways onto the table and held it there.

"See, you and us are both supposed to be able to feel when something is coming, so I should know when you're coming and I didn't. I also know that your kind is not always to be trusted because you are weak and refuse to fully take a side, so you do your little part for your own selfish gain and not to make better for your fellow earth dwellers. So, then I look into your eyes and notice the yellow coloring, and that means you are being influenced. So cut it out if you want a chance to live, and tell me why you are here," Dominick said coolly, as he held her face to the table.

The three male hyenas started to stir uncomfortably. They were much older than this young wolf pack, and didn't want to go up against such a young group with nothing to lose, but they wanted to protect their alpha, concerned these young wolves were not fully informed the way they should be. Wolves by nature were designed to take them out. Hyenas were more animal than human. They actually only could take on human form. Since the truce, they had tried to persuade the hyenas to join the side for good, but they always remained neutral, playing their part half-heartedly for the reward of human form and power of the life force within. They were too tied to each other and the earth , looking above was almost too much for them. It was a possibility they just hadn't evolve far enough. They had a difficult job, and it almost had to take a group of animals with no ties to eat the hearts of the slain. An empathetic soul would have a hard time doing so. But nonetheless, it was still hoped one day they would see the light and make better use out of their powers.

"Dominick, I know you own this bar, and the people around you are starting to wonder if you're a women abuser. Humans love to spread gossip, so for your own good you need to take your paw off my fucking neck," the female stated, calmly at first, until she reached her last couple of words, which turned into more of a hissing command rather than a request. Dominick quickly released, half shocked at the fact she knew his name, and half worried she was right.

He quickly scanned the room to find a few people stopped dead in their tracks at what they had just witnessed. Dominick knew he needed to play this a bit more coolly, and quickly took his hands off of her.

"That's a good boy," she said, completely unruffled by the strong hold he just had on her. "Now that my head is no longer pressed into the table, I believe you were asking me a question," she added, as if she were truly intent on answering.

Dominick didn't speak for a moment; he was trying to carefully choose which question he needed answered first.

"First off, how do you know my name?" He decided to decipher why she would even know that much. Sure she would smell he was a wolf, but how did she know who he was, and his father and grandfather.

"Now that's probably the question you would want to start with. We are old, very old, and you know you are supposed to treat you elders with respect. Let's just say I am a little bit older than your grandfather. I knew him and was one of the one's who helped make a treaty with us way back when. So, I always keep track of those from our world I know and those I don't know." She looked intensely at Dominick. "No matter what you think about us, we are scavengers, and we, like you, have a job to do, so we do it. Your kind, however, has treated us with little respect based on one time of us getting, manipulated, or as you seem to see it, carried away, but only getting carried away because of the way we were made. I am not expecting you to understand, you are still much too young. So, Dominick, I knew of you within the first year of your birth," she said as if she were a long lost family friend.

Despite the yellow in her eyes, Dominick did feel a bit bad for being so disrespectful to such an old being.

He thought a bit further before speaking again. "So, tell me why you are here then," Dominick asked firmly.

"Ah, the million dollar question! Bravo, young wolf. You have done all of your homework, and I can see you will certainly make a powerful alpha for your pack. Why are we here… that is not the only question you want to know. Your first question you want answered is why, if we haven't broken any treaties, do our eyes still shine yellow," she said, still smiling, and talking only to Dominick.

Everyone else seemed unimportant.

"Yes, why?" Dominick snapped quickly to the question, feeling like she was playing a game with him.

"It is a long story…" she started, before being interrupted by Dominick.

"I have time," he said quickly. The hyena let out a big laugh and clapped her hands together.

"Yes, I am sure you do. Perhaps I should just let your father explain," she said, looking past Dominick towards the front door.

Dominick turned to look towards the door to see that his father, and Mario's father, coming in through the door.

"Lazzaro, it's been awhile," she said, allowing Dominick's father Lazzaro take her hand and kiss it. "Santino, you haven't changed a bit," she then said to Mario's father, as he took her hand and kissed it, as well.

Dominick wasn't just confused, he was furious. He felt like he had missed something, and he glared at his father for what he saw as an embarrassment in front of his pack.

"I see you are early, I suppose that you have met my son?" Lazzaro said to the female hyena, smiling at the little bit of chaos he knew she had created just by walking in without Dominick's knowledge. He didn't always tell everything to his son, it was better for Dominick to be put into situations in which he had to learn how to think on his feet. Lazzaro knew it would only make him a better alpha male.

"We have not met. We were just doing so as you walked up," she said, and spoke more like royalty than animal.

"Dominick, this is Naki. She is queen of all hyenas. She is hyena royalty and, despite how young she looks, is currently the oldest hyena living. The four of them make up the last of the ancients," Lazzaro said.

"Dominick is such a big boy!" Naki said to Lazzaro. This made him smile proudly of his son.

"It's nice to meet you, and no disrespect, but you were just about to explain why the color of your eyes are yellow," Dominick said, instinctively trying to get down to the bottom of things. He was beginning to feel uneasy that it seemed as if his father had intentionally come there just to meet with her and what he assumed was her royal court.

Lazzaro stared at his son for a minute, realizing without all of the information at hand, Dominick was doing his job well. He put one hand on Dominick's shoulder and stared at him in his face.

"Not everything is always as it seems. Naki, Njau, Badru, and Iniko are all that remains from the hyenas that were manipulated a few hundred years ago. Their eyes are still yellow because what has been done cannot be undone. Their eyes will forever, as long as they breathe life, be yellow. It's the burden they carry. But these are the only ones still alive. When they were killing, the yellow was much deeper, and the whites of their eyes were absent. See how they have the whites of their eyes clear, that is how you can tell that they are still remaining neutral. See son, we don't hate hyenas, we just wish that they would join us. Which is why, I assume, Naki may have asked to see me," Lazzaro said, as he lifted an eyebrow and looked to the queen.

Naki started to laugh hysterically, almost flirtatiously.

"You never stop, do you?" She bent forward and said coyly to Lazzaro.

"Well, you did ask to see me, and you did say you were worried. Is this something the young pack can hear, or shall we talk alone?" Lazzaro said, seriously this time, to the playful hyena.

Naki looked at the rest of the pack and thought briefly.

"Well, if I send them away they will just position themselves to be able to hear, anyways. So I think they may stay," she said as she snapped her fingers for Iniko and Badru to offer up their seats and stand behind her.

The younger wolves surrounded the table as Dominick and Mario stood at opposite ends of the table, without stools.

"Well, Lazzaro, it has come upon me that there is something that has got both good and evil all worked up. It is interesting, though. I can't get a clear read on where this is. It just seems to be festering quietly around in dark places, and this has made me think long and hard about my people. I decided that after living many years, and seeing both my share of beauty and turmoil, it was finally time for us to try and take a stand, rather than just playing a small part in a machine, or there may be no earth left for us to be tied to. It has taken many years to undo what we had done to ourselves, but I am not stupid. I have evolved and I want more. Yes, my nature is selfish, and my nature is to crave life force much the way a vampire craves blood, but I am determined to have us be known as more than bottom feeders for good, or puppets for evil. As long as we remain status quo, my people run greater risk of manipulation and potential expulsion," she said seriously, looking for approval.

"I had a feeling you would come to that conclusion sooner or later," Lazzaro said and nodded in respect towards her. Santino did the same.

"You will be visited, then, by an angel who will help guide your people," Santino spoke, assuring her guidance would be given. "I want you to know that the spot on the council still is held for you, as it has been held for the past seventy-five years," Santino assured her presence as a welcome.

Naki smiled at both of them, seeming to be eating up the respect being shown to her. She was feeding off of it. Again, a selfish creature by nature wouldn't be able to help themselves feel anything less.

"Well, I do know that and I meant to speak with you sooner, but I came across something strange and I won't be able to guide my people until this problem is solved. I am pretty sure that what I am about to tell you will make you understand why else I am here. Three of my pack, young and all male, showed up a couple of weeks ago after missing for a few days. Their eyes were as yellow as ours once were. When I questioned them, they gave disrespect to me and gave me no answers. I can only assume one thing for sure; they have been manipulated and must have killed. Why they were picked on is because of their age, no doubt, and males are much easier to seduce. Why they came back to camp, I can only imagine was to try and form a larger pack. I tried to convince them to stay, and we fought to try and get them to remain with us until I was able to get help, but it was no use. They took off. I tracked them from Africa to the states and lost them in New York. That was a few days ago. I knew I needed to let you know of our decision to up our role, as well as let you know that three of our own have been tainted. I do not want them to be killed, if possible. I would like to save them, but I will need your help if they show up around here," she said, sounding even more like a queen.

Lazzaro looked at her and shook his head in agreement.

It was obvious she had more to add by the way she shifted in her seat. Having realized Lazzaro was happy to cooperate with her, she began to speak again.

"These boys are about to go on their last initiation, right?" She asked, already knowing the answer.

"Friday," Santino answered.

"I know you don't normally go into the upper peninsula for initiation because it is another wolf pack's territory, but would you mind spending one day to see if you can pick up their scent to see if they have trailed that way?" She asked.

"No problem, I will contact the chief of the pack up there and let them know when we will be around. They aren't doing initiation ceremonies this month, they are waiting until August because some of their pack haven't reached twenty one yet. This I'm sure will be no problem," Lazzaro said.

Naki smiled with pleasure. It seemed as if she was going to like the respect joining the good side would bring her, although Lazzaro and Santino had always shown her respect, hoping one day she would find she liked the way it felt to be treated in such a manner and make the decision to use their purpose for good and not just exist without any meaning for themselves and their fellow earthly beings.

Mario noticed his father looking concerned and, as he looked around, he noticed that Lazzaro and Dominick shared the same look. Mario knew something more was going on he wasn't aware of yet; he could see it from the shift of Lazzaro's eyes to his father, who was now wearing a look of worry upon his face.

"I see. I will do my best. For now, go back to your people and let yourselves be guided. I expect to see much greatness out of your people, my old friend," Lazzaro said, taking her hand and kissing it again.

Santino followed suit. Dominick put his best foot forward and bowed his head at the queen, taking her hand and kissing it as well.

"I am sorry for earlier, Naki. Please forgive me, for I am still young," Dominick said sincerely.

"Yes, spoken like a true leader," was all she said and smiled again, coyly.

She then bent forward and whispered in his ear. "You will learn much over the years, but remember one thing, not everything is always as it seems. Sometimes what you think is good, isn't always, and what you think is bad isn't so bad as it could be," she said with a look of desperation in her eye before speaking again. "You have good leadership skills, and take your role seriously, but young one, you must learn to tap into your instincts a bit more, for this will help you. I think you may end up being one of the greatest alphas of all time." She said and closed her eyes tightly and breathed him in, taking in his full scent. "Ah yes, you most definitely will." Naki added as she pulled away and refocused on the group.

Naki got up from the table and her subjects followed faithfully as Lazzaro and Santino followed them out. Dominick took a seat and sat silently for a moment. Mario pulled up a seat across from him, but said nothing, giving him a minute to think. Minutes passed by as Dominick's head was now resting in his hands, as if he felt helpless somehow. Mario knew for sure he wasn't aware of everything Dominick was.

They sat quietly for a few minutes more before Dominick looked up at Mario.

"I have to make a phone call. Let's go back to the condo." Dominick didn't wait for Mario to respond, he just got up and walked over to the door manager and said a few words to him before making his way up towards the stairs.

Mario followed behind him as he instructed the rest of the pack to go back to hanging out. Dominick didn't speed up the stairs, he took his time ,as if lost in thought, but they finally made it to the door of their condo despite the fact Mario was wondering if they were ever going to get there moving at such a slow pace.

19

They entered the condo to find Rowan on the couch, sifting through channels. Mario went right to her and kissed her on her forehead. He thought about how fragile she looked. She was small, and so beautiful, it almost hurt for him to look at her. Rowan smiled up at him, but somehow he knew something wasn't as it should be by the look in her eye. "What is it?" He questioned, without needing any further information to know something wasn't right. Before Rowan could speak, he heard Dominick yell.

"Damn it! Rowan, how did she get out? Where is she?" Dominick yelled, walking from his room to the living room, where Mario stood in front of her still tucked away on the couch.

"Just calm down, she was mad because you locked her in your room for talking to another guy. She called a cab and headed home. Relax, Dom," she said, rolling her eyes. Rowan never felt intimidated by Dominick, they were like brother and sister.

"Rowan, how did she even get out?" He asked, knowing she probably wasn't going to tell him, just in case this happened again. She just stood there for a moment, trying to think of a good excuse. This was the answer she was trying to come up with for the past twenty minutes, but still hadn't come up with a good one, that Mikayla had been gone.

"You know what, never mind," he said as he grabbed his keys and headed for the door. He then turned around and pointed at Rowan. "Just to let you know, I know how. The two of you can keep your little secret, but let's get one thing clear, I will always know more than you think." He then turned around and headed out the door, slamming it as he left.

Mario and Rowan watched as Dominick slammed the door shut behind him.

"What was he talking about? What does he know?" Mario looked at Rowan for answers. This night was getting more and more confusing for him. and now somehow Rowan, the one who was made for him, was seemingly tied into one more thing Dominick knew that he did not. She just looked at him and half smiled. "I need for you to talk to me, Rowan. I'm serious. Tonight has gotten a bit weird for me, and the last thing I need is for a wedge to come between us. Please Rowan, trust me. I plan on spending the rest of my life with you, so I need for you to tell me what Dominick was talking about."

Rowan was trying to think quickly. She wasn't sure whether or not she should tell him. She wasn't even sure if Dominick was talking about their powers, or if he thought it was something else. Looking down at her feet, she decided whether or not Dominick knew about her and Mikayla, a time was going to come when she would have to fess up to Mario. So, she finally concluded there was no time like the present.

"Ok, I will tell you, but you have to promise that you will not tell anyone, or commit me to some sort of mental hospital. I think you may want to sit down for this," she said, and took a seat next to him on the couch. She proceeded to tell him the story of when they were younger, the things they were able to do, and how, as they got older, new things would develop. Rowan confessed about their ability to communicate with each other telepathically. She then told him how, as of late, more things started stirring within them which led her to explaining just how Mikayla had escaped the room. When she finished, Mario didn't say anything, he just placed both of his hands over his face and tilted his body forward, leaning over his knees. He didn't say a word, he was now the one lost in thought and began feeling for what Dominick must be going through, if that's what had Dominick confused. Somehow he could see Rowan having powers would be obvious, with who her parents were, but his sister didn't make any sense. She should have turned into a wolf, but somehow had skipped the gene. He decided something went wrong in her genetic coding, and Dominick knew it.

Rowan was afraid of the silence and cuddled up closely next to him, needing for him to reach out to her, to tell her that he still loved her despite. Mario knew she was feeling insecure, he wanted to protect her and he needed her just as much, at that moment. He turned to her, grabbed her around the waist, and pulled her in tightly, still not saying a word. He leaned in and looked into her eyes and starred deeply into them. He felt hungry for her, and without a thought, grabbed her even tighter and began kissing her. She was relieved and overwhelmed at his response, and a tear started to roll out from her eye. This turned on every sense in Mario. He then wasted no time picking her up from the couch and taking her into his bedroom. He kicked the door shut and gently laid her down on the bed, still kissing her. They didn't speak with words; they spoke through love, leaving no part of each other untouched.

Mikayla had called a cab twenty minutes earlier. She had a call it was around back, but when she went out the backside of the condos, which technically really was the front, the cab was gone. She thought it was strange, but decided it was a warm night, and a two mile walk to her house wasn't that big of a deal. After all, she was wearing flip flops and not heels. At this point, she still had a bit of a buzz and figured the walk would be good to try and get rid of the rest of her buzz. She shook her head at the thought of the shots. "What the hell was I thinking?" She said aloud to herself and kept walking.

The night was clear and all the stars were shining bright. It was almost time for the moon to be full, and even though tonight it wasn't, the brightness from the stars created enough shine to light her way. The air was warm and still. She felt neither cold nor hot, she felt just perfect. As she headed down the road, she realized it was late and she was on her own. She had no time to feel scared, she surprisingly, at the moment, felt free. For a moment she thought it was from the liquid courage she partook in, but she knew deep down she was feeling free and she liked it.

It would take her another ten minutes to get home. She had been walking at a pretty good pace, and figured it was only about three quarters of a mile away if she cut through the park. Thinking about actually cutting through the park was the first time she felt nervous during her walk home. Sure she was alone the first mile, but she was also on streets with lights, buildings, and houses, as well as cars passing by. She hadn't truly been isolated yet, and the thought began to make her heart race a bit. The peaceful feeling was gone, and a feeling of dread washed over her. For some reason, she felt as if she was being watched. She felt like she had been watched the night before as she stood outside waving goodbye to Rowan, but it was different then from how she felt right now. Last night she just swore a pair of eyes was on her, and it could have been true with all the people out at the park playing ball, but this was different. Somehow she felt almost as if she were being stalked or hunted.

She picked up her pace as she headed down the paved path into the woods. Tall, thick trees lined the path. It was so thick, she couldn't see into either side of the forest. There was just enough light shining down on the path for her to see a couple feet in front of her. The smell in the air was warm and sweet, which was the only piece of comfort she was feeling at the moment. It was only a couple more feet until she reached the open field, and she would feel better then, she kept telling herself. That, to her, seemed less scary. Without the darkness of the trees blocking out the light, she would at least be able to see more than a foot in front of her. She was breathing a little harder now, having picked up her pace, but she swore she heard something rustling behind her, staying close, just off the paved path. Quickly she turned around to see if she could see anything, but it was too dark, and the only thing she thought she could make out were six yellow lightening bugs staying still and close together.

She turned around just as quick to keep her eyes focused on the open field in the park. It was close and in her sights. This made her feel better. She then started thinking about the lightening bugs, and thought how weird it was they had actually almost looked more like three pair of eyes. It almost helped her to not feel so afraid to think about something random like lightening bugs, especially with the open field just ahead. Then her instincts kicked in. Maybe those weren't lightening bugs. What if they actually were eyes, she thought to herself as her fear kicked back in to full gear, and every strand of fine hair stood straight up, like she had been electrocuted, on her arms.

Mikayla was just about to take her first step out of the wooded forest path when she knew now she heard something, and it wasn't just anything, it was a low growl. She decided now wasn't the time to turn around, and she started a full on sprint out into the open field. All of a sudden, it seemed as if a voice was whispering, telling her to do just that, keep her eyes on her house. Without questioning the voice, she put up no argument and focused. She spotted the lights of her house and tried to keep her eye on the prize, trusting if anything got too close behind her, she would be able to feel it. It was not the right time for her to take her eyes off of her house. If she made just one wrong move, she could trip and fall. No, now was the time to keep herself focused. Her heart was racing, and without even looking back, she knew something was running after her. She could hear the footsteps behind her gaining speed, but she had no idea what.

She picked up her pace even faster. It was almost as if she heard someone whisper in her ear to run faster. Listening to the voice now, she was moving her legs as fast as they would go. Every hair on her arms and back of her neck stood up when she heard the laughs behind her. She thought it almost sounded like hyenas, but she knew that couldn't be right; this was Michigan. Her senses told her there was still some distance between her and them. She kept focusing on her house and told herself over and over again don't look back. She heard another laugh and she almost let out a huge scream when all of a sudden she heard a yelp. Terror ripped through her body as she heard another yelp.

She was close to the street now, and felt as if she were no longer being chased as she heard a third yelp, now further away. It was strange, she suddenly felt like she actually had a chance of making it to her house as she approached the street. She didn't bother looking into the street for cars, completely forgetting cars usually drove down streets and ran right out in front of one. She quickly put her hands up at the car, as if that would stop the car, but the car slammed on its breaks and stopped, just inches away from hitting her. At this point, Mikayla thought she would pass out. Her buzz was definitely gone now.

The car door opened up and she saw a large figure getting out, but couldn't make out who it was because the bright lights of the headlights were shining into her eyes. "Oh my God! Kali!" She heard a voice say and knew right then it was Dominick. She didn't ever remember a time in the past few years where she was actually glad to hear Dominick, but at this moment she was. Afraid and relieved all at once, she started to cry and fell to the ground. As usual, Dominick didn't hesitate. He picked her up and put her in his car.

"What happened?" He asked, trying to sound calming, but Mikayla could hear the tension in his voice.

"I felt like some animals were chasing me, and whatever was chasing me was being chased by something bigger! It sounds strange, but anything else would just be a lie," she said through tears.

"No Kali, I believe you. I am not trying to use this as a means to get you to spend the night with me, but a lot is going on right now. Tonight, will you just please come back with me to my house. I will sleep better knowing that you are safe for the night." He said, buckling her in as if he already knew she would agree, and decided if she didn't agree she would just have to suck it up. Mikayla said nothing, and as Dominick suspected, shook her head in agreement. As soon as she was buckled in, he headed back to his condo.

20

Caleb realized the hyenas being there had taken some of the suspicion off of him, although it wasn't completely gone. The scout had only watched them for just about an hour. Caleb felt when he had left and knew he wouldn't be back. He couldn't help but want to see her again, so he slipped out of Jackson's party without his brothers knowing and orbed to the park by Mikayla's house. He landed in the open field just across the street from her house when he sensed something coming. The feeling wasn't that of a human, but an animal that didn't belong in these woods. He quickly made his way towards the forest when he realized what it was. *What are the chances of seeing hyenas twice in one night*, he thought to himself as he silently made his way towards the forest.

As he approached the woods, he climbed up into a tree, far enough in to not be detected but close enough to the opening of the clearing so he could still keep an eye on Mikayla's house. The light in her room wasn't on, so he assumed she was either asleep or hadn't made it home yet, and he wanted to watch for her in case she showed up while he was trying to figure out what this group of hyenas were up to. He was betting on a werewolf hyena war and hoped he was around to witness a good fight.

He waited, motionless, high up in the tree when he spotted a long, white dress flowing freely his way. *Mikayla*, he thought to himself surprised by her presence. He could see she was nervous and she could sense something was lurking in the shadows. It was like watching a mouse aware that it was being stalked by an owl, but it still tried to remain on its path to safety. His anger became almost unbearable as he realized it really was her they were after. They stayed in the shadows, slowly creeping towards her. It took every ounce of strength to not run to her right then, but he knew he still had to protect his identity, so he decided to wait for the right time to make his move.

She began to move even quicker as she approached the clearing. Little did she know Caleb was right above her, watching over her. One of the hyenas let out a low, evil growl. All of a sudden, Caleb watched as every hair on the back of Mikayla's neck stood as she busted into a full-blown sprint. He knew she heard the growl, and she was scared and running for her life Her instincts were surprisingly good, Caleb thought to himself as he waited for the hyenas to pass in front of him. The hyenas were no longer lurking deep in the woods. Now they were on the paved path, still inching their way quietly into position, until they realized she had sensed something was wrong and started to run. They picked up their pace as well and began to chase her. Their eyes were dark yellow and they went after her with their mouths watering. Caleb knew they hadn't killed since the 1700s and was baffled by what he was witnessing, but there was no time to figure it out now. Now he had to save her.

One of the hyenas let out a laugh and the other ones followed. It was definitely a hunter's cry, and Mikayla was their prey. Mikayla started to pick up her feet even faster. *That's a girl, run faster,* he thought to himself, trying to extend the thought out to her. The hyenas started to pick up their pace, as well. *Keep your eyes on your house. Don't look back,* he had another thought and tried to extend this one to her, as well.

One of the hyenas was getting too close and Caleb knew he had to make his move; he just hoped she would keep her eyes on her house and not turn around. He couldn't think about the consequences. Right now the only thing that mattered was keeping her safe.

Quickly he flew down on the hyena closest to her and grabbed it's neck and twisted until it snapped and the body fell to the ground, weightless. He turned around to take care of the other two when he was surprised to find Ali and Jamahl each take the other two and do the same thing. Without speaking to each other, they each grabbed their kill and dragged them off into the forest and watched as Mikayla nearly got plowed over by a car.

The car came within inches of hitting Mikayla, and Caleb watched in horror as if he, too, was about to be ran over by a car. He almost orbed over there when the car stopped. They watched as Dominick got out of the car. They were too far away to hear what they were saying, but watched as Dominick put her into the car and drove off. Caleb was both relieved and insane with jealousy. Relieved she was all right, and insane with jealousy when he realized she would be spending the night with Dominick after all. He knew Dominick was just trying to keep her safe, but somehow Caleb, not understanding it himself, wanted to be the one keeping her safe.

"What the fuck are you doing Caleb?" Ali asked point blank.

Caleb wasn't sure what to say. He didn't think he was even going to get caught slipping out of Jackson's party. "I don't know, man. I just wanted to see her again. I can't explain it," was all he could think to say, and it was the truth. He didn't know anything other than he wanted to see her.

Jamahl started to laugh.

"What are you laughing at, Jamahl. This isn't funny, this is serious. We obviously need her to get to Rowan, but we also don't need Caleb's judgment clouded," Ali said sternly.

"I think it's cute that Caleb found a puppy he actually wants to take home! Tell me, Caleb, what will you name her?" Jamahl said, teasingly.

"Shut up, man, she's not a wolf! I can't explain it, but she doesn't have a trace of wolf scent anywhere around her. She must be a defect of some sort." Caleb said as he trailed off, looking towards her window.

"Ok, well now all of us have used magic and orbed. We have to keep our magic to a minimum in case they have feeler's out there scanning for activity. Now we have to dispose of these carcasses in a human way," Ali said, taking control of the situation and focusing on the problem at hand. "Jamahl, you need to have Mary pick you up tomorrow to get the holy water and Caleb and I will take the carcasses in the jeep and drive them up north and bury them in the forest," Ali added, making the decision of what to do with the dead hyenas simple.

"Alright, sounds good to me," Jamahl said with a smile plastered across his face, realizing he was the one with the best job. He also was actually looking forward to hanging out with Mary. Even though she was just a human, Jamahl was getting the biggest kick out of her, and didn't mind at all having to spend the day with her. He thought if ,by the end of the day tomorrow, he wasn't ready to kill her, he would invite her out on the boat on Friday. Caleb shook his head in agreement.

"Alright, now that it's settled, we need to get these into the jeep before the pack runs through here searching for clues. They may pick up the scent, but if we are lucky, the air will fade their scent enough for them to lose the trail and not be suspicious that something else has happened to them." Ali said, still taking control over the situation. "Caleb, you orb back to Jackson's and get the jeep. Jamahl, go with him so that Mary doesn't notice that you are gone," he added.

"Well, that makes sense. What are we going to tell the girls about the dead hyenas when we drive them back to their cars?" Jamahl said, thinking about their reaction. It wasn't something they could cover up easily without using magic, and having orbed had already used too much.

"Just tell them we all drank too much and call and pay for a cab. You'll get twice the brownie points," Caleb said, finally breaking his silence.

"Well, thank you for rejoining us, little brother!" Jamahl said and slapped Caleb in the back of his head, jumping back quickly to avoid Caleb's right hook. They both started laughing when Ali, clearing his throat, interrupted them. They both looked and, without Ali having to say anything, got right to work.

21

Mikayla was beyond tired as she entered Dominick and Mario's condo. Rowan and Mario were locked away in his bedroom, which Mikayla thought was just as well. She had a rough night and didn't need to listen to her brother's lecture. Right now, what she really needed was sleep. It was a light work week for her, and right now she was glad for that. She didn't have to work the next day. All she had was work on Thursday. She was off the whole upcoming weekend.

She stood with her arms crossed, still feeling a bit shaken, waiting for Dominick in the hallway as he turned off all the lights and shut down the television. As soon as he hit the off button on the remote control, he walked over to Mikayla and grabbed her by the hand, leading her into the bedroom. Right now she didn't mind one bit. The warmth of his hand felt nice and she needed his friendship tonight.

They entered his bedroom and he started to go through his drawers and pulled out a white with blue writing Michigan Football shirt-shirt and a pair of white cotton Michigan boxers. Mikayla took them and headed into his bathroom to change. She washed her face and brushed her teeth with Dominick's toothbrush, which made her realize how close they still were, and wondered if it would ever turn into just a friendship without the wonderment of getting back together. She couldn't even think about getting back together at this point, not after today. Now she knew there were other people out there she could connect with, and Caleb had been in her mind all day. He represented freedom to her somehow, and even after the strange events of the night, she still longed for freedom.

She finished getting ready for bed in the bathroom and walked out of the door. Dominick headed towards her so he could get ready himself. He was already out of his clothes and was wearing only a pair of dark blue boxer shorts. He was tan and toned with big, cut muscles. Mikayla gulped at the sight of his body. It was that of a warrior, she thought.

As he passed her, he turned towards her. "Just to let you know, I do know how you opened that door," he said close and smiled, then quickly scooted himself into the bathroom and shut the door.

Mikayla was taken aback. Could he possibly know, she thought to herself. She started to go over other possible ways of her escaping to see if perhaps he was referring to that instead. Racking her brain, she crawled into the black satin sheets and curled up on her side and closed her eyes.

She was just about asleep when Dominick got in the bed with her. He grabbed for her and held her tightly as they spooned. Tonight, Mikayla needed to feel him close to her. It felt nice; safe. Like nothing bad was going to happen to her.

"You have to be careful when you use your special powers, Kali. It's not something you know how to use, so please, just while I am gone, try and be careful and do me one favor. If you feel unsafe at any time try and think of a safe place and use the same energy as you did tonight on my door to get you there. Don't ask how I know. Soon enough, we will have a talk, but I have already said too much," he said and kissed the back of her head. Mikayla's eyes were now wide open, she couldn't figure out how he knew. She sat stiff for a moment, and then had a thought, her brother! Of course her twin would most likely carry the same genetic defect, and it would be Dominick, out of any one, he would have confided to.

Thinking she was cleaver, she turned around to face Dominick. She could see his face in the moonlight, and he was so handsome. "Mario, too?" She said with a smile on her face, thinking she had just busted Dominick's all-knowing bubble.

Dominick was taken a back. He didn't think she would have made that conclusion, and the last thing he wanted to do was to mislead her, but after what she had done with the door and the hyenas showing up, and the fact Marcus hadn't called him back in the past couple of days, he felt like he had to say something to her. It was for her own good, he needed for her to be alright. He was conflicted on what to say back to her. He didn't want to lie to her. It was alright, in his mind, to keep things from her for her own good, but he didn't want to flat out lie to her. He had done that a few times back when they were together and it had cost him her. He couldn't afford to have her angry with him for lying once again, even if was for a good reason. The best he could come up with was to not answer at all.

He took his hand and started to rub her head gently. "Kali, I am so tired. Let's go to sleep," he said, avoiding having to answer, and kissed her softly on her forehead. She knew he wasn't going to talk anymore ,so she gave into her tired body and shut her eyes, falling fast asleep.

22

It was only 7 a.m. when Ali had awaken Caleb. He felt like he hadn't gotten quite enough sleep. He wasn't a full-blooded vampire, so he actually felt the effects from a lack of sleep, almost the same as a human would. He sat on the edge of his bed, watching Jamahl sound asleep in the bed next to him. "Aren't you going to wake him up?" Caleb snapped at Ali, grouchy from his lack of sleep.

"No, he doesn't have to be up until noon when Mary's picking him up. But we need to leave. We will be driving for five hours each way, plus the time it takes to unload the corpses and cover them up. If we leave now we will be lucky to make it home by eight," Ali said a bit more quietly, trying not to wake up Jamahl.

Jamahl was the worst person to wake up, and Ali wasn't in the mood to get his head slammed into the ground.

"Fine, but you're taking the first shift driving," Caleb said as he headed into the bathroom to take a quick shower.

It didn't take them long to make it out the door. It was only 7:30 and they were headed up Route 23. The sun was still making its way up into the sky and the air was warm and sticky. They were heading for the upper peninsula, and figured if anyone did find them, they would assume they were heading down from Canada. They didn't need any heat on themselves. It would hopefully only take a couple more days to find out whether or not Rowan was the one they were looking for, and they needed to buy just enough time.

Caleb looked out the window and sat silently, thinking back to the happenings from the night before. He still thought it was strange the hyenas were there. He wondered, had someone sent them? By the look in their eyes, they had already started killing, but he couldn't figure out if they just fell off the reservation, or the more likely scenario, been influenced by an evil outside force. Either way something wasn't right. Trying to go over the reasons in his head why they were after her, he decided it was probably because they had sensed she was a defect, she was born into a wolf family but carried no trace of wolf, and perhaps they were doing it for revenge of some sort. Wolves and Hyenas had a long history together. All of a sudden, he had thought of something and he had a sick feeling in the pit of his stomach.

"Hey, what's the likely hood that there were more hyenas in the area than those four from the bar?" He turned to Ali, suddenly awake.

"Probably not likely. If there had been more, they would have stuck together. They feel stronger in packs and would never enter a wolf den without all their pack intact," Ali said, matter of fact.

"Well, I was thinking, wasn't there four hyenas last night?" Caleb said, feeling pretty sure he had counted four.

Ali's eye's got big. He hadn't even thought about it. Usually he didn't miss a beat, but he had missed that with the sudden happenings of the night. "Oh shit, there were four, and we only have three! Damn it, one is still around somewhere!" Ali said, trying to calculate the next best move in his head.

"Well, we can't turn back now. We have to get rid of these three, but what if the fourth was hanging back and lurking around?" Ali asked, searching for the answer himself.

"No, man. I couldn't sense any but the three," Caleb said, surely.

"Well, I hope you are right, but the fourth is going to be pissed when she finds out that the three males she was traveling with are never going to show up again," Ali said, still trying to think of what to do, as well as thinking of what she might do.

"Do you think she will go to the wolves?" `Caleb said.

"She may, but they did seem really on edge that they were even there, so we might actually be alright. Besides, with the yellow in their eyes, they were under some kind of influence and they had definitely killed. Once that happens, the wolves cut them off and make them their prey. That is, unless…" Ali said and trailed off.

"Unless what?" Caleb said, poking Ali, agitated by him not finishing his sentence.

"Well unless those hyenas were some of the ancients, but it doesn't make sense for them to be here. They wouldn't have access to the knowledge about the half witch half angel. Unless they were here for another reason…" Ali trailed off again.

Caleb was even more agitated at this point. Ali had a habit of speaking to you, then going into thought, leaving you hanging in a conversation.

"Alright, first off, what do you mean if they were ancients?" Caleb said.

Ali looked ahead at the road, trying to make good time on the road, and started to tell him about the four oldest hyenas and how they were the only ones left from way back when. He told them they still carried the yellow in their eyes because of what they had done. After Ali had finished telling Caleb the story, Caleb was still unclear of one thing. "Is it likely that the hyenas in the park were not the same ones we saw at the bar?" Caleb rephrased his question.

"Again, it's unlikely, but perhaps they were. Perhaps someone else is aware of the powers the witch/angel has and either wants her dead or to capture her themselves," Ali noted the possibility was there, and he decided to put it on the table because, at this point, they really couldn't rule anything out.

They both sat in silence for an hour, each brother trying to figure out possible scenarios of what could happen as a result of what they had just done. Caleb was still thinking of other reasons they followed Mikayla home. He had wondered if it was possible they were not actually after her, but they were hiding in the park close by for whatever reason and just saw a free meal. He had to admit to himself it was a possibility. Finally, he grew frustrated when he realized with the hyenas dead, they would never have all the answers they needed to make a strong conclusion. They weren't fearful of hyenas in the least ,but they were afraid of someone else trying to do the same thing they were, or having someone on their trail.

"Well, I don't think that we are ever going to know exactly what they were doing, so I guess we need to just focus on our mission at hand and just be on the lookout for the fourth hyena, or any other immortal or mythical being that comes our way." Ali said, almost taking the words right out of Caleb's mouth.

"Yeah, only a few more days and we will have our answers," Caleb said unenthusiastically, thinking he may never get to see Mikayla again after they had the answers they needed. A few days wasn't enough time to convince a girl like Mikayla to drop her life and run away with him, he thought to himself.

He started to think if Rowan was the one they were looking for, then they could just take Mikayla, as well. He didn't think it would be too hard to convince them it made sense to take her friend. After all, they weren't planning on killing the witch. His father had other plans for her, and maybe having her friend along would serve as a comfort to her. He might be able to persuade his father of this idea. Then he realized, even if his father agreed, which Caleb knew was a long shot, Mikayla wouldn't be the same. She would resent him for taking away her freedom. The one thing he knew she longed for, and as selfish as Caleb was, he knew her feelings would shut off for him, and he would be left with an empty shell of beauty. Then another thought entered his head. It was simply just he couldn't do that to her. Caught without a net, he looked out of the window until his eyes grew tired and heavy. Shortly, he fell asleep.

Caleb was out for the rest of the ride to the Upper Peninsula. He even missed going over the Mackinaw Bridge, which he actually wanted to see. He wouldn't have woken up unless Ali hadn't woke him. Caleb only slept for a couple of hours before Ali had woke him at seven, earlier that morning. After they had put the dead hyenas in the back of the jeep and covered them up, they headed straight back to the hotel so Ali and Caleb could get some sleep for today's mission. Once Ali and Jamahl were sound asleep, Caleb snuck back out and headed for Mikayla's. He knew she probably wasn't going to be there. It was pretty obvious the wolf wasn't going to allow that to happen, but he couldn't help but want to check anyway.

When he approached her house, he could see the light in her room was still off. The whole house was dark and quiet. He came to the window to find the lock hadn't been latched. Without thinking of the potential consequences, he let himself in, as if curiosity was pulling at him without a thought sometimes it is curiosity that kills the cat.

The first thing he checked was to see if her door was open or shut. He saw it was shut and he immediately looked to the bed to find she was indeed not there. As if he couldn't help himself, he reached down for one of her pillows and held it up to his face and breathed in. It smelled like fresh laundry, with a hint of orange and vanilla, which was the way she smelled. He felt like a peeping Tom, but he couldn't help himself. Her room was clean and tidy. There was a place for everything and everything was in its place.

As curiosity got the best of him, he reached to open the drawer of the nightstand that had her alarm on it. It was the one furthest away from the window. In it he found a picture book and he started going through it as he sat on her bed with her pillow laid across his lap. He figured the picture book was from her college years. With each picture, he felt like he somehow knew her better. Of course the other wolves were in the pictures, as well as Rowan, but there were also a few pictures of just Mikayla. He was almost through the whole book until he came across a picture of Dominick leaning down, kissing her on the cheek so close to her mouth part of his lips touched hers. Caleb became agitated. It reminded him she was there with him right now, doing God only knows what. He wanted to take the picture out and rip it to shreds, but he didn't. Finally as angry as he was, he flipped to the last page. It was a picture of just her in a short, tight, strapless black dress and black strappy stilettos. Her hair was down with big waves and her makeup looked flawless, natural, and fresh. It seemed to be a picture at some sort of event and it was a single picture of Mikayla. Hesitantly, he took out the picture. He knew he shouldn't be taking it, but he couldn't help himself, and he slid it into his back pocket. Her house was still quiet, but Caleb knew he shouldn't push his luck any further, so he made his way quietly out the window and back to his car.

Once he was safely in his car, he took out her picture and stared at it for a few minutes, brushing his finger against her face before driving away. He grew more and more angry she was with Dominick, but he knew he had no right. He knew it didn't even make sense. He had only seen this girl for two days and talked to her only twice. The way he was feeling made no sense whatsoever, but he couldn't seem to help it. He was drawn to her without rhyme or reason. The night had grown so late, once he got back to the room, he found a couple of hours had passed and he knew he would suffer the next day.

That's just what was happening. He was suffering now, groggy from sleeping upright with the warmth of the sun hitting his face the entire time. Now they were getting out of the car in a heavily forested area. Ali had gone off road by the looks of the lack of road.

"Here looks good. We should lay them in the open so that the coyotes can easily find them and hopefully eat away the evidence. If we bury them then a tracker may find them and uncover them. But let's walk them in further away from our tracks," Ali said, still taking full control over the situation.

Caleb looked at him and lifted up an eyebrow. "We are half witch, you know. I can easily cover our tire tracks with just a flick from my wrist," He reminded Ali.

Ali stood there for a moment and looked at Caleb. "How do you know how to do so many things with your magic?" Ali said, surprised again at how easily using his powers came to Caleb.

"I don't know, I guess I see it as limitless and so somehow it is?" Caleb said, unsure of the real answer. "But you can do lots of stuff, too. Look what you did with the school stuff." Caleb reminded him.

"Well, if it has something to do with technology or information I do seem to have a knack," Ali said, suddenly proud of the things he was good at. Each brother had their own strengths, and they just happened to complement one another perfectly.

Ali opened the trunk and pulled out one dead hyena and looked at Caleb. "I drove," was all he said, meaning since he had driven, Caleb had to carry two hyenas at once.

"I'm not Jamahl," Caleb said, not budging.

"Just do it man, hurry up!" Ali snapped, still holding the dead hyena, which was starting to take on a strong, unpleasant scent. Caleb said nothing back, he just reached in and grabbed the other two. They walked a couple of miles away from the car, but they used their vampire speed to do, so what should have took thirty to forty minutes only took five.

They came across a heavily wooded area where the trees were packed tightly. Ali couldn't imagine a werewolf being able to get through this part of the woods with their size, so he decided it would be as good of place as any and he dropped the hyena.

"Are you sure they won't find it? What if they come up here on initiation?" Caleb asked.

"They don't come up this far. It's not their territory," Ali answered.

"Well, whose is it?" Caleb asked out of curiosity, knowing it had to be someone's territory.

"Don't worry, Caleb. I did research and the pack up here isn't having initiations until August, as far as I can tell from the birth records," Ali said, without answering Caleb's entire question.

Caleb was stunned by the research he realized his brother had done from last night until now, and was so stunned he forgot about his last question. He never could figure out how Ali could learn so much in such a little amount of time. "You truly are amazing, Ali. You should be working for the CIA or something." Caleb said seriously to his brother, giving him props. "Where the hell do you find the time?" Caleb added, not being able to let go of Ali's research abilities.

Once convinced Ali truly had thought things through, Caleb followed suit and dropped both of the hyenas he had thrown over his back. They quickly dug a large pit and pushed the bodies into it. They lightly covered it with the left over dirt. It was only a matter of time before the animals of the forest uncovered the pit and began to eat off the corpses, helping the bugs get rid of the meat and skin of the dead hyenas.

Once they were finished, there was nothing to stick around for, so they raced back to the car. Ali got into the driver's seat as Caleb worked his magic to erase the tire tracks behind them. Caleb had no idea how far into the woods they were; it took only about ten minutes to drive out. He was surprised by how little time it took to get out of the woods, and once they were out, they headed directly back to Ann Arbor.

23

The blinds were open, with the sun hitting Mikayla directly in her face. She squinted at the light shining brightly in her face. The sun was really high up in the sky, and she knew she had slept way past her usual wake time. She rolled over on to her side to find Dominick was no longer there, she thought that was just as well. The thought of having to be in bed during the daytime with him was worrying her a bit. She didn't want him to think this was the start of them reconnecting. Yes she slept in his bed, but that is all she did.

The house was quiet; she started to wonder if Rowan and Mario were up. She stirred a bit more before sitting up, deciding to see if they were up. She was hungry and needed some lunch, fast. It was way past breakfast, she thought as she looked at the clock shinning a bright blue 2:30 p.m.

She put her feet on the floor and stretched her arms above her head when she heard a voice talking. The voice, she could tell, was trying to be quiet. She knew it was Dominick's, and could tell he was trying to keep his voice down, but something told her it was more than trying not to wake others in the house. It was something in his tone, somewhere in between angry and scared. Angry was normal for Dominick, scared was not.

Mikayla was intrigued. She couldn't imagine what had the all mighty Dominick scared. As if she couldn't help herself, she snuck over closer to the door and quietly opened it a crack so she could hear better. The door barely made a noise. It was successfully opened unnoticed. She could see him pacing back and forth in the living room by the sliding glass door. Dominick took the phone and ended whatever call he was on, then put his hands on the back of his neck as he looked down and let out a deep breath. He then took the phone and hit one button; Mikayla assumed he must be redialing whoever it was he had just talked to. She sat quietly as she waited for whoever was on the other line to pick up. Her mind was stirring. Could it be a girl? She thought perhaps a girl he has been seeing found out she was there last night and was pissed off. This didn't affect Mikayla, Dominick had girlfriends off and on since they had broken up. Well, actually, before they broke up. She waited with intrigue as she remained quiet.

"Listen man, I'm sorry about the last message. It's just that I really need for you to call me back. Something is going on and I want to know if you have heard anything. I am leaving for last initiation in less than 48 hours and I want to make sure that she is not in danger. I figured with what I told you on the phone last night, you would have called back by now. So please, call me. Once I am at initiation it will be close to impossible to break free in order to come back here, not to mention that I can't bleep in the way you can. Call me back, ASAP," Dominick said and hung up the phone. He stood still, looking out the window at the small city, with his right arm supporting his body against the wall. Mikayla was even more intrigued then before. She decided it wasn't exactly a conversation he would be having with a girl, not to mention Dominick never called a girl "man." He then opened the sliding glass doors and stepped through to their over-sized porch and sat down, putting his head into his hands and rubbing the sides of his head, lost in thought. Mikayla decided now was a good time to come out of the bedroom. She thought he looked like he needed to talk and she wanted to be there. After all, no matter how possessive Dominick could be, he was always there for her.

"Morning, or should I say good afternoon!" Mikayla said cheerfully, still in a tee shirt and boxer shorts, coming through the sliding glass doors. Dominick said nothing, he just looked up at her with worry and what Mikayla decided looked a bit like resentment. "Are you mad at me?" Mikayala couldn't help but ask from the look on his face. Again, he said nothing. He just reached out for her hand and pulled her on top of his lap, wrapping his arms around her waist and leaning his forehead on her upper back. Mikayla felt like she shouldn't move, so she just looked out over the city. It was past lunch time, but there was still plenty of action. Students were getting out for the summer and starting summer break. Younger students had parents coming into the city to take them home for the summer, and then you had students graduating, which always brought tons of people into the city coming to watch their graduate walk across the stage with pride. It was almost like a home football game in Ann Arbor in the Fall. A usually descent influx of people becoming an indecent influx of people, creating traffic and parking problems. Days like these would take the locals much longer to do everything, and Mikayla knew Saturday would be even worse; that was graduation day. With so many colleges in one area, traffic would be unbearable. She winced at the thought, and was glad she didn't have to work that day.

Mikayla was lost in thought and almost forgot that she was sitting on Dominick's lap until he shifted his forehead, turning his head to the side and now placing his cheek on her back. "Dominick, are you going to tell me what's wrong?" Mikayla said, still looking down on to the busy city streets.

"No," was all Dominick could say.

Mikayla was agitated he had a hard time talking to her, but knew she could push it all day and he would still give her the same answer ,only he would end up getting angry and withdrawing from her. It was a no win situation, yet a game they often played with each other. She decided although he would be pissed she was eavesdropping, she might be able to get him to talk if she just asked a few questions about it.

"So, why did you say you had a last initiation? I thought you guys were going camping," was the first thing she could think of to comment on.

Dominick's jaw tightened. "How long were you listening for?" He asked calmly, as if he wasn't at all bothered by what he had just heard.

"Not long, just long enough to know that you had an initiation to go to and that you wanted to make sure she, and I assume me, was safe." She said back.

"Um, yeah. After last night I just want to make sure you are safe, that was weird." Dominick said, playing like he didn't hear the rest of the question.

Mikayla turned around and looked at him. "What about initiation? What is that?" She said, looking into his eyes, knowing he would have a hard time lying to her if he was looking directly into her eyes.

"Did I say initiation? That is weird, huh, I meant camping. Must be tired from last night still." He said, starring directly back into her eyes.

She wasn't intrigued anymore. Now she was pissed. He was always keeping things from her. She couldn't understand how she could feel so close and safe with him, yet at the same time feel so disconnected from him. It was part of why she couldn't bring herself to make another attempt at being with him. Ready to blow up at him, she tried to get up, but as usual his grip tightened and held her there.

"Where are you going?" He asked calmly as he kept a tight grip on her, preventing her from leaving.

"Dominick, just let me up. I am tired of you keeping things from me. You treat me like a baby and I am sick of it," she said, having lost some of her calm and cool composure.

"Kali, I am not trying to keep things from you. Sometimes there are things that you shouldn't know about and I am trying to protect you!" Dominick said, a bit less cool.

"Protect me from what, I just don't understand! Protect me from ever having a life while you date girl after girl! Maybe I would like to have a date, too, but you always seem to come in between! Just like last night. I was talking with Caleb and you flipped out and locked me in your room. Dominick, you locked me up like I was a prisoner. What the fuck is going on, and I want you to tell me the truth! Now!" Mikayla said, yelling at this point.

"Oh, so you were talking with Caleb. That's his name, huh, Caleb. Well I don't like him, and if you do want to date, I won't stand in your way unless I feel like he is a danger to you. Something is off about that guy! And for your information, if you hadn't drank yourself into a drunken stupor, I wouldn't have had to lock you up, but I didn't want you on the streets like that. We may not be together anymore, but I still care about you, and we are still like family, so excuse me for caring," Dominick said back, this time even more coolly than before. He was on the verge of yelling.

The two of them sat there, glaring at each other for a few minutes.

"Obviously we don't see eye to eye on this issue. You ARE keeping things from me, and I WILL find out what they are," Mikayla said, struggling to get free.

"Stop, just stop! Have you completely forgotten that you were being chased last night? Hello, it is why you ended up back here, or has the alcohol erased your memory?" Dominick shouted at her. He was now angry.

"I said I felt like something was chasing me, but I probably made it up in my head due to the fact that everyone around me keeps me so safe and tucked away that on my first night out by myself, in the dark, I became scared! I am convinced at this point a bodyguard is not what I need. What I need is a psychiatrist to help undo all the damage that you all have done to me over the years!" Mikayla screamed at the top of her lungs. She was furious, and never spoke that way towards her family and friends. She was at maximum capacity and it just came out.

"Kali, lower your voice," Dominick said, and held her tighter.

"Let me go, Dominick, I am serious!" She said, still shouting.

Dominick said nothing back. He just grabbed her and put his hand over her mouth as she began to shout again for all to hear. He quickly go up and took her into his room.

"Kali, calm down, please…I am sorry. Please calm down. It's ok, we will talk. I promise," Dominick said as he gently sat her on his bed and kneeled down in front of her.

She couldn't say anything, her face was hot and she realized she now had tears streaming down her face. Dominick reached up to wipe away some of the tears that had fallen. He just let her get it out, he knew she was hurting and he was part of the cause. He desperately wanted to tell her the whole truth, but he knew he couldn't. Sometimes he wondered if Marcus had planned it this way, and wondered if perhaps he didn't have all the facts right. Dominick felt it was more important for her to be kept safe over his own feelings for her, and so that is what he did, but right now, he just wanted to tell her the truth. When Marcus called him back, he would tell him he can no longer keep things from her. She was getting too old, and by this time next year, would be on her own. Dominick knew with the way they always protected her, she would probably choose to move far away, at least for a while, and then no one would be there to protect her. He decided her best protection was the truth. It may finally help them get back together, if she could ever forgive him.

Mikayla sat there sobbing. It was like an explosion, and she was sure last night's alcohol wasn't helping things. Her skin became flushed from the tears, and Dominick took his hand at traced the outline of the marks she would get on the right side of her upper cheek, just under her eye. It was like a birthmark, one dot on either side of what looked an ancient symbol, which came out when she cried. The blood flowed into her face, creating a mark that looked like a tattoo at the end stages of a removal. She couldn't seem to stop the tears. She remembered the last time she cried this hard, and that only made her cry even more.

"I just want to forget, Dom, forget all of this. I am so frustrated and I have no answers. Everyone but Rowan lies to me. I need something new, something different! I need something else. I wish you could be honest with me, and I am sorry that you can't. I have loved you my whole life, but you have changed since childhood. I don't want to feel trapped anymore," Mikayla said, purging her feelings and began to sniffle. "Last night you said that you knew how I got out of your room, how? How, Dominick? How do you think I got out of your room?" She said pleadingly, hoping he would tell her the truth. Dominick knew it wasn't the right time to let her know what he knew, and as much as it was killing him to see her like this, he knew he had to play dumb one more time. He had made a promise to Marcus, and Dominick never broke a promise, since he had broken them to Mikayla all those years ago and this was who he needed to face before telling her.

"My spare key, you found my spare key. See, I always knew you were smart," he said as easily as if it were true, but inside he was dying from another lie.

Mikayla felt exhausted. She had just poured out her heart to him and he was still playing dumb. She knew he would not give her any information. Her tears started to dry at the wall of defeat. She sniffled one more time, and half smiled. "A key, right. That's it, I found a key," she said, dropping her shoulders and getting up to put her flip-flops on so she could go home.

"Where are you going?" He asked as he grabbed her hand.

"Home, Dom. Home," she said, not even able to look him in the eye as her hand laid limp in his hand, absent of any feeling.

"Wait," he said as he felt his heart was being ripped out of his chest. She didn't even turn to look at him. She only waited for another lie to come out of his mouth.

"Mikayla, perhaps you do deserve for me to tell you some things. I just can't right now, I can't. But I promise you this, when I come home in a few weeks, I will have everything straightened out and you and I will sit down and have a talk. You might be mad at me now, you might be mad at me then, but this is the best I can do," Dominick said sincerely, and he meant just that. He was going to let Marcus know no more time was to be wasted, and he wanted to be the one to tell her. He earned that right. He knew Marcus might use the opportunity to swoop in and look like the good guy, but it had been Dominick all along watching over her. He deserved to be the one, and she deserved to hear it straight from him.

She stood still, looking away from him. "You promise me?" She said softly, hoping he was indeed telling her the truth, and she thought she could see the honesty in his eyes.

He picked her up into his arms and cradled her, placing his forehead on hers. "I am so sorry, Kali. I know you are hurting. I promise. Please remember that everything I did, I did because I love you. More than a girlfriend. You are and have always been like family. Learn how to forgive me," he said.

Right then and there, she felt like perhaps he was telling the truth. She wanted to kiss him, she couldn't help it. It was a mix of all the frustration and sadness she felt in her heart, and she was getting carried away in the moment. He starred down at her, into her blue eyes, his green eyes gazing. The heat from his body started to warm up. Mikayla hadn't kissed someone in so long, she started to tremble a bit. He put her down on her feet and bent forward and kissed her lips softly, gently. She barely moved her lips back. He stepped back and looked at her, her eyes were closed and her head was cocked back, waiting for another one. She opened her eyes and stared into his. The beauty and intensity of her eyes forced the animal inside of him to take over at the sight of her.

He shoved her up against the wall and leaned in for a deeper kiss, not asking, just taking. She sighed, swept away in the moment; feelings of sadness and defeat replaced by hope and acknowledgement. The feeling of his lips were familiar; a feeling of young love from childhood, yet somehow it was different at the same time. He was now a man, and she could feel that in his kiss. She didn't have time to think about what it was she was doing. It was only the moment she was going with. He kissed her mouth and her neck furiously, as if he had been waiting an eternity to do so. She was being attacked with passion, and was enjoying every moment of it.

Suddenly, things started to heat up even more. Mikayla couldn't think. Dominick slowly reached down at her shirt to pull it over her head. Mikayla was swept away in the moment and couldn't manage to fight against it. A new day was ahead of her, yet it was the second day in which she was taking risks she would never have before. Slowly he moved her shirt over her head and dropped it to the floor, leaving Mikayla exposed right in front of him. Without another movement, he just stood there and stared at her as if she were the only thing that had ever mattered. He had a look of hunger in his eyes. She started to shake as goosebumps fled across her skin. Mikayla was finally grasping the situation, and knew exactly where it was leading when they heard a knock at the door.

"Come on, Dom. Let's get some lunch," Mario said, still knocking on the door. Mikayla and Dominick just kept staring at each other. She came back into her own head further and realized what it was they were doing. As if automatic, she released her grip from around his neck, embarrassed by her lack of control and conflicted at what she was just doing. She was turning into someone she didn't know in the past couple of days. *What is the matter with me*, she questioned herself. She was still mad at Dominick, and hadn't thought of him that way in so long. It was a brief moment of insanity, she decided. She looked at him and could tell he had felt her break abruptly from him.

"Sorry," he said, looking hurt as he let go and reached down for her shirt, handed it to her, and then headed for his bedroom door. Quickly, Mikayla threw the shirt over her head.

He opened it, both Mario and Rowan were standing outside in lounge clothes and flip-flops, looking stunned to see Mikayla standing inside the room. "Ah, your back. Well come on guys, I am hungry. Let's get some food,"

Mario said with a smile plastered on his face. Mikayla wanted to scratch his eyes out at the smile upon his face.

Hmmm, Kali, what the hell is going on? Rowan thought to her so the boys wouldn't hear.

Don't ask… it's been a long couple of days and I briefly lost my head. But trust me, it is screwed back on now. She said back and headed into the bathroom to clean herself up quickly so they could go get some lunch.

She stared into the mirror at herself for a moment, brushing her teeth, and asked herself again what was the matter with her. She was lost in a moment. She didn't want Dominick to take that as a sign they were getting back together. It was just a moment. Her stomach started to turn as she spit out the last of the toothpaste and began to wash her face. She picked up her dress. It was full of wrinkles and a few dirt stains from falling in the street the night before. She hadn't anything else to wear. After getting the door unlocked, she decided a few wrinkles and stains would be a synch. She conjured up the energy from within her body as she did the night before and closed her eyes, focusing on what she wanted to have happen, happen. As she felt the energy build up, she released it towards the wrinkled white dress in her hand. The dress blew as if a strong wind had come through the bathroom, blowing only into the dress. As the dress finally stopped moving and stood still, she opened her eyes and looked down to find her dress wrinkle free and without stains. She was amazed. She never pushed these things she could do. It was as if she was scared to learn how far she could go, partly because it made her wonder if she really was just crazy. She was suddenly interrupted by a knock at the bathroom door.

"Hey, I have a tank top and some yoga pants you can wear to go out to lunch in," Rowan said from outside the door. Mikayla opened the door, glad to see Rowan had gone into her stash of emergency clothes she kept in Mario's room. Although her dress was fresh and clean now, she didn't like the idea of wearing the same thing as last night. She was afraid if anyone had seen her they would assume it was some sort of walk of shame. She was definitely not that girl.

Mikayla smiled and grabbed the clothes. "Have I ever told you how amazing that you are?" She said, smiling at her best friend.

"Yes, you have, and ditto!" Rowan said back as she winked. Mikayla shut the door so she could change.

She put her hair into a ponytail when Caleb's face flashed into her head. Her stomach knotted up even more. He was so beautiful and he made it hard for her to breath. What the hell had she done by kissing Dominick? It wasn't like she was cheating, but the thought of Caleb at that moment made her feel guilty. The thought of feeling guilty made her feel sick for Dominick. She decided to shake it off. Dominick promised her a talk when he got home, and then she would address the kiss. The two of them would finally get everything straightened out, and perhaps they would finally figure out a clear definition of their relationship. They would always have a relationship of some kind, it was the way their families were. They had gone back for generations and, besides that, she did love him. She just wasn't in love with him. She was pretty sure he wasn't in love with her anymore either, but he definitely loved her. It would only be three weeks away, and she had plenty of time to figure all of that out, she just hoped he would keep his end of the bargain.

Another knock at the door came. "What the fuck, we aren't going to a wedding. Put your freaking clothes on and let's go!" Mario shouted through the bathroom door.

Mikayla couldn't even be agitated. She actually welcomed Mario's bossy ways. It felt normal to her, and right now she welcomed normal. "Alright, don't get your panties in a bunch, I'm coming!" She shouted back, smiling. She loved her brother and at the right time he said something obnoxious to her as usua,l but it brought her back into reality and she was grateful.

She opened the door to find everyone waiting in Dominick's room for her. They were all on the bed looking half dead. Mikayla giggled, this made everyone else laugh. She tried to catch Dominick's eye, but he had already shut her out. Life had returned to normal as they made their way to the front door to get a late lunch.

24

The sun was fading fast. Caleb was searching for his picture of Mikayla. He couldn't find it anywhere. He thought it was in his pocket, but it wasn't, and continued to look for it on the way home from up north, but had no luck. It wasn't there. It only made him drive faster back to town in hopes he would find it in the pants he was wearing the night before, but sure enough, when they arrived back at the hotel the picture was nowhere to be found. This only made him feel frantic and partly crazy. He wondered if he actually had even taken the picture. He was sure he did, and was sure he had put it in his pocket just before heading up north. He wanted to stare at her picture. He wanted to see her face and he felt frustrated he could not. It was getting close to the sun being down and it was his chance to see her as he had done the previous nights before since they had come to Michigan. He would have a problem avoiding his brothers because they were going to go out with Mary again and some friends. He hoped they would allow him a pass for the night, or at least not follow him if he slipped out to see her.

They had only been home for a half hour or so before Jamahl finally came through the door. Caleb waited impatiently for him to arrive. He wanted so badly to check on Mikayla, to see if she was home, to see if all was normal again with her. So when Jamahl came through the door, Caleb snapped at him. "It's about time. Shit, what the hell, Jamahl!" Caleb blurted out. Jamahl and Ali said nothing, they just looked at him with confused looks on their faces and dismissed him.

"Alright, I have it here. I told her that we needed a young woman to get us holy water for our graduation scavenger hunt and she bought it happily. I actually think she was having fun with it," Jamahl said as he laughed at the thought.

"Well, it's a start, but I don't see how this can actually work. It would mean that there is one right religion and we all know that's not true, unless it's using that as one method..." Ali trailed off in thought. "I don't know... I just think this doesn't sound right to me, but I am not sure what else to try. The riddle seems somewhat simple, so I am sure that it is, but I don't think we have the right idea yet. Jamahl, I know I said I would go with you guys tonight, but I really need to do some research. You go ahead without me," Ali said as he wiped his hand against his forehead, showing he was about to take on an almost impossible task of trying to figure out the riddle.

Jamahl didn't look disappointed at all, Caleb noticed, which meant that Jamahl was actually digging Mary. Caleb knew this would make it even easier for him to slip away. He would insist Ali needed some alone time to figure out if they were even on the right track. Caleb started to fade off, thinking about Mikayla, when Jamahl started to say something which Caleb missed what he had said. "What?" Caleb refocused his attention back to Jamahl.

"I said, are you coming with me tonight, then?" Jamahl said for the second time.

"Uh, no man. I am tired and I want to check out somethings. I want to see if I can get any clues to why the hyenas were here so they don't fuck our shit up," Caleb answered back, thinking quickly on his feet. He wasn't being completely deceitful, either. He really was going to try and check on a few things to see why they were here and attacking Mikayla. It made no sense to him whatsoever. She didn't smell like wolf, so that couldn't be it, unless they knew her family and were retaliating against her because they knew she had somehow missed the gene which made her wolf.

The more Caleb thought about the weirdness of last night, the more things were not adding up. He knew it made no sense for Mikayla to just be missing a gene. If she was a werewolf, then she was a werewolf through DNA. It seemed almost impossible for her to not have that. He racked his brain and knew this would require a bit of work. The kind that Ali was good at, and at a time where it wasn't appropriate for Caleb to ask for his help. They were there for one reason, and Caleb knew Ali had a large task to complete at hand.

A knock came at the door. Ali knew it was the room service with their food. "Finally, I am frickin' starving!" Ali said and headed to the door. He then brought back with him three orders of cheeseburgers and french fries. Caleb realized he too was hungry, but couldn't remember Ali even ordering food. He shrugged his shoulders and sat at the table with his brothers to eat.

"So, where are you going to start looking for information on the hyenas?" Ali asked after he had swallowed a bit of his cheeseburger.

"I think I will start in the park and see if I can't pick up the scent, and see if it leads me back to anything. I'm thinking it was those hyenas we saw in the bar, so I am hoping that the scent leads me back there. If it doesn't, then we may have bigger problems on our hands," Caleb said again, honestly. Although he had his alternative, motive he had every intention of seeing her tonight, that was for sure. Thinking of her face, again he was lost in thought.

"Earth to Caleb!" Jamahl said, waving his hand in Caleb's face.

"Huh?" Caleb said, looking down at his hands holding his cheeseburger.

"Man, I think you do need sleep," Jamahl said, stuffing a fry in his mouth.

"Caleb, I said I thought that would be a good idea, but to be careful. If the wolves see you just wondering around by yourself it may draw attention, and from what I can tell from the hyenas last night, I think they did us a favor and may have thrown them off." Ali said, now repeating himself.

"Oh yeah," Caleb said quietly.

Jamahl started laughing and made a comment about Caleb's I.Q., which only made Caleb snap quickly back into himself. "I'm trying to eat, not have a romantic dinner with the two of you. I don't know why you guys keep harassing me," Caleb said as he took a bite of his burger. It wasn't his usual quick wittedness, but it would have to do. He was tired, low on blood, and completely infatuated with her.

Caleb took a shower after dinner and put on some clean clothes. He still was really tired, but didn't want to sleep because he wanted to get to Mikayla. It was now almost ten. Jamahl told Caleb to use the jeep and not orb around, Mary was going to pick him up so he would be fine. Caleb just nodded, not caring one way or another. He was ready to leave first, before Ali shared one more piece of information with him.

"Caleb, I thought about what you said earlier, and I have found us a three bedroom condo for rent. It's a summer lease, fully furnished. It looks to be corporate housing of some sort, perhaps university housing. Anyways, I talked to the lady when you were in the shower, she said it was ready to go right now. I made up a lie of why we needed it so soon and she assured me we could start moving in tomorrow. We are meeting her at 9 a.m. so don't stay out too late." Ali said, now playing a fatherly role. That was how it usually went. They were all brothers, but Jamahl was definitely the big brother while Ali slipped in from time to time to play the fatherly role. It was a much different feeling than what he had toward Cyrus. Cyrus was their father, but he was always at arm's length, which only made the three boys that much closer.

Caleb nodded his head as he headed out the door. Again, he had not one smart remark to make. He only took in the information and nodded at his brother's request he not stay out all night. Tonight he just didn't have it in him to be quick witted. Tonight he just wanted to see her and it seemed to be taking forever. He wasn't even sure she would be home. It was possible after last night she would be staying permanently at Dominick's house, he feared.

Caleb was driving the jeep towards the park and decided he would park on the other side of the park and make a walk through. First he would follow the scent of the hyenas, then he would go to her. The jeep wasn't all that fun to drive, right now he wanted his motorcycle so he could feel the wind pushing against him as he broke through it fearlessly. "Tomorrow I will get a crotch rocket, I don't care what they say, we need more than one means of transportation, anyways. I will go without them and just show up with it. Once it is bought, they can't say anything to me," Caleb said aloud to himself as he grinned, needing to take some control back. He felt like he was quickly losing control, partly because he was on this mission that seemed to be a bit on the impossible side, and partly because of her. Never had he felt such a lack of control and he needed to get some back.

He pulled up to the park on the opposite side of Mikayla's house. It was so far away he couldn't see her house from where he was at, blocked by acres of trees and separated by a large park with streams of water running throughout. He parked in a lot in front of a small creek. Caleb sat for a moment, staring at the light from the moon glistening on the water, and for a moment felt peaceful. Water always calmed him.

He got out after a few minutes and headed towards the entrance to the woods. It wasn't the same stretch of woods she had walked through the night before, but it was the quickest way to get to that stretch of woods and still remain unseen by anyone who would suspect him as being up to no good.

He was a quarter of a mile on the way in when he realized park patrol might be out this late and decided that wasn't a good thing. Despite his brothers warning of orbing, he decided to anyways, and made it back to the car. He stood in front of it for a minute, thinking with his arms crossed before it came to him. He took a deep breath in, channeling the energy inside of him. It swirled and stirred and he let it do so until he was sure he had full control. Once he knew the energy was his to use as he wished, he unleashed it through his arms and out of his hands towards the car as he said "for my eye's only." He zapped the car with the energy he held in his palms and the car disappeared for all eyes but his own. The jeep, to his eyes didn't look normal either, though it looked like a rough outline and Caleb smiled at himself, impressed with his work. He took a quick look around to make sure no one had come up while he was doing it, and once he determined no others were around, he orbed back into the woods, giving himself a couple of miles more than he had had before.

He reached the clearing from the opposite side where Mikayla had come out of the night before. Knowing he shouldn't, at that point, he looked at Mikayla's house and noticed her lights were on. He knew he shouldn't have done it, but he had, and he was so excited to see her lights on in her room, partly because he knew she wasn't with him and partly because he would be able to see her. As if a stronger force was at work, without hesitation he orbed once again and landed on the tree in front of her window, making himself invisible. Her window was open, he could see the breeze blowing the curtains gently. Only the white shear curtains were drawn and he could see through them perfectly.

First, he couldn't see her. He looked first to the right and then to the left. He knew she was around somewhere because music was playing. It was good music, too. Caleb decided it was one more good thing about her, she was playing a mix of music that had guitar and reggae beats. It was the music he would listen to on the way back from surfing or when he was chilling over-looking the water, on his iPod. He smiled at the thought of being with her on a beach somewhere. He knew she would love the ocean and he would teach her how to surf; he could watch her be free. All of a sudden something caught his attention; she was on the ground, lying face down with her knees bent and her feet doing their own thing up in the air. She was writing and drawing. This fascinated Caleb even further.

The drawings, from what Caleb could see, were magnificent. She was using pencils, with all different shading techniques. She was writing something all around the picture she had drawn, almost as if she were trying to draw some sort of conclusion. The picture was of her with a ball in her hand the size of a grapefruit, which looked like it had energy flowing through it. Caleb thought that was weird and started wondering if Rowan had let out her secret of being a witch, and perhaps Mikayla was wondering what it would be like to have that kind of power. He watched her further as one of his favorite songs came on the stereo, which surprised Caleb she even knew the band at all. They weren't a big name in most parts of the country, but they were great. He watched intently as she put down her pencil after writing quickly, as if she was trying not to lose her thought. She placed her hands on her cheeks, with her elbows planted on the floor, and looked off into space. Caleb could tell she was lost in thought about something.

As she was lost in thought, her feet kept swinging side to side and in circles as the rest of her body remained still. She was only wearing a pair of tight, white boy shorts cut way too short to wear out in public, and a tight midnight blue tee shirt with white and black tattoo type art work all over it. It was very trendy and Caleb thought about how great it was that it hugged every curve of her well-defined upper body, and showed off the slimness of her waist. He couldn't help but stare at her backside and the curve of her lower back. Her hair was tied tightly back in a high ponytail, showing just how high her cheek bones sat, which Caleb thought made her look even cuter.

She was fascinating to him. He was attracted to her physically more than he had ever been to anyone else before, but he was also intrigued by the little things she did, which never had happened before. It was her he was drawn to, not Rowan, as the seer had said. Perhaps it wasn't Rowan who he was referring to, he thought to himself The seer had only said I would be drawn to "her," and never said Rowan's name at all. This only made him feel a bit more out of control. It made him want to go inside of her room right then and take her away. It would give her freedom and he would get to watch her for as long as he wanted. He didn't even need to do anything with her, if that wasn't in the cards, as long as he just got to watch her.

Mikayla, still lost in thought, put her head down and then started to shake it like she was trying to decide on something, and then quickly got up and headed straight for her closet. The angle of the closet made it impossible for Caleb to see into, so he waited for her to come out.

She stood in her closet and grabbed a pair of workout pants. It wasn't too late at night, but she was determined to conquer her fear, which been high since what had happened last night. She wasn't sure if it was the alcohol and Dominick's paranoia that made her hear things in the park, or if it really happened. But she was determined to find out what it was. She was going to go into the park by herself and see if she could find anything out, or at least get a sense of what it was lurking behind her last night. Her smarter side told her she shouldn't go out there alone, at least she should have Rowan with her, but Rowan was with Mario on their "date" night. Dominick wasn't a possibility, he was managing his club and, even if he had been available, Mikayla decided he would just breed more fear into her. "I am not afraid," she said aloud to herself, as if trying to convince herself she was not afraid, but she was. *Trust in the strange power I have inside*, she thought to herself.

"What is she not afraid of, what is that girl up to now?" Caleb said quietly, out loud to himself as he watched her, now dressed in workout clothes, walk over to her sock drawer and pull a pair out. She finished with putting on some running shoes. *What the heck? Was she going to work out somewhere*, he thought to himself. He started to get excited at the thought of her being somewhere he could run into her at. The scent of the hyenas could wait. Still watching her until she turned out her lights and left the room, he knew he needed to get higher up, so again he orbed his way to the top of her roof so he could get a better view of where her car was headed.

She came out the front door and passed her car completely. Instead, she walked across the street to the park. "Oh no, that just isn't a good idea little girl. You definitely should be afraid after last night!" Caleb said quietly to himself again, with a smirk on his face. He knew she was trying to figure out what had happened last night and she was trying to get over her fear, but he even had to admit it wasn't the smartest move for someone with no powers to be doing. Although Caleb was pretty sure the threat was gone, he knew it wasn't a hundred percent. He smiled again, knowing he would be there to protect her if anything happened.

Mikayla approached the park fearlessly, marching towards it as if she was in line with a troop during boot camp. She knew she had to do it that way or she would lose her nerve. It was the entrance to the forest she was most interested in checking out, but this time she was prepared, this time she had a flashlight.

As she approached the entrance to the forest path, she started to slow down. It was the fear which was pulling her back. Her heart began to race and pound so hard, she could hear the beat of a drum in both her ears. She paused briefly, shining the light on the ground in front of the entrance to see if she could see anything strange or out of the ordinary, she saw nothing, though. She then shined the light into the forest to check out if she could see or feel anything. As the light was shining into the forest, a squirrel ran from one side of the path to the other. It scared Mikayla and she let out a quick scream. Every muscle in Caleb's body tightened in response, but quickly let go as he realized it was only a squirrel. He quietly laughed to himself and continued to watch her as he followed unseen behind her.

Mikayla was still for a moment. Caleb could hear her heart beating and his jaw began to ache at her vulnerability. Then she covered her mouth with her hand and laughed nervously at herself. That made Caleb smile, he realized her being able to laugh after what had happened last night was a sign this girl was a lot stronger than even she knew she was. As if being scared had given her confidence, she entered the wooded path, this time with much more confidence.

She wasn't sure what she was looking for. She didn't know if it was what she thought she heard last night driving her, or if she was just proving to herself she wasn't afraid. The last thing she wanted was to be so scared of life, when she graduated next year she would be stifled and stay put, never going anywhere on her own. Mikayla was determined to see the world and to be free. She wanted to prove to everyone who treated her as if she was so fragile she had much more spirit than they knew. Caleb understood what it was she was trying to do, and he watched intently wondering what it is she was going to do next.

The flashlight was bright and she was quickly walking through the wooded path as if she was a security guard checking out the grounds when she decided to go off the path and into the woods. Caleb quietly moved further to keep an eye on her. She shined the light over the ground, looking for tracks or anything that may give her a clue to what it was she felt was after her the night before. It had been about five minutes since she had been in the woods, stepping over shrubs and dodging trees, before she came across a muddy section close to the creek. She looked down, noticing animal prints in the ground.

"Holy shit those are big," she said as she knelt down to take a closer look. "Can't be coyote tracks…" she said aloud, again talking to herself as she trailed off trying to figure out what kind of animal prints that those were. She could have sworn she heard hyena laughter last night. "Could it really be hyenas?" She asked herself again, talking to the forest as if it would answer.

Yes, girl. It can be and it was, Caleb silently answered her question from afar.

"That is so strange…" she said, trailing off. As if her question had been answered, she decided perhaps some had escaped from the zoo and would check online to see if she could get any information about any escaped hyenas possibly running around the area. It wouldn't be the first time animals had escaped from a zoo. She thought further and knew a hunting club was also possible. There was no telling what some of those clubs were about, and was sure if they were missing any animals like that, they surely would never be reported.

Satisfied with her bravery and a possible lead to the mystery of last night, she decided to head out of the woods. She took her time walking on the wooded path as if she were reclaiming the forest as her own. Caleb smiled at her, but wished she would not return home yet. He then had a thought, he could glam her and then erase her memory of it, just to spend some time with her. Despite what he thought was a perfect idea, he couldn't bring himself to do that to her. He wanted her to come freely to him. With that, he then had another thought. *Perhaps I could just put the idea to come towards the jeep, it's on the other side of the park and wouldn't be obvious. I could pretend that I was reflecting on my life, when she asks why I am there. No doubt she will be suspicious of me,* he thought to himself, feeling his plan was a good one. Then he remembered he had a notebook and pen in the car, he grinned at himself, realizing it was the perfect prop.

As Mikayla slowly made it down the wooded path, she started to feel like the wind was talking to her; not with words but with emotion. She couldn't understand what it was trying to tell her at first, so she closed her eyes to try and concentrate. With her eyes closed, she saw a parking lot. She knew the parking lot, it was the one on the opposite side of the park by the creek, but she couldn't figure out why she felt like she was being pulled there. Whatever was nudging her was subtle, and felt as if she had been walking just a little bit faster, she would have missed the whisper of the wind. "Why should I go there, what is there?" She said to the wind. "Is there more clues there? Are there hyenas there? Should I be afraid?" She asked the wind again, as if she were expecting an answer. And why wouldn't she get an answer, she thought to herself. Her whole life, weird things seemed to happen around her, most of which came from herself. As she sat listening to the wind, she got a sense of calm, as if the wind was telling her not to be afraid. Mikayla thought about it for a minute and then decided this was part of being free and brave. Whatever was there, she was supposed to see, so she headed out of the wooded path and across the clearing to the other side where the wooded path picked up again and headed down it towards the parking lot.

Caleb knew he needed to follow her to make sure she was alright, and once she was close to the parking lot and within earshot of his car, he would orb himself to the car. She wasn't moving very fast, this only made Caleb long to be around her that much more, like a little kid on Christmas morning waiting for his parents to awake so he could open his presents as he sat staring at the beautifully wrapped packages with his eyes filled with wonder.

He loved watching her. She was perfect, and almost angelic, he thought. She moved gracefully through the wooded path, coming closer to him with every step she took. She had gone quite a while and was almost at the parking lot; Caleb knew this was his last chance to make it back to the car. Quickly, he orbed himself yet again towards the car, and just as quick removed the invisibility spell from the car. Again he looked around to make sure no one was around, but the parking lot was completely abandoned and hidden from the road that lead to it. He then opened his car and grabbed the note book and pen, then climbed on the hood of his car and sat down and waited for her as he made sure to listen for anything that may be going on in the woods without him overlooking her as she made her way out. Instead, he kept focused on his notebook.

25

The air smelled fresh and full of life. He could smell her, too. She smelled like citrus and soap, like she had just gotten out of the shower. His mouth began to water. She was coming out of the wooded path now, he could sense she was looking his way, just as her flashlight shined over his way.

Mikayla walked out of the wooded path, proud of herself for being brave enough to get all the way to the end without being afraid of things that go bump in the night. As she came to where the wooded path ended and the path along the creek began, she noticed there was still a car in the parking lot. She wasn't afraid before, but now she felt a bit startled knowing there could have been someone in the woods with her the whole time. Perhaps someone was even stalking her, she thought as her heart began to speed up again, having left over fear from the night before.

She shined the flashlight over towards the car and saw a boy sitting on the hood. Her heartbeat began to slow down, feeling at least the owner of that car wasn't stalking her. The person looked her way as her light was shining on him. She couldn't really make out his face from that far away, but something seemed familiar about him. He put his hands up over his eyes as if he was blocking the sun and Mikayla became embarrassed at the fact it was the light coming from her flashlight blinding this poor guy.

"Oops, I'm so sorry!" She called over to the boy on the hood of the car.

Caleb wanted to call to her, but knew she needed to make the connection first, so he called back. "It's ok, but could you please get that light out of my eyes? I'm trying to meditate over here," Caleb called back.

That was it, she suddenly thought to herself, and butterflies started to float around in her stomach. She now knew why he seemed so familiar, and once he spoke she knew for sure it was him. "Caleb, is that you?" She said, turning off the flashlight and heading over towards his car.

"Yeah, who is there? I'm now blinded, and it's dark out here!" Caleb called back.

Mikayla was a little disappointed he did not recognize her voice. She wondered if perhaps he was just a player, and he really wasn't as in to her as he made himself seem the night before. She didn't let that stop her though as she made her way towards the car without answering back.

Caleb played the part and watched her as she approached the car. "Well, I guess wishing on stars really does work," he said as she made it to the front of his car and in front of him.

"Oh yeah, what did you wish for? To be blinded in a park late at night by a flashlight," she said with a smile on her face, still embarrassed for having shined a light in his face. She was the one who was now feeling like the stalker.

"Nope," he said and stared into her eyes without as much as a smile.

Mikayla became a bit uncomfortable and started to fidget. "Well?" She said, trying to fill in the weird silence.

"Well, what?" Caleb said, staring down at her, making her even more uncomfortable and causing the butterflies to move furiously around in her belly.

"What did you wish for," she said, now really wanting to know what it was he was wishing for. Caleb just stared at her, or through her as it felt like to her, causing her to become a little more uncomfortable. He didn't answer right away. Mikayla wasn't sure whether it was a good thing, or whether he was annoyed of all the places in the city she could be this night, it was the same place as him. She started to wonder if perhaps he thought she was stalking him. *Oh for fuck's sake…he thinks I am a creeper. I'll just tell him that I am looking for my dog*, she thought to herself and turned to walk away.

"Well, I better get back to looking for my dog, see you around," she said, trying to leave as quick as she could, feeling stupid at the thought of her looking like a stalker. Caleb started to laugh at her little lie, which only made her walk a little bit faster towards the woods.

"Where are you going, Mikayla?" Caleb chased after her and grabbed her gently by her wrist.

"I was just, I mean, well I am not sure..." was all she could think to say. She was too lost in the magnetic feeling his touch had given her. Her whole body tingled. He turned her so they were facing each other and he looked down into her eyes.

"I didn't mean to chase you off. I was just shocked to see you here," he said in a sincere voice, and it was partly true. He knew she was coming, but it did feel like a shock to see her all alone in a park, where he could do anything he wanted to her, and yet he didn't do anything.

"Oh, I'm sorry. I guess I am shocked to," she said looking back up at him. "So, is it a secret or can you tell me?" she quickly added, trying to fill up any silence, not because she feared the silence part, but she feared what her body wanted to do and thought words were a great wall against doing things you shouldn't be doing.

"Tell you what," he said, still playing with her.

"What you wished on a star for?" She said, wondering whether or not he was being serious.

"Oh yes, that..." he said as he trailed off with a smile on his face, getting lost in her eyes and the shape of her lips, wanting so badly to drink her all in at that moment. She smelled so clean and sweet, it made his mouth ache. He wanted to take her right there and kiss her and hold her tightly against him for the rest of the night.

Lost in his desires, he was suddenly brought back to the current conversation from a nudge in his shoulder.

"Alright, you don't have to tell me," Mikayla said after nudging him in the shoulder. She became uncomfortable with his hand on her wrist, yet at the same time she didn't want him to let go, but if he wasn't willing to have a conversation with her then she knew she was doomed to do whatever he wanted with her. She felt weak against his charms. With every ounce of strength she had, she pulled free, and as she did he grabbed her wrist again, as well as the other one. She felt like her breath had been literally ripped out of her lungs, and her whole body tingled and ached.

"I wished that I would see you again," Caleb finally managed to spit out.

That was it, she was puddy in his arms. After he said it was her he had wished upon a star for, she couldn't help it, she reached for him as if she were trying to reclaim some of the air he had taken from her body back. She leaned into him on her tip toes, her lips were less than an inch away from his. "Well I am here, so now what?" She said playfully.

Caleb said nothing, he just looked down at her and his heart began to race as his stomach was doing cartwheels. She smelled so good, and his body started to ache. Not just his gums, but his whole body tingled. "So, I am happy," he said in almost a whisper as he looked down at her, and upon the word happy, his bottom lip came within a millimeter of her top lip. It was so close, she could feel the energy coming from him.

The distance between the two was now almost none existent. Both were frozen, each too scared to make a move for fear of a lack of control. Mikayla decided to fill the gap again with words. "What are you doing out here, anyways?" She said, making sure not to get any closer.

"Meditating on a few things," he answered, still focused on her face. She was now feeling a huge lack of control, and thought she needed to get free, but when she tried to break out of his grip and back off a bit, he only held on tighter, which only made her body tingle more.

She tried one more time to get some space by talking, but right as she opened her mouth to begin to talk, he leaned down and very gently, and even slower, traced the outside of her mouth with his tongue. The taste of her exploded in his mouth, and the thrill of her made him ache for her.

Her whole body stiffened up the instant his tongue had touched her lips, but quickly released as the pleasure set in. She just stood there, motionless, as his tongue made its way around the outline of her lips. It was soft, slow, and steady, like he was tasting her. It was erotic. When he finished, he pulled back for a minute and she just stood there, not sure what she should do next. He led the way and pulled her closer to him, still holding her wrists, and bent down and gently kissed her once. She didn't kiss him back at first, but then he came down and kissed her gently again, and this time she managed to make her lips move, and even more gently than he had kissed her, kissed him back.

He came up again, still looking at her, and came down again for another single, gentle peck on the lips. This time she responded equally. Again he came back up, briefly pausing before leaning down one more time.

This time after he had gently kissed her, he didn't take his face away from hers, he just stayed there, giving her little pecks on her soft, tasty lips as she reciprocated. He was getting hungrier and hungrier for her with every kiss. He didn't long to drain her of blood, he wanted to be one with her. He wanted to make her feel good and fulfill his own desires, and with that he couldn't help but taste her some more. The kissing became more frequent as he started to incorporate his tongue, tasting her lips and trying to get her tongue to come out and taste him back.

It took a few minutes of him gently tasting her before he felt the silky wetness of her tongue, which tasted of fresh mint, glide over the smoothness of his own tongue. This sent Caleb into a frenzy as he took a double breath in. He moved his hands off her wrists, wrapped them around her body, and kissed her fiercely as she reciprocated with desperation and longing. The kissing grew heavier and heavier. Mikayla couldn't even listen to her rational brain screaming something she couldn't quite make out, nor wanted to, while the other part of her brain was saying she needed more. They stood there for what seemed like an eternity as the whole world kept passing them by before Caleb retracted. He wanted more, he needed more, but somehow knew if he didn't get control at that moment, there wouldn't be anything else he could do to stop things from happening.

There was something more to Mikayla than just a one-night stand. He couldn't help himself but respect her. He could tell she wasn't the kind of girl who just kissed anyone, he would have been surprised if she had actually kissed more than a few people her whole life. It wasn't from her technique, that was by far the most sensual kiss he had ever had, but there was something pure about her aura and, for whatever reason he could read that about her. This made her even more precious to him.

Mikayla still had her eyes closed when Caleb backed off. She stood there for a few moments, waiting for more, and didn't open her eyes until she was sure he wasn't coming back for more. She longed for him to dive back into her mouth again, but the rational part of her brain was now speaking louder, this time she could understand what it was saying, and it was saying enough, Kali. Take this slowly.

She saw him looking down at her, still staring at her and breathing hard. Without knowing the right thing to say, she averted the kiss and focused on his notebook. "What are you…" she cleared her throat, trying to sound in control. "Um, writing about?" She asked.

Caleb smiled down at her, amused at her efforts to try and avoid anything to do with addressing the kiss. "Things…" he said with a cocky grin plastered on his face, again making her nervous.

"What kind of things?" She asked, feeling like she was right back to the same kind of conversation they were having before the kiss. Again this made her uncomfortable, and she began to shuffle her feet around as she crossed her arms, looking for a safe position to be in. Caleb tilted his head up in the air and laughed briefly before bending down and kissing her on top of her head.

Mikayla wasn't sure if he was truly smitten with her, or if he was just playing games with her, having caught on how into him she felt.

"Come on," he said, taking her hand and leading her to his car. She followed as they approached the passenger side of the car.

"Where are we going?" She asked hesitantly.

"To the water," he said.

"But we are by water," she replied, wondering what he had in mind.

"This is a creek, we need a lake," he said as she smiled up at him. This truly felt like freedom, and she was exhilarated and readily hopped in the passenger seat, feeling like at any moment she was going to bust at the seams as he shut the door behind her.

She watched him as he passed around the front of the car to get to the driver's side. She noticed how sexy he was. She hoped she would be able to control herself around him.

He climbed in the front seat and looked at her. "Well?" He said, still looking at her.

"Well, what?" She said, confused.

"How do we get to your lake?" He asked.

"I thought he have been there before," she said, looking confused.

Caleb couldn't believe how stupid he was. He did tell her that, but he got so caught up in the moment he totally forgot about the scheme. Quickly he thought of something, he was always good at that. "Well, I usually don't drive, and besides, it's a big chain of lakes and you grew up there. I didn't and I thought you might know of a good place for us to take a swim. But I do realize that we might need to find your dog first." He said, and the lie just flowed freely out of his mouth as he threw her lie back into her court to distract her.

"I…I think I heard off in the distance my mom grab the dog," was all she could muster up, having remembered the lie she had told him. Her cheeks flushed with embarrassment.

"Yeah, I am sure you did," Caleb said as he gave her a look that told her he knew better than to believe that.

Mikayla couldn't start things off with a lie. "Alright, I wasn't looking for my dog. I just didn't want you to think I was somehow following you. I happen to live on the other side of the park, and please don't ask me why I was out here. It's stupid and I don't want to talk about it," she said quickly, already feeling better she had told the truth. "There, I said it! Do you feel better now?" Hoping he wouldn't be too disgusted at the lies she had just confessed to.

Caleb grinned ear to ear. "Much better," Caleb said, looking at her in amusement. This took the pressure off of her and she suddenly felt better.

She looked at him and smiled. She was so beautiful he thought, and she also had an air of innocence about her that made her cute, as well. Caleb bent forward and gently kissed her on her cheek. All was well again, she thought. She giggled, which only made him think she was even cuter now, and switched sides to plant another kiss on the other side of her cheek. She let out a deep breath and Caleb's body started to tingle again. This only made him grab the back of her head and gently tilt up her neck to expose the pulsating veins underneath her olive smooth skin. He placed his tongue on the base of her neck and slowly followed the pulse all the way up to her ear. The ache in his jaw became almost as prominent as the tingling of the rest of his body. Usually it was the opposite, the ache in jaw was usually much more prominent in these types of situations, but this was different, she was different and he felt different.

As she felt his wet tongue making its way slowly up her neck, she relaxed into it, letting out a deep breath. She felt helpless in his arms and she knew it was dangerous, but she didn't care. He was exactly what she needed tonight, and not because of all the kissing, but because of the freedom she was feeling. Never had she been so careless before. She seemed to have a babysitter around her at all times. No one would ever expect her to leave her house and travel out to the park this late, let alone thinking she would be with some guy who was a stranger. She thought about that for a minute, and realized even though this guy was a stranger, he did not feel like one. He felt familiar, somehow. It wasn't something she could explain, she just knew he did.

Caleb could feel his canine's starting to lengthen, so he paused briefly to gain control over them. He was shocked at how easy it was for him to control them around her. This only made him want her more. Happy at the fact he was feeling normal for the first time, he changed the sensuality of him kissing and licking her neck to a soft peck on her forehead. She said nothing for a moment, just blinked at the sudden change. It was a change of pace, but she liked not knowing what he was going to do next.

He pulled back, still looking down at her. "Well?" He said, as if there wasn't a brief break in conversation so he could explore a little bit more of her. Mikayla knew she needed to compose herself quickly, so he wouldn't think she was a ditz who had no control over her own self.

"Alright..." she said with a sly smile coming to her face. "We are going to play a game," she finished, still grinning.

Caleb raised one eyebrow. "A game? What kind of game?" He said, seriously having no idea of what she was up to.

"Here's how it goes. We are going to play hot and cold. When I say hot, it means you are on the right path. When I say cold, it means you are on the wrong path," she said, pausing to see what he would say so far.

Caleb started to laugh. "That's cool with me, I will make a lot of colds just to spend more time with you," he said, laughing at his attempt to foil her plan.

Mikayla didn't get discouraged, she had more up her sleeve.

"Yes, Caleb, you could do that but here is the deal, you said you want to go swimming. I will give you 30 minutes to find it. if you cannot find it within the allotted time, then you must drive me back immediately and no more kissing tonight. Not even as much as a hug. But if you can find it, then I will go swimming with you. I may even let you kiss me again," she said, satisfied the task at hand could be close to impossible for someone to do who doesn't have a good idea of where it really was, not having actually driven it himself. It was all back roads and very dark, as well. The turn offs were very easy to miss. She waited for his reply looking, not at him, but straight ahead.

Caleb was surprised by the game she was playing. He liked it, a lot. Without saying a word, he put the car into reverse and sped towards the exit of the park. He looked at her as he put his right turn signal on.

"Cold," she said coolly, and without putting on his left turn signal he sped out taking a left hand turn.

They came up to the first light. Instinctively, Caleb knew it had to be towards the north. He put his left turn signal on and looked at her.

"Warmer," she sai,d still not giving as much as a smile.

Caleb decided he would out smart her a bit and head for the highway to make his way quicker north. He took a quick U-turn and Mikayla looked at him and squinted her eyes. She wasn't sure what he was doing.

"Cold!" She said, now a bit ruffled by his erratic driving and his lack of following the rules.

She couldn't stop looking from the road to him to try and figure out what it was he was doing. He went through a couple of green lights and made a couple of turns until he ended up on one of the main roads, and then she knew what it was that he was doing. She hadn't even thought about the highway. She was going to try and take him through all back roads. She had almost hoped he wouldn't find the lake so it would give him more reason to find her on Friday, although the thought of being with him alone tonight was thrilling.

Caleb entered onto the highway and headed north. With a cocky grin on his face, he looked at her, waiting for her to call out either hot or cold. Mikayla gritted her teeth, feeling a little bit out smarted.

"Warmer," she said without enthusiasm, feeling like he was now the one with the upper hand.

Caleb shook his head and let out a cocky laugh.

"Shut up," she said, not having a more cleaver come back. "It's not over until the fat lady sings, just remember that, and by my watch you only have 20 more minutes to find this place," she said, taking back some of the control and hoping once they were off the highway he would miss some of the turns that were hard to see.

"Plenty of time," Caleb said confidently. He could tell by her reaction he had made a good move, which upped his chances.

They were on the highway for ten minutes before he noticed Mikayla glancing a little too hard at an exit coming up. Caleb's instincts told him this was the right one. She was being too quiet and he knew she was hoping he missed it so she would win her little game. Caleb wasn't about to let that happen. Besides, if worse came to worse, he would cheat his way to winning and put on his magical GPS and find it. He hadn't done it yet though, because this way was much more fun.

He waited until the last possible second before exiting to try and make her feel like she was winning, just to take away her win at the last second.

"Thought I was going to miss it, didn't you?" He said to her, still looking ahead as he flew off the exit.

She had to laugh a little bit, but quickly recovered. "Whatever, warmer," she said and rolled her eyes.

He came up to the stoplight at the end of the exit and looked at her, trying to get a sense of left or right. He first put on his right turn signal, but she said nothing. Then he put on his left signal to see if perhaps silence now meant cold, but she said nothing.

"Well, am I hot or cold?" He said, waiting to see which way to turn. She kept looking forward.

"I cannot tell you. You have yet to make a choice," she said, proud of yet again taking back control and putting a check mark in her winner's box.

Caleb was confused for a moment, she had been telling him hot and cold before with just his turn signal, and now she wasn't giving up the information, but he realized he must be closer to getting there and she was trying to stall, all in the name of winning. He decided he liked her even more and was now more determined than anything to make it there without the help of magic. It was almost as if he had something to prove as a man.

He thought quickly and decided he would go left, since his first instinct was to go right, and she chose not to tell him hot or cold. So, he assumed it was cold, but she was hoping to stall by having to have him turn around. His assumption was right, and as he straightened out his wheel after he took a left, she called out, "warmer." Mikayla was trying hard not to let herself seem ruffled.

Caleb smiled and sped down the road. He rolled down his window to try and get a sense of where the water was by way of smell. He could tell by doing it his next move would be towards the north again, on one of these back roads. It was now even more obvious to him she had given him a pretty impossible task. A normal human would have a hard time seeing some of the turns on these back roads, but he wasn't human. Being part vampire made his night vision remarkable. He could see better than any creature with has night vision. All of the turns were clear to him. He grinned even harder at the game she was playing.

Oh your so gonna loose this battle, He thought to himself, gripping the steering wheel with confidence.

Mikayla was wondering what was happening to her skills. She thought for sure a half of an hour was almost impossible to make, even if you knew where you were going, at this time of night. He still had ten minutes, and he was only a few away. She thought perhaps he had lied about not knowing exactly how to get there. Mikayla decided perhaps it was a double or nothing kind of moment, as Caleb turned into one of the public beach's parking lots.

Caleb lost his smile and gave a serious look as he looked at her. "Well, looks like you are going swimming." He said with complete control over his emotions.

Mikayla thought quickly. "Well, yes. We could swim here, but you said for me to take you somewhere that I thought was a good place to swim, and I think this is not a good place to swim. I will tell you what, if you can pick the right spot without me telling you hot or cold, on the first try, I will let you pick what I get to swim in. If you can't, then you owe me some french fries and a coke on the way home!" She said, realizing by some small chance with all of the lakes connected, he could pick out her secret space, she may be baring more than she was really willing to bare.

Caleb thought about it for a moment. Should he let her win and give her the satisfaction? Or should he incorporate some magic and make her put her money where her mouth was. He decided he wanted to have the upper hand. "Ok, I will take that bet as long as you stay true to your word and swim in any thing I ask you to!" He said, thrilled at the idea of her squirming. Hesitantly, Mikayla agreed to the deal, now hoping for french fries and a coke. She hated losing, but took the challenge knowing it was unlikely he would pick the spot.

Caleb sat quietly for a moment as Mikayla watched him as he centered himself and tried to tap into her aura. Once he found it, he followed to where it was being pulled. There was a couple of places, but one pull was stronger than the others. He decided that must be the place, and he drove straight there. Mikayla took a big gulp as he pulled into the right parking space now. She was baffled by his luck.

26

"Alright, lucky for you I have some towels in the back!" Caleb said teasingly at her.

"I am not going swimming!" She protested.

"So, you don't make good on your word. That's all right, you're scared, I understand. I guess it is good that I find this out ahead of time," he said, taunting her.

Mikayla quickly opened the door and headed for the back of the jeep to take a towel out of the back. She actually always made good on her word, and he knew just the right thing to say to remind her of that.

"Whatever," she said, agitated at loosing as she grabbed a towel.

She headed down the path to a very small beach area. It was completely deserted and lit only by the moon and stars. The night was clear and hot. Surprisingly the water was warm for the first week of May, due to April and March having been unseasonably warm, Mikayla thought as she knelt down to check the temperature with her hand. She hadn't been out on the water yet this year, but was glad the water was warm. The first week of May, despite temperatures, people started to use their boats, having been cooped up all winter. "That's Michigan weather for you," she said, too low for Caleb to hear as she pulled her hand out.

Caleb followed behind her, not needing to check the temperature himself because his body didn't feel the cold or the warmth the way humans did.

Caleb kicked off his flip-flops and put them on top of the towel he had thrown on the ground. Mikayla was still crouched down by the water as she looked back at him, and watched as he then peeled off his shirt. Her hands started to shake; it wasn't a bad nervous feeling, but a good nervous feeling traveling all the way from her head to her toes. He threw his shirt on top of his flip flops and looked her way with a look of "well, what are you waiting for," displayed across his face. She was busy staring at his body. He had a few large tattoos specifically placed around his body; it was too dark to take a look at the artwork. The first one she noticed covered his whole upper right arm, which balanced the second tattoo that covered the lower part of his left leg.

It wasn't until he turned around to place his flip-flops on top of his shirt, to prevent it from blowing away, she saw the third tattoo, which covered the middle and upper part of his back. thought how symmetrical it all looked. Although it was too dark to see what the tattoos were, she could tell they were intricate and somehow all seemed to go together. It wasn't like the tattoos on Dominick and the other boys, which were more sporadic and overly done. She thought it made her even more attracted to him, not that she needed tattoos to be attracted to someone. Marcus had no tattoos and she doubted he had any now, yet she was completely smitten with him. She shook her head at the brief thought of Marcus, irritated he had even crossed her mind and instantly came back into the moment.

"So, are you chickening out or what?" Caleb said tauntingly.

Mikayla got up quickly and folded her arms in front of her as she tilted her head to the side.

"No! I don't chicken out. I made a deal. So what am I supposed to swim in?" She asked, knowing he was going to push her to the edge. It was obvious he was mischievous, so undoubtedly he would make her squirm.

"Hmmm...let's see?" Caleb said, squinting one eye while he rubbed the bottom of his chin with his right hand, which made the definition in his biceps seem unreal.

Mikayla tried to cover the nervous breath in she had taken, although Caleb had taken notice.

"First take off those pants. They will just weigh you down," he said, still standing a ways away from her.

She walked away from the water slowly, and a bit closer towards him, not wanting to get her pants wet. Like Caleb, she threw her towel down and pulled off her gym shoes, tucking her ankle socks inside so as not to lose them. She then bent forward a bit and started to take down her pants.

"No, slowly," he said as if he held all the control.

"That wasn't the deal! You aren't allowed to tell me how to undress, just what to undress!" She said, and quickly took off her pants, wanting that part to be of her control, and before he could say anything else, she started to take off her shirt when she heard him start to say something.

"Mikayla I…" Caleb said, but was quickly interrupted by Mikayla.

"Like I said, this isn't a strip tease, but I will take part in my losing the game, but I control how it gets done!" She said, irritated as her shirt came off.

"But I…" Caleb started to say, putting up both hands. Mikayla was now getting a kick out of thinking she was ruining his big game plan of having her do a sexy strip tease in front of him.

"Shut up!" She said, feeling victorious in her state of embarrassment as she now unhooked her bra and threw it on top of the rest of her clothes.

She was standing there, tan, sporting nothing more than a ponytail and a pair of very short, tight, white, boy cut underwear. Caleb was taken back at just how perfect her body was and immediately his hormones responded to seeing the nakedness of her breasts as she flung her bra on top of her clothes. She quickly covered her breasts with one hand as she started to take off her shorts, and with the speed of light they were off. Caleb thought he was going to lose every ounce of control. He had no intention of letting her take off her clothing. He was only going to have her get down to her underwear, since that was basically the same thing as a bathing suit anyways, but she was now naked and slowly heading for the dock.

He watched from where he had set his stuff down as she slowly made her way to the end of the dock. She stood there looking perfect and looked back at him and stared for a few moments before jumping in. Caleb took off his shorts, but left his boxers on to act as a barrier between the two of them, and then ran to the dock and down to its edge and jumped in.

The water was quiet and peaceful. He stayed down for a moment before being grabbed. He came up to the top of the water and found her right in front of him. The water seemed to be a few inches less than 6 feet. The sand on the bottom was hard and free of muck, rocks, and seaweed. It was definitely a great choice for swimming.

"Hey, that's not fair. You still have clothes on!" She said, looking agitated at him as she felt his boxers against her skin.

"Hey, no one told you to take your clothes off!" Caleb said seriously to her.

"What are you talking about, you said to take off my pants!" She said.

"Yes, but I was going to stop after your tee-shirt. You are the one who kept stopping me from telling you, so that is your fault, not mine! I was just going to make you get down to something that resembled a bathing suit, that's all." Caleb said honestly.

Mikayla felt her cheeks get all hot. She was completely embarrassed. No one got to see her naked, and now twice in one day two guys had seen her without a top on. She let this stranger have a free peek at her, despite the fact it wasn't what he was even after in the first place. What was she turning herself into, she thought to herself, embarrassed at her behavior.

Not knowing what to do, her first instinct was to get out of the water and put on her underwear before getting back in, and without thinking about the fact she would only be exposing herself more, she started to swim towards the dock.

"What are you doing?" Caleb called after her.

"Going to put on a swim suit, just give me a minute," she called back to him, having already grabbed on to the dock ladder. Just as she was about to climb up it, she felt his hands wrap around her waist, and it felt good.

"Don't get out. I promise when we are done swimming, I will go grab a towel and shield my eyes from seeing your beautiful body naked anymore tonight," he said quietly behind her.

She all of a sudden felt safe, like he was trying to protect her from embarrassment.

"I have to say, I do like you like this though. I have never seen anyone as beautiful as you and forever I will have the image of you in my mind," he added as he pulled her closer to him.

She felt like she was going to melt at any moment, and having a bit of a hard time speaking because he, yet again, removed the air from her lungs and began to speak.

"Why, because I am naked?" She said, trying to figure out if it was a perverted thing he was saying or sincerity.

"No, simply because you truly are the most beautiful thing I have ever laid my eyes on," he said, completely honest.

She had always had people comment on her beauty, but never had a guy said words to her like that. Her whole body started to tingle and there was nothing in-between she and he besides a pair of boxer shorts. She hoped that was enough to keep her head on straight. It was as silent as a night muffled with a heavy snowfall for a few minutes, as they remained still. Mikayla wanted to say something to him. She didn't want him to think that she was ungrateful.

"Thank you," she said sincerely, still not moving.

As they sat spooning in the water, with Caleb's arms wrapped around her and her hands on the ladder of the dock, they heard a motor from a boat approaching. Mikayla knew this particular chain of lakes, people usually just used as a mean to get from one of the bigger lakes to the other. There weren't any houses for a good eight miles or so on this side of the lake. It was a hidden swimming area her and Rowan would sometimes come to for swimming, and to get away from the crowd. They started coming after Mikayla first found out about Dominick's unfaithful ways their senior year of high school. It irritated Dominick that summer she was still going out to the lake, but staying far away from him, at the point she wouldn't even look his way.

"They are probably just passing through," Mikayla broke the silence. Caleb looked towards the boat, his eyes were keen in the dark and he watched as the boat approached closer. They could hear the faint voices in the distance. Mikayla turned towards the boat to see if she could hear better. The voices sounded familiar. She turned towards the boat and Caleb noticed the look on her face was fear. Not the kind of fear you would have for your life, but a fear of being caught, which made Caleb look at the boat now coming closer. It looked as if the boat was passing through, but it was coming awfully close to hugging the side of the lake where Mikayla and Caleb were. As it got closer,

Mikayla stiffened. "Oh shit, that's Lucio, and he's with Tony and a few others, including some girls whose voices I can't recognize." She couldn't see them, but she could make out the shape of the boat and recognized it's lights as well hear them.

Caleb didn't have to look again to know she was right. Unlike her, he could see in the dark, and had already spotted them moments before.

"Just stay behind me," Caleb said as the boat approached further.

"What if they see us and come this way? I won't ever see the light of day again. They would probably put a lock on my bedroom door, keeping me in for the night," she said, half serious half kidding, but fully worried.

Caleb just looked at her, and then back towards the boat. "They are getting a little too close for comfort, lets quietly move under the dock, just in case they spot us and decide to get curious," Caleb said quietly as he noticed the boat now getting even closer, and slightly turning towards the dock.

"They are heading over this way, do you think they saw us?" Mikayla quietly whispered as she waited for Caleb's cue to get underneath the dock.

"No, I don't think so. Come on, we better get under," he said, keeping an eye on the boat.

They both slowly forced themselves underneath the water and made their way undetected underneath the dock. There was enough room underneath for them to put their heads out for air. Sure enough, the boat was headed towards the dock.

"Shit!" Mikayla said with a forceful whisper.

"Shhh…" Caleb motioned his finger to his lips for emphasis.

The boat made its way to the dock. The radio was blaring and Mikayla could tell they had been drinking beer. Apparently the boys had picked up a couple of bimbos, Mikayla thought as she listened to one screaming.

"Oh my god, I have to pee so bad! Thank you, boat guy. I just can't pee-pee in the lake when it's dark. It's way too scary when it's dark. You are a superhero; hold my beer, here, superhero of the ladies room! Maggie, come with me!" The drunken girl said at the top of her lungs.

"I'm coming, too! Hey, we need a look out!" Another one said.

Mikayla heard Tony start to laugh.

"Fucking just go pee, we are right here!" She heard Tony call out to the girls, who were already on the dock stumbling towards some trees.

The boat was so close to them, if it weren't for their blaring radio they probably would be able to hear them breathing. They waited as the girls were somewhere over by the trees using it as a restroom. Caleb and Mikayla were motionless. As the girls finished up, they were making their way back towards the boat when Caleb and Mikayla heard one of them yell.

"Hey, someone left their clothes!" The one girl called out.

Mikayla's eye's opened wide. Caleb stayed calm.

"We should just take them!" Another one called out as they started to laugh.

Mikayla started to move towards the edge of the dock, as if by instinct she was ready to defend the taking of her clothes. Caleb grabbed her hand under water, and with a stern look in his eye, gently shook his head no. Mikayla was completely nervous she was going to have to enter her house naked and wet. The thought made her feel panicked.

"Just leave them. Come on, we have a party to get to," Tony called, which made Mikayla start to relax a bit, knowing people usually did as any of those guys said to do.

"You all have about ten seconds to get on the boat or we are leaving your asses, so hurry the fuck up!" Vince added, obviously annoyed at the drunk bimbos.

The other boys on the boat started to laugh as they watched the stumbling girls, dressed in bikinis, try to hurry back towards the boat. Mikayla smiled at what Vince had said, and Caleb smiled to.

They heard the drunken stumbles above them as the girls passed over their heads. Mikayla thought to herself , *bimbos*, as they were passing over top of them. She then remembered she was naked and at least the bimbos had suits on.

Oh my god, I am naked... she thought as the motor of the boat started to move away from the dock.

They waited until the boat was far enough away before moving from underneath the dock. As they reached the other side of the dock, Mikayla and Caleb looked at each other and started to laugh.

"I thought you were about to get out and smack those girls down!" Caleb said, laughing.

"I was, but you stopped me!" Mikayla said back and giggled at the end of her sentence.

"Well, I can't say I wouldn't have loved to see the naked you rip off another girls bikini, but I thought it might cut your night short!" He said.

Mikayla splashed him for his comment. "Typical male!" She said, still splashing him.

He was laughing and splashing back at her while making other jokes about naked girls and wrestling as she laughed and splashed at him, trying to get him to stop. Caleb was relentless and took things as far as he could go. Mikayla decided to act like she was just going to leave then if he was just going to make fun of her, and started swimming towards the dock, hoping he would stop her once again.

She had, yet again, reached the dock when she felt his hand grab her just below her waist by her pelvic bones. Electricity shot throughout her body.

"Don't be mad, I will stop," he said, sincerely.

"Fine, no more naked girl jokes. You have told one to many," she said flirtatiously.

"Want some truth then?" He asked.

"What truth?" She said back, unsure if this was just another trap for another one of his jokes. Either way, she was having a blast.

"Truth is I stopped you because I didn't want any other guy to see you naked," he said, and he meant it.

Right now he wanted no one else to see her naked but him, and he hoped he would get to again.

As if the voltage was kicked up a notch, the electricity in her body traveled furiously. She couldn't help herself. She turned around towards him and put her legs around his waist, her arms around his neck, and planted a kiss on him. His whole body responded. She could feel it through the only thing between them that prevented them from becoming one, his boxer shorts. The firmness of her wet breasts against his chest was almost unbearable. He wrapped his arms around her waist, trying not to feel all over her body. He had respect for her, and didn't want to just take advantage of her in this moment of freedom for her. They kissed for a good five minutes before Caleb pulled her away.

"What is it?" Mikayla asked, dazed by the moment.

"We aren't going to do this, not now," he said honestly.

Mikayla understood what he meant, and felt good about it, but was still a little out of it.

"So, how good of a swimmer are you?" He quickly changed the subject, using every ounce of control he had.

"Pretty good, why?" She said, squinting her eyes at him, wondering why he was asking.

"Let's have a race to see who is going to buy who something to eat after we finish swimming," he replied.

Mikayla started to giggle.

"Alright, you're on! Name the start and finish," she said, determined to give it her all. She really was a great swimmer.

Caleb pointed out the start and finish lines, but let her call out the "on your mark, get set, go!" They both swam their hearts out, as if to prove to each other what they were made out of. Caleb was impressed by how closely she stayed behind him. Normally he would have smoked someone in a swimming race, but she was fast. However, as fast as she was, she was no match for him!

They raced a few more times, with the outcome the same each time. Caleb joked around with her, telling her all the things he was going to order to eat after they were done swimming, which made Mikayla laugh and splash him. She even tried dunking him a few times as he defended himself and tossed her in the water. Mikayla was having the time of her life. Caleb was having the time of his.

As they both were out of breath from laughing and playing around, Mikayla had an idea.

"Alright, double or nothing," she said with a smile on her face.

Caleb started to laugh.

"What is it with you and this double or nothing business, didn't you learn your lesson the first time? If you had stuck to the original bet, you wouldn't be out her in the dark without your clothes on," he said, and turned his body as she flung a huge splash of water towards his face.

"Well, double or nothing?" She said, stopping her splashing long enough to hear his answer.

"Alright, what now?" He asked.

"Alright, let's see who can hold their breath longer underwater," she said.

Caleb knew he would win this, too. He was half vampire, which meant he could go a really long time without having to take any kind of breath at all.

"Alright!" He said as he raised an eyebrow at her.

She counted down to one from three and they both went under. It was a good minute she was under the water, and forced herself to stay a little bit longer to make sure she would win. She came out of the water, taking in a huge breath, but he was still underwater. A few more seconds passed by before he came up. At first he barely seemed winded, but quickly started breathing harder. Foiled by her own plan, she decided to once again change the rules.

"How about the best out of three?" She said, desperately wanting to win at least one time before the night was over.

"Fine," he said, and quickly counted down to one and they both put their heads underwater. Caleb quickly came up, he decided to let her win the next two rounds to give her an ego boost. He knew there was no way she could ever win against him, but he wanted to see the satisfaction on her face after beating him in something. He could slightly see her underneath the water. *She looks so peaceful*, he thought to himself. Mikayla held her head underwater and decided to concentrate on the quietness of being under the water. Everything was muted, even the quietness around her, as she felt weightless. She concentrated on this, hoping it would help her stay under longer. Just as she felt she was about to lose all consciousness, she headed for surface.

She was so excited to see Caleb was already up.

"Alright, it's one to one! One more time to see who is paying for food!" She said, excited she may actually win something after all this night.

They both counted down together and plunged their way into the water. Caleb only stayed down for a few minutes before coming up and waiting for her to finish. Mikayla was losing breath a bit quicker, and again headed for the surface, only to find Caleb already up again.

"I won! I won!" She shouted.

Caleb smiled, he was amused at her lack of sportsmanship.

"You owe me a chocolate shake, a big fat cheeseburger, and some greasy french fries!" She said as she was doing a little dance, forgetting she wasn't wearing any clothes and not knowing Caleb could see fairly clearly in the dark.

At first Caleb thought she looked adorable and free. His heart swelled a little at her innocence. Then as her body came out of the water, with her hands raised in the air doing some kind of winners dance, he could see her for the women she was. She was truly perfect, and again his body responded. He quickly reached for her as if it was second nature to him to take her in his arms.

"I will get you whatever you want," he said, grabbing her as he gently spread her legs apart with one foot, while grabbing underneath her backside to wrap her legs back around him. The movement was fast, and soon he found her tucked around him in an embrace.

Again they were kissing uncontrollably. She could feel just how much he wanted her and she couldn't help herself, she wanted him just as much. His hands started to move around her body as if he had done this before, several times. He slowly made his way around to the front of her stomach and made his way up. This made her let out a sigh from the pleasure of it all.

It was dangerous; he was starting to lose control. She started to lick the side of his neck gently, and then bit it playfully. That sent Caleb over the edge and he felt his canines lengthen, which was his only saving grace. He just didn't want to hurt this girl or use her in anyway. He felt a bit of shame for the teeth coming out, which was just enough to make him cool things off again.

Caleb put his hands on her waist and pulled her off gently. "Alright, we need to get you some food and get you dried off. Your body is starting to feel cold," he said, which her body honestly was starting to feel cold.

Mikayla smiled at him and he thought about how innocent she looked.

"Ok," she said again without an argument. She was still on a high from the risks she had taken throughout the night.

"Stay right here. I will get you a towel," he said, and quickly headed up the ladder and down the dock towards her towel. She was amazed even after she had remained naked in the water this whole time, and made out with him like a bimbo, he was still willing to protect some of her virtue.

It was amazing to her how respectful he was being after she had put herself out in a way which should have made her feel cheap, but somehow it didn't. All she felt was excitement and hope. Most of all she was exhilarated from the freedom she was feeling. Even though she was twenty-one-years old, she somehow felt like a teenager who had snuck out of the house on a forbidden adventure. The feeling was thrilling as she felt in one night. she was taking some of the control others had over her back. No matter what, she would not allow herself to feel ashamed, she told herself as she waited for Caleb to return with a towel.

Caleb was back in no time with her towel and held it up and opened it towards her as he tried to look the other way. It took all of his strength to not take one more peek. Mikayla quickly made it up the ladder and into the towel. Once she was safely covered, she reached for his hand as they made it off the dock and back to the beach were the rest of their clothes were.

"Thank you," she said as she reached down for her clothes.

Caleb smiled at her. "No problem," he said back to her while he was pulling back on his own clothes.

They made it from the beach to his car and from his car to a 24-hour diner for cheeseburgers, shakes, and french fries. Mikayla was so hungry, she ate every last bite. Caleb was always hungry and ate every last bite himself. The conversation seemed to flow so naturally. The talked about places they had traveled and beliefs they have. They made each other laugh. It truly was the best night Mikayla ever remembered having. It was also the best night Caleb had ever had. Neither wanted the night to end, but it was already three in the morning, and soon she would have to get up. She had to work a short day, only a four hour shift the latter part of the day, but she needed to be well-rested, and she was determined to get her run in beforehand. It had been a few days since she had worked out last and she was itching to go. Her workouts were her place of meditation.

Caleb settled the check and they got back into his car and sat in silence, with nothing but a CD playing for noise as they held hands on the way home. As they approached her neighborhood, Caleb played like he had no idea where she lived and played along with her directions. He was a bit worried. He had wondered if it was such a good idea he drop her off in front of her house, yet he knew she was tired and didn't want to make her walk through the park.

"Should I drop you off a little further down the road?" He asked.

Mikayla thought about it for a moment before answering.

"I don't think anyone was aware that I left. If they were, they would have called me. Besides, after last night I think everyone just expected me to stay holed up in my room," she said, smiling at him.

"What was last night?" Caleb asked as if he didn't know.

"Oh nothing…" she said, trailing off for a moment. "I just normally don't drink that much and last night, well, let's just say I was in rare form. I slept half the day away today." She added, telling him the truth without telling him the strange part of the night before, not wanting to seem crazy.

Caleb smiled genuinely at her, wishing he knew her better.

"This is far enough. I will get out here, just in case," she said a few houses down from hers.

"Are you sure?" He said, wishing he could just carry her up the stairs and tuck her in for the night, only wanting to take care of her.

"I'm sure. I will be fine," she said and leaned towards him and gave him a soft and gentle kiss on his cheek.

"I will wait for you to get in. Can you flash a light or something so that I know you really are alright?" He said, trying to seem normal and not like a guy who would more than likely be sitting in a tree watching her sleep for a while before heading back to his temporary home himself.

"Yes, see that room upstairs, the one on top closest to us? That's my room, I will turn on the light to let you know that the coast is clear," she noticed he had a worried look on his face. "Don't worry, my brother doesn't live here. He won't be waiting up, and Dominick is stuck at his club tonight, he will be busy trying to make sure everything is caught up over there before he leaves on their camping trip. Long story, I will explain later, but the answer is no. I am not going," she said thinking that may have been what it was he was looking worried about.

He smiled at her and softly kissed her forehead.

"I will see you Friday," he said, looking away from her.

She leaned in to give him one more kiss on the cheek, and he turned his head and caught her lips with his and gave her a couple of goodnight kisses. Both of them felt shivers throughout their blood streams. Again, Caleb was the one who used his strength to pull away. It almost killed him to do so.

Mikayla finally got out of the car and made it quickly down the street before reaching her house. It was only a matter of seconds before he saw her bedroom light switch on. Caleb sat there for a few minutes before starting the car to head back towards the hotel. He wasn't in the mood to spy on her for the rest of the night; he was feeling a little out of control and weird. It only made him want to get back to the hotel just to take a step back and catch his breath. He was too easily wrapped up in her, it was something he wasn't able to help. As he made it half way there, he remembered he had done none of what it was he was supposed to do.

"Fuck, I'm never going to get to sleep," he said as he made a U-turn and headed back towards the park.

The whole reason he was supposed to be gone was to follow the scent of the hyenas and there was no way he could go back having been gone this long without any information at all. It was decided, for the second night in a row he would be getting very little sleep, if any, and he let out a defeated breath at the thought as he made his way back towards the park.

27

Caleb stared at her for a long time. He studied the outline of her almond shaped eyes and thought about how they reminded him of the ocean the first time he looked into them less than a week ago. He ran his finger over her high cheekbones and then looked at the perfect structure of her nose. *She's absolutely perfect*, he thought to himself. Then he carefully traced over her full lips, slowly. He closed his eyes and breathed in. *She definitely doesn't smell like a wolf*, he thought, again.

Outside the sun was starting to come up and Ali and Jamahl would be wondering where he was, so he decided it was time to go. The benefit of being half witch is nobody needed to invite him in. As he turned towards the window, Mikayla started to shift. Nervous she might open her eyes, he hid behind the long dark blue and white curtains. She turned onto her side facing the window and seemed to settle in after moments. Caleb waited a few more minutes until he was convinced she was back asleep before he would sneak out.

He decided to take the long way home and walk instead of orbing, which he had been forbidden to do by Ali, but seemed to keep using his powers in small doses when he felt it was the best choice for him. *A walk would be good for me*, he thought to himself as he made his way down the street. He was trying to figure out two things. First thing is what was with this girl? She didn't smell of wolf, yet she didn't smell quite human either. Sure, today she smelled like fresh oranges on top of creamy vanilla ice cream with a touch of brown sugar and cinnamon, but she also definitely didn't smell human. Secondly, why was he so drawn to her?

He couldn't come up with any conclusions, which only frustrated him and made him angrier with each step. *What the fuck is wrong with me? I am here for one purpose and one purpose only, and she is clouding my judgment and getting in the way of my job… I should just drain every ounce of blood out of her and be done with it*, he thought to himself, but all of a sudden he felt sick to his stomach just thinking about taking her life.

"Apparently this is not an option for me," he said aloud to himself, half-crazed, thinking of the night before when they were kissing as her wet, naked body was pressed up against him.

Right then and there he could have taken her, but he didn't. He wanted things to be on her terms; wanted the right moment and he hoped he would have another chance. He knew she wasn't "that" kind of girl, and realized it was the first time she had ever skinny-dipped. She put on a brave face that night, he thought to himself.

He made his way a couple of miles into the woods. The park was empty and still mostly dark underneath the trees. The sun was slowly making its way out today. He climbed upon a big rock which looked over the small river and began to think about the past week since they had been in Michigan.

The sun started to raise higher and Caleb put his thoughts about that first night aside and realized he had resulted in feeding off a bird and a couple of squirrels to get his strength back up. *Nasty*, he thought to himself. He started on his long walk back to the hotel; it was too light now to fly or teleport and risk being seen, even if he had wanted to go that route. For part of the walk, he had cleared his mind, taking notice of small things like the smell of spring in the air and the sound of birds flying overhead, moving tree to tree. As he headed down the street, images of her stuck through his head as he began to go over the past week since they had arrived.

Caleb made his way towards their new condo. The day before was spent moving into the condo, which they paid in full for the summer all though they may only be there a couple of weeks. He had also went out and purchased a motorcycle and justified it to a complaining Ali by saying they may need two vehicles. Ali didn't buy it, but dropped the conversation after realizing it was a losing battle. He kept asking Caleb how he was going to get it home if the girl turned out to be the one they needed to take. Caleb told them he would drive it back or orb it back. Ali laughed at the thought of anyone having enough power to orb an object that heavy, that far. The purchases they made were big, but they were trying to go undetected and fit in. They were going to purchase a boat, as well, but found there was a place to rent boats at the lake and, despite Caleb feeling like a pontoon boat was beneath him, he realized getting rid of a boat in a couple of weeks was a much bigger deal and had to agree it wouldn't be something that could easily be done. However, if he had not purchased the crotch rocket, he may have argued the point.

Looking around, he noticed again how good the air smelled. Closing his eyes, he started to sense other small things, like the warmth of the sun on his face. He began to wonder what life would be like if he were a full vampire and could not live life out in the sun. It made him and his brothers the envy of a large number of vampires, who half of them would have loved nothing more than to rip out their throats because of it.

He could see the condo from down the street and hoped Jamahl and Ali were not up yet as he made his path down the street. He finally came to the entrance of their temporary home, made out of tan colored bricks. It reminded him of what happened after he had first seen her and he started to go over it in his head.

Caleb stood outside on the front porch for a moment, thinking about the past week again. He shook his head and started to laugh at how they were worried their idea wasn't going to work that day on campus, and it ended up working out even better and faster than they had hoped. Then he focused on the fact that today he would get to spend time with her. He was hoping to have her to himself, as Ali and Jamahl did their thing with the holy water. A solution to reveal an angel's wings Ali felt would not work, but they would try it until they could find another way.

What is wrong with me, he suddenly said to himself. *I cannot get her out of my head... All I can think about is her, I am not focused. What the fuck is happening*, he added, plopping himself down on the top step of the porch.

Spiraling down without a parachute was how he was feeling. Mikayla was a distraction, but one he couldn't seem to get away from. Hoping it all would just pass, Caleb tried to put her out of his mind, but all he could see was the color of the ocean in her eyes and the fullness of her lips and the bright perfect smile that lay within. Shaking his head, with his palms pressed up against his face, he tried one more time to put her out of his head. Again, the thought of the smoothness of her skin, tan, soft, and smelling of oranges and vanilla with a mix of soap and fabric softener, made his stomach do cartwheels.

"Why?" He asked out loud, as if he expected an answer.

But it was useless, he would have to come up with a plan B, he decided.

Hmm...a plan B... Not at all a bad idea, he selfishly thought to himself. If he couldn't get her out of his system during the time they were there, he would just have to convince her to go with him. Never before had he felt like this for someone. It's nothing he wanted, but here it was and he felt possessive, like somehow Mikayla belonged to him; like, perhaps, she was made specifically for him. *Plan B, yes that could work!* He thought again.

It was now close to nine and they really needed to get to the lake. Ali would for sure be up now, and Caleb knew he was going to have to hear about it. Today he decided he would just take whatever Ali dishes out and not make a big deal. He knew his head was clouded and didn't need anyone pointing that out to him. The best he could come up with is to just allow Ali to say what he would and not argue back, things would go much quicker that way.

Caleb got up off the porch and headed inside for his tongue lashing.

28

The sunrise shone through Mikayla's room, waking her. Her heart began to race, remembering the feeling she had in the middle of the night someone was watching her. Strange, she had felt as if someone was either behind her or watching her all week. She decided it must be from all of the stress from the past week. Taking in a deep breath to slow down her heart rate, she closed her eyes to bring herself into the present. *Easy breath…just breathe…* Her heart began to slow down as she brought herself into the present, almost forgetting the gnawing fear she had just been feeling. Slowly she opened her eyes again, studying the warm sun shining through her window.

She lay there for a moment trying to decide whether or not she was ready to get up, until she thought of Caleb. She was worried he wouldn't end up showing up, thinking to herself she may have already shown him enough. The thought made her bite her bottom lip in embarrassment.

Two days had passed since she had seen him last. The day before was pretty boring in comparison to the two nights before that. She worked yesterday and went straight to Lucio's house for a barbeque for the boys who were leaving later on in the evening.

At the barbeque, her and Rowan had brought up, again, the two of them getting a place together on campus for their last year. She felt it was better than asking to live close to the boys, who would control her every move. Their parents just laughed it off alongside of the boys at the barbeque. Her mother became a bit agitated after a while and whispered to her, tight lipped, for her to not talk about it any further at Lucio's. She told her it wasn't the appropriate time. Mikayla knew it wasn't, but she had hoped that someone would be on her side and help pursued them.

Squeezing her eyebrows together, she realized she had a headache just thinking about it again. The argument didn't stop there, and she, like the discussion, was not yet closed despite that they said it was.

She was still angry with her parents and her twin brother about getting an apartment with her best friend Rowan. Rowan was in the same boat; her parents weren't budging either.

What are they so afraid of, Mikayla thought. Which only made her briefly think back to the feeling someone had been watching her all week. *That's it right there; it's got to be. My parents and brother are so afraid to let me grow up that it's manifesting my paranoia. Ok, that's it. I will not give in to this fear...I will not become one of the people so scared something may happen I forget to live life.* Her decision was made; she would put all of those silly thoughts out of her mind and concentrate on the present. Concentrate on what she could see, and ignore what she could not. She was not stupid. She knew how to keep herself safe, and no way was she about to let their fears affect the rest of her life.

Immediately she returned to thinking about the argument from last night. How unfair it was her brother and his group of friends got their own condos in downtown Ann Arbor as they just took a class or two here or there; not at all taking school seriously, unlike Mikayla and Rowan. But she then remembered it was expected of them to take over the family business; a responsibility Mikayla didn't have, and she began to think maybe, in the grand scheme of things, she was actually the lucky one.

Mikayla and Rowan lived in a small neighborhood in which a good portion were family or close friends who went back many generations. They were rumored to be mafia, which made outsiders leery of buying in that neighborhood, which helped to keep it a clean and safe neighborhood in which very few outsiders lived. Sometimes even Mikayla herself thought the possibility of mafia was there. They all owned restaurants, jewelry shops, liquors stores, clothing stores, a couple bars and various businesses, as well as some condo lofts they rented out to young professionals and grad students.

Which brought her back to the thought it was unfair the boys lived in the condos above the stores and restaurants, while Rowan and her couldn't even get a small apartment on campus together. They had outstanding grades and even put in some hours working downtown at one of Rowan's mother's stores.

That was her argument against her parents the night before, it was unfair that while the boys all were able to have complete freedom, they were stuck at home like a couple of young teenagers. It was absolutely stupid, but it was their parents who paid for their colleges and employed them at a much higher rate than they would get working at the mall. Ultimately they had the say so. Nonetheless, it stilled frustrated both her and Rowan beyond words.

Mikayla was up and staring out of her window when her cell phone rang.

"Hello, Rowan, I didn't know that you even owned a cell phone," she answered, jokingly. Rowan almost never called her anymore, it was so much easier for them to converse telepathically. That way they never had to wait for the other to answer while they listened to an obnoxious ring.

"Kali, it's our first day of summer. You know what that means! It's just you and me and perhaps a certain good looking stranger!" Rowan said cheerfully, not addressing Mikayla's joke.

"Just you and me, huh? What about your boyfriend? Are they still out for the day?" Mikayla said, questioning.

"He and the boys are plotting out their three week retreat...and I think after last night we could use the day to explore all of the things we are going to be able to do next year after we graduate! They won't be able to stop us then!" Rowan always had a way of turning things into something positive.

Mikayla knew it was why her brother was so in love with her and would never leave her. She was like the sun to him.

"Ok, as long as Romario, Dominick, and the rest of their minions don't show up, I'm in. I could totally use a day to dream of what it will be like leaving in the free world!" Mikayla said jokingly.

"Are you kidding, with what time? They are leaving tonight!"

"That's true... Ah to explore the ins and outs of being an independent woman!" Mikayla sighed.

"You also mean exploring being a normal girl looking for romance?" Rowan said with a giggle.

"Whatever, I don't even know him. I was just saying that he was really cute, that's all, and brave. Plus I think it was weird that I saw him twice in the same day and never once before," Mikayla said defensively.

Mikayla still hadn't told Rowan about her encounter the other night, she wasn't sure if or when she would say something. The thought of having this secret thrilled her.

"Bla, Bla, Bla, Kali. That's not all you said. Just be ready in an hour, love ya bye!" And Rowan hung up quickly to avoid anymore of Mikayla's lame attempt at denial.

Mikayla was still looking out the window, studying all of the leaves which had recently blossomed all over the trees, and the blue of the sky; it was such a bright, beautiful day. It was supposed to be a hot one. As she started to shift off into a daydream, a hard knock came at her door.

"Kali, you have a letter here... You want me to read it to you?" Romario yelled teasingly from outside of the door.

Mikayla quickly opened her door, laughing. "No, Mario. I do not need your help, and what are you doing here anyways? Don't you have your own home now!" She grabbed the letter lightning fast, and just as quickly shut the door.

She looked down at the letter addressed to her and, in disbelief, tried to focus again on the sender's name. *Marcus J. Rodriquez*. She was taken aback for a second. Her first instinct was to open it quickly and tear through the letter as fast as she could, to see if all her questions over the past three years would finally be answered. Questions like, what happened to you? Where did you go? Why didn't you call? Did I say or do something that had offended you? Why did you leave a week before graduation? And why did you stand me up for prom?

The minutes flew by as she stood with the letter in her hand and it dawned on her the letter was light. It couldn't have been more than a page, at best. Now switching gears from wonder to anger, she thought, *it must be a pity letter...sent three years later.* Agitated, she threw the letter on the bed.

Perhaps I will open it later, she thought. *Perhaps I won't open it at all.*

Looking at the clock, she realized she now only had forty minutes to get ready. She headed into the shower. As the warm water drenched the top of her head and soaked into her long dark hair, she was suddenly drowning in memories of the past… Marcus had moved to town her senior year. She befriended him. He was in all her classes, every semester. She always thought how strange it was every class they had was together. She noticed how he would watch her and she was flattered but couldn't do anything because she had been going out with Dominick since junior high school. Everyone always thought her and Dominick would get married during their college years… how wrong they were.

Dominick changed the summer before senior year. He grew tall and his muscles filled out. He was the star quarterback for the football team. His strength seemed unmatched to all the other high schools boys, including his own group of friends; including her brother. They all seemed to go through a change that summer, but none of them had filled out as much as Dominick. Dominick's attitude changed, as well. He became cocky and aggressive. He no longer focused on her, except for possession. During the summer he had cheated on her a few times, but somehow wooed his way back in during the fall. Perhaps it was her hurt ego that had let him back in, proving to all the other girls throwing themselves at him in the end she was the winner, but just what had she won?

He constantly left her out; leaving her to form new friendships, but the friendship with Marcus was one he tried to forbid. However, three girls later and an unopened Christmas present for him under the tree finally determined she was done. Dominick spent the next half of the year trying desperately to woo her back, but she and Marcus had become close. They were very good friends and spent all their free time together. It was undeniable, the chemistry they had was real, and Dominick could see it as clear as day.

Despite how close they had become, Marcus had waited until Valentine's Day to kiss her for the first time. She felt loved, cared for, and adored. Her knees were weak as he leaned in, and her breath taken away as he took her mouth into his. Electricity shot throughout her whole body. They hung out every day…they even went to the same place for spring break, and despite the constant hovering, especially at night, from Mario and Dominick, they had a wonderful trip down in the Bahamas.

The prom was just a couple months away from the time they got home from vacation. Mikayla and Marcus had planned to go to prom, alone, since Rowan would be with Romario, and Romario couldn't seem to go anywhere without Dominick, Lucio, Mikey, Tony, Vince, and Ricky. This was her chance to spend some real alone time with him since the boys would be distracted with their own dates… She wanted to give herself to him on that night. Such a cliché, but nonetheless she had planned everything. She had convinced herself he was the right one and it wasn't something she was doing to get back at Dominick.

She was excited and took her time to find the right outfit. Her dress was white with random pearl beading. It tied around her neck with a low cut back and clung to her body until it reached mid-calf, where it started to flow out to the ground like a mermaid. The white on her athletic, tanned 5'6" frame was eye catching. She wore her long hair down, with large loose waves tied loosely half back, with a small white flower donned with a pearl center on the right side of where her hair was fastened. Her jewelry was simple, pearl drop earrings laced in silver and a silver arm cuff with a few pearls woven in here and there. Of course she kept her toes painted at all times, for the night of prom she had spent the money on a French pedicure and matching French manicure. Mikayla was known for her beautiful feet. She was known for being beyond beautiful all the way around, though she never gave much thought to it. She truly was a knock out. That night was one of few in which she stopped to take notice and smile at the outcome… Of course not for her sake, but for his.

The water was still warm on her head as she thought further of the day of prom while under the warm, even pellets.

She felt beautiful, not as a girl but as a women, and she was ready to go… She was supposed to have been picked up an hour and a half before all of Mario's clan came over. She waited…and waited… A half hour later she called him, but his phone was shut off. She waited another half hour, this time trying his house… That phone too was shut off. Before she knew it, Mario's friends had arrived along with their limo, all except for Dominick. She stood in for pictures, hugged Rowan farewell, and watched them all pile into the limo. As the Limo pulled away from the house, a familiar black Mercedes SUV was parked across the street, and a handsome man stood in a tux, holding a white rose corsage in his hand with a smile on his face. "Dominick," she said quietly under breath. A tear ran down the right side of her face and another one followed. A tear because it wasn't Marcus, and a tear because Dominick came to save the day.

Mikayla let the water from the shower hit her face as she realized Dominick always came in to save the day. For a moment she started to feel guilty for the past few days, until she was lost back in remembering that day.

Despite her heart being ripped out from her chest by the fact Marcus never showed, called, or made any attempt on letting her know what was going on, she had a good time. It was like the old Dominick; he was familiar, and he was like family. At the end of the night, when he tried to kiss her, she turned her head and said, "I'm sorry…" Dominick, despite being turned away from her again, understood his part and understood things had changed. However, he always kept a close watch over her, chasing off many a caller, some rightfully so.

The following day was Sunday. There was only a week of school left and then she would graduate. She decided before she had to face the humiliation of seeing him in school the next day during finals, she would march over to his house to make sure everything was all right, and if they were, demand an explanation. But when she got to the house it was empty. She stood knocking at the door for several minutes before she decided to peak in the front window, and was surprised to find out everything was missing. Not even a piece of trash on the floor. It looked like a brand new house waiting for someone else to move in. She looked on the front lawn, but there was no For Sale sign. She thought it was strange and wanted to investigate, wondering if she made Marcus up all together in her head just to get over Dominick. Then she remembered Marcus kept a spare key under a rock by the front porch. How strange, she thought because he had just told her that a week ago. Sure enough as she lifted up the rock, there sat the key.

Mikayla held the key in her hand, wondering if she should go in. Her heart raced out of fear for entering a house uninvited. Staring at the key in the palm of her hand, she decided she would go in.

The door opened just fine, and despite a cold case of nerves, she was determined to at least take a look around. She made her way around the house and every room was just as empty as the front living room she peaked in on from the outside. Finally she made her way up the stairs to Marcus's room. As she approached his room, a feeling of nausea waved over her. She felt frozen, as if she shouldn't go in. From the hall she could see the door was opened and, sure enough, like the rest of the house, his room was also empty.

Out of defeat, she fell to the floor in tears, not knowing what had happened, or if she was crazy and she made the whole thing up. She curled up into her knees, with her arms wrapped tightly around them, crying in frustration. Only a few minutes had passed as she sat in tears, when all of a sudden she felt a slight breeze at the back of her hair, like the gentle blowing of a small child. She froze for a second, hoping it was him. She turned around to find nothing when something from above caught her attention. Freaked out, her heart started to pound into her ears as she witnessed a letter falling from above. Without hesitation, however, she grabbed the letter and read the note…

> *Dear Mikayla,*
> *I'm so sorry. One day I will explain…but for now, just know this was beyond my control. By the way, you looked beautiful in your white dress, baby. I will contact you as soon as I can. For now, live your life and please be careful… Stick closely to Dominick and your brother, they really do love you.*
> *Love, Marcus*

The tears began to fall faster and harder. She felt heartbroken, even more than when she had been stood up. She didn't understand and cried herself to sleep right there in his bedroom. Daylight turned into nighttime before the feeling of large arms scooping her up with ease awakened her. Mikayla opened her eyes to find Dominick's face. He was saving her again. How did he know she was there? She wanted to ask, but she was too upset and too tired to speak. So she just clung on until he had her home, taking her shoes off and tucking her into bed. Dominick was the only man her parents would ever allow in her room, even after all the girls he had throughout the last year. She fell asleep with a dim light on by her bed. Dominick watched her for a couple of hours before leaving. He had tears in his eyes…somehow she knew that when she woke up the next day.

Deep in thought, as if she were watching a movie of her life, she had forgot she was in the shower until the water went from luke warm to cold.

"Shit!" She screamed, turning off the faucet as fast as she could.

She quickly put a towel around her and rubbed the steam off of the mirror and stared at herself, remembering the other strange things which had followed in the weeks after, and still continue to happen. She wanted to confide in someone, but she thought they might think she was crazy. She was just grateful Rowan seemed to have the same strange things about her, as well. Because of Rowan she would never be alone.

"Maybe I am crazy…" she said still looking at herself in the mirror when she heard a knock on the door.

"Kali hurry up! You've had your hour, now let's go, chica!" Rowan shouted from the other side of the bathroom door. Mikayla blinked at herself and began to finish getting ready.

"Almost done," she assured Rowan, and within a few more minutes she was lotioned with her bathing suit on, hair up, and teeth brushed. She opened the door

"What's taking you so long?" She said to Rowan with a big smile on her face.

"I don't know, I guess it's just the diva in me!" Rowan replied, playing along with Mikayla's attempt at a joke.

Mikayla grabbed her bag, ignoring the letter sitting on her bed. She knew it was there, but decided to deal with it later. For now she needed a day alone with Rowan.

29

The temperature was already in the low eighties and it wasn't even noon yet. Mikayla had already forgotten about the note sitting on her bed as they pulled up to her family's lake house. The excitement of being curious of a good looking stranger, and three whole weeks, starting the next day, without all of the hovering from the boys was just the right medicine for her to forget about the note.

They parked the car in the garage and walked into the house. It was a large house on a small chain of lakes; their house was on Baseline Lake and was connected to other lakes, like Portage, Strawberry, and Zuki Lake. Her family owned this house. The house on the left of her house Dominick's family owned. His house was equally as large. To the right of her family's lake house, Lucio's family also owned a house. They had put up a fence on one side of Lucio's family's home, and another fence on the far side of Dominick's family home.

This blocked in the three houses' backyards to make one large backyard, and accessible only by way of water or through the houses' back patios. The families wanted it like this for privacy and to keep their children safe and contained in one area during get togethers.

Each of the houses had seven bedrooms, two master suites, and three and a half bathrooms along with a bathroom in each master bedroom. Mikayla had a bedroom of her own that had two beds, one for her and one for Rowan. She always considered it both of their room and they collaborated in the decorations.

Rowan's family was always invited and had full usage rights, along with Ricky, Vince, Tony and Mike's families, although Ricky's and Vince's families stayed at Dominick's, and Mike and Tony's family stayed at Lucio's. Tony's family also had use of Mikayla's family's home. This was how it had always been. There were also others who would come around. Mainly other families they saw as distant relatives who owned other businesses on the same block that Mikayla, Dominick, Lucio, Ricky, Vince, Tony and Mike's families owned.

The families essentially shared the houses. They had the same thing going on in Florida where they would vacation during the cold winters. Only down there, on the southern gulf coast, it was Ricky, Vincent, and Tony's families who owned three homes all next door to one another. They had done the same thing with the backyards in Florida, as well. Creating a magical, safe, blocked off community yard. They had built one large pool equipped with waterfalls and three hot tubes. The grounds in Florida were plush and tropical, and equally as beautiful as the lake houses in Michigan.

Rowan and Mike's families were not without, owning a vacation spot everyone could enjoy. Their families had made a purchase of two large cabins in Aspen for another vacation spot. The boys and Mikayla loved going there to snow board. The cabins were just as beautiful as the other homes. They were close enough to each other their families had built a large joining room they called the common area, which turned the two cabins into one massive lodge. It had two large fireplaces and warm colored oversized and over stuffed furniture, and a large flat screen with surround sound. They were almost always there on Super Bowl Sunday. They would all gather in this one large common room to watch.

Rowan and Mike's moms combined their kitchens into one large kitchen, and then made one large dining area, as well. The two homes separate were already beautiful, but when Rowan's and Mike's mom got done with the renovations, they turned out so beautiful some other people in the neighborhood selling their cabins were able to get much more money for them because neighbors on either side of the one's selling the homes were trying to buy the second house to do Rowan's and Mike's family had done. Obviously in this crowd, money was no issue, and it made for a great place to rent out to others for the long winter months.

Mikayla always felt a bit funny about it, but realized it was money handed down to her family, and her family really worked hard. Her family also paid their employees very well, and made sure benefits were good and available for their employees. They also did a lot of good things for charity, not just with money, but with time.

Mikayla's own mother didn't work at any of the family businesses. She spent her time doing volunteer work. She was heavily involved in several projects. Mikayla admired her mother for this and let her know she, herself, could make her own choice to do something else outside of the family business. It was her mother's commitment of helping others that led Mikayla into wanting to become a teacher.

Mikayla didn't have any dream of working in any of the family businesses herself. She really wanted to teach children. It was now her dream. She had so many ideas she couldn't wait to get out there, and she only had a year left to go. Besides, to her it seemed as if the businesses were mostly geared for the boys to take over.

She sometimes wondered if her parents were only okay with her becoming a teacher because they had assumed someday her and Dominick would still get married. They still, four years later, said things to her about it. Her father even got into a few fights about how stubborn she was and Dominick was a good man and I had made him suffer enough. Some supportive father he was. Who knew, perhaps she should forgive him for what he did as a teenager. But her feelings had changed for him and, stubborn or not, she knew a part of her heart which had been hurt repeatedly had been blocked off from Dominick.

Now her feelings were also blocked from him because of how controlling he was. Even with them having been broken up, he still acted as if she belonged to him somehow. All the boys were. She felt they had too much machismo and needed for someone to come along who could take their belts down a few notches. Not that she would ever want to see them hurt, just humiliated a tiny bit so they would back off.

For the next three weeks, starting late tonight, the boys would be gone, she thought to herself. It would be her first chance at a taste of freedom. This would be a good dry run of what it would be like to live on her own, which she planned to do as soon as she graduated. As a matter of fact, she envisioned a moving truck pulling up to the parking lot at graduation, her getting into the driver's seat with her things in tow, and tossing her cap out the window as she pulled off into the sunset for her first chance at freedom. It was a great daydream, but she wouldn't be quite so cruel to her overprotective, but loving, parents.

Mikayla and Rowan entered the house and the first thing they noticed was the quiet stillness. It was empty. Nobody was at any of the houses. They had the place all to themselves. "Let's put our stuff upstairs!" Rowan said to Mikayla, who was in a bit of a daze thinking about the fact this was the first time she had been here on her own without anyone around. The emptiness was the benefit of an early day on a Friday. She didn't have to work the whole weekend, and already it somehow seemed perfect.

Mikayla currently worked for Rowan's family at Rowan's mom and dad's herbal shop.

Rowans mother was an herbalist and ran her own practice while her father ran the store. The practice was also an herb, candles, books, music, and strange knickknacks store. Mikayla loved the magic of it all.

The store itself was painted several different shades of earth tones, with dark wood furniture, bright colored cushions and pillows, and dimly lit with soft, glowing lights and candles. The smell in the store was Mikayla's favorite. It was one of those smells good enough to eat, and one no matter how many times you breathed it in, you never grew tired of it. A mixture of sweet fresh citrus and backed by various smells like sandalwood and patchouli filled every corner of the store. The smell wasn't heavy, it was just lightly in the air without being too over powering. It often made Mikayla refer to the smell as the white noise for the nose.

The store was one big room with an upstairs you had to have a special card to go up into because of the rare items sold upstairs. That, along with Rowan's mom, Mrs. Munoz, whose practice was also upstairs, was the reasons for the cards.

In the practice office there was a separate waiting room and three private practice rooms, which she used for consultations, massage, acupuncture, and other rituals Mikayla didn't understand. The practice rooms had darker walls with hints of bright colors in accent pieces which tied into the waiting room's burnt orange couch and oversized ottoman, which went well with the three bright yellow and burnt orange striped chairs. The brightness from the accents and furniture made the dark wood of the store that much more magnificent. In the same dark wood, there was also two long wood counters attached together which aligned two of the walls that held jars and jars of different specialty items. It wasn't like the vitamins and herbs they carried in the public downstairs part of the store. Mikayla thought it was the coolest place on earth.

But today was not a day to focus on work; today was for fun, and for the first time Mikayla and Rowan had the place all to themselves. It was daytime, so neither of their parents had worried much about them being there alone. They had planned to spend the whole weekend at the lake house. Mikayla realized she had been in a daze ever since she woke up.

"Am I awake?" She turned to ask Rowan.

"Um, I'm pretty sure you are not, cuz you are acting strange, girl!" Rowan said jokingly back. This made Mikayla smile and feel a little more at ease.

"So, do you think that Caleb and his friends will show up?" Rowan asked, having a feeling Caleb was part of the reason Mikayla seemed to be in a bit of a daze.

Mikayla's stomach felt weak at the thought of seeing him, and a tingling sensation suddenly burned throughout her entire body.

"Which guy?" Mikayla said with a smile on her face. She was now red, but trying hard to seem indifferent.

"Really, I know you want him to. It's all you could talk about for the rest of the day," Rowan said, provokingly, as she saw right passed Mikayla's poor attempt at indifference.

"Well, maybe if he shows up it wouldn't be the worst thing that could happen," Mikayla giggled at her own joke and thought of how he had cornered her at the bar the same night and promised to see her Friday, which then led to a strange meeting in the park. She hadn't yet told Rowan what had happened, she wasn't sure she wanted to. Again, it was almost as if she wanted to keep that night all to herself, partly at the shock it would cause because she actually skinny dipped, and partly because something about keeping the secret made her feel in control over her life.

Suddenly she thought about his lips and the way he had leaned into her hair, taking in a deep breath, and the feelings of butterflies swirling around in her stomach. Just the thought brought goose bumps to her skin. Mikayla went tingly all over just thinking about the moment again. She took a deep breath in, trying to regain her composure. The thought of how that made her feel scared and excited her all at the same time. The thought of being in the water next to him, naked, thrilled her even more and scared her even more. But what scared her the most was the last time she had those butterflies it broke her heart and damaged her spirit. It took her some time to get over, but she vowed never to feel that vulnerable again, so she kept people at arm's length. That wasn't such a problem, anyways, because if a guy was trying to get too close, Dominick would step in anyways.

She tried the best she could to get him out of her head, but it was useless. She found herself wondering if he was going to show up, especially after the secret night at the lake and Dominick's threatening ways. After the display her brother and Dominick put on, she thought he might not show and tried to use that as an excuse to shove him aside so she wouldn't find herself disappointed at his absence. However, it was useless, she would remember as clear as day the look in his eyes as he said, convincingly, he wouldn't let Mario or Dominick get in the way of him going out on the lake, and she was right back into feeling butterflies. He said he wasn't worried about it, and he did seem just as happy to have ran into her at the park as she was. They had so much fun that night, sure some of the kissing got a little heavy, and he did see her naked, but once they were in the water they behaved as if they were young teenagers, holding their breath for as long as they could under water and having swimming contests. It was the best night she ever remembered having and she felt truly free that night.

That ended up making her feel excited all over again, which only led her to her fear of having her heart ripped out a third time. This only started her thinking cycle over again, repeating itself and she couldn't make her brain work around it. So, it was settled today. Either she would see him or she wouldn't. "Let fate decide," she told him and herself. If he was there, she wouldn't worry about anything but getting to know him even better, and hopefully having a normal twenty-one-year old's life, for once. If he wasn't...she didn't want to even think about it. It only made her feel embarrassed at her actions from the other night. She finally let out a sigh from the teetering game her mind was playing.

"So, are you sure your Neanderthal of a boyfriend won't be showing up?" Mikayla thought she should ask, so she could be prepared for the worst.

Rowan was so in tune with Mikayla, she heard her hesitation. "You'll have fun. Stop letting the boys' negative behavior make you give up. You are a tough cookie, but lately you seem to be dealing with a case of defeat. That is so not like you. So shake it off there, missy, and RELAX," Rowan commanded.

She always had Mikayla's best interest at heart. It was as if they were linked somehow, and not just by the secrets they shared between each other of all the strange things they could do, but also by the care they had for each other. They kept their secret so tightly safe between the two of them, not even Mario was aware of the things Rowan could do. Afraid they would be locked up in a phsyche ward, they decided it was best to keep it to themselves.

Mikayla was feeling grateful for Rowan and drifted off into thought. She remembered her and Rowan being able to do strange things when they were very young. At the age of four and five they could do simple things, like make their dolls and stuffed animals dance without touching them. They could draw pictures on the wall with chalk by just lying in bed and controlling the chalk with their minds while they giggled with their little dark heads sharing a pillow.

Looking back through the magical eyes of a child, it all seemed like just that, like they had made it all up and it just seemed real. As they approached the tween age years, boys and clothes became more important than dolls and drawing. Somehow their powers seemed to dissipate. They never talked much about those days of being children until they reached eighteen and strange things started to happen again, only they were no longer children whose worlds bordered between reality and dreams. They were old enough to know what they were seeing and doing was actually happening, or they both were in desperate need of medication.

Mikayla had the first encounter during finals week of her senior year. She had been so distraught over Marcus and his disappearance. She had no answers and was left heartbroken and confused. Two times in one year she had her heart broken. It took her mom peeling her out of bed in the morning to go to school that week, and Mario literally carrying her to the car, driving her in, and forcing her inside of the school.

She couldn't study because her mind was spinning and her heart had been shattered. It was breaking for Marcus and for Dominick. She felt torn between being angry and sad. It was Marcus she was sad for and Dominick she was mad at. If he had never decided to be the horny, big man on campus, she wouldn't have felt like that. She would probably be planning a wedding for the summer with him before college started.

Her brain literally felt like it was going to explode the first day of finals. She had always been a straight A student. Her school work was important to her, not because she felt the need to prove herself to others, only because she put a standard on herself to learn as much as she could. But the task of taking finals seemed impossible. She knew with as much as she worked during the semester, she could mostly likely ace those finals, even having not studied. That, however, wasn't the problem.

She sat in her first class of her first final of her last semester of grade school and was given the test. Her hair wasn't brushed and she had a yellow t-shirt on inside out and backwards with an old pair of ripped up jeans and her slippers on. She was a mess inside and out. The test sat in front of her and she squinted her eyes to try and read the questions, but they all looked like one big blur. She tried to remind herself of how important these tests were to her and if she let one person ruin what she worked hard for, then she was to fault. But still the page seemed a blur. She read and reread the first question a dozen or so times before she looked up at the clock. The test had fifty questions and according to the clock she was under the gun with only fifteen minutes left, which wouldn't have been enough time for even the most prepared and fastest test taker. She began to feel a panic swell up inside of her which only made the blur on the page start to spiral before her eyes.

Out of fear and frustration, she closed her eyes and let out a long sigh to try and center herself. When the lungs had finally cleared themselves of air, she spoke five words in her head, *answers appear on this page*. She then looked up hoping to find the page, indeed, filled with answers. To her utter disbelief and surprise, the whole page was covered in answers. Whether or not they were the right answers at that point didn't even matter, her page was filled and at least she had a shot of having answers right, which was better than none at all. Sure enough, she was either making this happen or she was insane. With no time to think fully about what was happening, she repeated this page-by-page and class-by-class. She would never normally cheat, but she knew under normal circumstances she would have aced all of the tests. She was a straight A student and she was just happy to have her page filled. Sure enough she aced every test she took and never again did she use that method of taking tests. College was important to her, and so far she spent more time studying than she needed to, partly out of guilt from that time and partly because she had a thirst for knowledge.

That was also around the same time she and Rowan realized they could communicate telepathically with each other. Rowan would wake up in the middle of the night to loud sobs from Mikayla, who wasn't even at her house. Mikayla would be so upset, she knew it was too late to call Rowan, but focused on what she would say to her if she could talk. Eventually Rowan actually started to talk back.

Rowan's heart would break for her, and she would reach out with words of love. They weren't sure if they were dreaming until after the second day when each had confessed of dreams that they were communicating with each other telepathically. It was too much of a coincidence and deep down they knew it was true, but decided right then and there to test it. Rowan thought to Mikayla, *are you hearing me*, and Mikayla responded with a short and simple, *yes*. It worked and they had been doing it ever since.

Everything started happening for them around the same time. A week before the prom, Rowan kept seeing visions of Mikayla going to prom with Dominick. She never told Mikayla about the visions until after graduation, when Mikayla had confessed what she did during finals week in order to pass the tests. They agreed to keep what was happening to them a secret from everyone else. They also tried hard to not use these magical urges they had inside them for fear of the unknown. The only thing they allowed themselves to use freely was the telepathic communications with each other.

They didn't see any real harm in doing that, besides the fact it seemed natural to them somehow.

Mikayla was making her and Rowan a couple of sandwiches while she was deep in thought, but soon snapped out of it, startled by the ringing of the phone. Everyone these days had cell phones, so the home phones rarely rang, but when it did she was often startled. Especially when she was in moods of reflection as she had been all day. Perhaps she was trying to take her mind off of Caleb, just in case he didn't show up.

She didn't want to get her hopes up of hanging out with a guy, completely uninterrupted, who was gorgeous, witty, brave, and had Mikayla replaying his smile in her mind for the past couple of days.

"Hello," she answered.

"Put my girlfriend on the phone," Mikayla heard her brother bark over the phone.

She didn't know what it was, but he and his friends seemed to have a monthly issue, along with all the women of the world. Once a month they would get ten times worse than usual. Mikayla always thought it was the stress of going into the family business, but as a joke experiment she kept track of their odd mood swings for three months in a row and found indeed, without fail, every four weeks or so they seemed to have these crazy mood swings, and always during a full moon. Perhaps there really was something to astrology, she thought. After getting bored with keeping track of the boys' moods, she decided to stop keeping paper track, but once in a while would notice there always seemed to be a full moon when they were more controlling and barking more orders than normal.

"How about a, 'hi Mikayla, how are you?' Then you can let me answer, in which I will ask how you are back. See, that's how this goes. Once we have finished proper phone greetings, then you may ask to PLEASE speak with Rowan, in which I would then say, 'just a minute please' and I will get her," Mikayala said sarcastically, while looking at the calendar by the phone.

She squinted her eyes at the date and started laughing. Her brother was already yelling at her, but she had tuned him out and interrupted him.

"Oh wait, it's a full moon. You are always grouchy on a full moon! In that case, I will get your girlfriend, but in the meantime you might want to take some PMS medication." Mikayla smiled as she quickly took the phone away from her ear and yelled for Rowan.

She could hear her brother yelling on the other end of the phone, but chose to listen to the information coming out of his currently loud mouth.

Rowan came down and grabbed the phone, but in the middle of her saying hello was immediately cut off by Mario. She looked at Mikayla and rolled her eyes. Mikayla started to laugh and pretended to stick a gun to her head and pull the trigger. Rowan, trying to keep her laughing quiet, pretended to tie a noose and put it around her neck and pretended to jump. Mikayla started laughing even harder, which only made Rowan laugh harder. All of a sudden Rowan straightened up.

"No, we are not laughing. Why would we be laughing when you are obviously having such big issues?" She said to Mario as seriously as she could while holding in her laughter.

He became more enraged and hung up the phone. As soon as he hung up they both busted out laughing. Mario really was a good guy, and he loved his sister and Rowan, but again, once a month for the past four years he seemed to have a meltdown. It was totally out of character for him, usually he was much more controlled.

"What the heck is his problem this month?" Mikayla finally said as the giggles started to fade out.

"I don't know, something about him wanting us to wait for them to get done, that it would only be a couple of hours, but I know that's not true because I saw their schedule for today. They are busy until 7 p.m. and they leave shortly after that. I think he might suspect that we might be meeting Caleb out. For some reason he said that Caleb had rubbed him the wrong way, but that he couldn't put his finger on it," Rowan said back.

"Now I am ticked off," Mikayla said. "These guys all think I am a moron. They think I can't take care of myself. I have been babied for way too long and I am sick of it. How am I ever going to be a role model for other kids when at the age of twenty-one I myself seem to still function as a twelve year old?" Mikayla was now pissed.

She felt much more angry than she had in a long time. She felt, at this point, she was actually more angry than she had ever been her entire life. She was at the end of her rope, holding on by just a thread and ready to let go. Enough was enough, she was going to have to set some firm boundaries with the guys and with her parents. As soon as they came back from the camping trip, she would set the boundaries and put her foot down. She would work on her parents while her brother was gone. She hoped doing this would get them onboard before Mario had a chance to put in his two cents. Perhaps this was just their way of hoping her and Dominick would reconnect, she often thought. But she couldn't dwell on the reasons why they were so protective of her, she just had to try and get them to stop.

All these thoughts running through her head came to a stop when she looked down at the sandwich she was making and realized she had been spreading the peanut butter over and over across the bread until there was no bread left, just a clumped up glob of goo. She looked at Rowan, who just stared at her wide-eyed.

"Um, I think I need to redo this one," was all she had said.

Rowan started to laugh.

"I guess you really are fed up! But perhaps you shouldn't take it out on the PB and J, it's not it's fault!" She and Mikayla started laughing at the ridiculousness of what was a sandwich. "Well, three weeks of freedom and maybe when they see that you haven't gone off the deep end they will all start to relax a bit more." Rowan added before she stopped laughing to smile at her with hope and reassurance.

"I hope you're right. But you know what, I am not going to let this thing ruin our day! Let's just hurry up and eat and get out there," Mikayla said back as she finished remaking the sandwich she had destroyed.

They sat down to eat their sandwiches and make a checklist of things they were going to need on the boat. This was the first time they got to take the boat out themselves, so they wanted to make sure they weren't missing anything. The last thing they needed was someone telling them they could never do it again because they weren't prepared. Rowan added some wants on the lists, such as music and a cooler filled with some beer. Mikayla was more practical and added things like emergency kit, extra fuel, sunscreen, and life jackets.

After lunch they started to fill the boat with all the things they needed. Mikayla checked the fuel and made sure they had extra onboard. She also made sure there were flares on the boat. Rowan glanced at her side ways, thinking she truly was over prepared, but said nothing to her about it, afraid it would set her off. She had enough people telling her what to do. Rowan, herself, had people telling her what to do, but somehow everyone was twice as bad around Mikayla. So she just let her do her thing and, before she knew it, they were ready to head out onto the water.

30

It was a pain in the ass to rent the boat, Caleb decided. Use to being able to buy whatever he wanted, new and trend setting, he felt it was a step below him to have to rent an old pontoon boat, plain and white with green carpeting. They had to pay the guy a few more dollars just to get the boat with the extra seating. The first boat they were supposed to have only had a few seats as part of the stock of the boat, and lawn chairs for the extra seating. It was brown with cream stripes, which made Caleb's nose turn up.

Looking around at all the other boats for rent at the dock, he found one of the newest ones to be more appealing. The marine operator tended to save the good boats for the older, more responsible crowd, and left the older ones for the young hotshots. Persuaded by cash and assurance from Caleb, he allowed them to have one of the new boats. Still, it was a pontoon boat, not built for speed. Today wouldn't be a day for wake boarding, Caleb thought as he paid the man.

"Snob," Jamahl teased as he watched the look on Caleb's face turn sour.

"Dude, it's a pontoon!" Caleb tried to defend his snobbery.

"You're a snob," Jamahl said again.

"But it's a pontoon!" Caleb said again, realizing he did have an issue with it, but somehow couldn't help but be embarrassed. He wasn't ever considered an Average Joe and right now he felt like one. Boiling down to one of the main reason's came Mikayla. He was worried she would think less of him for rolling up in such a contraption.

"Man, who cares. We needed a boat, we got one. When you get home you can drive your little speed boat all you want and show off for the world to see, but right now you are a college kid who just wants to be on the water." Jamahl, no longer teasing, tried to put his brother in check.

Caleb was always the one who wanted the fastest, shiniest things. It was part of his down fall. His brothers did not share in his love of things. He was a bit spoiled, something he knew he should work on, but something he had not yet tried to do.

"Whatever, I am just saying that we won't get to do any water sports, that's all," Caleb tried defending himself once more.

"Why do you think we are here on vacation. You were supposed to be the lead on this. Cyrus thinks that you are somehow a leader, but you can't see past your own wants to complete one single mission. You need to get your head on straight," Ali scolded.

"Whatever, man. I am not listening to you. You don't care about things because you have no hobbies except for nerd stuff," Caleb snapped back.

"You're right, I don't place value on things. Thanks for the noticing," Ali said and smiled with satisfaction.

"You do realize you just made yourself sound stupid, right?" Jamahl antagonized.

"Would you two just fucking shut up," was all Caleb could think to say, but realizing both of his brothers were right. He did place importance on all the wrong things. The only two things he ever truly cared about were standing right next to him on the rented, plain pontoon boat, and at the end of the day he was glad they were by his side. Not even their father was someone who he truly cared about. He loved him because he was supposed to, not because of who he was as a person.

"Man, Caleb, we are just saying that the man makes the thing, the thing doesn't make the man. So quit acting like a pre Madonna teenager getting ready for her sweet sixteen party and throwing a temper tantrum because you got a brand new BMW when you wanted a Bentley," Jamahl replied.

"Fuck, I do sound like a bitch," Caleb said and started to smile, realizing he did indeed sound like a whining teenager.

"Alright, Dr. Phil time is over, you guys. Let's get the boat loaded," Ali instructed.

Lately Ali was getting better at leadership. He was a natural, not just because he was so calm, but because he was smart and remained consistent. Truly, he was reliable and always pulled through. Caleb never understood why he was overlooked the way he was by Cyrus, but he figured it was because he was so quiet and always seemed to do things that were good.

Caleb started thinking further about his father. Cyrus was always trying to shape Caleb into the alpha of their trio, when in fact an alpha wasn't needed with their trio, unlike Aidan's group which really did have a hierarchy. Caleb knew deep down the reason he was picked was because of his ability to utilize his powers, and because he was so self-centered and self-serving. Mostly he never thought about it too deeply until right at that moment, and thinking about it was actually making him start to feel uneasy.

"Alright, little brother. Do your thing…find your girl," Jamahl said, interrupting Caleb's thoughts about himself.

"Uh, yeah, ok," Caleb said, feeling a lack of energy to do so.

He let out a big sigh, trying to get his head clear enough to tap into her energy. Closing his eyes, the day disappeared as Mikayla entered his mind. Unable to help himself, he smiled at the picture of her face. Now he felt centered. Lost in the beauty and perfection of her face, he floated inside his own energy and, for a moment, he felt peaceful. He felt like he wanted to be more then he was.

"Well…" Jamahl tapped him quickly on his shoulder.

Caleb ignored Jamahl, still trying to feel where he was feeling drawn to. Only moments passed before his eyes flew open and he knew exactly which direction he needed to head.

"Man, do you have it or not?" Jamahl tried again.

"Yeah, I got it," Caleb responded, taking hold of the wheel, as if somehow this would help him to gain back some control, as he shoved Jamahl aside.

Jamahl didn't mess with Caleb back as he usually did. Instead he pulled out his cell phone from his pocket and started to dial his phone. First he called Mary to check when she was coming out. He then called over to Jackson's to see when they were coming out. Ali had rented a second boat for the boys. They wanted to make sure they looked like a few regular guys, just in case anyone such as the wolves or anyone else potentially watching could see. The more they fit in, the better.

"How far is it from here? Which lake?" Jamahl said, wanting to figure out how and when he could get Mary and her friends on the boat.

"I don't know, but it's not on this lake. We have to travel through at least one of the channels." Caleb replied. "When are the other guys getting here and picking up the second boat?" Caleb added, not really wanting to know for the sake of the mission, but for his own reasons. He thought the more people there, the better chance he would have at spending more time with Mikayla. Everything seemed to come directly back to her.

"They were just waiting for James to get off of work, now they are on their way. They said they would be out here in a bit. I told them we already paid for the boat, so they just had to get here," Jamahl said, playing the cruise director.

Ali said nothing during this time. His nose was stuck in an old book. The book was tan and old. The pages were slightly worn and torn. The ink had faded as the pages grew darker. The language in it was Latin. Ali was still trying to figure out the mystery of uncovering an Angel. The holy water was not setting right with him. Jamahl wasn't worried about it, he would only worry after there was something confirmed to be worried about. Caleb didn't think about it at all, the only thing he could think about was whether or not Mikayla would actually show up. He felt like his heart was being pulled, not to Rowan, but to Mikayla. This he found strange. He thought the seer meant he would be drawn to Rowan, but he wasn't. He knew it was Mikayla he was drawn to, and by the way, he was feeling he knew she was there.

Jamahl's phone rang. "Hello…Yeah…no…yeah there…just park, we will come get you." Jamahl then closed the phone, realizing Caleb had already started to drive the boat forward.

"Wait a minute, what are you doing? We gotta turn back. Mary parked at the marina, we have to turn back," Jamahl said, pointing towards the dock.

Caleb rolled his eyes, annoyed. He knew Mikayla was out there, he could feel it, and waiting for Mary and her friends to pile on the boat would take them another twenty minutes before he could see her again. Caleb was hoping they would just wait for Jackson and hop on their boat, but no such luck.

Frustrated, he grabbed hold of the steering wheel so hard all the blood rushed out of them as he cut the wheel fast and hard.

They hadn't gone very far, so it only took a couple of minutes to head back to the dock of the marina. Mary was there wearing oversized sunglasses and short cotton shorts with a tank top covering her bikini and sporting a large beach bag. She was waving as she spotted them coming in. The two friends she was with the other night were right by her side, similarly dressed, each with a beach bag as well. They had a cooler sitting in front of them with a bag with what looked like munchies, from what Caleb could tell. Seeing the effort Mary made for the day softened Caleb's edge a bit. Again, he knew he liked Mary, guys weren't good at thinking of things like that.

"Hey you guys, I have plenty of munchies and sandwiches and fruit in the cooler, so make sure you help yourselves so my nurturing skills don't go to waste!" Mary said, rolling over the cooler as her friends followed behind with the bags.

"Good looking out!" Jamahl said as he hopped off the boat in order to help her with the cooler.

"Thanks," she said, smiling up at him as he grabbed the cooler and motioned all of them to walk ahead of him.

"No problem," Jamahl then smiled.

Caleb could tell Jamahl actually liked this girl. He wondered how it was going to play out when they left. Partly he wondered because of the way he felt about Mikayla, and wasn't sure exactly how it would play out, despite of his plan B.

Just as they had settled into the boat, one of Mary's friends claimed she had to "pee" before they took off. The other girls joined in with a "me too." Caleb rolled his eyes, he was back to being annoyed as he let out a long sigh to match.

"What's your problem?" Jamahl said, smiling at Caleb because he knew he was getting frustrated.

"Nothing," Caleb said as he looked out onto the water and noticed how busy it was.

The girls came back almost ten minutes later. Caleb couldn't imagine what would take ten minutes, but shrugged it off as they climbed back on the boat.

"I cannot believe it has been so warm this spring. We are lucky to have an early onset of summer!" Mary said, obviously happy it felt more like the middle of summer than the beginning of May.

"It's not always like this in May?" Caleb, not thinking, asked.

"Hello, California boy. You have been here for four years! Don't you remember last year when it was unseasonably cold?" Mary said, looking at Caleb sideways.

"Oh yeah, that sucked," was all Caleb could manage to say. *You are losing it, Caleb*, he thought to himself. He couldn't believe how careless he had been since they came to Michigan. It was something he couldn't help. all he could seem to think about was Mikayla and it was screwing with his ability to function. Normally he was real sharp and very cool; his movements were calculated and performed to perfection.

Ali, who had been ignoring everyone, lost in his book, looked up and shot Caleb a disapproving look. He caught the slip up and, while it wasn't that big of a deal, he started to worry about Caleb.

Caleb just looked back at him. *What?* He said telepathically back to Ali.

You and me will have a talk later, Ali replied the same way back.

Caleb knew it was unavoidable at this point, so he just turned his head away and gripped the steering wheel tighter.

Jamahl started to untie the ropes from the dock when they heard a horn honking.

"Hey man!" Jamahl called to the parking lot, waving. It was Jackson and his friends.

"Fuck!" Caleb said out loud, not mad because they were there, but because he knew it was now going to take another twenty minutes, that is if the girls didn't have to pee again, and somehow he knew they would indeed have to pee again. Caleb started to bang his head repeatedly on the steering wheel. The girls were startled by Caleb and looked at him with shock. "I um…I stubbed my toe," was all he could think to say as he lifted his head off of the steering wheel. It wasn't until Caleb banged his head on the steering wheel for the third time he noticed the girls looking at him. He hadn't meant to say "fuck" so loud, but he was growing more impatient by the moment and it ripped out of his throat uncensored.

The need to get to Mikayla was building stronger with every moment. It was like he hadn't fed in over a year and needed to feed, and anything getting in his way would greatly feel his wrath. He didn't even know for certain she would show up. His wonder turned to certainty once he felt her energy coming off of the water.

It was taking them so long to get it together, he was afraid she would think he wasn't going to show up. Especially after what happened the other night. She wasn't the kind of girl who did things like that, this he knew for sure. He was afraid with every second he wasn't there it might make her feel like he was just another guy having fun when he could. That is the last thing he wanted her to feel.

As Caleb suspected, it took over twenty minutes before the girls were settled on the boat. Sure enough, they did have to pee again. Caleb tried to talk them into using the water, making a case they would be doing it the rest of the day anyways. They shot him dirty looks and let him know it was different when they were on the water than when they were at the dock. This made no sense to Caleb, but it was three against one and he was pretty sure he wasn't allowed to kill them. In the meantime, Jackson and his friends had loaded themselves on the second boat they had rented.

Finally everyone was ready. Both boats were loaded as Caleb led the way through the chain of lakes towards the sandbar where he could feel himself being pulled, as if Mikayla was holding an invisible rope and guiding his boat towards her.

An hour had passed since Rowan and Mikayla had been out at the sandbar. Due to the warm weather and the end of classes, the sandbar was busy. It was mostly college students who had all pulled up to the sand bar with their boats, blasting music, drinking beer, and playing various games of catch as boys tried to catch the attention of girls, and girls did their best to reciprocate. The sandbar was seaweed and rock free, and the water was fairly clear as far as lake water can be. It was a party on the water made for having fun. Mikayla was trying to have fun, but she worried because Caleb hadn't shown up yet. Perhaps she had been too wild the other night and gave him a wrong impression, she thought to herself. Maybe she shouldn't have made good on her bet, she wondered further.

"What's wrong, Kali?" Rowan asked as she sipped on a bottle of water.

"Nothing," Mikayla was short.

"Not nothing, I know it's because he hasn't shown up, but I saw the way he looked at you and I am pretty sure that he will be along sooner or later." Rowan tried to assure her, but she was feeling insecure. She still hadn't told her about the other night. Right now she wished she had so she could get her honest opinion. She kept the secret because she liked the thrill of having a secret, magical moment all to herself. Now she was afraid to tell her out of the embarrassment of being stood up because of it. Rowan wouldn't judge her, this she knew, but somehow she was still too ashamed to tell her.

The sun was bright and the weather was warm. Mikayla and Rowan both agreed they hadn't seen warm water this early in the year in a long time and they were grateful for it. Mikayla decided to refocus her attention back on to the weather.

"I wish the beginning of May was always this nice," Mikayla quickly switched subjects.

Rowan knew what she was doing.

"Yes, May should always be this nice," she replied, allowing Mikayla to stay off the subject.

"Look, I don't want to be a downer. It's just that this is the first guy that I have been interested in, well, since you know who." Mikayla said, referring to Marcus.

"I know, and maybe he is the one and maybe he is not, but somehow you need to be able to move on. If you and Dominick are really never getting back together, and I doubt that you are, then you have to learn how to date and have relationships with other people. It's not that I would oppose you and Dominick, it's just that you were young and everyone put so much pressure on you that no one ever thought to ask what it was that you were looking for. But I know what you are looking for, and I am not sure that Dominick, with the way he is, is what you are looking for. You have never been free, neither have I, but I know how much you long for it. If this guy doesn't show up, and

I am not saying that he isn't, but if he doesn't then it's still going to be alright. You have taken the first step just by allowing yourself to be curious. Marcus has nothing to do with you moving on if you don't allow it. What he did was crappy, but you can't go through life expecting the worst out of people because of what Marcus or Dominick did." Rowan said, finally taking a breath as Mikayla listened.

What she said was making Mikayla feel better until she remembered what Mario had given her earlier in the morning.

"Oh, no!" Mikayla said as her eyes widened, looking directly at Rowan.

Rowan was lying down and shot up. "Oh no, what?" Rowan said, alarmed by the way Mikayla had said it.

"No, sorry, not an emergency, but I got something today and I can't believe I almost forgot about it. Maybe I really am over Marcus!" Mikayla said, trying to process out loud.

"Ok, you are not making sense. What happened?" Rowan asked.

"Today your Neanderthal of a boyfriend knocked on my door and told me that a letter came for me..." Mikayla trailed off, thinking of how strange it was a letter came for her that early in the morning, she didn't remember the mail ever coming that early. She shook her head at the thought and focused back on the conversation.

"Anyways, the letter that came for me was from Marcus," Mikayla was quickly interrupted by Rowan, whose eyes were as large as saucers from shock.

"What? Oh my God! Well, what did it say?" Rowan asked, now sitting up even further. It almost looked as if she was about to tip over in her seat.

"That's just it! I didn't even open it and, until now, I practically forgot about it!" Mikayla said, feeling like she had finally realized he was out of her system; something she worried would never be possible.

"You didn't open it? Why?" Rowan asked, wishing she had opened it for her own curiosity.

"I don't know. I held it there in front of me for a moment, just starring at it. Then I realized that there couldn't be more than a page written, which pissed me off. The last letter he wrote said he would contact me soon and tell me why he left the way he did, but Rowan, you know that he never did! So now, four years later, he writes? I mean, was it his explanation? A sorry? I don't know, but I do know that what I went through warranted more than a one-page pity letter four years later. And I just didn't have the energy to open it, it actually really made me mad." Mikayla explained.

"That's crazy! Wow, I guess you really are over him. Even a year ago you would have been tearing through that letter while it was still in Mario's hands." Rowan said as she cupped her face with her hands.

"Yeah, and when I was in the shower I thought about that year; about him and about Dominick, and the whole thing made me sick. I guess I just put it out of my head."

"Well, do you think it has something to do with Caleb?" Rowan had to ask.

"No, I don't. I should hope not. I don't want to be that girl who can only get over someone by having someone new. I think it's getting close to graduation, as well as how lately I have been feeling even more imprisoned than usual. I mean, we are old enough to drink, get married, have children, work, and pay taxes, yet I am still treated like I am in middle school. What the fuck is that about? I am feeling so trapped lately and I am ready to just bust out! I want to feel independent and I want to be independent. I love my family, I even love Dominick, but I am an adult and I want to be treated like one. Not like some dumb, snot-nosed teenager. Marcus and his false promises and feelings were just one more thing making me feel imprisoned. He used to tell me that he would never hurt me the way Dominick had, and yet that's just what he did!" Mikayla's voice was getting louder and louder as she spoke.

"Well, that's good. I mean that you feel like you were over him on your own accord. Don't worry, we only have one more year and then we will prove to everyone that we are responsible, smart, independent, and hardworking young women. I still have never understood the way they are with us, either. Even the younger girls from our friends and family circle don't have it as bad as we do, not by a long shot." Rowan said, starting to get worked up herself.

"I know what you mean. I mean, maybe it's just our families that are so strict. Rowan, you're an only child and I am the only girl out of two children. Dominick has only younger brothers and his attachment seems to be me. Lucio's sisters never get the treatment or restrictions we get, and they are in high school. Come to think of it, Mikey's older sisters never were treated like this, either. Maria even went away to school in New York before she came back to live here. I can't even get my parents to agree to an apartment with you! So weird ,if I didn't know any better I would guess there was something more to it." Mikayla said, thinking about all the strange things amongst their families, and how Rowan and Mikayla seemed to have the most rules and people always looking over their shoulders. It was strange.

"Do you think that they know about the things we can do?" Rowan started to put the pieces together, and began to wonder if their parents reasoning of being protective had something to do with the powers both she and Mikayla possessed.

"I never thought about it…" Mikayla started to trail off, putting together the pieces. "They must. Maybe they saw what we could do when we were kids, and they think that we are freaks and that we are half a step away from the psyche ward. I mean, why us? Really, within our circle of eight families there are how many girls? Seven? All ages ranging from fifteen to twenty eight, and not one of them has it, or had it the way we do. It doesn't add up," Mikayla lightly bit the corner of her lip, lost in thought.

"Well, plus all the extended family we have. I don't remember anyone complaining of the same things that we complain about. It seems as if everyone just laughs it off. I just don't find it amusing anymore." Rowan said, agreeing with the way Mikayla felt.

Rowan felt she wasn't treated quite as unreasonably as Mikayla, but it was close enough for her to be in the same boat.

"See, there are thirteen boys and seven girls. So it seems perfectly reasonable that the boys would naturally feel protective over their sisters, but they don't seem all that protective over the other girls…we should ask our parents about our childhood. We should see if they knew we could do things." Mikayla was trying to figure out a way for them to get some answers.

"We should, but I think we shouldn't come right out and ask if they knew we had special powers when we were younger, just in case they aren't aware. If they didn't know that then, I can only imagine what the rest of our lives would look like once they found that out. We need to be sneaky about the whole thing to get the right answers without outing ourselves," Rowan said, also trying to come up with a plan.

The two sat quietly thinking amongst the loud music and constant flooding of voices draped with the random sounds of people splashing in the water. Suddenly, a different thought popped into Rowan's head, having exhausted herself of finding a plan for the moment.

"Oh, by the way, I have some other gossip..." Rowan said, quickly changing the subject. The counting of the boys and girls of the eight families made her remember what she accidentally found out, and probably shouldn't have a big mouth about, but she couldn't help it. It was Mikayla and the secret was about her mother, anyways.

"Gossip? What gossip?"

"Well, this morning I overheard my mother on the phone. She didn't know that I had come home from Mario's, so she didn't think to keep her phone conversation quiet. All I heard was; "That's wonderful, you really are pregnant. Giving birth to a second child, finally, after all these years, it's a miracle!" At first I thought nothing of it, but then I heard her say; "Teresa don't worry, you had Mario very young, plenty of women are having babies in their late thirties and early forties. Your kind seems to be able to have them even later. I know it's not exactly how you pictured having your children, but how wonderful you get to do it all over again! And finally this will make twenty one." It was a bazaar conversation because she mentioned Mario and not you... I just wonder..." Rowan trailed off.

Mikayla was in shock and took a few minutes of silence. Her mom was pregnant; actually it was a good thing, Mikayla decided. What a wonderful mom she did have. Mikayla loved her very much. She was always so nurturing to her and always wanted to spend time with her, but a second baby she thought, what would that mean?

"I'm going to have a little brother or sister?" Mikayla spit out.

"Looks like it!"

"Wait a minute, why did she say giving birth to a second child?" Mikayla asked, wondering why she said a second child when her mom had both her and Mario, and Rowan's mom only mentioned Mario.

"That's what I thought was so weird… Perhaps your mom is further along than we know and she already has it confirmed that it is a boy. That's the only logical scenario I could come up with," Rowan said, trying to make sense of the conversation. "That, or maybe the fact that you're twins counts as one birth," Rowan quickly found another reason that fit.

"Yeah, I guess that does make sense…" Mikayla now trailed off.

"What is it?"

"I just feel weird that's all. I mean, technically I could be having a child, and my little brother would be an uncle before he was out of diapers! It's just weird. I mean, I am so happy for my mom, but it is just shocking. I am shocked!" Mikayla blurted.

Rowan started to laugh. Mikayla was now shocked by her mother! What a role reversal, Rowan thought.

"What?" Mikayla said confused.

"Well…now you sound like the parent, I am shocked!" Rowan started laughing.

Mikayla started laughing, too. "Well, I am shocked," she said between giggles.

"Well, I think it's pretty cool," Rowan encouraged.

"You know what…me too. I am happy for my mom, she should have had like ten kids. She really is a good mom." Mikayla agreed, complimenting her mother.

Mikayla almost forgot who she was waiting for, all she could think about is what it will be like to have a little brother. It would be the first time a boy in her family wouldn't be able to boss her around, and it would probably be her chance at being a boss for once. Mikayla started shaking her head and smiling at the thought.

"What?" Rowan asked her.

"I am actually getting excited about having a boy around that I can boss! So, this baby better be a boy!" She replied, giggling.

"Yeah, that probably won't happen. He'll be running you in no time!" Rowan laughed.

The conversation helped Mikayla to relax and stop thinking about whether or not Caleb would show. Rowan and Mikayla decided to change gears and take themselves from tanning to getting into the water. As they slipped in, they felt the warmth of the water welcome them in. Despite the busy sandbar, they managed a spot on the outer perimeter so they could save enough room for Caleb's boat if indeed he did show up.

They were splashing around and enjoying the water. Mikayla had brought a Frisbee and they had started tossing it around. As they tossed the disc, Rowan mentioned she had to admit she missed Mario; Mikayla turned her nose up at the comment and splashed Rowan with a small wave before throwing the Frisbee back towards Rowan.

More time had passed and still Caleb had not shown. Mikayla decided to get out and eat her feelings by breaking open a bag of chips and washing it down with a cold can of soda. Rowan joined her. They were busy munching down on their chips and soda and didn't much pay attention to anything else around them, at this point they were just having a girls day out, drying off as they stuffed their faces. Mikayla had written off Caleb, and instead was enjoying the sun's rays and the company of her BFF. All of a sudden, a nerf football soaked in water hit the inside of their speed boat. Mikayla had just stuffed a large amount of chips into her mouth and was startled as she scanned for the owner of the ball.

31

"What's up!"

Mikayla recognized the voice and looked up as crumbs were spread out across her mouth like sand, as her cheeks were puffed out from having shoved in one too many chips. She quickly turned her head to wipe off her mouth and swallow the rest of the chips in her mouth. "Oh my God," she said quietly to Rowan as she finished dusting off the last bit of crumbs.

Rowan only laughed at Mikayla and her embarrassment from having food face.

"Hi!" Rowan replied while Mikayla swallowed.

Mikayla watched as two pontoon boats slowly made their way towards her. It was more people than she had expected. Somehow, in her brain, she imagined it would just be Caleb and maybe his two brothers, but it wasn't just them. She counted the heads and realized there was thirteen people all together, three of them were girls. Feeling a bit overwhelmed, she turned towards Rowan.

"I didn't know he would be with so many people," was all she could think to say, feeling uncomfortable.

"I think it's great, especially for me. Now I have some other girls to talk with!" Rowan said, feeling the opposite of Mikayla. Rowan was relieved. The thought of her having to entertain two strange guys while her boyfriend was unavailable made her a bit nervous, but now there were other girls she decided the day would be much better and she would no longer have to feel guilty. Either way she was determined for Mikayla to move forward with her life.

Mikayla said nothing back, she understood immediately why Rowan was happy about the situation. Still, she felt nervous and shy. She still hadn't looked his way. It was her embarrassment from the other night and the feeling of being put on display as a large group, all focused on her boat. was coming her way. Mikayla didn't like to be the center of attention.

The boats finally came to a stop. One boy from each boat jumped out as the motors were cut to walk the boats in closer. The water was only waist high. She finally got enough nerve to look Caleb's way as she heard the motor cut off. Caleb was no longer at the wheel, his brother Ali was now there instead. Desperately she looked around, trying to spot him, when something in the water caught her eye. It was the color of a tropical sea which captured her attention when she caught his eye and, as it had before, all sound was cut off and she felt her arms tingle as she rubbed them, trying to keep herself from shivering. Yet again she noticed there were goose bumps.

He was guiding in one of the boats. Caleb had no shirt on and, in the daylight, Mikayla could really see his physique. She decided it was even better in the light. Letting out a deep breath, she closed her eyes to center herself. *Stop being a dork...* she thought to herself.

"*Just breathe,*" Rowan thought to Mikayla.

"I am," Mikayla replied out loud.

"No you're not," Rowan commented back. With that, Mikayla let out a long deep breath, the one she had been holding in.

The boys anchored the boats right next to Mikayla and Rowan. They tied the boats together, lining up the gates and making use of both boats. All were back on the pontoon except for Caleb, who was walking through the fresh, warm water towards Mikayla.

"Hey, I told you I would be out here," Caleb called out.

"You are," Mikayla said, knowing she sounded stupid.

"*Awkward!*" Rowan thought as she nudged Mikayla slightly.

"It's nice to see you again, Caleb," Rowan said, trying to break the ice.

Caleb nodded to Rowan. "Nice to see you, too."

"Hey, Mikayla. How's it going?" Caleb said, standing by the side of the boat, placing his arms on top of the boat.

"Good. Um, so who are all your friends?" Mikayla said, making small talk.

Caleb pointed to people, one by one, and told Mikayla their names, except Mary's two friends who he couldn't for the life of him remember. He shouted towards the newer pontoon boat everyone had climbed on. "You guys, this is Mikayla and that's Rowan," he shouted. Everyone waved Hi and quickly went back to opening beers and passing them around. Caleb refocused his attention back to Miakayla.

"How long have you been out here?" He said, now making small talk himself. He could tell she was nervous and he guessed it was because of the other night. His guess was right on.

"A couple of hours, I guess." She said, feeling like a dork because her sentences were short.

Rowan rolled her eyes behind her sunglasses. "Well, Caleb, why don't you climb aboard, we have snacks, beer and soda and you are welcome to help yourself." Rowan stood up from the chair.

"Where are you going?" Mikayla said nervously.

Caleb smiled at her uneasiness, watching her struggle a little around him was almost a turn on due to his predatory nature.

"I am getting in," Rowan said confidently as she climbed down the ladder and into the water.

Caleb didn't use the ladder, instead he opted for the side of the boat, pulling himself aboard with ease just as Rowan made her way out of the boat. Mikayla couldn't help but admire his strength as he pulled himself with ease.

Mikayla knew she was acting nervous, but she couldn't help it. She had resolved he wasn't going to show up and had just relaxed into her day when all of a sudden he just pops up. It wasn't that she was unhappy to see him; it was she was overly excited and filled with the rush of a million different thoughts.

At first they sat silently, making a bit of small talk. Caleb tried to make it easier for her by not looking her way. Instead he looked towards the other boat. Jamahl and Ali were both eyeing Rowan, who was now on a float close to Mikayla's boat.

"Yo, Rowan, right?" Jamahl called from the boat as his arm was tightly placed around Mary's waist.

"That's right! You are?" She called back smiling.

"Jamahl, and this is my...well this is..." Jamahl paused, not really knowing what to call Mary.

"Mary! Sorry, we just started dating so we are in that awkward stage of not knowing what to call each other. Want to come aboard? We have some beer and snacks," Mary said.

Jamahl grinned at Mary. She was so helpful, and never even knew how much. It was easier if it came from a girl. He had a feeling if one of the boys had asked her, she would have quickly declined. His hunch would have been right.

Before she replied, she looked to Mikayla's boat and saw her and Caleb were struggling a little bit. She frowned, knowing it was only because Mikayla had gotten nervous. It was a system overload for her. Rowan climbed aboard the pontoon boat, hoping a little alone time would allow Mikayla to open herself up.

"Do you have any light beers?" Rowan said, flashing her beautiful, warm smile as she reached the deck.

"Of course we do! What self-respecting girl doesn't have a choice of light beer?" Mary said, pleased to have Rowan take her up on the offer.

Rowan made her way to a beer and the other two girls on board as some of the boys jumped into the water to check out the scene. Ali made his way over. He was there for one reason, and one reason only, unlike Jamahl and Caleb who both seemed to have distractions of the female persuasion.

Back on Mikayla's boat, silence fell. Caleb could tell Mikayla was still acting strange. "What's wrong?" Caleb asked.

"Oh nothing, I am fine," Mikayla said back, slapping herself in the face mentally.

"Alright, I think I know what this is about. The other night right? I just want you to know that honestly, that was one of the best nights of my life, and I couldn't wait to see you today." Caleb said honestly.

Mikayla smiled, she felt much better. Her nerves began to fade away. She was surprised all it took was for Caleb to say a few words to put her mind at ease.

"I am sorry that I brought so many people with me," he added.

Mikayla looked at him and smiled. "That's not it," she said, letting him know she wasn't ruffled by all the people, and admitting without verbalizing his first instinct was right. Although his side thought was also correct, she was too ashamed to admit it for fear out of seeming antisocial.

"What is it then?" Caleb asked, starring into her eyes.

Mikayla's heart beat sped up.

"Well, I am glad that you had fun the other night, and I did too…" She trailed off, trying to get up the courage. "Ok, the truth is I had more than fun with you. It was one of the best times I ever had as well." She looked at him to gage the look on his face. "And today, after an hour passed, I thought you weren't coming and I was really disappointed. I thought it had something to do with me, well…me being naked, alone with you, at night while we made out left and right. I was afraid you thought maybe that I was a wild, party girl and I didn't want you to get the wrong impression," she added.

"I loved you naked," Caleb said and smiled towards her.

Her body tingled all over. An ache came over her, as well.

"I feel it too," he said instinctively, knowing how it was she was feeling.

A little embarrassed, she blushed. She wondered if he really could know how she was feeling.

"Nothing to be embarrassed about. I feel it too, maybe even more then you do. All I seem to do these days is think of you and if that was the only time I will ever see you naked, I can live with that as long as I can still see you," Caleb said, saying the exact thing she needed to hear.

She smiled at him and placed her hand over his. Now his body was tingling and aching, yet his canines seemed to be intact.

"When I thought you weren't coming and then you showed up, I was in shock. It was like in an hour's time being really excited to see someone to getting over them. I really thought you weren't coming," she said.

"I am here," he said back, and leaned in to gently kiss her on her forehead.

She felt so nurtured at that moment. No more worried feelings of insecurity about him seeing her naked.

"I am really glad you are," she said and gave him a smile that melted his soul.

The ice was now broken and they went back to talking freely. Their conversation went from one thing to the next. Caleb decided he could never tire of talking with her. Mikayla felt the same way. They joked a bit in between, sharing things about themselves with each other; they were both having a good time just sitting on the boat talking with each other. Truth was, they could have been sitting at a bus stop and had just as much fun as they were having out on the boat. The world around them seemed insignificant as time stopped while they were together.

Back on the pontoon boat, things were getting rowdy. Beers were being cracked open and passed around as laughter filled the boat. Rowan was just finishing her second and having a blast making some new girl friends with Mary and her friends. The boys were joking around as they tossed around the football. Some were out in the water while a few others were still hanging around on the boat as the music blared, competing with the surrounding boats.

Ali knew he had to splash the holy water on Rowan. He had her right where he needed her, but he also couldn't risk chasing her off. She may or may not be the one, and this could be a stupid move, he thought to himself. Despite his doubts, he took the tiny container of holy water and began to empty it into the plastic gun he got at the drug store. With the small water pistol now loaded he reached for a second gun which was much larger and filled it. There was no way he could justify just shooting her, and there was no way there was enough holy water in the smaller pistol to waste on the others. As per usual, Ali had thought about the logistics ahead of time and he couldn't have had it come together any more perfect than if he had scheduled the play by play himself. He tried to get Jamahl's attention, but it seemed as if, for the moment, Jamahl was under the impression they were on vacation and not on a job. Looking around to see who was near, he spotted Carson.

"Carson, come here for a second," Ali said nonchalantly.

Carson, with a half empty beer, made his way towards Ali.

"Aright, let's get the girls in the water to liven up this party. I have two water guns, here, you can have the bigger one. Why don't you go after Mary's friends. I will go after that girl from the other boat. What's up, are you down?" Ali said, trying to seem as juvenile as possible. Even if he weren't on a mission and was on vacation, this kind of partying wasn't his style. He often went along with his brothers, but usually had his nose stuck in a book half of the time while his brothers acted like what he thought was a couple of jackasses. No matter though, he loved his brothers and accepted them for who they were as they did for him.

"Right man! Good idea! Dang this gun is monster!" Carson said, laughing slyly as he admired the super soaker.

Ali decided it was too easy. Never would he be that excited to shoot someone with a water gun, yet here he was, about to do so because they didn't have a better plan. They didn't have all the information. His father hadn't thought the whole thing through. They shouldn't even have come until they knew exactly what it took to reveal the mark of an Angel. Ali had been furiously doing research on Angels and what happens when they give a person life energy, but most of it was hard to understand. He did decipher one thing, the mark would never be duplicated. The mark was significant to the Angel and would appear, somehow, but exactly how was unclear. He wished he could figure out which Angel had jumped in, because then he might be able to find something about angelic symbols that would give them a clue as to what to look for. He found out the marks were given to each Angel as a way for the spirits above to keep track of them on earth.

"So, what's up man? On the count of three?" Ali tried hard to sound like Jamahl would, but had to admit to himself he only ended up sounding awkward.

"Your count!" Carson said, seemingly he hadn't noticed the awkwardness of Ali.

"All right, on three," Ali said. "One…Two…" Ali quietly counted. "Three!" He shouted, and he and Carson unloaded on the girls.

They all got up and started to scream, but they were laughing as they did it. Even Rowan was laughing. She started to feel like a normal college student herself and she was having a blast.

"Stop it you guys!" One of the girls shouted.

"On one condition!" Carson said, holding his fire.

"What?" The now wet blonde stood with her arms folded, but still smiling.

"You guys have to come play some catch with us in the water," Carson said.

"Fine! We will play some catch!" The other girl beside the blonde said pretending to be mad as she tried to salvage her now dampened hair.

Rowan, wet herself, reached for a towel. She felt a couple pair of eyes on her back as she reached down and grabbed a dry towel. Quickly she turned to see who was staring at her. Jamahl and Ali were looking intently at her. She had a creepy feeling. What the hell are they looking at, she thought as she tried to look around her body to see if perhaps something was hanging out. But she didn't find a thing.

"What the hell are you two starring at?" She said, now facing them.

Neither one spoke for a moment, they were busy now scanning the front of her for any mark or change in skin color.

"That's my towel!" Ali said, quickly thinking on his feet.

"No man, I think that is my towel!" Jamahl had to use the same excuse, because he didn't have another one.

Ali couldn't help it, he rolled his eyes.

"Well, it became my towel when you decided to splash me with your tiny little gun!" She said and smiled, letting them know there were no hard feelings.

"So, are you gonna play some catch, too?" Ali asked.

"Sure, why not!" Rowan said, after having looked back at the speed boat to find Mikayla smiling and talking, and Caleb who seemed to be interested in trying hard to impress Mikayla. She liked that, someone trying to impress her friend. Mikayla deserved the best and she wanted a guy for her friend who was willing to put forth the effort. A guy who would actually make an effort to try and impress her best friend.

Jamahl and Ali looked at each other.

"No marks," Jamahl said.

"I didn't see any either, but that might not mean anything," Ali said.

They all jumped in the water and started to play catch, laughing and enjoying the sun while Mikayla and Caleb enjoyed spending time alone.

After a while, Caleb and Mikayla also jumped into the water. They had a rematch on their swimming race and holding their breath under water contest. This time, Caleb wasn't as kind. He didn't let her win at anything. Mikayla was furious she couldn't win, but was having fun despite as the silky waves renewed her childlike spirit. The sun was shining, warming the water that glistened over their skin as both of them felt they were right where they belonged.

The day went on and eventually Caleb and Mikayla joined the rest of the group. Everyone was laughing and having fun as they tossed around the football and made waves, diving in and out of the water to catch the ball. Mikayla was having the time of her life. The exhilaration of meeting new people brought out a part of herself she had lost somewhere along the way. She decided this is what it must feel like to be free and independent. This is how her college years should be, she thought to herself.

The sun was starting to drop from the sky, changing the angle of the sun. Mikayla started to feel a bit cold as a gentle breeze arrived, so she climbed out of the water and into the boat where she wrapped an extra-large, hot pink beach towel donned in tropical flowers of a lighter pink and green leaves around her shoulders. Caleb followed her and dried himself off with a towel similar in style, but a much more masculine color of dark blue with light blue and orange. He then took a seat right next to her and, without even thinking about it, wrapped his arms around her and kissed her on top of her head. She was shaking a bit. This made Caleb agitated at the slight wind which began to pick up. He couldn't help it, he felt so protective over her, but he knew the feeling was stupid. Nonetheless, he tried warming her up as he glared at the wind every time it struck Mikayla's body.

Mikayla thought his arms felt good and she was beginning to warm up. The way he was warming her up felt almost as good as a massage and she let out a slight moan accidently. He then began to knead her muscles to give her a massage. She moaned again with her eyes closed. Trying hard to control himself, he focused on the massage and not on her moaning. Finally he could feel she had stopped shaking.

"Better?" He asked.

"Perfect," she responded, looking at him, hoping he would softly kiss her again.

Caleb responded gently, perfectly. First he gave her a soft peck on the forehead, and then on each cheek. Then he kissed the right side of her neck, just under her ear. She giggled because it had tickled and without being able to control himself, he quickly found her lips and kissed her passionately, as if he had been waiting for that kiss for two days. And he had been.

"Excuse me!" Rowan said, interrupting them as she climbed into the boat. "Sorry guys, but I need a soda and some munchies. Too much sun, beer, and water. I am exhausted," she said, wrapping herself in an orange towel with peach and tan flowers, then she grabbed a bag of chips and a can of soda.

"No problem," Mikayla said, smiling at her friend as she grabbed another bag of chips and two sodas herself, one for her and another for Caleb.

"Did you have fun?" Caleb asked.

"Actually, I did! Your friends are nice and those girls are really cool! Mary, especially, I like." Rowan said through a mouthful of chips.

"Yeah, Mary is pretty cool," Caleb said, honestly.

Rowan grabbed her bag and pulled out her phone. "Shit," she said.

"Shit what?" Mikayla said, almost not needing an answer.

"Mario called me three times, and then left me a text message. It says that they were done early and that they are going to meet us on the water for a couple of hours before they had to leave and were wondering if we were still out," she said reading off the text message.

"How long ago was that?" Mikayla said, sitting upright and leaning towards Rowan as her heart sank into her stomach.

"Shit! That was almost an hour ago, they might be out here any minute. Caleb they are so going to give you a hard time." She said, shutting her phone and looking at the two of them.

"I am not scared of them, if that is what you think," Caleb said, defending himself, but he knew they should be leaving because he didn't want to raise any suspicion, which would make them cancel their trip and make it near impossible to get close to her again.

"Don't leave, they are going to have to get use to you being around sooner or later." Mikayla said matter-of-factly.

"Yeah?" Caleb said, smiling at the thought Mikayla wanted him to stick around for a while. This made him feel even more protective over her.

"Yeah!" She said and smiled.

"Well look you guys, I am all for the two of you, but if you want time to get to know each other uninterrupted so you can decide whether or not the two of you really like each other enough to endure what they are going to dish out, then I suggest that Caleb needs to skidattle." Rowan said, trying to help.

"I hear you," Caleb replied and stood up. "Thanks Rowan, I would like to get to know Mikayla better." He then winked at Mikayla as he stretched his arms over his head.

"Wait, don't I get a say?" Mikayla said, expecting them to both say no, since that was how people usually treated her. But no one said no, instead, they turned to her, waiting for what she was about to say.

"What I have to say is…" she paused, waiting for an interruption but still there wasn't one. "Is that…that's a good idea!" Finally she spit out, knowing what Rowan said was the truth.

"Tomorrow I want to see you," Caleb said and quickly kissed the side of her cheek before jumping into the water.

Mikayla watched as he entered the water. "Wait, we never exchanged phone numbers!" She called to him.

"We'll do that tomorrow!" Caleb called back.

"What do you mean?" Mikayla was now confused.

"Meet me tomorrow at two at the place where we first kissed," he called back.

Mikayla just smiled as she watched him round up his friends and pile them into the boats.

"First kiss, huh? Looks like Kali's been hiding a big fat ole secret!" Rowan said teasingly, but understood Mikayla needed to have some secrets of her own.

Rowan grinned from ear to ear, waiting for the story, as did Mikayla when all of a sudden Rowan saw Mikayla's beautiful, child-like grin turn into a look of disgust. "Tell you about it later, look who's coming on Lucio's boat." Mikayla said, pointing at another speedboat which had all seven of the boys on it.

"Here we go," Rowan replied, watching as Caleb was pulling up the anchor on to the rented pontoon boat.

The boys sped in fast. Dominick was at the front of the boat and Mikayla could tell they had been watching for a while and must of seen Caleb jump off the boat.

"Well, by the look on Dominick's face I'm guessing that he saw Caleb on the boat, he looks pissed," Mikayla said, not taking her eyes off of Dominick.

Caleb had just pulled the anchor up when he looked towards Mikayla and saw her staring intensely out at the boat Dominick was on. It made him angry the way she had to watch herself around him. It made him even angrier at the thought of how protective Dominick was over her. He wanted to get rid of the alpha, because the alpha was in his way. He was worried about Mikayla, he could tell she had feelings for him. It was something he couldn't change, because it was something she would always have from childhood. Her heart was passed him though, he tried to remind himself as h secured the anchor on deck.

Rowan squeezed her eyes tight to see if she could catch the look on Dominick's face. "Yup, he is pissed. He's doing that nostril thingy with his nose," Rowan said still squinting.

Dominick, Mario, and the rest of their friends had finally pulled Lucio's boat up to the sand bar as Carson and Ali had turned on the engines of the two rented pontoons. Jamahl and Jackson were still working on untying the two boats, preventing them from making a quick exit.

"What the fuck are you doing out here?" Dominick shouted to Caleb as he jumped out of the boat before the motor had even shut off. "I thought I told you to stay away from her," Dominick finished as he glanced at Mikayla, whose mouth had dropped open.

"Man, she is not your girlfriend, and besides, we just kinda ran into her today," Caleb said, trying to sound tough and innocent all at once.

"Kinda ran into her today, huh?" Dominick repeated in a tone which suggested he didn't buy it.

"Yeah, I guess you could say that it was fate," Caleb said, knowing this would instigate him and was counting on it. He knew Dominick would blow up, which would only piss off Mikayla more, which would mean her running much faster towards him.

"Look, you little punk, I am not playing with you. Why don't you get off that boat and let me show you how I see your fate," Dominick said, clenching his fists as the water that surrounded him began to slightly vibrate.

"Dominick, stop!" Mikayla said horrified.

Dominick ignored her. "Come on man! Or are you too much of a pussy to get off your rental boat?" Dominick antagonized as the small vibrations in the water continued to move around his large muscular frame.

Caleb realized what this kind of threat actually sounded like and decided perhaps his own attitude should change. "Nope, man. I am good." Caleb said, opening a beer.

"That's what I thought," Dominick said trying to provoke Caleb to come out to the water so he could beat the shit out of him.

"Really?" Mikayla shouted. "Stop it now!" Mikayla shouted, now getting off the boat and swimming towards the pontoon boat to get in between it and the speedboat.

"Get back on the boat Mikayla," Dominick shouted to her.

"She's twenty-one years old, why do you keep telling her what to do? She is perfectly capable of taking care of herself," Caleb said, antagonizing him even more. However, he also wanted to scream at Mikayla to get back into the boat, knowing what was starting to transpire. He didn't want her in between if things exploded. But he refrained from giving her an order. She had enough of being ordered and knew it was also the quickest way for her to cut him off.

Mikayla ignored Dominick's warning and instead stood in the water right in front of Dominick. "Can I talk to you…NOW!" Mikayla said, asserting herself.

Dominick said nothing for a moment, just starring at Caleb while everyone watched on in silence. Both groups knew it was between the two and needed to let them settle it.

Finally he looked down at Mikayla. He couldn't help but take notice she looked so cute in her hot pink bikini with camouflage strings tying it all together. Her skin was glowing from the sun and her hair was damp and long and tousled. She looked like a Tropicana model, he decided. He couldn't really blame any other guy for trying, but something was irritating him about Caleb, but he couldn't put his finger as to why. Mikayla's hands were on her hips and her head was tilted to the side. *I really pissed her off this time*, he thought to himself.

Caleb didn't like the fact Mikayla was about to have another moment with Dominick. The way Dominick looked down at her with love, possession, and a history Caleb would never know started to make his blood boil. He wasn't into sharing, and this to him was sharing. His instinct told him to get in between the two and fight the battle himself, but he kept on reminding himself of the bigger picture. It wasn't the right move for him to make currently, if he had hopes of getting his job done and making Mikayla his. Instead, he motioned to Jackson, who was navigating the other boa,t to go as he made his way towards the other boat as it followed, leaving her alone to deal with him. He's going away tonight, Caleb kept telling himself, trying to calm down the urge to rip out Dominick's throat.

Everyone on the pontoon boats were so dumbfounded by the overgrown muscle bound Dominick's behavior, no one said a word. Well, no one except for Mary.

"That guy is such a jerk; looks like an ex-boyfriend. You handled yourself the best you could with the way he was acting and, trust me, she noticed. This will fall into your favor. Don't let a guy like that make you give up, I see the way you look at her." Mary said quietly, for Caleb's ears only, as he climbed aboard and then smiled at him.

"Oh, I am not giving up Mary. Not by a long shot. I am just letting that guy dig his own grave, until then I am playing it cool." Caleb said back, looking down and giving her a sly smile.

Mary, still looking up at him, winked. Caleb's sly smile turned into a genuine smile. He really did like Mary. Something was different about her, she was really likable for a mere human, and they all felt it. It was only a few short days, but she seemed to fit in perfectly, and his brother seemed to really be into her.

The sun was starting to make its way slowly down as they headed back to the dock. He doubted he would get to interact with Mikayla later on that night, but he would for sure get to see her, even if she couldn't see him. He hoped Ali wouldn't start to harass him about his nightly disappearances, but he knew Ali wasn't stupid and probably already suspected what it was he was doing. Ever since they had been in Michigan, he had been acting strange, and they knew it was because of her, but so far they had kept most of their comments to themselves. Whatever was going to happen would happen, and right now he couldn't help what was happening between him and Mikayla.

"I thought we just cleared the air! But NO! Here we go again!" Mikayla shouted at Dominick with her hands still pressed against her hips.

"We did, but I also told you that we had to talk when I got back. So, the way I see it is, until then I need to look out for your best interest!" Dominick, still pumped up, shouted back.

Everyone else started to roll their eyes and went on about their business, paying no mind to another one of Dominick and Mikayla's fights.

"Dom, I just don't get it at all! Whatever you feel you need to tell me, just tell me so that we can move on!" Mikayla said, realizing the words were a bit hurtful.

Dominick's jaw tightened as he hung his head. He couldn't take more of her rejection. She had no idea there was more behind why he was so protective over her than him wanting to get back together. He did still love her, and the idea of getting back together was definitely on his mind, but slowly he was starting to let go of that. Whether they were together or not, he loved her as family and as a friend, if nothing more ever happened he was settled with that, but he knew with the way he acted she was getting the wrong idea all together. To her he seemed like a jealous boyfriend, but in reality he was given a large responsibility which tied him to her more than love. He was angry at the position he was left in. It was part of what kept him from getting her back, but her safety was his first priority, even over his own wants and needs.

"Mikayla, when I get back we will talk," was all he could manage to say. What he needed to tell her was going to take a whole day. It wasn't going to be a five minute conversation.

"Whatever, fine. I am trying to understand Dominick, I really am, but I hope you can see that this is very confusing to me." Mikayla said, feeling a bit calmer now, and partly guilty for being so harsh just a moment ago.

"I promise you will understand, and thank you for being patient," Dominick replied, letting out a big breath.

Everyone else was now in the water, leaving the two of them alone. Dominick leaned against the boat, silent, and Mikayla made her way over to him and took a place next to him. Her heart was tightening and her eyes started to sting at the way he looked. It was as if they were back in time and seventeen again, before he had changed and cheated on her repeatedly. He was fun-loving and adorably awkward, nothing like he had become. She thought things would be easier if they just got back together, but now she couldn't stop thinking about Caleb, even if it had only been a few days. She didn't know what would happen, but she felt butterflies every time she thought about Caleb. This made her feel even guiltier.

Her head was so clouded, she didn't know what to think. She just wished someone else would come along and steal his heart, it was the only fair thing. It would hurt for a while, but the right girl and her could get along, and then everyone would feel whole. Mikayla was convinced she wasn't Dominick's true love, she knew him well and felt even at a young age if his true love came along, wild horses couldn't even drag him away with how loyal she had seen him be to everyone else except for her. It was one of the things which always played in the back of her mind when she would think about giving their relationship another chance. Perhaps she was living in a fairy tale world, but it was her world and she still believed in true love, even if she knew it hurt a lot trying to find it.

Mikayla was still staring at Dominick as he looked out on the water. He could feel her eyes on him, so he turned to meet them with his own. She smiled and grabbed for his hand. He smiled back and squeezed her hand gently. The touch sent tingles through her hand and into her chest. She could cry right there, but the comfort of him made her feel stronger. No one could make her feel as angry as he could, but no one could comfort her the way he could, either.

32

Mikayla and Rowan had slept at the lake house. They saw the boys off after a quick barbeque and a long make out session for Mario and Rowan. It was late and they were tired. Mikayla was making Rowan's favorite kind of pancakes, blueberry, while she was still asleep. Once they were finally ready, she put everything together on a tray to bring her best friend breakfast in bed. As she approached the room, she heard sneezing.

"Rowan, wake up. I made you your favorite!" Mikayla said cheerfully, entering the room.

Rowan was laying down, but her eyes were open and she was blowing her nose into a tissue. She took a big sniffle. "I think I have a cold," Rowan said, sounding plugged up.

"Oh no! You don't look so good," Mikayla said, realizing Rowan looked a little pale. "Why don't you eat your pancakes and I will take you home," she finished.

Rowan sat up, taking hold of the tray. "Thanks for the pancakes." She forced a smile and started to eat.

Mikayla headed back down to the kitchen and grabbed a plate for herself but decided to eat in the kitchen so she could clean as she ate and Rowan could get home sooner.

She finished cleaning the rest of the house while Rowan stayed in bed and only woke her when it was time to take her home. Rowan was looking even worse, which only made Mikayla drive faster. She hated to see her friend feeling awful, and somehow felt the faster she could get her home the faster she would heel. Rowan felt worse as the minutes dragged on.

After Rowan was dropped off, Mikayla headed for home herself. She was in need of a shower and a cold can of soda. It was already one and she was supposed to meet Caleb in an hour. The thought swallowed her breath as she finally pulled into her driveway. She hurried inside to get ready.

Mikayla took notice it was sunny and warm again. Flowers were blooming, releasing fresh floral scents which filled the air as she made her way through the park. It was a couple of miles, but she decided to walk rather than take her car. Anytime she could walk, she did. The air was a little sticky, so she was glad she chose to wear her light blue sundress and flip flops. The park was busy with people biking, walking, and playing sports, as well as children's laughter coming from the playground. All the action was comforting and signified summer was truly here, even if the pools weren't open yet.

She finally made it to the parking lot to find Caleb waiting there for her with a flower in his hand. This made her a bit uncomfortable, she wasn't the flower type, but somehow she liked he had one for her. It was a single white flower.

"This is for you," he said, handing her the flower.

She wasn't sure what to say. "Thanks," she said, feeling a little stupid taking it.

"You don't like flowers?" Caleb observed, but didn't feel insecure at all, only curious. Mikayla took notice he wasn't ruffled at all by her lack of enthusiasm.

"No, no. I do like flowers, I just feel weird about getting them," she said, accidentally opening her big mouth.

Caleb reached for the flower and grabbed it out of her hand and ran to the playground where a little blonde girl was playing. Mikayla was in shock and started to giggle as he made his way to the playground.

He reached the playground and headed to a little girl with blonde pig tails wearing a pink short-sleeve shirt and a pair of short overalls and handed her the flower. She looked up and smiled at him as her mother looked on in amusement. Mikayla started to laugh at the whole thing.

"Alright, let's start again," Caleb shouted as he ran, returning from the playground.

"Well this sucks, now I have no flower!" Mikayla teased.

Caleb turned towards the forest and, without saying a word to her, ran towards it, stopping at a patch of white flowers next to the entrance of the path. He quickly bent down and picked another flower that looked identical to the one he had previously given her. She threw her head back with laughter.

Once he had the flower in hand, he made his way back towards Mikayla with a serious look on his face. She grinned from ear to ear.

"This is for you!" He said, handing her another flower.

This time Mikayla wasn't uncomfortable. She took hold of it and knew exactly what to say. "Thank you!" She said still smiling.

"You're welcome!" He said, and finally broke a smile.

Mikayla started to giggle again, which made Caleb start to laugh. He thought she looked so cute, as she was giggling he held his laughter in for a moment, long enough to bend his head down and kiss her softly on her forehead.

"So, what are we doing today?" Mikayla said as he pulled away from kissing her.

"We are going on a ride!" He said, and grinned a grin Mikayla thought looked like a mischievous grin. "Probably not the best choice of outfits, though." He added, looking her up and down in a way which was anything but innocent, the thought made Mikayla swallow out of nervousness.

Mikayla was offended for a moment, feeling as if he had just slapped her across the face, and her smile faded as she tried to decide if what he had just said was an insult.

He grinned. "Not what you think. You look beautiful. But the ride I am taking you on, wearing a dress… isn't the best pick." He said, leaning in towards her neck and taking in a deep breath to smell the fresh soap and lotion on her skin. He then backed away, but still remained close.

Her knees started to shake as goose bumps caressed her from head to toe. She swallowed with even more nervousness, not understanding what he was talking about.

"What do you mean?" She said after she had caught her breath and began looking around the parking lot when she noticed his jeep wasn't there. "Wait, where is your car?" She then asked, starting to put two and two together as she fixed her eyes on a crotch rocket motorcycle in black and gunmetal, highlighted with chrome.

Caleb noticed she finally figured it out. "Yup," he said, smiling at her while answering the question she was about to ask but hadn't yet.

Mikayla felt excited and thrilled. *Another step towards freedom*, she thought to herself as she made her way over towards the bike as Caleb followed. This was definitely different than riding with Dominick, who would have chosen the biggest SUV, dark and tricked out. Caleb's choice was sleek and fast, Dominick's choice was big and flashy. Right now the only thing she wanted was sleek and fast. She thought it was funny how the choice of car fit both of their personalities.

"Can you handle it?" He said, lifting up an eyebrow.

"Can you handle me?" She said, climbing on the back without waiting for him.

He laughed as he grabbed a helmet and handed it to her. She quickly put it on as if she couldn't wait. He loved the fact she didn't complain about the dress, instead she climbed on ready to go.

Caleb climbed on the bike. "Hold on tight and don't let go," he said before putting on his helmet.

"I wasn't planning on it!" Mikayla joked, which made Caleb laugh.

The bike was loud, but the vibrations felt like smooth waves underneath her body. She felt like this was going to be a better ride than any roller coaster ride she had ever been on. The wind felt good against her warm, sticky skin and she was grateful then the helmet was shielding the damage it could do against her hair.

Caleb had followed the speed limits until he got to the back roads. Then he floored it. Mikayla felt a little bit scared, but at the same time thrived in the excitement of it all. Again she was with him and somehow it made her feel safe as she relaxed and let herself enjoy the ride as they cut through the wind. The back roads weren't very busy with cars but were over grown with trees full and green, creating a feeling of privacy, as if her and Caleb owned this road and all the trees. One by one they passed each tree as Mikayla watched them all start to distort beautifully into a blur of soft green in various shades as they flew by.

Mikayla didn't know where they were going and she didn't care, she just held on tight. Caleb loved the way her arms felt wrapped so tightly around his waist. Her touch was unlike any he had ever felt. He had plenty of girls to fulfill pleasure and blood, but never had he had these types of feelings where just the touch of someone holding on behind him made him feel protective, excited, and whole. This girl was going to be the end of him, he remembered the seer saying, and now he understood. He would forever be different because she made him different. This was definitely the girl who could ruin him as he was, and he could already see it happening, but somehow it didn't seem like such a bad thing. Caleb chose not to fight it, as if he actually thought he had a choice in doing so.

They drove for an hour before stopping at some pub overlooking a beautiful lake lined heavily with trees. It wasn't on the same chain of lakes Mikayla's lake house was on; it was a different lake about thirty minutes away. Her lake was towards the north and just slightly west of her house, this lake was much farther west and slightly south of her house. Caleb turned into the parking lot.

"Hungry?" He said after taking off his helmet. Mikayla thought he looked even sexier than he had before he put the helmet on. Now his already short hair was tousled from the helmet, she thought it made him look mysterious and dangerous.

"I am," she said after taking off hers.

Caleb couldn't help himself, he leaned in without permission and grabbed her face gently and began to kiss her. As if he had deflated a balloon, she let out a long slow breath as she kissed him back and he felt her legs tremble. That sent him into a frenzy and he was glad they were in a public parking lot because if they hadn't been, he didn't know if he would have been able to control himself.

He pulled away, knowing he needed to get a hold of himself. Then he grabbed her hand as they walked into the restaurant.

It was an old wooden building, probably a lake house back in the day before someone had turned it into a pub. They took a seat outside by the water. Caleb ordered a beer and, after a brief pause, contemplating whether or not to partake, Mikayla decided to order one too.

By the time the food came Mikayla had already finished two beers as Caleb sipped on his third. She felt a little tipsy, which made her lose her manners as she dug into her barbeque, eating much faster and losing some of her poise. Caleb laughed at how uninhibited she was. She was stuffing her face and she looked cute doing so.

"Sorry, I am so hungry and this tastes so good!" She said with a bit of food still in her mouth.

"You're so cute," was all he could manage to say.

She smiled and kept on eating, truly enjoying herself. The deck they were eating out on overlooked the water and nature and, even though it was remote, there were tons of things to look at. As Mikayla stuffed her face, she enjoyed looking all around at the beauty of it all. Caleb ate slower, paying more attention to her than his food, and zero attention to the nature that surrounded them.

They finished eating, but decided to stay for a while because they were lost in conversation with one another. The more they talked, the more interested they became in each other. The conversation flowed with ease and it seemed as if they would never run out of things to talk about. Mikayla felt free and Caleb felt normal, a first for each of them.

Time had flown by so fast, but before they knew it, it was already six o'clock, so they finally cashed out. Mikayla still had a little bit of a buzz, but Caleb had none, it would take more than a few beers to affect his senses.

"Thank you for dinner!" She said, walking towards the bike. "I really had a good time," she added, as if it were the end of the night

"Do you have plans tonight?" He said, picking up on the fact it sounded like she was saying good night.

"No..." she said, hoping he wasn't ready to take her home yet.

"Good," he said, handing her the helmet.

She grabbed it and put it on as he lifted her on the bike.

He didn't go out the way he came into the restaurant. Instead he headed even further west, following the lake until he spotted a hard to see parking lot blocked with heavy trees on either side and poorly marked. He decided it would be a good place to take a walk and pulled in.

They got off the bike for the second time. The parking lot was empty; it seemed as if they had the place all too themselves. Caleb gently led the way as they took a walk and picked the conversation back up. Again it flowed so freely. He reached for her hand as she was saying something about an art project she was working on. As their hands touched, they both felt electricity jolt through them. They both felt so drawn to each other.

They came across a man-made path in the woods and decided to track it through to the water. As they approached the water, they noticed it was remote. Blocked off by trees and a bend in the river, it seemed like a perfect secret spot. The water was clean and ran over smooth and silky firm sand. They dangled their feet in the water as they looked out onto the water and talked.

A couple more hours passed and the sun decided to make it's exit. They quietly watched the sun set as Caleb held her close to him. He smelled so good, she thought to herself. Caleb thought the same thing about her as he held her, occasionally kissing the top of her head.

The sounds of night quickly surrounded them as the last of the sunlight left and the full moon made its way up into the sky, giving them more than enough light to see each other. The air was still, warm, and sticky.

Caleb got up and took off his shirt, putting it by their shoes. He then took off his shorts and placed them on top of his shirt.

Mikayla, still sitting on the ground, watched in silence as he stripped down to his boxers. "What are you doing?" She said.

"Swimming, you coming?" He said, stepping into the water.

Mikayla thought about it for a moment, but didn't answer. Instead she stood up and took off her sundress. She didn't have on a bra, the sun dress was tight enough against her skin she didn't need one. There she stood in a pair of light blue cotton boy shorts, cut high on the butt and lined with dark blue. Caleb was glad he was wearing shorts to hide his obvious excitement from her. She stood in front of him, still on the bank. This time she wasn't feeling self-conscious. This time she felt in control of herself, she felt free and truly happy. She was making her decisions, not others doing it for her, and right now she decided to go swimming topless.

After standing in front of him, allowing him to look at her topless, she slowly made her way into the water and right into his arms. He grabbed hold of her and began to kiss her as they each stood waste high in the water. Her breasts squished against his chest and Caleb lost control. He moved up her waist with his hand and found himself just underneath her breasts.

Mikayla sighed in pleasure, which made him gently rub over her breasts with his hand as if he were just testing out the waters. Never had he been so careful before. As he found her nipple he stood there, just kissing her for a moment and felt her skin turn into goose bumps. He took that as a good sign and started to kiss and lick her neck. Not once did he want to bite her as he made his way down towards her chest, but before he tasted he looked up for permission. Mikayla's head was tilted back slightly, but her eyes were slightly open and watching him. Caleb was now turned on even more and took her nipple into his mouth. Mikayla groaned slightly, sending chills throughout Caleb's whole body.

As if the wanting to be fair, he made his way towards the other one to give it equal time before making his way back up towards the other side of her neck, which he felt was equally as lonely.

She grabbed his face and started kissing him passionately before kissing the side of his neck and making her way down towards his chest, giving back to him what he had just given her, and then made her way back up the other side of his neck.

They started kissing again before he turned her around and started kissing the back of her neck and then the upper part of her back. Every nerve in her body tingled with pleasure. He slowly led her to the bank and laid half of her body face down on the bank as he began to massage her back. She didn't know whether to give herself to him right there, relax and enjoy the massage, or tell him to stop. He threw in a few soft kisses slowly around her neck, traveling down her back as he lightly brushed over her skin, causing the smooth texture to fill in with tiny little goosebumps as the tiny blonde hairs on her arms stood up.

His hands were getting lower and lower. Finally she gulped as his hands got to her underwear. Slowly he grabbed hold of them and pulled them halfway down very slowly, then suddenly stopped, waiting for her to tell him no.

She didn't. Mikayla thought about it for a moment as her heartbeat began to speed up even further. Caleb smiled wickedly at the racing of her heart and, since he hadn't heard her object, he began to gently massage with soft, feathery strokes the lowest part of her back and the top of her glutes. She gulped again and then moaned as he began to trace his tongue along her spin.

Caleb's instincts kicked in at the pure and helpless sound of her moan. For an instant, he lost hold of his composure and grabbed hold of her underwear, yanking them down around her ankles and over her feet, then he threw them on the bank by their clothing. Mikayla felt scared for a moment before the feeling of pleasure set in and a sudden trust for him overwhelmed her as she laid there naked, face down in front of him.

He moved himself back up towards her ear as his chest pressed firmly against her back, while he moved his hands along the sides of her breasts pressed into the sand on the bank. Lightly he sampled the firmness of the sides of her breasts, exploring what he wanted to be his. Then he moved his hands back down towards her thighs and started to gently massage her whole butt and back of her upper thighs.

She moaned a little bit louder. He took it as a good sign and started to gently massage the front of her thighs, getting closer and closer with each fluid stroke to her private place. The lower half of her body was submerged in water, and finally his hand was close enough and he finally touched her, gently and softly. Her eyes shot open as she threw her head back with pleasure. Again he took it as a good sign. He began to massage gently, on the exact right spot, first making slow soft circles as his other hand continued to massage different parts of her body with a fluidity that made Mikayla both nervous, recognizing he was truly experienced, and excited, with a lack of control because of the intensity of pleasure radiating throughout her body. The slow, soft circles gradually got faster and faster as the heat throughout Mikayla's whole body started to rise as her muscle's began to tense. Mikayla moaned with pleasure as he watched. Her hips began to slightly move in rhythm with the growing intensity.

Her breathing started to become deeper and Caleb knew she was about to explode as he kept a steady pace watching. All of a sudden, Mikayla moaned even louder as her hips moved a bit faster before suddenly stopping as all of her muscles tightened and held briefly, steadily, before letting go. He could feel the contractions, warm and wet, on the palm of his hand and he just stood still, not moving his hand until he felt the contractions had ended.

After a few moments of stillness she turned around and climbed a little more out of the water and so she was sitting on the bank. As if she were out of breath underwater, just inches away from the surface were she could find air, she grabbed for Caleb. She leaned in to start kissing him without thought of anything but him and wrapped her legs around his waist. Time had stopped, reason had stopped, and all of her usual self-control had fled as she tugged at his pants. He felt helpless against her, consumed by how much he wanted her, and slipped them off the rest of the way.

There they were, both naked, starring into each other's eyes in silence. Not a sound was heard by either one of them but the hard, steady breathing of the other as if they were in synchronicity with the other. Caleb was holding himself up with her wrapped tightly around him and began to move the both of them up out of the water and onto the bank. Gently he laid her down as he kept his eyes connected to hers. Neither of them blinked as she lay beneath him.

"I've never felt like this before," Caleb said, surprised by his honesty. The sentence came out without him having even a split second to think about it. It was pure.

"I feel so connected to you, it's crazy. I just meet you but somehow I feel like this is meant to be," Mikayla said without even worrying about how it sounded, or the possible repercussions of saying something like that to a guy she had just met.

They started to kiss again with nothing between them. Caleb slowly kissed her face, taking his time to study every detail of her beautiful features. With every peck Mikayla felt a warmth rush over her. Then he moved just as slowly and kissed every inch of her body. He liked knowing she was feeling pleasure. She tilted her head back as her body tensed again while Caleb made his way back up to her mouth.

Again they starred at each other in silence as Caleb tried to decipher if he should take it any further. Every inch of his body was saying yes, but his soul was throwing up caution signs which were getting harder and harder to read.

"It's ok, I want you to," Mikayla said in a timid voice, as if she had read his mind and his breath was taken away. He was caught between her timid answer, which brought forth the predator in him, and the fact this beautiful woman was giving him permission and he knew it would mean something to her as much as it would to him.

He bent down to kiss her gently, again looking into her eyes to make sure she was all right. She seemed to be fine, but there was something innocent behind her eyes and she was lightly shivering. It was almost as if she was scared. He knew he needed to be careful with her.

Caleb moved his hand down to find she was still wet. He ached to be inside and carefully moved her legs a little further apart. Once again he looked at her face, he was about to enter her and he wanted to make sure she was still ok. She looked up at him with complete trust and anticipation. Caleb took it as the final go ahead as his heart melted at the trust she was giving him.

He slowly slipped partly inside of her as he watched her moan. He couldn't be sure, but he thought this moan sounded different, as if she were slightly in pain. Even slower he entered her further, only to come across something blocking his path and a bell rang in his head.

"You've never actually done this before?" He asked, almost shocked she hadn't yet done it, and half shocked a girl like this would allow someone like him to take her virginity from her.

"I was waiting," was all she said, a bit embarrassed.

Caleb didn't move any further.

"Are you sure you want to?" He said, looking down at her and questioning his own actions.

"I'm sure," she said trembling, which told Caleb a different story.

After thinking about it for a moment, Caleb couldn't seem to move. "Mikayla, we should wait," Caleb said, looking down at her and, for once in his life, actually caring for someone besides himself and his brothers.

"We should? For what?" Mikayla asked, confused by his wanting to wait. Maybe he no longer found her interesting now he knew she really wasn't that kind of girl, she thought, waiting to see what his answer was and hoping with everything in her heart she was wrong.

"For a bed, for one thing, and for a special occasion," Caleb paused and looked deeper into her eyes. Mikayla swallowed hard, as if instinct told her he was about to say something else. "Mostly, I want to wait for you to tell me that you love me," Caleb said, still a quarter of the way inside of her, not moving an inch.

"I don't need a bed," Mikayla started quietly. "This to me is a special occasion. I am free for the first time in my life." She, too, paused at the subject of love, wondering what he would say to her question back to him. "And… why not wait until you tell me that you love me?" She said back, still wanting to give herself to him in that moment, and partially grateful she didn't have to go through with it yet.

"This is crazy," he said so quietly she could barely hear him.

"What's crazy?" She asked just as quietly back, not knowing what he meant.

I do…I don't know how I even know it…but I know…I love you, he said honestly, only to himself, and shocked by the fact it almost came out of his mouth. Never had he told someone that. This was the first time he felt it and he knew the moment he saw her he was in love with her. The theory of love at first sight had now proven itself to exist.

Caleb controlled himself not to blurt out those three little words. He suddenly chose his words carefully. "We have something special, something unique, and I will only do this when and if you tell me that you love me." Caleb said standing his ground, still not quite believing what was coming out of his mouth.

She starred up at him and felt just how strong their connection was. It was as if they were meant to be. *Could I really be in love with him? It's too soon…isn't it?* She thought to herself.

More than anything she wanted to be one with him, but she couldn't manage to say the words. She wasn't convinced the love she felt for him could be true. Less than a week couldn't possibly be enough time to tell, she decided, although she felt it throughout her whole heart. So she simply accepted his rule.

"Ok," She finally managed and flashed him a smile of youth and innocence.

In that moment, despite his own wants, he was glad she agreed. As the moments passed it was getting harder for him to remain in control, and if she had refused, it would have been really easy for him to lose control and go through with it.

He still hadn't let go, instead he was a quarter of the way inside of her and bent forward to kiss her gently. She could feel his feelings for her were strong and it felt good. He made her feel free and like her choices were her own, which only made her feel closer to him. She also noticed he had actually put her before himself. The trust grew tenfold in that brief moment.

A few minutes of gentle loving kisses passed before he backed off her gently, as if he didn't want to hurt any part of her. He stood in front of her, smiled down at her, and gave his hand to help her up.

Her skin was cold, and as if he had done so a thousand times before, he started to rub her arms with his hands to warm her up. She felt truly cared for by someone who actually treated her like she was an adult. It was a given]having the boys leave would allow her a certain amount of freedom, but she had no idea what she was in store for and right now she was ready to experience everything.

The words started to swirl around in her mind about him only wanting to make love when she told him she loved him. She started to think it seemed a bit unbalanced, unless he already loved her. Again she asked herself if that was even possible. He hadn't said it, but his touch had made her feel loved.

"What about you?" She said as she grabbed her dress and shook off the loose sand.

Caleb knew what she was referring to, but decided to play dumb, not wanting to admit to her how he felt because it seemed too soon and because he didn't quite believe it himself yet, although he knew it was the truth.

"What about me?" He said, pulling his shorts on.

"Well, you say you want to wait until I tell you that I love you… So, what about you? Shouldn't we wait until you tell me that you love me, too?" She said, slightly hesitating out of fear of what he might say and what he might not.

Caleb seemed to be lost in thought for a moment as he pulled on his shirt. Mikayla stood waiting for him to answer.

"Caleb, did you hear what I asked?" She said feeling like he was trying to dodge the issue and she was not about to let him. Too many people seemed to dodge her questions and dismiss her and she was no longer putting up with any of it, no matter what the cost.

Caleb stood facing away from her, now dressed. His head was bent down and his hands were on his hips. She couldn't help but think how handsome he looked, even underneath the moon's dim light. Finally he turned towards her.

"Mikayla…look I…I mean…you are right, we should wait," he said, wanting to tell her but feeling out of his element he couldn't seem to make the words come out.

Mikayla lifted one eyebrow, she didn't believe what he was saying. It was more than a hunch, she knew he wasn't telling her everything and she suspected at that moment more was going on than even she knew. She started to think pushing him wasn't fair, since she was also holding back.

"So, alright then, where do we go from here?" She said, feeling slightly stupid sounding needy.

"We keep seeing each other," he said as he grabbed her and pulled her in close.

"I like that idea!" She said, sounding light hearted as she smiled up at him, glad everything seemed to be alright between the two of them.

He bent down and started to kiss her again. This time the kiss was even deeper and more connective than the previous kisses. Both of them longed to be with the other. Someone had to pull away before they started all over again, having forgotten the talk they had just had.

"Mikayla…" Caleb whispered as he pulled away.

"Yeah…" Mikayla whispered back.

"I…" he began, but trailed off as she came in for another kiss.

There they stood, kissing lovingly as moments passed by, only interrupted by a few cold rain drops forming in the sky. Mikayla looked up into the sky and noticed the full moon was now covered up by a blanket of clouds which had quickly moved in. She wrinkled her nose, knowing the sky was getting ready to open up and pour down on them.

"Come on, we gotta go! It's about to pour…" she said, trailing off as she realized they came on the motorcycle and not the car. "Shit!" She added.

Caleb threw his head back and started to laugh. Not being able to do anything about the rain, Mikayla started to laugh along with him. He grabbed her hand and they quickly made it back towards the bike, running and laughing carelessly at the wet drops as the rain started to pick up. Despite the increase in rain drops, they laughed harder, trying to dodge as many as they could.

33

The ride back was long and wet, but neither of them cared too much they were getting hammered by the rain. They were much to content with being close on the bike; Caleb in control as Mikayla held tightly onto him. His body felt tight and strong in her arms, and the feeling of her arms wrapped around his waist made him feel like he had a new purpose for existing.

They finally reached the city limits when Caleb took a left turn where he should have taken a right turn. They were still on the bike, so she couldn't ask him where they were going. He made his way down a few different streets before pulling into some condominiums. A garage door to one of the condos opened as Caleb continued to pull into the empty space.

She hopped off the bike and realized he had taken her to his house. Without saying a word he lead her into the dark house. He didn't bother turning on any lights, instead he lead her into his bedroom.

The room was still dark, she could barely see him. He flicked on a very dim lamp which only slightly helped her to see. From what she could tell the room was sparse, as if he hadn't lived there very long at all. There was only a large bed with one night stand the dim lamp sat on top of. The only other thing on top of the night stand was an mp3 docking station. There wasn't any alarm clock or books of any sort. There wasn't anything else in the room. Mikayla thought it was strange but didn't judge him for it. Despite it being sparse it was clean and the bed was neatly made.

Without saying a word, he offered her a seat on the bed. "I will be right back," he said and turned out of his room for a short moment before returning with a couple of large towels. "Here you can dry off with this and I can put your dress into the dryer so it's dry when you get home." He said, handing her the towels.

She hadn't even thought about being wet, but now he had handed her the towel she realized she wasn't just wet, she was cold. She wrapped one towel around her body and the other around her arms. Only the ends of her hair were wet, the helmet had kept the majority of her hair dry, and right now she was freezing.

Caleb grabbed her dress and took it into the laundry room and stuck it into the dryer. He knew his brothers were going to kill him. He was supposed to bring Rowan to Jackson's party, but it was late and he couldn't bring himself to break away from Mikayla yet. He hadn't even done what he was supposed to do during the day and set things up for them to go to the party.

Ali felt it was a long shot, but they were hoping to try and get Rowan to drink the holy water and see if anything would happen from that. Caleb was too preoccupied with Mikayla, right now he could care less what his father wanted or needed. The only thing he cared about was Mikayla. Normally Caleb would have been irritated being sent to do a job with no real way of deciphering what it was they were looking for, but right now he was glad. The more time it took to figure out how to show the markings of a soul living off the breath of an Angel, the more time he would have to spend with her. He needed as much time as he could get.

He came back into the bedroom to find Mikayla asleep, laying on top of his bed wrapped in towels. She was still shivering a bit from the cold rain and wind from riding on the back of the bike.

Caleb stood over her for a moment and watched her breath. He never had seen a more beautiful woman in his life. She was cute, sexy, funny, and smart, and a lot tougher than she even knew she was. He bent down to pick her up and held her as he pulled back the covers. Then he removed the towels as she lay passed out in his bed. Not caring about the towels at the moment, he threw them on the floor and climbed in bed next to her. He pulled her in close as he wrapped his arms tightly around her. She nestled right into him; he couldn't deny she was his perfect fit.

Just like that they had fallen asleep in Caleb's bed, neither caring where they were supposed to be, only feeling like they were where they were meant to be.

Caleb had no idea how much time had passed when he was woken by a hand gently shaking him. His instinct took over and he grabbed the hand and twisted as he looked up to find his brother, Ali, standing over him. Ali made a hush motion with his index finger over his mouth and then nodded towards the door.

There was no clock in his room, so he couldn't tell exactly what time it was, but he knew it must be late. He quickly checked Mikayla to find her still sound asleep. He checked her skin to find it was now warm. Bending forward he smelled the back of her hair which still smelled like it had just been washed, and then he kissed her softly before quietly getting out of bed.

He made it to the door when Ali grabbed the door handle behind him to close his bedroom door shut as to not wake up Mikayla. Caleb already knew this wasn't going to be good.

"What the hell are you doing?" Ali asked through his teeth, pointing his finger towards Caleb's bedroom.

"I can't help it," Caleb felt was all he could say. He knew he had messed up big time, but somehow he just didn't care.

"Where is Rowan?" Ali asked getting down to the point.

"I don't know."

"What do you mean, Caleb? Were you ever with her today or not?"

"No."

"What do you mean no, you were supposed to convince them to come over to Jackson's house but you never showed. I know I said that it was a long shot, but that didn't mean that you had a choice of whether or not you wanted to show up. Remember why we are here in the first place. This girl has got you screwed up in your head," Ali scolded.

"You don't understand!" Caleb shouted.

"What, Caleb. Tell me what I don't understand? That while we are here on what is supposed to be a mission, you and Jamahl are gallivanting around town pretending to fall in love as a young college grad? What the fuck is going on?" Ali matched Caleb in volume.

"That's just it! I am not pretending!" Caleb shouted, surprised by what he had just let slip out of his mouth.

"Tell me you signed up for classes and that you are no longer pretending to be a college student because you actually are one now. Tell me that is what you are not pretending, please!" Ali said shaking his head.

Caleb could tell his brother was struggling with what he had just let slip out of his mouth. Feeling defeated, as if his football team had just lost the championship game, Caleb crouched to the floor and put his head into his hands.

"Nope, I am definitely not enrolled anywhere," Caleb said without looking up for fear of the look on his brother's face.

"You aren't serious…" Ali tried one more time to snap him out of it.

"Like I said, you don't understand. I don't even understand it. I have never loved anyone, well besides you and Jamahl, and neither of you are quite my type. It's as if she were made specifically for me. This is the girl the seer said I would be drawn to. I wasn't drawn to Rowan, I was drawn to her." Caleb said, feeling a little relieved he was able to get that out.

"Shit…" Ali said as he threw his head up to the ceiling before looking down again. "What's your plan?" He then asked, wondering just how much thought Caleb had actually put into it.

"I am hoping to have enough time with her to convince her to come with me, I mean us." Caleb said irrationally.

"What the hell are you going to say? I am an evil vampire/witch raised by a super demon vampire and I am here to see if your best friend has the soul of an angel so that my father can use her for the advantage of evil! He will use her powers and then probably dispose of her after he has extracted all that he needs, but hey, until then you can still visit with her between her bleedings!" Ali said sarcastically, trying to show Caleb how ridiculous his plan sounded.

"Fuck…" Caleb said hopelessly. "What am I supposed to do? I can't be without her. Maybe I will just leave the coven and live my life with her," Caleb said, trying to make it sound simple.

Ali could see his brother was in pain, which only made him feel pain. The three of them were all each other ever had. None of them trusted their so called father much, he was pure evil, and while he favored the three of them, he never gave them love or support, so they had given it to each other.

Letting out a large sigh, Ali put a hand on Caleb's shoulder as he bent down. "Alright, I don't think this is a good idea, but if you really can't be away from her we will figure something out, but until then we have to complete our mission. If we don't and Cyrus knew what you were doing it wouldn't be a question of how you were going to be able to be with her because she would already be dead. You hear me?" Ali asked, lending him hope and support.

"Thanks," Caleb said, glad his brother seemed to have come around fast. He was happy to know even in this strange, new, vulnerable place his brother still had his back.

He wondered at that moment why they worked for evil. Thinking about it more, he realized it was Cyrus they worked for and not necessarily evil. Away from him they all had tendencies to do good things, which was opposite of what Cyrus had taught them from such young ages. Instead he taught them about their powers and how to use them. He also instilled in them they were higher on the food chain than humans, and they should be looked upon as mere food and pleasure sources. Cyrus felt humans should be wood animals, they're only to feed the needs of vampires. Once he told them his ultimate dream was to have a large farm where he kept humans for food, work, and pleasure. He told them one day he would make it happen, turning his land into a hunting ground for human gaming and slave trading.

Despite all of the propaganda Cyrus spread, they still had natural tendencies towards goodness, which was noticed heavily by only those who were close to them. They got away with most of it by telling people it was all part of the master plan. No one questioned them as long as they got whatever job they were given done, although from time to time they did raise a few eyebrows. That is what Cyrus counted on, he knew the good part of them is what made them so loyal to him. Caleb's head was spinning, like he was on a fast looping rollercoaster. He didn't know what was going to happen, and for the first time felt a bit of insecurity from the unsureness of it all.

"Where is the big guy at?" Caleb said, just now really noticing Jamahl was nowhere around.

"He's another one!" Ali chuckled.

"Mary?"

"Mary," Ali confirmed. "What is it with Michigan, it's like the love state, and here I thought it was supposed to be the glove state," Ali joked as he stood up.

"Well, I guess that means you are next then, huh?" Caleb joked back.

"Right," Ali said as he rolled his eyes.

"Despite the fact that you didn't do your job tonight, I still did mine, and I think I found some things out." Ali said, walking into his bedroom and over to the desk which held a laptop and a couple of the old books he had on the boat. Caleb noticed the books where even older than he thought. They were more brownish in color than he remembered, and the pages looked worn and smelled of dust and mildew. Not all the writing was legible, leaving way too much room for interpretation, Caleb thought. Ali had done a lot of work and it showed from the amount of book marks placed throughout them.

"I knew that the prophet said that this girl would swing the balance in the way of good, leaving us defeated, but I don't think that is exactly what he is after. I found an ancient text and deciphered what I could of it. Basically it says that a human who is given the breath of an Angel will live not by the constrictions of earth, but the openness of the heavens. It then said that man walks between two lines, but a man who has been given the breath of an Angel is able to walk limitless, without lines but within his own strength." Ali said, fascinated by the information.

Caleb didn't quite get what it was that he was saying. "So…" Caleb prompted Ali to get to the point.

"Basically, what I think it is saying, is that whichever of our witches has the soul of the Angel, her powers will be limitless within her own abilities. It means she would actually be able to create things instead of just being able to manipulate things. Basically I think that Cyrus wants to use her to gain more power for himself. I think she might be able to give him the power to walk in the daylight, which would make him more powerful than he already is. There is more going on to the story than the balance of power. If the only reason he wanted her was to prevent the good from being triumphant, then why don't any demons know about this? Why keep her alive and why were the six of us sworn to secrecy?" Ali said.

"So basically she will be the most bad ass witch anyone has ever seen. Like she could take us out if we weren't all together, huh?" Caleb said.

"That's the jest I'm picking up on." Ali said. "Also, I found out that the mark of an Angel is specific to the specific Angel that gave its breath for a life to live, and it seems that each mark is unique, so there isn't a way for us to figure out an exact thing to look for without knowing what Angel it was and what his or her mark was, which is a much more impossible task. So we might not know what to look for exactly, but whatever it is will be small and inconspicuous," Ali said.

"If they're trying to be all inconspicuous, then why have a mark at all?" Caleb asked, now looking down at the text he couldn't understand whatsoever.

"Because once an Angel has entered into a body they basically go into hibernation, cutting them off from the heavens. This mark is a way to ensure to another Angel the Angel who has placed themselves in the body of a human still exists. Angels who give their soul become vulnerable to the choices humans make. If a human decides to sell their soul, for example, if the Angel isn't extracted out of the body before the human dies, then the Angel's soul will go to hell along with the human, turning them into a slave and fallen Angel for all of eternity. The mark is basically a way for Angels to keep track of and monitor the Angel's soul as long as it is inside a human." Ali said, completely enthralled in his fascination of the subject.

"So basically it won't be something like holy water that reveals it, then," Caleb was catching on.

"Right, which means that the holy water in a bottle trick wouldn't have worked anyway. The passage I found translates a bit differently than what the seer had seen in his vision. This text translates roughly; If upon a choice has been made to give a human life, an Angel will give its soul for that life time, allowing the human a chance at life. The energy force within the human will be of the heavens, but the Angel lies asleep hibernating until being released upon the human's death. Through the tears of purity, or by bloodshed of a pure silver knife, an Angel's mark will surface, allowing the heavens to keep watch over them." Ali read off what he was able to translate.

"So blood or tears will show the mark, but we have no clue what the mark is. We just know that it will be small and specific to the angel that has given its breath." Caleb said, actually interested in what Ali had found out. "So this isn't a chick that is half angel, she is just living on the life force of an angel?" Caleb then asked.

"We already established that last weekend, Caleb, thank you for joining the party." Ali said grinning at Caleb. He knew Caleb hadn't paid much attention to this task, but it seems as if his attention had now been awoken.

"Shit! That seems almost impossible that someone could actually be walking around out there with more power than us," Caleb said, suddenly thinking of the implications of enhanced powers which seemed limitless. Perhaps she could strengthen our powers while we are at it!" Caleb added, getting a little excited at the possibility of holding even more power than he already had.

"Yeah I think that is exactly what Cyrus doesn't want to happen," Ali stated as a fact. "He's so consumed with power these days that I would bet that anyone who tries to fuck with his mission will feel his wrath." Ali said, shaking his head in disapproval.

"He doesn't have to know." Caleb replied, still looking through the text he couldn't himself read, but that seemed to hold so much knowledge and access to things of limitless power all of a sudden Caleb became interested.

"No, he raised us, and no matter what we feel about him we owe him that much respect." Ali said, trying hard to convince himself.

"You know for one of the bad guys, you sure do seem to do a lot of the right things! A bad guy with ethics, that's what you are all right," Caleb laughed, knowing how absurd it sounded and how even more absurd it was actually the truth.

"Whatever," Ali said, brushing off Caleb's teasing. "At least I didn't fall in love with a virgin wanting to buy a white house with a picket fence!" Ali shot back.

"How did you know she was a virgin?" Caleb asked, he had no clue she was one and wasn't sure how Ali knew that.

"Was?" Ali smiled.

"Is! How did you know?" Caleb asked with a look of complete confusion.

"Vampire skills! Remember Caleb, we are half vampires. I am surprised you didn't pick up on it being that close to her?" Ali said, looking at Caleb as if he had lost his mind. "I could smell it a mile away," he added.

"You know what, I didn't…I didn't pick anything up other than I just wanted to be near her… Why would I even have to ask how you knew. I must be losing it…" Caleb said, trailing off, thinking back through the week.

He realized everything which normally came instinctually to him was suppressed around her. He dropped what he was and became who he was. She clouded his judgment, but the clouds felt good, as if he could float from cloud to cloud in the blue sky alongside of one other person on this earth. He could have kicked himself for not taking away her virginity at the lake at that moment. Had he done that, it would be easier to make her feel tied to him, but there was something inside of himself which spoke louder and the voice was telling him to make sure she was sure and really ready. He wanted her to be ready. Her first time needed to be special, and so Caleb would wait.

Images of Mikayla's face swam through his mind as he thought of how things went that night. He really couldn't believe he actually had enough strength, respect, and love to hold back. Never had he experienced that kind of pleasure, and it wasn't as much what they were doing as it was just being near her. Never had he wanted anything more than he did that night, but she was more important to him then his own desires. His biggest desire of all was to see her happy. This shocked him, and he tried several times to shake this thought out of his mind but it was impossible, her happiness was as natural to him as breathing. He was in love with her; he knew this for a fact. No matter how short of a time or how stupid it sounded, he knew he loved her the minute he laid his eyes on her, before she had even seen him.

Mikayla! Mikayla where are you? Answer me! Rowan said, frantically trying to call for Mikayla, who seemed to be missing. Mikayla was tired and groggy as she heard Rowan calling for her.

"What?" She said out loud, still half asleep and completely unaware of where she was.

Where are you? Rowan called one more time, making Mikayla take notice Rowan wasn't in the room, but calling from a far.

She opened her eyes to find she wasn't at home. She looked around the darkened, sparse room and then realized she was in Caleb's bed. Mikayla sat up and realized Caleb wasn't in the room. She rubbed her eyes for a moment, looking for a clock but couldn't find one and remembered he didn't have one in his room.

What time is it? She finally managed to answer back.

Oh my God, Kali. Thank God you are alright! Rowan said with a sound of relief.

What time is it? Mikayla asked one more time.

It is almost three and your Mom is freaked out! My parents just woke me up and asked if I knew where you were. I assumed you were with Caleb so I covered for you when they told me that your mom had found your phone in your room but that you were gone and hadn't been around for hours! Rowan said.

Mikayla scratched her head, trying to figure out what she would tell her mom. She didn't want to give the boys any reasons to come home from their trip. Right now life was feeling perfect for the very first time in a very long time, and she wasn't willing to have that taken away from her. *What did you tell them?* She quickly asked.

I told them that we had a friend from school named Mary who was having an end of the year beauty night. I told them that you probably fell asleep with a mask on your face watching a chick flick. They bought it, I think, but I was worried because I have been trying to call to you for fifteen minutes. Where are you? Rowan demanded.

Caleb's. I fell asleep, Mikayla managed.

Fell asleep? Is that all? What the hell? I am sick for the day and you end up in some guy's bed? Rowan joked. *I want to hear everything!* She then added.

How are you feeling? Mikayla asked, remembering how she was sick earlier that day.

Crappy, I was in bed all day. I really don't feel any better. I actually feel worse. It seems to be spreading into my lungs. I tried to use the energy inside to clear myself but it only drained me and seemed to make me feel worse. I think I used too much energy, Rowan replied, now sounding weak.

You need to go to sleep! I will have Caleb take me home so that I am there when my mom wakes up. She must be worried sick with my Dad gone and all," Mikayla said, having woken back into the present. As much as she wanted to stay right where she was, she knew her mom was in a delicate state and no amount of freedom was worth putting her mom in jeopardy.

Alright...Kali I am glad you are ok. I want a full report later, Rowan said, sounding even weaker now.

Get some more sleep, Mikayla said, sitting herself up in Caleb's bed, wondering where he had went to.

The floor was cold beneath her bare feet as she stood up, ready to look for Caleb until she realized she was sporting a towel and not her dress. Searching the floor for the missing blue sundress, it finally dawned upon her Caleb had put it into the dryer. It was too risky to walk out with just a towel wrapped around her if Caleb's brothers were home. Sure she had been traipsing around naked in front of Caleb, but he was the first man to see her fully naked and, despite the fact she was ready to feel the thrill of freedom and walk slightly on the wild side, becoming a nudist wasn't on her to do list.

Quietly she made her way towards the bedroom door and put her ear up to see if she could hear anything going on. At first it sounded quiet, but as her breath steadied she became more in tune with the energy going on outside the room as she started to hear voices. One was definitely Caleb and the other she thought had to be Ali. It was late and she assumed their conversation couldn't possibly take much longer, so she decided to make her way towards the bed and wait for him until she heard something strange that caught her ear. Normally she wasn't a snoop, but as if she couldn't help herself, she steadied herself to try and make out what they were saying.

"Vampire skills..." Mikayla whispered to herself, wondering what the hell they were talking about. She had hoped it wasn't in reference to her. *Oh God! What if he is in there telling him what happened!* She then thought to herself, turning bright red. She couldn't help but feel a little paranoid, she never did things like that but heard lots of stories of girls who did and hoped she was not becoming a story.

Her mind raced for a couple more seconds until something inside her convinced her he could not and would not deceive her. She might not have heard him say the words, but he made her feel loved, even if it had only been a week of knowing him. Perhaps her instincts were wrong, but they didn't feel wrong, so she quieted her mind and began to listen again. He started saying something again about "how he knew…" but knew what, and suddenly Mikayla's face was flushed with a red warmness which seemed to beat heavily into her ears as she felt a lump form in her throat. Never had she been talked about like this before, and granted she didn't hear the whole conversation, but her instincts told her they were talking about her, and from what she heard she felt it was pretty safe to assume what it was that he was referring to. "I am so stupid…" She whispered to herself as tears formed in her eyes, wetting her lashes.

After a few minutes of silence, she heard footsteps coming towards the door. Not wanting to get caught eavesdropping, she quietly but quickly made it back to the bed. She plopped down just as the door handle turned and the door was pushed open.

Caleb could see from the light shining in from the hall way Mikayla was now sitting up. He couldn't see her face, but he could sense a feeling of sadness emanating from her. Instinctively he asked her what was wrong.

Mikayla shook her head.

Caleb shut the door behind him and made his way towards the bed.

"What's the matter?" He asked again, grabbing for her hand, but her hand felt cold in his hand as she pulled it away.

"Nothing," she said as she folded her arms in front of her.

Caleb sat quietly for a moment, trying to figure out why the sudden change. It wasn't anything she said, or a look on her face, he could just feel she was upset.

"I can't explain it, Mikayla, but I know something is wrong and I can't fix it if I don't know what it is," he said, trying to get her to talk.

"I need to go home," was all she said back.

With those words, Caleb felt a rip tear through him. The connection they had all of a sudden felt suffocating, like someone was stepping on his chest. She was trying to push him out and he could feel it, but he wasn't ready to let go, and he didn't understand why she was until it dawned upon him.

"How much did you hear?" he asked, sure as anything that's what it was.

"Not much… just the part where you blabbed about me being a virgin, that's all." Mikayla said as she stood up, trying to get some distance between them.

Caleb shook his head, trying to remember exactly what was said at the end of the conversation. He needed a way to spin it. This was not going to end and he would use whatever measures he could to prevent her from walking away from him.

"You didn't hear the whole conversation, I take it," he started out, trying to gage just how much she did hear so he would know how to spin it.

"No, I just heard the last part, where you didn't know but should have known…" she said as a tear ran down her cheek, feeling embarrassed and wanting to be at home in her safe little world.

Caleb didn't have to have light to notice the tear streaming down her cheek. He had vampire senses in the night, and although he couldn't see the color in her cheeks, he sensed blood was rushing into her cheeks. The outline of her face was so beautiful he couldn't help but get up and move towards her, but she quickly turned the other way.

Not fazed by her sudden cold shoulder, he reached around the front of her face from behind, wiping away the tear. Mikayla, despite feeling hurt, couldn't help but feel comforted by the gesture. How could he still make her feel so good after he had betrayed her trust, she wondered.

"Don't," she whispered.

But he did not listen; instead, he wrapped his arms around her waist. For a moment she sank into his arms, comforted by the feel of them wrapped tightly around her as if he would protect her at all cost. She felt dizzy with confusion.

"Come back and lay down," he said, trying to lure her back to the bed and make her forget what it was she just heard.

Mikayla quickly broke free, coming to her senses. "It's obvious you thought I was that kind of girl, and now you know that I am not you seem to think you need help dealing with that from your brother! That is sacred, Caleb, and while I may be stupid as to think that these kinds of things might actually be able to happen this fast, I am not so stupid as to put any more time in with someone who values so little what I have that I happen to value a great deal! I don't know why you told him you didn't know, but it sure sounded like locker room talk to me. I shouldn't even be mad at you, I should be mad at myself for being so carefree, so unlike myself. I learned my lesson and if you can just get me my dress I will catch a cab home," she said firmly.

"No!" Caleb shouted at her.

"No? No you won't get me my dress?" Mikayla shouted back at him.

"No, you are wrong. I do value you. No, you aren't taking a cab back. I will drive you." He said, trying to control his temper, which was hard because he was starting to feel a lack of control but he knew he had to keep it under wraps or he could lose her forever. He could feel just how angry she was.

Mikayla stood there and said nothing. Caleb then brushed passed her and forced his door open, walking down the hallway to the laundry room and grabbed her dress from the dryer. He stormed back into the room and slammed the door, but held on to her dress tightly before handing it to her.

This time she was modest, pulling the dress over herself as the towel stayed wrapped around her body tightly. It was killing him she had closed herself off to him so quickly. He was feeling vulnerable and he knew she was too. Somehow he had to make her see things differently.

He struggled, stumbling over his words, trying to explain things to her but she only stood there dressed with her arms crossed in front of her as if she weren't even listening and just waiting for her ride home. He became more and more angry as he felt her shut down. Something needed to be done and quick, he thought, and the lies he was telling wasn't working, so he decided he needed to play on the truth and shocked himself at what came out at the end of his partial truth.

"Alright, you did hear me talk about it, but it isn't exactly what you think!" Caleb shouted.

Mikayla relaxed a little, appreciating his attempt at finally telling her the truth as her arms, still wrapped around her waist, eased a bit.

"I have exactly two people in this world that I consider family and that is Ali and Jamahl, and that is ALL I have. When something is important to me, they are the only ones I can turn to, or would want to. Anything I tell them I tell because I can trust them. So don't think I am so stupid as to believe that you aren't going to go back to Rowan and tell her!" Caleb said as he paused, hoping the first part would sink in.

Mikayla did think he sort of had a point, but was still guarded because she still thought it was sacred and they had only known each other for a week, which made her realize no matter what she felt around him, she really didn't know him.

"I really don't even know you," she surprised even herself at how cold that sounded.

Caleb was even angrier now. "You don't know me? I have never let a girl in before you. I know it's only been a week, but that is long enough for me to know that you are different. You are special, Mikayla. Can't you feel the way I feel?" Caleb said, coming closer towards her.

"Why? Is it because you never had a virgin before, and you need to check it off your things to do as a male list?" She asked smugly, still feeling guarded.

Suddenly angered by the wall she had built around her, he grabbed her by her upper arms and looked into her eyes. "I needed to toss around my feelings for you. The part of the conversation that you didn't hear and it led into what you did hear was something I needed good advice on because it is important to me to be responsible to you because…" Caleb said and trailed off.

Mikayla felt flushed, her body started to radiate as if she could almost feel what was coming next. She knew she was being a bit unfair and overly sensitive, but these were all uncharted waters to her. "Because why?" She said softly as she swallowed to catch her breath.

"Because…" Caleb froze with fear.

Mikayla tried to struggle free, agitated he wasn't spitting out what it was she had hoped he would say. The one thing that, if it were true, would make it all better, but his grip was like steal. Not only did she hope he would say it, but the thought also frightened her.

He bent forward quickly. His lips were only millimeters away from hers as he looked into her eyes. "Because…" He said, softly this time as she heard a slight smile in his tone.

The coolness of his breath and a slight brush of his lip against hers made her knees weaken. Again she swallowed her breath. "Because…" she whispered, this time without pulling away.

Quickly he lifted her up, with his face still locked on hers. "Because, Mikayla…I love you." He said honestly, looking into her eyes.

Her whole body tingled and radiated an energy she had never felt so strong before. It wasn't hormones or wishful thinking, it was pure and magical. Another tear formed in her eye, but before it could slide down her cheek, Caleb kissed it away with his full, perfect lips. The room was dark and still, yet full of an explosive energy. Mikayla wanted to tell him back, but he literally had taken her breath away and before she could form the energy to say the words, he kissed her gently and lovingly on the lips.

Softly she kissed back as the kiss grew deeper and deeper. As they stood there kissing, he gently laid her down on the bed and stroked her hair, looking into her eyes for a moment before kissing her again. This time he was putting soft little kisses slowly on every inch of her face and neck. It was the best feeling Mikayla ever had. It brought forth goosebumps so strong it was on the verge of feeling almost like a tickle. She couldn't help it, she believed him. *I do love you…* she thought to herself.

"I know," Caleb said back, having heard her but didn't realize the words hadn't actually left her lips.

Mikayla was in a state of pleasure and didn't care to even think she hadn't actually said it out loud and continued on with Caleb, kissing him back. She realized she had not actually said the words out loud, but at that moment she was lost in him and words were not important to her at this point.

After a long make out session, Caleb spooned her as they feel asleep again. Mikayla forgot all about going home. The only thing she could think of was spending as much time with this beautiful stranger she felt she had known her whole life, who loved her and who, despite the short time, felt she loved back. Tomorrow would come and she could deal with the consequences then, but until that time she wanted to soak up as much of Caleb as she could get.

34

The next morning was sunny again. Caleb had dropped her off early the next day before Mikayla's mom awoke, but this time in the Jeep and again a little down the street, so no one would notice who had dropped her off. They made plans to see each other that night. Caleb's brother Ali had been up early that morning as well and had invited her and Rowan to a party he said they were having at their house that night. Mikayla knew Rowan was sick, but said nothing at the time. Caleb looked sideways at Ali, but went with the flow. Mikayla said yes for herself and asked what she should bring. Ali named a couple of things and then added again that Rowan was welcome as well, and to please make sure and ask her to come. Mikayla thought it was a little too persistent and offered a warning Rowan was taken. Ali seemed to back pedal and assured her it was just an extension of hospitality and nothing more. Mikayla couldn't help but think it wasn't quite true and she couldn't put her finger on what she was picking up on, but she knew something was there. She knew it was pointless to push the issue so she dropped it and told him she would ask before heading out the door with Caleb.

The morning was quiet around her house without her father around. Her mother was still in bed. Mikayla noticed her mother was still sound asleep with the cordless phone in her hand as she tiptoed past her parent's bedroom. Not wanting to make too much noise, she slipped off her dress and put on a nightgown quietly and climbed back into bed. She was exhausted and needed more sleep, anyways. As soon as her head hit the pillow, she was out.

The sun had changed positions since she had fallen asleep. She wasn't sure whether it was the presence of her mother standing in her room or the sun from the outside that had awaken her. Rubbing the sleep from her eyes, her mother began to speak.

"Where were you last night?" She said calmly.

Mikayla took a minute before answering, trying to remember what it was Rowan had told her. It didn't take long before it came to her.

"Mary's; Rowan was supposed to show up but got sick. She was to be my ride home. We did a beauty night and watched movies. I feel asleep and forgot my phone. Sorry if I worried you," Mikayla said and was surprised, and a bit guilty, at the ease with which the lie came out.

Her mother seemed to buy it but still looked worried.

"What's wrong?" Mikyala asked.

"It's just that I wish that you could be a little more careful, especially with your father gone. I don't mind you living your life, and I know we are strict, and technically as an adult you are able to make your own choices, but please keep me informed and I would appreciate you doing me a favor by sleeping at home while your father is gone." Her mother said again, calmly.

Mikayla felt guilty, she knew the secret her mother was currently keeping about another baby, and the last thing her mom needed was to worry about her. It was decided in Mikayla's mind her mother was feeling vulnerable because of the pregnancy with her father gone. Despite her three weeks of freedom, Mikayla knew she had to be responsible and vowed to herself to not sleep another night away from the house, no matter how much she longed to sleep next to Caleb. She would put a curfew on herself and that was that. Her own happiness could wait a little while longer, but until then she would respect her mother and sleep at home.

After a few minutes of deliberating as her mother sat on the end of her bed, Mikayla decided she needed to assure her.

"I am sorry, that wasn't very responsible of me. I won't let it happen again. I will be here with you every night! Even if I go out, I promise that I will be in by 2 a.m. Can you live with that compromise?" Mikayla asked lovingly.

Her mother smiled at her and placed her hand on Mikayla's foot.

"You are very patient, and you have a heart of gold, Mikayla. I am very proud of you. I think I can live with that compromise." She said as she gently rubbed her daughter's foot, as if Mikayla were still a toddler.

A sadness was behind her mother's eyes as she gently rubbed her feet. Mikayla thought perhaps it was because the rules put on her were unreasonable and she knew it, but somehow just having her mother understand that made all the difference in the world.

"You're a really good mom," Mikayla offered with a smile of assurance.

Her mom said nothing back, only strengthened her smile as her eyes teared up. She then made an excuse to get up by saying she was going to make some lunch, and for Mikayla to come down and eat once she was up and moving around. Mikayla shook her head in agreement and smiled as she watched her mom walk out of her room.

The day grew cloudy but it was still warm. In the air Mikayla could smell rain coming again. She didn't mind the rain as long as it was warm out, it was peaceful to her. After spending a lazy day around the house, she had dinner with her mom and got ready for the party over at Caleb's. Mikayla had told Caleb about the conversation she had with her mom earlier that day, and Caleb came up with a plan so her mother wouldn't worry so much. He would have Mary pick her up. Hating to have to lie to her mom, Mikayla decided to think about it for a moment before deciding under the circumstances, with her mom being pregnant and her dad being gone, it was for her mom's own good and agreed.

Sprinkles started to pellet lightly on the windshield just as Mikayla climbed inside of Mary's car. She was alone, which was nice for Mikayla. She was a little nervous about being stuck in a car with a group of girls she didn't know. Surprised by the easy conversation and the wit of Mary, she immediately liked her and settled into the passenger seat of the car.

They finally arrived at Caleb's and just as soon as the rain began, it stopped, in true Michigan style. The clouds had left behind a sunny blue sky.

Caleb greeted her at the door with a kiss on her lips as Mary scooted through the door and was greeted by a swat on her butt by Jamahl, which started a flirtatious game of chase.

Out on the back porch, Mikayla could see the other guys from the boat and a few random girls. They were drinking beer and barbequing hamburgers and hotdogs as they listened to music while laughing and talking. The rain was light and had lasted only a couple of minutes and obviously hadn't affected the barbeque any, Mikayla thought to herself as she made it out to the porch holding Caleb's hand.

She opted for a soda instead of a beer, she thought it wasn't a good idea to make drinking a regular habit and she had already had beer two times in one week, which was way more than she normally had. If she drank once a month it seemed like too much to her. Caleb smiled at her opening her can of soda as he took a sip of his beer.

Over by the grill, Ali was cooking, he turned his head and said hello.

"Hi," Mikayla said as she waved.

"Hotdog or Hamburger?"

"No thanks…maybe later, I just ate with my mom," she answered.

Ali looked around for a moment and wrinkled his nose. "Where is Rowan?" He then asked.

"She's really sick… She said if she wasn't feeling better tomorrow that she was going in to see her doctor," she answered

Mikayla couldn't help but notice the disappointment in Ali's face. She couldn't place what it was about the look, but it wasn't quite that of someone who was looking forward to seeing a crush, only to find out they weren't coming. Instead, it was more of mechanical frustration, like she was supposed to drop off something to him he needed.

He tried not to make it obvious he was frustrated and took a moment to choose his words carefully. "That's a shame. I hope she feels better soon. Let me know when you want something to eat and I will put fresh meat on the grill for you," he said then smiled, changing back into a regular guy.

Mikayla felt uneasy but couldn't put her finger on it, so decided not to focus on it, feeling like she may just be interpreting things the wrong way. The more she thought about it, she realized it was a new thing for her to spend time without her family and friends, and mainly Rowan. It was just a part of freedom, she thought to herself and moved on, spending time on the porch with everyone while stealing precious glances with Caleb. Every time he caught her eye she felt a warm sensation enter her veins.

Caleb felt the same warm sensation flowing through his.

The night was fun. Her and Caleb even stole some snuggle time in his room. This time it was only kissing as they held each other, fully clothed, listening to music. It was getting late and Mikayla could feel herself falling asleep. She knew if she didn't get up and get moving, she would lose herself in his arms and fall asleep. It was there in his arms she felt the most peace she ever remembered feeling.

Mary and Jamahl were still hanging out with the party crowd. Mikayla knew she had been drinking and wasn't comfortable with her taking her home. Drinking and driving was the last thing she would do or ever allow anyone else to do. Without having to point out the obvious, Caleb noticed the same thing and grabbed his keys then took her hand protectively.

She felt so cared for at that moment. He was protective, but still respectfully recognized her freedom, treating her as he should, an equal.

As he pulled into her neighborhood, he sat quietly, turning off the car for a moment. There was a look on his face Mikayla didn't understand. It looked as if something was wrong.

"What is it?" She asked.

Caleb just shook his head and then tilted it up towards the roof of the car as he let out a sigh. "Nothing." He said rather unconvincingly, she decided.

"Hmmm…" Makayla sounded as she looked at him. "Well I need to go," she added and went to open the door handle. If he didn't want to talk, then she was not going to push him. She was determined to show him the same amount of respect he had shown her, no matter how badly she wanted to pester him until he talked.

Caleb quickly reached over and grabbed the door before Mikayla could push it open. "I just will miss you. I wish I could spend all night, every night with you. That's what's wrong. Sorry if I gave off the wrong impression," he told her truthfully.

Mikayla was impressed by his confession and his ability to leave the games behind. She smiled at him and kissed him softly on the cheek. It was the most nurturing feeling Caleb had ever had. He reached for her and held her tight as he held a kiss softly on her forehead.

"I would stay with you if I could," she whispered before kissing him one last kiss goodnight.

She got out of the car and tried not to look back, afraid seeing his face one more time would have her forgetting about her mother's condition and she would run back, telling him to floor it back to his house so they crawl back into their little world together. It was hard, but she managed to stay focused as she made her way down the street.

Caleb watched her, wanting to go after her but knew he couldn't. He would stay longer than she knew, he decided. If he couldn't be with her, then he would watch over her a little bit, at least until she finally feel asleep.

35

The next day, Mikayla called Rowan to see how she was doing. Rowan didn't answer so she communicated telepathically to her. *How are you doing?* She asked.

Sicker than a dog, I am at the doctors now. They say I have pneumonia! I can't believe it! I must have been stressed out about the end of school and Mario leaving that my immune system is down. He is prescribing me some meds, but looks like I will be out for at least a week or so. Could you help cover some of my shifts at work? Rowan asked.

Of course, I will take all of them so your parents don't have to worry and can make sure they have enough time at home with you." Mikayla assured her best friend. *Do you need anything?* Mikayla added.

If you can think of how to use that power of yours to cure me, that would be great. Rowan joked.

Mikayla thought about it for a moment and actually felt like she could before realizing just how crazy it sounded and pushed the thought out of her mind.

Yeah, I wish I could. You get some sleep and call if you need anything. Tell your mom I will work both shifts today, and any others she may need until you are feeling better. Mikayla said, reassuring Rowan.

Thanks., Rowan thought back.

Mikayla wasn't supposed to be at work for another four hours, but she knew Rowan was supposed to be there in just a few minutes, so she hurriedly got ready for work and ran out the door to the shop.

It was another nice day, no rain in sight. The store was slow. It was a Monday, but Mikayla always brought in books as a pass time. After she stocked things and cleaned around the store, she sat on her stool, picking up her latest read and began to dive in. Hours passed without a single person entering the store, so Mikayla was startled when she heard the jingle of the store door opening.

A middle aged man dressed in black, walked into the store accompanied by a young guy maybe only a few years older than Mikayla, also dressed in black. There was something mysterious about the man. He looked familiar, but she couldn't place it. His eyes were as blue as the ocean and, like Mikayla, he had olive skin and hair just a little bit darker then hers. His eyes met hers and they were locked on one another for a moment. She felt he was sensing something, too. The uncomfortableness of it all made her speak up.

"Can I help you?" Mikayla quickly blinked her eyes to break the connection with the man staring so intensely in front of her.

The man had a deep, strong voice Mikayla noticed as he answered.

"I have an appointment with Mrs. Munoz," he said, then made his way towards the stairs as the young man quietly followed behind. "I have been here before," he added as he made his way up towards Mrs. Munoz treatment room and herbal store.

Mikayla watched as they made their way up the stairs. She couldn't help but think he seemed familiar somehow. Her mind was trying to place it, but she couldn't help sensing there was something to it. Just then, the shop doorbell rang open again. Mikayla snapped out of her trance as she glanced at the door.

He walked in with a devilish smile plastered on his face. It was Caleb, and all of her thoughts about the strange man dressed in black were forgotten.

"What time do you get off?" Was the first thing out of his mouth.

"At seven," she answered with a questioning smile.

"Good. Jackson's having a party tonight and I would like to take you, if you are up for it," he said.

"Sure, but I can't stay out to late. Rowan as pneumonia and I need to cover her shifts this week." She said smiling at him.

Caleb didn't know if he should feel agitated because Rowan would now be inaccessible for a week, or happy because it guaranteed him more time with Mikayla. Being honest with himself, he admitted he was happy his trip wouldn't be cut short and he could now spend more time with her. He wanted to get to know her as much as he could. Caleb wanted her to fall so much in love with him, the thought of them ever being apart was too much for her to bare. It was the way he felt, and the only way he could convince her to follow him wherever they went. He knew with the wolves it wouldn't be possible to stay much longer around Ann Arbor, so he needed to find a way to convince her to come with him, and the best way he knew how was to make her feel the way he felt.

"That's too bad about your friend. I promise to have you home early. Can I pick you up here or should I pick you up by your house?" He asked.

Mikayla briefly thought about her mom before answering. "Could Mary pick me up?" She asked with a look that told him she hated to put him out by asking.

"Not until after midnight. She's working," he said with a slight worried look in his eye at the possibility of her turning down the invitation out of fear of her mom finding out.

"Alright, pick me up at my house but in the jeep. My mom would freak out if you showed up on a bike," she said and smiled.

Caleb quickly leaned over the counter and kissed her before turning towards the door and leaving.

Mikayla watched him as he made his way through the door. He was so athletic and beautiful. She thought she would never tire of watching him. As she looked out of the window, she got a text message from Caleb, it read, *you're so beautiful.* Mikayla's heart skipped a beat, she was amazed even when he wasn't in her presence, he could take her breath away. Looking at the clock, she realized she still had a few hours to spare and picked her book back up to pass the time.

Her book was great and had actually made the time fly by. Before she knew it, it was seven o'clock and time for her shift to end. Mrs. Munoz was still upstairs. It dawned upon Mikayla the strange gentlemen had never made their way back down the stairs. Mikayla felt a little uneasy and used the intercom to check on her.

"Mrs. Munoz, it's seven, would you like me to lock up?" She started.

Without any hesitation Mrs. Munoz answered. She sounded perfectly fine and told her to lock up shop; she was still in the middle of an important meeting.

Mikayla felt better. The strange men were probably just business guys and perhaps she had seen the older gentlemen before after all. Without a second thought she grabbed her purse and headed out of the shop, locking the door behind her.

36

Caleb arrived home from downtown as Ali waited for him.

"Well?" Ali asked impatiently.

"Well I have some good news and some bad news. Which do you want first?" Caleb said with a mischievous grin plastered on his face.

"Caleb!" Ali shouted, unamused.

"Alright fine, bad news is Rowan is out sick and will be for at least a week. Good news is that I will have more time with Mikayla. I intend to make sure she will go away with me, of her own free will, of course." Caleb shot it straight.

"What do you mean sick?" Ali questioned.

"Pneumonia, I think Mikayla said," Caleb answered as he put his helmet on the kitchen counter.

"Fuck! Someone needs to tell Cyrus. You need to call him. He made you lead so you need to call him and let him know where we are with things," Ali ordered.

Caleb had no desire to call Cyrus but he knew Ali was right. Without hesitation he pulled his cell phone from his pocket and dialed his father as he took in a long deep breath.

The phone conversation didn't go as bad as expected. He found out from his father Aidan had come into a time issue, as well. The other witch was gone for another week, so it turned out they had some time to spare. Caleb didn't mention to Cyrus about Ali's findings. He didn't think of it, having been glad Cyrus was being calm because of Aidan's situation, and Caleb wanted to get off the phone as soon as he could for fear he would sense something in Caleb and start asking questions. He couldn't let Cyrus know about Mikayla, at least not yet. Caleb wouldn't put Mikayla in a vulnerable position, and anything to do with Cyrus would put her in a vulnerable position, especially if Cyrus suspected he wasn't doing his job properly because of her. Cyrus would have no problem coming around and snapping her neck just to get rid of the distraction.

No sooner did Caleb hang up the phone did he see Ali folding his arms, giving him a disapproving look.

"Why didn't you tell him about the information I found?" He asked.

"I didn't want him to pick up anything about me and Mikayla. I don't want him to know because if anything else goes wrong he will blame her as a distraction and kill her before we even know he is here. I will wait and tell him after we have completed the mission. Ali I mean it, don't say anything to him. Please," Caleb begged.

"Of course I would never, Caleb. I just don't see why you couldn't have at least told him the 'how' so he could pass it along to Aidan. I will call and tell him tomorrow so he doesn't get suspicious. This girl better be worth it." Ali shook his head and grinned a friendly smile at his brother.

"Thanks," Caleb said, now feeling reassured his brother was still behind him.

As the day came to an end and night fell, Caleb picked up Mikayla. He watched her walk towards the jeep in a tight pair of bootcut dark jeans and open toed heels with a tight white strapless top that looked more like a corset then it did a shirt. She wore her hair long with gentle flowing waves. Mikayla was dressed more for a nightclub than a party. As Mikayla made her way down the street, he decided she needed a night out and quickly texted Jamahl to round up the gang and meet downtown at a nightclub, and not the one Dominick owned.

Mikayla reached the door and flashed him a smile. Her teeth were perfect and white. Without any words at all, she climbed into the passenger seat and smiled.

"Change of plans, you look too good to go to a party, so I texted them to meet us out at a night club instead. Do you have a suggestion of one not owned by Dominick?" He asked.

Mikayla was excited. She wanted to go out dancing, especially when none of the boys were around to control her every move. "I do! Tell them to meet us at Fantasia's, it's a couple of blocks up from Dom's club, so I don't think I will be spotted," she answered. "Not that I care about being seen with you, but I want as much time with you uninterrupted until…" She started to explain but trailed off.

"Until what?" Caleb asked, but already knew the answer.

"Well, until I hook you in so you will think all the abuse will be worth it. But I have a feeling that after they see that you are not going to be pushed around, and that you are going to be sticking around, you will be in with them in no time. I think Dominick will even eventually come around." She said, thinking to herself Dominick would be the toughest one to convince.

Caleb just looked at her and smiled as he texted Jamahl which club to meet them at. The sound of Dominick's name had stirred up anger inside of him he couldn't explain, but he was determined to put it aside for the night and concentrate on the only thing that mattered to him, Mikayla. She looked beautiful and as he took off towards downtown, he had a hard time keeping his eyes off of her and on the road. Mikayla giggled as she noticed, especially when he drove over a curb, not having paid close enough attention to his driving. Despite that, they somehow made it safely downtown.

The night was perfect. Mikayla danced so freely on the dance floor as Caleb stood by and watched. He even danced a few times with her, but mostly he enjoyed watching her. Caleb thought she looked so powerful on the dance floor. He also noticed every guy in the club had their eyes on her, but he knew something about her they didn't, which was that she was a virgin who decided she was soon going to let him have the rights, and he would make sure he would be the only one who would ever have those rights. It gave him satisfaction they could only ever admire her from afar. He couldn't blame them.

When Mary and Jamahl arrived it only seemed to bring more joy to Mikayla, who danced mostly along with Mary. The two of them got along very well, it seemed as if they had been friends for quite some time, though they really had just met. Caleb couldn't help but notice Jamahl was looking at Mary with awe. Caleb thought back to what Ali had said about him and

Jamahl coming to Michigan for a love connection and laughed. At the moment, neither Jamahl or Caleb seemed much like hard core predators, instead they seemed like a couple of fools in love. Caleb wanted to rip his skin off at the thought, but caught sight of Mikayla smiling and dancing with Mary and it made the thought fade out until the thought was gone.

It was getting late, Caleb was trying to keep track of time, despite a selfish voice inside telling him to just keep her all night. The voice was telling him to make problems between her and her mother, it would only ensure her coming to him faster, but he knew in the long run she would only resent him. Looking at his watch, he knew he needed to get her home.

"Mikayla, it's a little after one. I need to get you home." He came on to the dance floor to tell her.

"Already?" She questioned as she picked up his wrist to look for herself. "Time flies, I guess," she said, looking disappointed.

Right then Caleb knew he had made the right choice. It's better for him if she gets fed up on her own, it will only make her run faster towards him. He grinned slyly at the thought.

"What's that look for?" She asked, having noticed.

"Just thinking that you are lucky we are in a public place. You look way too sexy and I don't think tonight I would have enough sense to keep myself off of you." He said and looked deep into her eyes.

Mikayla could feel the heat rise into her face. She thought she was lucky at that moment, too, after what he said and the way he looked at her she didn't think she would be able to either.

"I guess we better go then." She said, still looking into his eyes as her heart beat faster.

"I guess so," he replied, still burning his eyes into hers.

The ride home was quiet. They were both thinking of the same thing; of how they longed to be in Caleb's bed holding each other. Neither of them wanted the night to end, but the end was here Mikayla thought, as Caleb pulled into her neighborhood.

After they spent a good five minutes quietly kissing the windows steamed up. Mikayla giggled at the sight, breaking the moment ,and drew a happy face on the side of her window. Caleb laughed and told her to take that off so he wouldn't have to be seen with it driving down the road. Mikayla refused, which started a playful fight of Caleb trying to get past her to erase the smiley face, and Mikayla using all her might to prevent her happy face from becoming destroyed. The two laughed until, finally, Caleb made his way quickly past her and smeared the happy face with his hand as he held a laughing Mikayla down in her seat.

"I win!" Caleb teased.

"You only won this time!" Mikayla joked back.

Caleb took the smile off of his face and looked at her with mischief in his eyes. "Actually I always win!" He said with the utmost sureness.

Mikayla, for an instant, became uneasy. Caleb sensed that and put the smile back on his face. Mikayla then relaxed and smiled back.

"Well, I will help you learn how to lose a little!" Mikayla added.

"Ok, we will have to see about that one," Caleb said back.

Mikayla loved his confidence and his positive attitude. Most of all, she loved how playful he was but at the same time treated her with so much respect. She knew it was late and despite the fact she didn't want to leave, she knew it was time to go.

"I better go," she said, and opened the door quickly before she changed her mind.

Caleb understood and nodded towards her and smiled as she slipped out and closed the door behind her. She paused for a quick moment and blew him a kiss. Caleb actually put his hand up to catch it. He wanted to catch it, it was his kiss from her. He was glad he was not being observed by either one of his brothers as he placed the blown kiss to his heart.

A sudden instinct came over Caleb as he held his kiss close. He quickly got out of the car and ran after her. He was so quiet, being part predator and all, he snuck up on her without a sound. Mikayla started to scream. Quickly Caleb covered her mouth with one hand as he grabbed her from the waist with the other.

It took Mikayla a minute to realize it was just Caleb. Her heart was beating twice as fast as normal. Caleb couldn't help but feel bad at the way he made her scared. He knew it was caused from the night she had been chased by the three hyenas.

"Sorry," he whispered. "I didn't mean to sneak up on you like that," he then offered.

Mikayla nodded in understanding but couldn't speak because his hand was still covering her mouth. Caleb noticed the nodding and slowly uncovered her mouth.

"Geez! You scared the shit out of me!" She said with a smile on her face, partly amused at the thrill and the other part just relieved she really wasn't in any danger after all.

"There is something I want to ask you," he came right out with it, not wanting to stall her anymore.

"What is it?" She asked gently, wondering what it was he was about to ask.

"You say Dominick and the other guys are gone for a few weeks, and that would be enough time for me to decide whether or not you are worth all the grief they will give out. I already made my decision, I made it the minute I saw you, and you are worth it. So what I want to know is if, when you are not working or committed to your mother, if I can please have the other time. All of it, I want to see you every day, so I am making plans with you now. I think it would be a good idea for us to have a strong foundation for when they get back, and the best way for us to do that is to get to know each other as fast as possible." He said, sounding like he was organizing a military operation of some kind.

"Really?" Mikayla asked as she giggled with nervousness.

"Really, I can't imagine not seeing you, even one day," Caleb said honestly.

Mikayla looked into his eyes and saw the sincerity in them. As if she was led by pure instinct ,she threw her arms around his neck and jumped on him, wrapping her legs around his waist. She said nothing; instead she buried her head in his neck, kissing it softly.

"Is that a yes?" He asked, but again already knew her answer by the ticklish, tiny kisses she was applying to his neck. He smiled as he chuckled a little, pleased at her obvious answer.

"Yes," she softly whispered into his ear, sending soft chills running down his back and firming his front.

Mikayla felt that too and started to giggle. "I guess you are both excited about that!" She joked.

Caleb started to laugh and acted as if he was going to drop her. She gave a playful scream as they play wrestled in the street for a couple of moments before he grabbed hold of her and kissed her lovingly. At the moment, neither cared who saw them, they were too wrapped up in each other.

"You need to go now," Caleb looked down at her with a serious face, hating to see her leave.

"Yeah…" was all she said back as she forced herself away from him and headed towards her house.

"I will see you tomorrow," he said as she walked away. Caleb stood in the street watching her enter her house and kept perfectly still until he saw the light in her bedroom turn on. Quickly he orbed himself into the tree to watch her until she fell asleep.

Inside her room only one soft, white, dim light was turned on. Mikayla was inside of her walk-in closet. Caleb knew she was changing out of her clothes and into nightwear of some kind. He had watched her enough times now to know her routine. Sure enough she came out of the closet in a tight white cotton tank top and tight matching short shorts. The material was thin, which Caleb couldn't help but be thankful for. Then, like clockwork, she put her hair into a pony tail so she could wash her face and brush her teeth. After that she put lotion on her face. Now it was time for Caleb's favorite part, her putting lotion on the rest of her body. She had several different lotions, all scented. Mikayla would look at them for a few moments before deciding which one she was in the mood for, sometimes she even mixed scents, like vanilla and mandarin orange, which is what Caleb noticed she was now reaching for. He loved the motion of her rubbing the lotion in, not in a perverted way, but because she looked so graceful while doing it, almost like watching a dancer. It was hypnotic.

Now she was all ready for bed, she did something he had not seen her do before. She stood in front of the mirror over one of her dressers and stared intensely for a few minutes before a smile broke on her face. He hoped that smile was her thinking of him. She let out a little scream as she jumped towards the bed like a little girl on Christmas Eve being scooted off to bed, but much too excited to sleep. Caleb's heart softened in that moment and knew now the smile was, indeed, for him. He couldn't help but smile as he watched her crawl up towards the pillow and slip under the covers. She reached to turn out the light, then turned on her side facing the window and shut her eyes. Caleb noticed she was still smiling, feeling exhilarated as he sensed by her heart beat, then she fell quickly into a deep sleep.

He stared at her for a while, watching as she softly breathed, still smiling. Finally he knew he needed to get back to the house. He didn't want to keep pushing it with Ali, right now he was on his side and he wanted to keep it that way. Not that Ali would ever turn his back on him, but turning his back on Mikayla was a whole other story.

37

The week seemed to fly by as Mikayla and Caleb spent every moment they could with each other, separated only by Mikayla's work schedule and her having to sleep at home at night. They made sure Mikayla's mom wouldn't have much to worry about by having Mary pick her up or Caleb pick her up down the street in his jeep. Mikayla offered to drive to him, but Caleb didn't like the idea of her walking into her house without being able to watch her after what had happened with the hyenas the week before. Of course she didn't know what had happened, and had soon put it out of her brain, convincing herself she just got scared because of the way Dominick had acted that night mixed in with too much to drink.

She told Caleb of the story and that she thought the entirely over protective behavior had made her paranoid. Caleb saw this as a chance to discredit Dominick and not reveal the truth, so he told her he thought she was probably correct, nothing was chasing her but he could see with the way they treated her, especially Dominick, how she could become so paranoid. He used it as a way to let her know he would never make her feel that way. Caleb made sure she knew he saw her as a woman, not a little girl, implying Dominick only thought of her as a child despite being the same age. Mikayla half defended Dominick, but stopped as she noticed Caleb's jaw tightening. As she let go of defending Dominick, Caleb's jaw relaxed. She realized there was a little bit of jealousy there and she had no right to push things. Caleb, on the other hand, realized he needed to back off of trying to deface Dominick, he could see it would only work against him and chose not to mention it anymore.

As the days went on, they were getting to know each other more and more. Caleb could be very funny, never before had Mikayla laughed so hard in her life. Around him she felt truly free. When she was at work she would watch the clock, counting down the minutes until she could be with him. Caleb did the same thing, keeping watch of the time, trying to find things to do just to pass the time until he could be next to her. He never went to her work after the one day; Ali knew what kind of shop it was and thought it was much too risky to have his presence in a shop like that. For once Caleb listened, for fear of losing her.

Having to fill up the day as the clock dragged on, Mikayla started to thumb through some of the books in the upstairs part of the shop. She was amused some of the books seemed to have spells in them. If only these people knew, she thought to herself, referring to her and Rowan. She started to read about crystals and started to become a bit interested in their properties. When Rowan gets better I will show this to her, she thought as she thumb through it.

She would buy things from the store from time to time, today she had purchased a beautiful blue and white stone called laminar. It was supposed to hold properties of finding one's true love and she loved the color, she knew it was a long shot but she thought it might be a way for her to confirm her feelings about Caleb.

When she got it home, she slipped it into her top dresser drawer where she kept all the goods she collected from the store. She wasn't sure how she was going to use it, but having thumbed through some of the spells in one of the books, she knew she would figure something out. It wasn't even something she thought would necessarily work, but it was a beautiful stone and fun to think about.

As the weekend approached Rowan was still sick. Mikayla had the whole weekend off and was glad for it. She was excited to be able to spend more time with Caleb.

Saturday came and they spent the day on the boats. This time she didn't go to her family's house because the wives were there with other family, enjoying the sun. Instead she was on the rented pontoon boat with Caleb hanging out on another lake. Again the day was fun. She interacted more with Mary this time and was much more comfortable with Caleb, making the day somehow seem magical.

It had been a long day, but Jamahl, Mary, and the rest of the gang were still living it up on the water. Caleb saw this as his chance to spend some alone time with Mikayla, so he convinced Jamahl to drop them off at the dock a few hours early. Then they got on the back of Caleb's bike and drove back to Caleb's to spend alone time there in the privacy of his room and their magical little haven.

The house was empty; they had it all to themselves. Caleb was making her laugh as he sang songs from the radio with a mischievous passion. It was some hardcore Screamo band Mikayla had never heard of, but loved every moment. His voice was beautiful and every note was sung to perfection, despite the fact he was doing it just to make her laugh.

Again they found themselves in Caleb's bed, but they still hadn't made love yet. Caleb was sticking to what he had said. *Not until you tell me that you love me*, was what he said and he meant it. Mikayla knew she was in love with him, but was too afraid to tell him. She was afraid of what could happen if she did. It wasn't that she was changing her mind about giving herself to him, it was the fear of telling him and him walking away. Her life was so happy right now, she was afraid to let the words escape, but Caleb already knew the truth, he could see it in her eyes, the same way she could see the love in his.

Time seemed to stop when they were together. Although they had a couple of close calls in the bedroom messing around before, Caleb would remind her of the deal. They also had a lot of peaceful, innocent moments of spooning in the bed while listening to music and talking, as well as a fair share of play wrestling and naps. It was perfect, and neither of them wanted it to end.

When Saturday night came it was time for Caleb to drop her off. When he did she paused before getting out of the car and looked at him.

"Pick me back up in a couple of hours, my mom will be asleep then. We can set an alarm clock and have me back before she wakes up," she said and ran towards her house as if she were trying to make the time go by faster.

Caleb didn't come back, he never left, and was right there waiting in the same spot he had dropped her off at. He watched as she made her way down the street in an oversized black hooded sweatshirt with a skull and cross bones on the front and writing on the back. On her legs were some tight black leggings made for running and only came a little more than half way down her calves, which showed the tightness of her curves. Caleb thought she looked sporty and really cute.

Once she got to the car he noticed that she had not a drop of make up on, with a fresh clean face, and took notice of how beautiful she really was. Here in this moment, in sweats, no make-up, and a pony tail, he found her to be more beautiful than he had ever seen her look. He smiled when she got into the car, giving her a curious look.

"What?" She said as she fastened her seatbelt.

"You're even more beautiful without makeup…" He said, trailing off as he became lost in her eyes for a moment.

She thought it was the sweetest thing and didn't know how to reply, so she flashed him an approving smile and placed a soft kiss on the side of his face. It was a very sweet and innocent moment. The two of them had a lot of moments like these.

That night they went back to Caleb's house and back into his bed again. It was another night they came close. Again Caleb had to back off as Mikayla tried to pull him in closer. This time Caleb almost gave in until he realized it would be more meaningful for her if she told him first she loved him, and it would make her trust him if he kept true to his word. If he had any hope of luring her away from home, then he needed to make sure he played his hand carefully. He also couldn't help but feel a truth in his heart it would only mean something once she admitted to him she loved him too.

Mikayla was so hard to resist, there wasn't anything in this world he wanted more than her. She was so beautiful and sexy and always smelled so good. Caleb still had no urge to bite her at all, he only desperately wanted to make love to her and be near her. He decided if all he could have was a little fooling around and spooning, then that was all he needed as long as she was there. To be honest with himself, he didn't even have to fool around with her, he just needed to be near her no matter what that meant.

They tried over the next few days to do the same thing with sleeping over at his house until Tuesday morning came and Mikayla was almost too tired to see him that night. Instead of doing something they just slept, well, Mikayla slept as Caleb watched her and held her close.

38

Wednesday finally arrived and Mikayla finally had a short work day. Rowan was better and was working that day, as well. Mikayla was working the morning shift and Rowan was working the later shift. She was so happy to see Rowan walk into the store, she worked an extra hour just to stay and fill Rowan in on the details of what she and Caleb had been doing. Rowan listened with pure excitement. She was so happy for Mikayla and could see she was truly happy, which was the only thing she ever wanted for her best friend.

The spark in Mikayla's eyes was finally back. Rowan couldn't remember the last time she had seen it, but it was there and in her mind she silently thanked Caleb.

The days with Caleb just kept getting better, she felt so close to Caleb and she knew she was finally ready to tell him. She thought it would be important for her to do it before Dominick came home so she and Caleb could face the boys as a united front, a couple in love. Nobody could deny them if they were truly in love, not even Dominick. She decided Saturday would be the day, again she had the weekend off, which meant Sunday would be a day of exploring each other. The thought sent chills through her whole body. She was both scared and excited. *Definitely I will tell him Saturday, no matter what!* She said to herself as she made her way home from work.

Caleb had told Ali Rowan was better. Ali thought it was best if they all met out at a dance club, he thought it would be easier to get her friend to go dancing than to a party. Caleb agreed and made the call to Mikayla on Friday.

"Hey, I'm hungry, did you eat yet?" he asked.

"Actually, my mom is having dinner at our restaurant with some of the other families so I haven't," she said, glad to have someone to eat dinner with.

"Good, I will be there in twenty…oh, but before I forget, Jackson's band is playing tomorrow night at the Front Room. Will you please come? And why don't you invite Rowan so I can get to know her? If I can get her on my side perhaps that will help us out with your brother." Caleb said, hating to lie but having no choice.

"Sounds like a great plan, actually. Let me give her a call and I will be outside in twenty," she said, hanging up the phone to finish getting ready.

Cell phones were too much of a hassle between the two, so Mikayla used telepathy with Rowan instead, asking her about Saturday. Rowan was on it. She didn't have to be asked twice to get to know Caleb. From the change in Mikayla, she was already a fan, but she still wanted to watch it with her own two eyes.

Alright, we will drive together tomorrow. Come to my house and we will get ready here, Mikayla said, finalizing the plans.

Sounds like a plan, but I haven't had much of a chance to spend time with you. How about we go lay out in the daytime for a little girl time together, just you and me! Away from the family so we can really talk. The boys will be back soon and I think it would be a great time to just have some time to ourselves! Rowan said, hoping Mikayla liked the idea.

That sounds perfect! I could really use some Row time! Mikayla said, getting excited to have Rowan all to herself for part of the day. She was so glad her friend was now feeling better.

Mikayla was glad Rowan was being so encouraging. Caleb was right, she would need as many people as she could get on her side so her relationship would be supported. But despite all the support, she knew dealing with Dominick would be hard. The sudden thought of him crushed her.

Out of nowhere, she had an idea. She had no clue if it would even work, but she was going to try it. No matter what she would always love Dominick, and she wanted the best for him, those were the exact words going through her head when she decided to try and do something about it. I want the best for him, kept ringing through her ears.

She went into her drawer of collected crystals, herbs, and candles she collected from the store and took out the laminar crystal she had just purchased a few days earlier. It was her intention to try and use it for herself, but right now Dominick seemed more important than herself. Without a clue of how to use any of them, she would try to follow the patterns she saw in some of the spells she had come across at the store and the rest would come from her heart.

First she purified her room with sage and a blessing ,much the same way she had witnessed Mrs. Munoz do weekly at the herbal shop. Then she lit a white candle with the scent of linen and placed it in front of her as she sat with her legs crossed in front of it on the floor. With her right hand she held the Larimar crystal tight and held it against her heart. She knew it was a stone which held properties of helping to find true love, it is partly why she bought it in the first place, counting on and hoping it would work.

As she sat in front of the candle with the stone in hand, she closed her eyes and thought of Dominick. She concentrated on him until she felt she had tapped into his energy, which was her instinct and had nothing to do with anything she read. It also wasn't something she had ever done before, but she felt desperate to try and make things right for him.

The room around her seemed quiet, Mikayla wasn't sure if she was really tapped into his energy, but the buzzing sound which started getting louder and softer and louder again in uneven tones in her ears was telling her she may actually be tapped in. Without second guessing herself, she decided to go with it. Somehow it felt natural to her. She held the energy, which seemed to be zooming in and out, trying to get it to stabilize, so she wouldn't lose it when she performed the next step.

A few minutes passed by as the buzzing in her ears stabilized into a low humming, holding Dominick in her mind and his spirit in her heart. She felt it was time for the blessing, not knowing how long she could keep hold of the energy swirling all around her. Freely she let the words flow out of her using a spell from one of the books as her guide.

"By wind, through fire, over ocean, on earth, bring him his true love to make his heart no longer hurt. Bless him for he is a good soul and make his true love appear. Bring forth a girl with the heart of a lion and the face of a goddess, bring forth a girl with the soul of an angel and the faithfulness of air, bring forth a girl wild and brave. I ask whatever energy it is that I possess to please bring forth Dominick his one true love, his soul mate." She said passionately, with every ounce of energy she possessed.

When she was finished she sat with her eyes closed until she felt the energy leave her body and mesh with Dominick's energy. For a moment she could hear wind sweeping by her ear. Then she heard the burning crackles of a flame followed by the waves of the ocean. Last she heard what sounded like a single pair of footsteps slowly walking away from her, and although she couldn't see it she could feel whatever it was had taken Dominick's energy with it. Somehow it didn't worry her, it was a warm peaceful feeling and as it was finally gone, the humming she had heard stopped. She opened her palm to find her hand around the stone had changed shape. It had been in an polished oval shape and now it was unpolished in a natural state. Mikayla could hardly believe it, but at the same time was willing to believe it just so Dominick would be happy one day. She really did love him, but it was time for them to move on, and now she was in love with Caleb, so in love she felt she would be with him forever.

However, despite her feeling as if she had done the right thing by Dominick, she couldn't help but feel a loss when she heard the footsteps walk away. Looking down at the changed stone, she couldn't help but feel uneasy at the thought she had finally let Dominick go. Tears filled her eyes as the memories of Dominick throughout her life passed quickly through her mind, as if she were watching a movie on fast forward. The last image to come into her mind was the kiss they had shared just a couple of weeks earlier. The knot in her stomach tightened as she stared down at the Lamina. She reminded herself it was the right thing to do, selflessness was always better no matter how much it may hurt, she reminded herself as she took in a deep breath and blew it out. It was the right thing to do and, at the last thought, she smiled at the thought of Dominick's happiness.

The time had gotten away from her. She looked up at the clock and realized Caleb had probably been waiting for her for fifteen minutes. Mikayla was never late and quickly reached for her phone to dial his number.

"I am so sorry, I lost track of time. I am coming right out," she said, embarrassed by her lack of consideration as she explained before he could even finish a hello.

"No worries, I would wait forever for you if I had to," Caleb replied, having meant every single word he said.

Mikayla rushed out the door and down the street to his car. After apologizing again, she tried to explain she was in the middle of doing something important without telling him exactly what it was she was doing. He would think she was crazy, and it was too soon for her to tell him about these little things she could do. She wasn't sure she would ever actually give that information out, but whether or not, now wasn't the time.

Since they were going out as a group the following night, they decided to spend the night alone together. Ali was tucked away in his room with his door shut, and Jamahl was hanging out at Mary's work hanging out with his new BFF Jackson until she got off of work. Jamahl had been just as absent as Caleb, having fallen for Mary. Caleb wasn't sure what to make of it, but he knew all of them couldn't help but like Mary, and Jamahl seemed to like her even more.

Caleb took Mikayla out on to the porch and put a couple of logs in the fire pit. He offered her a soda as they settled into a couple of lawn chairs in front of the fire. It smelled so good, it reminded Mikayla of spending summer nights at the lake and the bonfires they would make at night so they could roast marshmallows to make s'mores. Thinking of those times, she smiled and shared some of those stories with Caleb.

Listening to the stories, Caleb realized just how different the worlds they came from were. He had no childhood memories so sweet and innocent. The best memories he had were of Ali and Jamahl. They had been raised by one of the most evil beings who walked the earth. Needless to say they didn't get much love, however they did get encouragement, and out of that encouragement they grew into immortal men capable of deceit and murder, just to name a few. Had it not been for the company and love for and from his brothers, Caleb knew he would be much worse than he already was. However, that was all he knew, and he enjoyed listening to these stories picturing what it must have been like. He never knew his parents and often wondered what it would have been like if they hadn't died, but whenever he thought Ali and Jamahl would then not be in the picture, he stopped himself from wondering; for the thought of life without them was something he couldn't fathom, nor wanted to.

Caleb smiled at Mikayla, who was apologizing for going on and on about her childhood.

"Don't apologize, I love listening to your stories. It helps me to get to know you better," he said and reassured her with a smile.

She smiled back, feeling lucky to have someone who didn't mind when she babbled on and on.

"What about you? Did you ever make campfires as kids?" She asked with wonder in her eyes.

"Not really. We started fires, but never a campfire. Our father never took us camping, I guess you could say his idea of camping is staying at a mediocre hotel and he is not into that, so pretty much camping was out," Caleb said, trying to be honest without giving too much information of his childhood.

Mikayla thought she noticed a sense of sadness in his voice, which made her reach for his hand. He smiled at her as he took it. He knew what she was thinking, but she didn't have it right. It wasn't because he didn't get to go camping he was sad, it was thinking about his birth parents being around as a tradeoff to his brothers was always something which conflicted him.

"What happen to your parents?" She blurted out before thinking. Nervously she fidgeted with her can of soda as she felt the blood rush into her cheeks out of pure embarrassment for bringing up the topic. "I am sorry, you don't have to answer that," she added.

Caleb started to laugh. "Relax, Mikayla. I am fine," he said, which Mikayla thought was surprisingly nonchalant. "I don't know and I don't really care," he explained.

"I don't mean to pry, but how can you say that you don't care?" Mikayla asked, shocked by his answer, realizing she didn't read him well at all on that subject. Her mouth was partly open as her brain raced to figure out the next thing to say to him.

"Look, if my parents had raised me then I wouldn't have Ali and Jamahl. I grew up with them as brothers and no amount of blood relations could ever replace that bond. I can't miss what I never knew, but I do know Ali and Jamahl and I don't know what I would do without them." Caleb spoke honestly as he shifted the logs in the fire pit around to make the fire flame higher.

Mikayla was taken back with what he said, it made sense to her, but now she was left without words. "Wow, that is powerful," was all she could manage as she watched him make the flames burner higher.

You have no idea, Caleb thought silently to himself.

Silence fell between the two of them for a few minutes as they watched the flames underneath the stars.

"I think I owe you some dinner, you hungry?" Caleb broke the silence, remembering he was supposed to feed her.

"I am," she replied and was glad he had said something and broke the silence.

"What do you want?" He asked and shot her a smile to reassure her the conversation really didn't bother him and she was worrying for nothing.

"I don't want to leave, so how about we just order a pizza!" She suggested and smiled back at him, letting him know she understood.

"That's my girl," he said, taking out his cell phone to order one.

Mikayla thought how peaceful it was there on the porch with a fire, waiting for dinner to arrive next to Caleb. If another night came and was never any different than it was right now, then her life would be perfection. More than anything, she wished she could see his face every night before she closed her eyes and every morning when they opened. His energy consumed her.

Her energy consumed him.

They spent the rest of the night after dinner under the stars by the fire talking. They didn't go into Caleb's room once. It wasn't that they meant to keep away from the room, but they were talking so deep and enjoying every moment, the time got away from them and before they knew it, it was time for Mikayla to be taken home.

That night she decided she would sneak back out, having missed their daily cuddle time. She wanted one more innocent night with him because she knew after tomorrow those nights would be gone.

Caleb held her tighter than normal that night, worried Saturday night things could possibly go wrong. He hoped with every ounce of his soul Rowan turned out to not be the one and finding out would be fast and easy with no harm done. One wrong move could leave Mikayla hating him and that was something he wouldn't be able to live with. Fear made him stay up all night, watching her in his arms as she slept. Whenever she moved in her sleep, he scooped her right back into his arms, tightly aligning her body perfectly next to his so he could feel as much of her as possible.

"I love you, Mikayla," he whispered in her ear while she slept. "Follow me when I go," he added and kissed her softly on the top of her head as he held her just a little bit closer.

The sun was starting to rise. Caleb knew he needed to wake her up and get her home. He didn't want to take her home; he worried about what would happen that night. During the night he decided Jamahl, Ali, and he had to have a talk to try and make things run as smoothly as possible. He knew he couldn't take the chance of losing her, but he also knew from talking with Ali it wasn't going to be pretty. It wasn't as if they could charm her, that didn't work on witches, so they would have to figure some other way of doing it on the sly. Nothing came to his mind yet, but he was counting on the three of them to be able to figure something out. Perhaps a spell of some sort, but that would require getting her alone and it wasn't looking like a good possibility. For now he put it aside to focus back on the present with Mikayla gracefully asleep in his arms where she belonged.

The gentle stroking of her hair by Caleb woke her up. As she opened her eyes, she saw Caleb laying over her, staring down as he brushed his hand gently over her hair. The look in his eyes was pure love, not only could she see it but she felt it, and there had never been a time before she saw someone look at her with that amount of intensity. She shivered at the power of it. Time around her seemed to stop as she stared back into his eyes, reveling she loved him too, but still she didn't say it. She wanted to wait until that night and make it special so they had the rest of the night together afterwards. This would be her first time and she wanted it to be special.

"It's time," Caleb whispered, still stroking her hair.

"No," Mikayla said, looking sad because she didn't want to leave.

"Believe me there is nothing I want more than for you to stay with me. I would take forever, but I can't ruin things with your family before I have a chance to build a foundation with you. I have to take you home." He said, but still didn't move. Instead he leaned in further and kissed her softly and slowly.

With every movement of his lips and tongue, Mikayla could feel energy travel throughout her veins, vibrating gently, causing the goosebumps to come forth in a domino effect, as if she could feel each one separately as they made their way to the surface of her warm, soft skin.

"I really do love you," he whispered, breaking the kiss and lifting himself up knowing, if he didn't break it now he wouldn't be able to.

Mikayla desperately wanted to tell him, but she really wanted tonight to be a surprise. It took every ounce of strength for her to keep it inside and not just throw herself into his arms and tell him she felt the same ,but that would only ruin the surprise for the night, so she bit her tongue and opted for silence as she stretched, trying to get her body to move out of his bed. A task which seemed easier said than done.

Silence filled the jeep on the ride back to Mikayla's as Caleb grew worried about the night and as Mikayla yearned for it at the same time. When he made his way into the neighborhood, he grabbed her hand and squeezed it tightly, as if he were trying to tell her something. Instincts took over as she assured whatever it was he wanted to tell her she would be there. She affirmed it further by smiling her beautiful, white smile as her full, perfect lips parted. Caleb then pulled her hand to his mouth and breathed in as he pulled up to her usual drop off spot.

They really had pushed the time and Mikayla's mom would be getting up soon. So without any further hesitation, she opened the door and got out, turning towards him. "I will see you tonight and I have something to give to you then!" She said nonchalantly as a teaser, wanting him to wonder all day what it was.

"Oh yeah, what's that?" He raised an eyebrow, looking dangerous.

"It's a surprise, so I guess you will just have to wait," she said teasingly, and quickly shut the door so she could have the last word and made her way towards her house.

As Caleb did what he usually did, watched her walk to her house, he smiled. No one had ever had a surprise for him before; he couldn't imagine what it was she got him. He laughed when he decided she must have bought him an alarm clock. The only alarm clock they had at his house was his cell phone. Mikayla had mentioned on more than one occasion it was weird he didn't have a clock in his room and threatened to go out and by him one. It wasn't a sentimental gift, but Caleb thought definitely practical and showed she planned on being around a lot more. The thought made him laugh as he turned the car around and made his way back towards the house. He had a lot to figure out that day so he wouldn't lose her and the more time he had to try and get a plan together the better. He had to make sure things went flawlessly, the future of he and Mikayla depended on it.

39

It didn't take Mikayla long to fall back asleep. She had slept more irregularly than she ever had before. It was now early morning and the sun was starting to shine through her window. As the sun grew brighter, she fell deeper into sleep until she woke up in the middle of the park wearing a red ball gown...or so she thought.

It was strange to see the park with large white tents and tables decorated to the nines. Usually people kept their barbeques simple, but this was anything but, Mikayla thought as she looked around taking in all of the flowers and the other décor. She couldn't remember how she had got to the park, or why she was in the red dress. She never remembered even buying a red dress. The only people she noticed in the tent were the wait staff and a lady in business attire ordering them around as they set silverware around the table. Mikayla finally figured it out. The tent set up was for a wedding taking place. She smiled at the thought.

The smile quickly faded when she remembered she was in the red dress. She wondered if she had been sleep walking, everything seemed so real she didn't think she could be sleeping. It had to be something else, something she was forgetting. Just then she heard the soft music of a quartet starting to play just beyond the tent. Curiosity got the best of her and she made her way towards the beautiful sounds of string instruments being played to perfection.

She came around the side of the tent to find rows and rows of white chairs perfectly aligned divided by an aisle. At the front, off to the right, she saw the quartet. he hadn't looked at the audience or the groom yet because she was so intrigued by the music. It was melodic and smooth. A smile formed across her face as she watched.

Suddenly, out of the corner of her eye, she noticed something waving. Mikayla focused on a lady dressed in black with long white hair. She was beautiful, but looked to be quite old. It looked as though she were waving at Mikayla. Just to check, Mikayla looked behind herself to make sure it wasn't someone else she was waving to, but there was no one behind her. Mikayla put up her hand to wave and noticed the lady stopped and had a sudden, cold look on her face. It was as if no one else was noticing what was happening. All the other guests were oblivious to the lady standing in front, waving at her; not one person turned around. The lady's face then turned grim and she charged at Mikayla, moving faster than anyone her age should ever have the ability to, Mikayla decided.

There was something about the way the lady moved which frightened her. It was creepy and quick. If Mikayla didn't know better, she would have guessed she was actually floating, but if she were then the others would notice, and still no one else seemed to be paying any attention to the lady coming at her.

Mikayla took her eyes off of the floating lady for a moment longer to see if perhaps the groom and his best man were even paying attention. At first it didn't register to her what she was seeing. A tall handsome man built of strength and pride standing handsome with a single red rose pinned to the side of his jacket ,standing next to another nice looking gentleman, also full of muscle but a bit shorter than the groom. It helped to take her mind off of the lady who seemed to be moving fast towards her, but strangely had not yet reached her. She looked at the lady and saw she was barely half way to her. Mikayla scratched her head, having a hard time understanding what it was she was witnessing. It was making her uneasy so she focused her attention back on the groom and was startled when she realized who it was she was looking at.

"Dominick?" She said out loud, as if she had said it first and thought it second. Next to him she noticed her brother. They seemed to not be able to see her.

She was completely confused, so she started to walk down towards Dominick. As she took her first couple of steps, the lady in black suddenly appeared in front of her. Seeing her brother and Dominick had made her completely forget about the woman.

The woman appeared to be yelling at her, although Mikayla heard nothing coming out of her mouth.

"I am sorry, I don't know why you are angry, and for some reason I cannot hear what you are saying…" Mikayla trailed off, noticing the woman was holding something and shaking it at her.

Mikayla tried to focus on the blue thing in her hand. Finally she recognized it. It was the blue lamina stone she had used earlier that day to perform what she thought may be a true love finding spell.

"My stone?" She questioned the women.

The women stopped her silent yelling and handed Mikayla the stone. When Mikayla took it from her, she threw her head to the sky and let out a tremendous scream. This time Mikayla could hear it. No one else in the area seemed to notice. Mikayla felt, at that moment, she had to be dreaming.

She tried to put a hand on the woman's shoulders to try and comfort her pain. The lady stopped screaming and began to weep.

"Are you alright?" Mikayla asked, but the lady did not respond, she only kept weeping.

Mikayla did the only thing she could think of and that was to pull the lady closer to her. The weeping became quieter and quieter as the lady started to fade. It was the strangest thing she had ever seen and, as if she had never been there, she was gone.

She then looked back to where Dominick was and began to walk down the aisle towards him. Mikayla finally decided it must be a dream and knew she really wouldn't be interrupting anything by heading forward.

She was almost to Dominick when he finally seemed to notice her.

"Stop!" He shouted as her brother looked at her with hate in his eyes.

"Dominick it's me!" Mikayla said, shocked even though this was just a dream he would be so cold.

"Stay back, far back! I don't know what you have done, but stay back!" He shouted.

Mikayla couldn't help but feel the lump in her throat swell. She gulped back the tears before they could fall. "I don't understand!" She shouted back, feeling angry at the rejection.

"Oh you don't? You did this!" He said with venom in his voice.

"What is it that you think I have done?" She asked.

"You set forth a motion that now cannot be undone," he said with just as much venom and looked at the rock she was holding in her hand.

Mikayla starred down at the rock for a moment. Finally the tears she held back started streaming down her face. "I am sorry. I just wanted you to be happy," she said softly to him.

"No Kali, you didn't. You wouldn't let it happen. I was willing to have my offspring take on a new legacy to be with you," he said stonily.

"I don't understand what that means…" she said, approaching him.

"No!" He said, putting his hand up. Everyone else around began to chatter, making it seem as if the world was turning faster.

"Why? Is this because I want you to move on?" She asked.

"It's what will become of you. I would have protected you, but you didn't find forgiveness in your heart so it is you who will now suffer long term. My suffering will soon be over," he said, warningly.

"What suffering?" Mikayla was now angry at being threatened.

He said nothing back to her, instead he turned his head to Mario and started whispering to him while pointing at Mikayla. Mikayla couldn't help but feel all the others around her doing the same thing. She scanned the room to find indeed that was exactly what was happening.

"What are you all talking about?" She found herself getting overly caught up in the dream. No one answered her. "Stop it!" She cried.

All of a sudden a little girl stood dressed in a pink dress and pigtails with hair the color of night and eyes as green as emeralds which popped off her olive skin tone. "Hello," Mikayla said trying to be kind amongst the craziness.

The little girl smiled up at her and held out her hand. Mikayla reached for it. The little girl then began to speak. "I will take care of him, I waited my whole life. Thank you," the little girl said. Mikayla was completely confused, but she liked the little girl. She couldn't put her finger on it but she felt connected to the little girl.

All of a sudden the little girl was holding a leash. On the other end of the leash was the largest dog she had ever seen. It was a husky, she thought, although it's legs were much longer than she ever remembered seeing a husky have. The wolf was white with green eyes.

"What,s your doggie's name?" Mikayla asked.

The little girl didn't answer, instead she covered her mouth and giggled.

Mikayla couldn't help but giggle at the little girls reaction. All of a sudden she heard Rowan screaming from behind her. She turned, and sure enough it was Rowan screaming and running towards her.

"No!" Rowan said, trying desperately to get to Mikayla.

"Rowan!" Mikayla let the little girl's hand go and began to run to her friend, who was obviously upset.

Just then, from behind, her brother appeared and grabbed Rowan, who was now reaching out towards Mikayla crying.

Mikayla stopped in her tracks, stunned. Then out of nowhere she began to feel extremely warm. It was making her dress drenched with sweat. Rowan then let out a blood curdling scream as she pointed at Mikayla's arms.

Mikayla looked down to try and figure out what she was pointing and screaming at. Her red dress was now white and red, she first noticed, then she looked at her arms. There seemed to be tiny little bite marks all over her arms as blood gushed out of them. It was Mikayla's turn to let out a blood curdling scream. As she did she scanned the rest of her body and realized it was a white dress she had been wearing and the red in the dress was blood. Her blood, and she began to feel tiny marks all over her body and the wetness of the blood as it poured out.

"Look out!" Rowan shouted to her as Mario still kept hold of her.

Mikayla didn't have a chance to turn around before she could feel him. It was Caleb. She felt safe in his presence and turned around to bury herself in his arms. He smelled just as good in her dreams as he did in person. The comfort of him made her racing heart beat slow down. For a moment she had forgotten about the blood and the other craziness until she heard a familiar voice.

"Kali! I said I would be back and this is what you do to me!" Marcus's voice came from a seat amongst the people in the middle of a row.

She was stunned and didn't know what to say. She watched in silence as he made his way towards them. All the while Caleb kept a safe hand on her.

"Let her go, Caleb," Marcus said.

Before Caleb could answer, Rowan let out another scream pointing at Caleb's face. Quickly Mikayla turned around and found the skin around his eyes had changed. Mikayla blinked a few times, trying to clear her view. Once she refocused, he looked like the same Caleb she had got to know; beautiful, strong and caring. Mikayla turned her head back to face the crowd.

"What is going on with you people?" She screamed. All of a sudden she felt a sharp piercing on the side of her neck. The pain was intense and she could feel herself start to fade. Soon she faded into darkness and all stood still.

40

It had been only a few days since Layla and her family had returned from Lebanon, but she had taken those days to recuperate from the trip so she could enjoy the concert she, her brother and some friends were going to. It was Friday and she was ready to let loose. They had just spent the last couple of weeks around family and it felt good to be home so they could really let loose and have some fun. Lebanon was great, but she was ready to come home.

Layla was Lebanese and Italian. Her mother was Lebanese and her father, who was killed while her mother escaped with her in the womb, was from Italy. She was raised in southern Florida until she was seventeen, then her family relocated to Lebanon for a year and then to Italy and had been there for the past few years since. Her family had intended on moving back to the states eventually, but her mother wanted her children to have experiences in both her home country and their father's, so during Layla's college years her mother decided it would be the best time for them to do so.

Layla's mom was a powerful witch with much patience. Her father had also been a powerful witch, but he was also half werewolf from his mother's side of the family. This made for an interesting mix for all three children. She was not an only child. Layla had two brothers.

Her oldest brother, Ra'ad, was in training to become one of the members of the Seven Points of Light Council. It was the witches' hierarchy; it was their lawmakers and rulers. The future for his spot on the council was far away, but nonetheless, he was in training for it along with one other young man and a young woman around his age.

During their training, they were put through a combat training program first, which would get them ready to spend time with the Dark knights. This was considered the police force of the witch world. Some of those picked for training would stay only with the Dark Knights, and others would be handpicked as apprentices for the council as they still served as part of the Dark Knights. This is where they are then shaped to eventually sit on the Seven Points of Light Council. Ra'ad was in transition to move into the apprentice council.

Ra'ad was the oldest and strongest of his siblings. He was able to channel into his wolf side and worked hard to utilize it into shapeshifting, unlike his younger brother who showed more wolf than either Ra'ad or Layla. During a full moon, Ajay would lose control over himself. His temper would rise and it caused him to make a lot of bad judgements. When he was seventeen the problems started. His mother tried to send him off to some distant cousins in hopes he would learn how to control the wolf within him, but he was too rebellious and refused. Over the years he managed to get to a point where he learned his own way of working with it. Still, it was not under control. Layla though had no signs of having to control herself during a full moon. Instead, her wolf side came to her in visions, like a spirit guide, who always kept a close watch over her. She was recently beginning to learn how to communicate with the shadow of the wolf that followed her. After college was finished, she was going to learn more about the shadow wolf by spending some time herself with her distant cousins from her father's side of the family.

Her other brother was Ajay, the middle child, also older than her but only by two years, which is what they all were, two years apart. He was the prankster in the family, a bit of an adrenaline junkie, but Layla and him were the best of friends. He had a heart of gold but was always getting into trouble, unlike Ra'id who was well-spoken, strong, and perfect. Ajay had an edge, perhaps he got lost behind the great expectations of his brother to follow in his father's footsteps, alongside with growing up without his father. He was only two years old when his father died. The wolf within him was restless, unlike Ra'ad who had completely conquered the wolf within. Again it was only one more thing Ajay felt inferior to his older brother for. Although both were strong, they were like night and day.

Layla's life growing up was different than Rowan or Mikayla's. Unlike them, she was told of her powers. She was also told of the other witch, Rowan, who had survived as well, but she, like everyone else besides a few people, didn't know about Mikayla. Her mother wanted to make sure if anyone ever came back she knew how to use her powers so she could protect herself.

Her mother, Diya, was a ball of fire. She was strong and independent and she would do nothing but make sure her children survived. She had never remarried. She loved Layla's father and decided until she met him up in the heavens, she would remain without a partner. She could always feel him looking down and they would meet in her dreams. Diya was bound by true love for all eternity.

Her household was a tough one; Layla was treated like one of the boys, although she looked like a princess. She, too, had long dark hair like Rowan and Mikayla, only her hair was much darker, it was almost black and her eyes matched her hair, although during the a full moon they would shine a bright green. Her skin tone was a beautiful olive which showed she belonged to the Mediterranean. Her brothers were equally as attractive as she was. Ajay took full advantage with his looks, while Ra'id felt he had no time or want to move from girl to girl. Layla knew when the time was right, Ra'ad would do things the old fashioned way and not the way of the humans, but of the witches. On the other hand, she prayed Ajay would practice safe sex and not bring any unexpected children into the world. She hoped one day his rebellious heart would find the one who would tame him and make him finally feel full. Ajay and Ra'id really were like night and day, which is what her mother referred to them, calling them Sole figlio and Luna figlio. She called them her children of the sky. She called Mikayla the child of her heart.

It was a beautiful night and she was going out to enjoy it with her brother. He shared an apartment with her. They were only miles away from their mother's house, but wanted the experience of being young and independent ,so they took up an apartment together closer to the downtown hotspots and Layla's school. It was a small two-bedroom apartment with a living space and small kitchen. Their porch was much larger than the kitchen and it was big enough for a table and chairs, as well as a small lounge area. This is where they would have most of their meals. The porch over looked the sea and it was peaceful. Tonight they were going out to a club to go dancing. A famous DJ was in town and they couldn't wait to dance into the night.

Layla looked through her closet, trying to find the perfect outfit. She chose a pool colored, short, strapless dress and paired it with a summer heel in the same color. She pulled her long hair back into a ponytail and put on a pair of silver earrings that looked tribal hanging from her ears. She was all set to go when she heard a knock on the door.

She reached the front door to peak out and saw it was Ra'id. Layla opened the door.

"What are you doing here? Isn't it past your bed time?" Layla said jokingly as she grabbed to hug her older brother. Ra'id hugged her back before speaking.

"Something has been brought to my attention today. I am not supposed to say anything to anyone, so don't ask, but it just made me want to see you," he said honestly.

"Well we don't keep secrets in our family Ra'id, you know that, so talk," Layla said, going into the kitchen to grab him a bottle of water.

As she entered back into the living room from the kitchen he had taken a seat on the couch. She brought back the bottle of water and handed it to him.

"Talk," she said, as if she knew he would have a hard time not telling her.

He said he couldn't tell her, but it only made him want to come and see her. This told her he wanted to at least tell her something. She wouldn't push him too much, allowing him to keep what he needed to keep safe, but tossing around whatever was going on in his head. Ra'id let out a big sigh.

"Nothing is as it seems, it wasn't just one thing I found out tonight, it is two things, and I really cannot tell you, not yet. A couple of weeks ago a couple of other things were brought to my attention and tonight I have learned another piece that is making my heart feel unsettled. Once I learn more and understand the threats I will know if I can tell you. But the information has left me baffled. It seems as if nothing is as it seems. There is storm brewing in the air. Promise me to be careful and call on me if anything weird happens, and I mean anything. What we think we know isn't all that we know and what we think is good sometimes strays for various reasons. The world I know is starting to tilt upside down and I will not be part of any of it. I will always honor our family and our father, this I promise you ,and I want you to always know that," Ra'id said.

Layla thought it sounded a bit cryptic, but she would take it and she knew just how to give him a little piece of comfort.

"I will always call you when I need you and I am always careful. I know you have told me what you can, but when you are able to tell me more I want you to come right to me." She said to him as she grabbed his hand in promise. Just then the door flew open.

"Let's go! The night is ours!" Ajay shouted from the front door, bringing in a case of beer and what looked like tickets.

As he came through the door, three of his friends followed. He looked shocked to see Ra'id sitting quietly on the couch.

"What are you doing here?" He asked rudely. Ajay was ready to have fun and he thought his brother repelled fun. Tonight he was not in the mood for one of his brother's lectures.

"I just came by to see Layla," he said, getting up from the couch.

"Was nice to see you," Ra'id said and headed for the door.

Layla shot Ajay a dirty look as she followed her oldest brother to the door.

"Remember, be careful," Ra'id said to her before walking out. She grabbed and hugged him goodbye and promised him she would. She watched him walk towards his car and wondered what all of it meant.

As she was standing outside, she realized the weather truly was beautiful and the night would be great. She closed the front door and grabbed a beer from her brother. Layla joined the party as everyone in the crowd was talking about the other DJs who were opening for the headlining act. It was going to be a great night and not the night she would try once again to repair the broken bond between her two older brothers.

Aidan, Ahiah, and Rory where waiting patiently across from the apartment, the terrace seemed to be busy, they thought. "Tonight is the night, I can feel it. I haven't seen any other people around that we need to worry about in the past couple of weeks, so I think we might be still under the radar. The only question is how do we get her alone?" Aidan said, slicking back his jet-black hair with both of his hands. His skin was creamy white and he had green eyes bright as jewels. Aiah looked much like Aidan; however, Rory was a redhead with brown eyes and freckles.

The boys had been back from France for a little over a week, making sure they kept a close watch on people coming and going from the apartments just in case the missing witch from the light council who Cyrus beheaded had been able to send warnings out before she died. It wasn't even clear if any of them knew about the Angel's Breath, so the fact the witch was missing, well, now dead, wouldn't necessarily have them tie anything to these girls. The seer was the one who was channeling the prophecy, and he was the only seer still in existence who was known. Perhaps they saw prophecies another way, but they didn't see the first one about the girl witches, and if they did, they sure as hell didn't do anything about it to help any of them, hence only two from that year survived. Obviously it was a waste of time to kill so many witches and not end up with the right one, but Aidan knew it was a good thing she hadn't been killed. There was much she could help him with and he would make her do it. He would find her weakness and use it to get what he needed out of her. He hoped they would not have to go any further, that the girl standing outside on the terrace was the one they needed and the ticket for their freedom.

In the meantime, he had sent the wild hyenas to Maine, mapping out a path for them to take to get to Ann Arbor Michigan where Caleb, Jamahl, and Ali were. He hadn't heard anything about the hyenas from any of them, though. He tried to get a hold of them but there was no response. He had assumed perhaps some hunters got to them first, or that their elders had found them and had them held somewhere trying to bring them back into reality. This worried Aidan a little bit, but he figured no news at all was better than news that the hyenas had screwed everything up and ratted him out. With that, he shrugged his shoulders. Perhaps they have been wreaking havoc and the boys just don't want to tell us, he thought to himself, deciding it was another good possibility. He thought about it for a few more minutes as he watched Layla, who was out on the terrace laughing and drinking a beer with her friends.

They sat silently watching the action across the way on the terrace, trying to decipher what it was they were doing. It wasn't going to be at her apartment, which was obvious, because it did look like they were getting ready to go out for the night.

"We can't come up with an exact plan because we do not know what she is doing, so we are going to have to follow her and see what transpires. It's going to be a split decision, so we need to keep tight tonight. This is our only focus," Aidan said.

"We will follow them. Perhaps if we slip something in her drink it will take the worry about sneaking up on her. She could give us a run for our money if she is strong enough," Aiah said.

"Yes, but she has to be quick enough. We are quicker in movement than they are, even with their orbing. They need to get refocused, even if it only takes a brief second and that second is enough for us to make a move. We don't have that, we never have to get refocused, and it's in our nature to be in constant motion." Aidan answered back. "But I do like the idea of slipping something in her drink to make her groggy. Yes we will follow her," Aidan added as he watched the girl out on the terrace, who was now looking at her brother who was shouting something as he held his drink up.

"Let's move out people!" Ajay said, holding up an empty beer bottle in the air.

Everyone quickly sipped down the last of their drinks before they headed out the door. Layla was the last to leave, locking the door behind her and putting her keys into her little purse. She then kicked off her heals and bent down to grab them as she hurried to catch up to the group already heading down the street.

Aidan rubbed his chin as he smirked. "This won't be hard, they aren't even driving. I think I know where it is that they are heading and it is a good ten minute walk, which is close enough for her to walk home alone. The key is for us to make sure she leaves alone, or at least with one of us," Aidan said as if he knew this task wasn't far from his reach. He just had to be creative, that's all, he thought to himself.

They watched the group walk down the street towards a busier part of the street where a few nightclubs were. It wasn't until they had watched them take a left that they decided to move from their watchtower and head closer towards

Layla, staying far enough behind as they kept a close eye on the group strolling on ahead.

It wasn't more than a ten-minute walk, just as Aiden suspected. As usual, Aiden was right, they saw the group heading into a line at the night club which he had suspected. It was busy and the line was long. Aidan hated waiting in any kind of line. He hated waiting for anything and he hated feeling like a commoner, which is exactly what he felt like as he, Aiah, and Rory made their way to the back of the line. They were only about seven people behind them in line.

Aidan stood quietly as Aiah and Rory made small talk, quietly picking out who they would drain and kill and who they would drain and have fun with. They were getting a little too carried away and Aidan shot them a look, they knew what the look meant and quickly quieted down and switched subjects.

They had waited in line for almost fifteen minutes before getting up to the front of the line.

"Tickets," the bouncer said in a thick, Italian accent.

It was obvious to the bouncer these three boys were not Italian. Aidan looked around realizing everyone in line had tickets. Quickly he grabbed a couple hundred euros out of his pocket and slipped it to the bouncer quietly.

"Are these the right tickets?" Aidan asked discretely.

The bouncer looked down at the money and the corner of his mouth turned up.

"I see two tickets here, but I can't seem to see the third one," the bouncer said antagonistically. Aidan reached back into his pocket and pulled out another hundred.

"Oh, sorry man. here it is," he said, restraining himself, trying to memorize the guy's face just in case they ran into him later so he could take his money back and drain the bouncer (who he had sized up as an overly grown meathead) of every last ounce of blood.

"I believe it is," the bouncer said, slipping three hundred euros into his pocket as he motioned with his hand for them to enter.

41

They walked into the large club and saw the place was packed. It was obvious the club had been sold out and Aidan was glad the bouncer was greedy enough to take his money. The dance floor was packed with people who were facing a DJ who was spinning on a stage above the crowd. Aidan focused his attention on the bars and they were also packed. He then scanned the room for Layla and spotted her in line waiting for a drink. That was perfect, he had thought to himself, and headed towards the bar as Aiah and Rory followed.

Aidan was very good looking, as was Aiah and Rory, and Aidan thought he would use that to peak her interest so they could get close enough to slip a sedative into her drink. They were just a couple of people behind her in line, but they wanted to be right behind her to make contact. Aidan tapped the smaller of the two guys who stood in between them and Layla. The smaller of the two guys turned around and Aidan just looked him in the eye. He used his hypnotic power to suggest to him the other bar was quicker. The guy said nothing, he just left the line. His friend watched as he walked towards the other bar and, as if he had no mind of his own, stepped out of line and followed his friend. Aidan, Aiah, and Rory laughed.

Now they were right behind her. Aidan noticed just how beautiful she was. She was olive skinned with long, dark, silky hair. All her features were perfect and she was slender and toned. He thought it was going to be a waste if it was her who had the life force of an Angel running through her. He couldn't let anyone have that kind of power unless it was himself. Wondering how to approach her, he decided accidentally bumping into her was the best way to get her attention without seeming obvious. He could then offer to purchase her drink.

Without warning the others, he stumbled forward and lightly bumped her. Layla turned around with an evil look on her face.

"What the fuck?" She said, turning around to look at who had just bumped her. Aidan put on the best innocent expression he could.

"I am so sorry, I was talking and didn't realize that I had gotten so close," he said. Layla just stared at him, although he was gorgeous, she was completely unaffected by his charms.

She had never had a boyfriend before. Her parents were so in love and had been each other's first everything, from first kiss to first and only love. Her mother told her it was just something she and her father knew. Both her parents never wasted time on people they felt were a maybe, they both believed when they found the right person they would just know, and they did. Layla felt the same way. She was sure it was a true feeling, and not just something she convinced herself of from the stories of her parents. She felt it was true for her because she could feel it deep in her gut, she would know immediately when she found the one she would spend forever with. It took only one look at this drop dead gorgeous man standing in front of her, practically perfect, to know it was not him. So she said nothing to him and turned back around without saying anything.

Aidan was baffled, she should have been happy to see his face. This should have been the easiest part of all. Taken back, he had to think for a moment. They were getting closer to the bartender. Layla was the next person in line for a drink. Aidan decided he better do something quickly before she decided to avoid him like the plague for the rest of the night.

"Hey, you seemed pissed that I bumped into you. Again, I am sorry, it wasn't intentional." He said, stepping next to her.

She didn't look his way at all.

"Yup, mmm hmm," was all she said.

"Seriously, let me make it up to you. I will buy you a drink. After all, by your accent I can tell that you are a fellow American, so if not for me, do it for your country. Let's keep the peace at home," he said with a smile on his face.

Layla started to laugh, she knew she was acting a bit harsh but she was use to guys pulling tricks on her just to get her attention. But it never worked because she was saving herself for the magic spark. She didn't expect the person she would find would do the same thing, or even be aware of what it was she was aware of. It was kind of a special gift that ran on both sides of her family, but she wasn't so stupid as to think the person who would be right for her would have the same gift of knowing. She decided it would be a good idea for her to lighten up just a little bit.

Layla turned towards Aidan. "Fine, you can buy me a drink, but don't think that means I owe you anything." She said, now looking at him.

"Of course not, just trying to be a gentlemen," he said, holding up a scouts honor gesture.

Layla laughed again as he smiled, which made her stiffen. Something about him when he smiled seemed dangerous. She watched him for a minute as he shuffled around nervously, which made her relax a bit more, thinking perhaps he was just nervous. It had been a couple of months since they had bought tickets to the event and she really didn't want to deal with things that seemed off. She would simply take her drink and try and stay away from these boys for the rest of the night, just in case her instinct about them was right. It was definitely not something she would bring to Ajay's attention because they would for sure be kicked out and the DJ line up was so sick she wouldn't chance it. Besides, they look innocent enough, she thought to herself.

That was the problem with vampires, there was always something about them which reeked of danger, yet they were such good bait for their pray you always ended feeling they were somehow trustworthy. It was one of the things which made them so dangerous. It worked just as well on immortals as it did humans. The bartender broke her train of thought by asking her what she wanted to drink. She had started out with a couple of beers at home and thought about it for a moment.

"Well, this guy's buying so what is your most expensive drink?" She asked with a grin on her face. The bartender answered her as she tapped her finger to her mouth in thought.

"In that case, I will have a tall light beer," she said as she smiled at Aidan.

Both the bartender and Aidan laughed. She acted as if she was going to make Aidan pay for a very expensive drink only to turn around and order the cheapest drink next to soda. Even the water was a little more expensive in a place like this if you wanted bottled.

Aidan added three more to the order, shaking his head still smiling as he thought about what a firecracker this girl was. He wouldn't mind at all keeping her around awhile for the pure entertainment of it all, not to mention she was stunning to look at. Aidan decided she would definitely make a great toy to play with for a while if he could figure out how to bind her powers without draining her energy. He knew there was a way to do it, but the knowledge was beyond his reach, it was also beyond the reach of Cyrus' knowledge, which is why they only had moments to get the names of the girls. It had also taken them months just to capture one of the members of the Dark Knights of the Light Council. There would definitely be some hell to pay for that one, but her death was at the hands of Cyrus, not him, and he was glad for that.

The bartender proceeded to grab four tall glasses and fill each one with the cheap light beer quickly so he could move on to the next person in line. He held up his fingers indicating the price. Aidan grabbed some money and handed it to him.

"Thanks for the beer," Layla said and smiled as she grabbed her beer.

"You are welcome," Aidan said and smiled back. Layla wanted to move, but she felt the least she could do after being harsh and letting him buy her a beer was stay for a moment of small talk.

"I think I'm gonna do a shot, I love the next DJ on the line up," Aidan lied, having no real clue as to who was next.

"Me too, I have seen him before and he is even better live than when you hear him on CDs." She said, appreciating where he was coming from since she was a music lover herself. Aidan held up his glass at her to toast her last comment. She reciprocated the move as their glasses clinked together in a cheer for the DJs who play good music.

Aidan looked to his brothers and asked if they wanted a shot. They both smiled and agreed it was definitely a good time for a shot. Aidan then looked at Layla and with just a look gestured with his finger as if to ask if she would join them.

"No, I think I will stick with the beer," she said hesitantly.

"Are you sure? I'm buying and I don't always offer free shots." He said honestly.

Layla squinted her eyes at him trying to size him up, she was already a little buzzed but tonight was her night. She was letting loose and enjoying the night. "Um…" She paused briefly. "Fine I will do one shot with you," she said, and lifted her glass to his.

"Alright, what kind of shot do you want?" Aidan asked.

"I don't care, just surprise me," she said as she focused her attention towards the DJ on stage.

The bartender came over quickly when Aidan signaled for him. Then he order four shots of tequila. Layla's head was still turned as she was enthralled with the DJ. It was obvious she couldn't wait to get out onto the dance floor where her brother and friends were. She decided she would take the shot and make a couple more minutes of small talk and then bail. It wasn't that this group of guys weren't attractive, they were, it was that she knew none of these guys were the one she was supposed to be with. Because she felt like that, she was able to blow guys off. She wasn't much into flirting and all though she looked like a girly girl, she was more of a tomboy at heart.

Aidan was getting a bit antsy, wanting the bartender to hurry up and bring forth the shots while her head was turned. Although it didn't take but a minute, Aidan felt like it was going in slow motion. He could tell from her personality this was the only chance they would get for the night to put a sedative into her drink. When the bartender put the shot glasses down on the counter, Aidan had the sedative placed between his pinky and ring finger on his left, which was the side, Layla was standing on.

As he reached for her shot, he slipped it in, keeping his hand on it to hide it as it quickly dissolved into the liquor. He paid for the shots then looked down at the one for Layla to make sure that it had indeed dissolved and it had. Then he tapped her on the shoulder.

"Bottoms up!" He said, handing her a shot.

He then gave the boys their shots.

"To long nights, great DJs, and new friends to take shots with!" He said as he held up his shot glass.

Layla really wanted to be on the dance floor but she played along and held up her glass. "To a great night!" She added, trying to seem friendlier than she currently felt.

They all tilted their heads back and threw the shots into their mouths, then they all slammed them on to the counter in unison. Together they all laughed. Even Layla thought it was funny, thinking about what that must have looked like to anyone standing around watching. It was as if they had practiced this together before.

Layla made some small talk as she finished her beer. When the beer was gone she motioned the bartender for one more as she proceeded to make more small talk with Aidan. They talked about the DJs and about why she was living in Italy. Aidan couldn't help but be a bit smitten with her. He could tell she was a tough cookie and that impressed him. She was the first girl ever who didn't fall for his charms. The bartender soon came with her beer and she settled up.

"Well, thanks for the shot and for the beer, I really need to get back to my friends but I am sure I will run into you later," she said, politely exiting.

"No problem, perhaps I will find you on the dance floor later." Aidan said as he smiled.

"Yeah, absolutely. If you see me come and dance." She said as she began to walk away.

"Oh, I will be seeing you later." He said as the look on his face went from innocent to devious.

Layla noticed the look on his face and it made her uncomfortable. Something was off about this guy; she all of a sudden could feel it in her gut.

Layla headed towards the dance floor where her brother and friends were already feeling the beats the DJ was spinning throughout the club. They were all in a state of trance, dancing in a group facing the stage. She finally got there and sipped on her beer a few more times before joining in.

"What took you so long?" Her friend Franco bent down to ask her.

"Oh, someone wanted to buy me a drink," she said casually.

"Oh, anyone good?" He asked curiously.

"Not for me," she said simply.

"Girlfriend, you are so picky. You are on the fast train to never getting any," he said as he laughed.

"As opposed to you, who will take anyone who is willing?" She bantered back.

"Honey, everyone is willing!" Franco said as he smiled and wagged his eyebrows.

Layla laughed. Franco was her best friend and they loved to joke around with each other.

The song changed with the next DJ and the lights got dimmer. Layla's favorite DJ came on and she finished the last of her beer and set it down on a high table off to the side of where they were all dancing. She immediately started clapping as she held her hands high up into the air and her feet began to move. Her brother and friends were all doing the same thing. Franco stood out the most. Layla started to check out the scene. She loved the way the crowd looked on the dance floor when there was a good DJ, it was as if the music literally was putting people into a trance, hence the name Trance, she always thought. Across the way she noticed the boy and his friends who bought her a drink watching her from across the dance floor. Franco noticed her looking at them and her looking back.

"Girlfriend, don't tell me that's who bought you a drink? If a guy looked like that and offered me a drink, I wouldn't care what instinct my gut had about meeting the right guy. I would settle for the guy right now. He is hot!" Franco said, admiring Aidan from across the room.

"Well, he is pretty, perhaps he plays for both teams. Want me to hook you up?" She said, smiling at Franco. Franco turned around and made a couple of full slow circles with his hips mimicking what he would like to do with Aidan if he had the chance. They started to full out belly laugh as they danced to the music.

42

The music was jamming and the dance floor was packed. Layla never looked towards Aidan again, she got lost in the music as her feet flowed freely underneath her. She had a small buzz from drinking a few beers and the shot and was feeling pretty good until a wave of dizziness came over her. She tried to ignore it at first. It was probably drinking the beer that did it, she thought to herself. Usually she never drank more than two drinks, but tonight she had already had four beers and a shot, which was a lot for her. Get a hold of yourself, she told to herself. It's really not that much alcohol, she then tried to convince her spinning head and turning stomach. Her dancing started to slow down as she heard the music speed up, making her feel even dizzier. She needed some fresh air, she thought to herself again. Fresh air would help her feel better, she thought. Not wanting to cause a scene, and not being in her right mind, she decided she needed to step out briefly and catch her breath.

"Hey, I'm going to get a water and go outside for a moment, I'm getting a little hot." She said to Franco, who was the closest, dancing right by her side. Her brother and the other boys they were with had a group of girls they were hanging around trying to impress. The last thing Layla wanted to do was bring drama to a great night, she wasn't that girl and she really could handle her own. It was still pretty early and the party would be going on for another five hours easily, so stepping outside she felt was her best bet.

"Are you ok? Want me to go with?" Franco asked.

"NO! You stay here, I will be back shortly," she said as she patted him on his back, really not wanting anyone to follow her around. She wanted him to stay right where he was and enjoy the DJs. Franco nodded and placed a kiss on top of her head.

Layla made it towards the door. The closer she got, the dizzier she became and she stumbled out of the front of the club, bumping into a few people on her way out. No one said anything to her because they could tell by the way she was moving it was completely unintentional. She made her way to the sidewalk and felt her stomach start to turn; she thought she was going to throw up any minute as she looked down. The sidewalk was spinning faster and faster. At that moment Layla knew she was in trouble. She couldn't even think about going back inside right now, she needed to go home.

She tried to focus long enough to get a clear picture of the path she would take home. More than anything she wanted to orb home, but the streets were crowded and it wouldn't be a good thing if she were seen doing so for many reasons. She knew she needed to suck it up and try and make it home, or to an empty alley which would allow her privacy so she could orb from there. With an alley in mind, she headed towards home as fast as she could, which, by the way she was feeling, wasn't fast at all. She kept her eye out for an alley the best she could as she concentrated on not passing out, but it was getting hard to keep the world from spinning around her.

Layla was to the end of the street, she made a right. That street was a little less busy than the street the club was on. She managed to walk a little bit faster, hoping she would be able to find an alley. It was looking to her as if she didn't try to orb home, she may actually not make it home. Her eyes were getting heavy, as if she had sand bags glued to her eyelids pulling them shut and the ground was spinning fast. All of this was almost enough for her to forget about the nausea, until she started to dry heave as she stumbled on. Layla looked desperately down the second alley she came across. The first alley was much too open and she had no real way of being discrete.

The second alley would have to do, she decided. It had a couple of large dumpsters she could hide behind and it was also not very well lit, which would help to conceal her even more. Her only hope now was she would have enough concentration left to actually orb. She made her way as quickly as she could into the alley. It took everything she had to scoot herself as fast as she did into the alley.

The alley smelled like trash and the brick street was damp from the rain which came through just hours earlier. She made her way to the side of the large trash can and tried to get herself to focus, but she was quickly loosing moments of time as she felt herself going in and out of consciousness. Then her knee's buckled. Layla grabbed the side of the dumpster for support as she crumbled down into a crouching position.

Fearful she would pass out in an alley, where god only knows what could happen to her if she blacked out, she tried harder to center herself. Unable to reach a place of balance, she decided to try to orb without being centered, but nothing happened. She knew it was a long shot. Having the gift of magic was an awesome power, and truly was a gift, but the energy had to be drawn from within. She braced herself and tried to will herself to orb again, and this time was knocked to her butt from the spark of energy trying to come forth. The spark quickly fizzled out, sending an electrical current back into her which was what knocked her over. She stayed there for a moment before trying to get to her feet again. Layla managed to get back into a crouching position when she felt a hand on her shoulder.

She was starting to black out now and hoped it was Franco or her brother standing over her. She looked to her left and saw a couple of pairs of feet, none of which she recognized. Right then she knew there were at least three of them, two pairs of feet to her left and one pair behind her. Instinctively she knew she was in trouble. She tried to draw some energy from within to defend herself and could feel it stirring within as she saw one of the pairs of feet move in front of the little space she had in front of her between her and the trash can. Another moved to the other side of her. She was cornered.

All of a sudden, she had a small window of clarity and was able to use the energy to zap the one who was now to the right of her. He flew back and his whole body crashed against the side of the brick building, which sounded violent because he was so close.

Rory felt the bricks against his back push back and he let out an "Oomph" as he hit.

She quickly tried to muster up enough energy to do the same thing again when she felt her self being lifted to her feet by a single hand, and then she knew she was in even more danger than she had thought. Though she was tiny and light, she knew there was no possible way a mere mortal could lift her to her feet as quick as this guy did, and by a single hand. She tried to remain focused on centering her energy through the cartwheels of her spinning brain. Again she was briefly able to tap into her energy out of fear.

Focusing with every ounce of herself she could, she took her left hand to conjure up a ball of energy to throw at the guy on her left. She then turned her head towards him to make sure she wouldn't miss. Layla noticed something that made her hold the power at her fingertips for a moment. Though it looked as if he was spinning, she recognized him as one of the guys who bought her a beer. She realized at that moment she hadn't had too much to drink, they had slipped something into her drink. With a fury, she released the fire. He held up his hand and, with energy of his own, blocked it, sending the flame into the air where it dissipated.

*Ajay, Ra'id...*She mustered up enough energy to communicate to her brothers. But she knew it was faint, and hoped they could hear her as she felt her head being tilted to the side and her hair being pushed aside, exposing the veins in her neck. She knew what was about to happen and then she felt two sharp punctures into her skin. Luckily whatever it was they had put into her drink had masked the pain, and she knew without a doubt it was them who had spiked her drink. She could feel the blood being drained out of her as she thought about how dumb she was to have taken her eyes off of her drink, something she had never done.

She tried to struggle and draw energy from within but she couldn't even feel as much as a spark. It was true, vampires could drain witches of their power by drinking their blood. It was only temporary, lasting only as long as the witch was strong. Some witches could be affected for a few days or more trying to regenerate their power. Other witches who were stronger may be only drained for a matter of hours, and it's been said there are a select few who only take a matter of minutes to regenerate. She had hoped coming from such a strong line of witches on both sides of her family would allow her to heel fast if they didn't kill her.

Her knees became even weaker now, as he had finished. She wasn't dead yet, perhaps they weren't going to kill her after all, she thought. The two other boys came over to help hold her up as Aidan, the boy who had bought her drinks at the bar, stepped in front of her, holding open an intricate silver blade of some sort. He looked at her and grabbed her arm. Slowly he sliced the front part of her forearm, opening a cut about ten inches long. Aiden seemed to enjoy the look of pain on her face as he dragged the blade across. He was fascinated she found no pleasure in being bled; he had never seen anyone immune to the pleasure. Her arm immediately began to bleed as she felt her arm begin to throb. Whatever they had put into her drink unfortunately wasn't strong enough to block all the pain in her arm. She let out a cry as a tear dropped from her eye.

Aidan grabbed her by the face and checked over for any marks. Although he could see as clear as day at night, he held up a tiny flashlight, carefully looking over every spot on her face, neck and chest. He then pulled the front of her dress down forcefully to her underwear line. She could do nothing while he carefully checked over the front of her as she stood there with nothing blocking her chest but her bra.

"What the…fuck are you…doing…you…sick…fuck," she managed to get out. But he just ignored her, checking every inch of her. Layla, barely coherent, could understand enough of what she was going to understand, he was looking for something but what she did not know.

Then he opened the front of her bra, but he didn't make any snide remarks, he just checked around like he had done to the rest of her, closing her bra shut after he had finished. Layla was mortified. He proceeded to check the rest of her, covering up any private areas after checking, as if he was a doctor, not a monster, but still he made no comment. He made his way around her backside and did the same thing. Layla wanted so badly to zap these guys into oblivion, but she was too weak and her brain was now spinning out of control.

"Nothing, she hasn't got a mark anywhere. We have bloodletting and tears and still nothing. She isn't the one," Aidan said, turning off his tiny flashlight and sticking it back into his pocket. She managed to open her eyes as he came back to face her.

That's when she noticed her blood was staining the corner of his mouth. It made her stomach turn as he wiped it with his index finger and licked it off, as if he had just stuck his finger in the frosting on top of a cake.

"Mmmm..." He said, looking at her and letting her know just how tasty he found her. Then he stepped in closer.

"By the way, between you and me...Nice. You are definitely one of the sexiest women I have ever seen, and believe me I have seen a lot over all these centuries." He said with an evil grin stretched across his face.

His voice was so low she was sure the other's wouldn't have been able to hear him if they weren't vampires and whatever else they were, she thought to herself as she thought about the way the other one was able to block her fire, sending it up into the air.

"What are you?" She asked, expecting him to answer.

"We were half-breeds, warlock and human, who were bitten and turned to vampires. We are some of your kind's worst nightmare." He said, feeling victorious.

"But I could ask you the same thing, Layla... You're more than a witch... you taste different and you are immune to bloodletting pleasure... Very interesting..." Aiden said, and then came into her neck again to take in a long whiff of her blood. Layla's sleepy eyes opened wide as she looked at him, feeling fearful of what he was going to do to her next.

"Let's kill her," Rory said, breaking the conversation off.

"No, we can't. If they find her body then we may tip them off. We are going to take her with us. Perhaps she will even stay with us after a while." Aidan said as he winked at her, and then proceeded to slowly look up and down the front of her body. Layla was enraged. It wasn't that she felt violated; she felt violent and wanted to hurt this creep.

"How are we going to move her from the alley to somewhere safe without people noticing?" Aiah asked the important question. They couldn't orb, so that wasn't an option. Aidan looked up, vampires were good at scaling up walls, but they used all fours to do so and he tried to think how they would do so with her.

"Let's tie her hands and feet and I will fling her over my shoulder and we'll make our way up," Aidan said, pointing to the top of the building.

"What if she gets her powers back? What do we do then?" Aiah then asked.

"Simple, we keep draining her," Aidan said, looking at the puncture wounds in Layla's neck.

"Eventually that will kill her, wont it?" Aiah asked.

"No, witches cannot be killed by bloodletting, but wouldn't it be interesting to see if we could take someone of the witch blood and turn her into a vampire?" Aidan said, looking deeply into Layla's half opened eyes.

"Is that even possible?" Aiah asked.

"I don't know, but we now have a Guinee pig." Aidan said and began to laugh as the others joined in.

They didn't have anything to tie her up with, so Aidan pulled the front of her dress down, unhooking her bra for a second time tonight. Layla wasn't even coherent anymore, she had passed out. Aidan ripped the bra in two after quickly pulling her dress back up to cover her. He didn't want the other two to see her naked, he didn't know why, but he didn't. There was something about this girl he admired, it was her strong spirit accompanied by her beauty. Whatever was driving him he put aside, as he began to tie her feet together. At the same time, Aiah tied together her hands as Rory held her up so she didn't fall.

They were all done tying her up and Aidan flung her over his left shoulder. Rory scaled the building first and made his way up before Aidan followed with Layla. Aiah was going up after him so he could catch her if she fell, and Rory would help pull her off of Aidan's shoulders when they reached the top.

Aidan was almost to Rory when he heard a zap hit the wall a few feet away from him. He knew instantly they were caught and he sped quickly up the wall as Rory grabbed Layla. Aiah was closer to the ground and jumped down, then turned around to be able to defend himself.

"Put her down now!" Ra'ad said as Marcus followed behind him. Aidan didn't respond as he handed off Layla to Rory.

Aidan looked down at Aiah and realized that he was cornered. There wasn't much hope of him getting up unless they started throwing power balls at the two witches below while Aiah tried to make his way up. Aidan thought Aiah had a good chance, being he was so fast.

Looking at the two witches from above, Aidan realized he had seen the one who spoke go into Layla's apartment earlier that night. The small mark on his neck imprinted from tattoo ink caught Aiden's eye, he knew the boy was part of the Dark Knights of the Light Council. The other guy standing next to him was also marked. They were young though, and didn't have as much experience. Aidan thought they might be able to pull it off after all. It wasn't as likely they would make it away with the girl, however, unless they could somehow drain all of her powers long enough for them to escape. But on the upside, they were three, with Layla as a bargaining chip, against two and that upped their chances, Aidan thought.

Just then, the other witch threw a power zap at Aiah, who was prepared and sent it right back at him mid-way.

"Marcus, look out!" Ra'id called as he sent two power zaps, one towards Aiah, who was able to block again with ease, and one up towards Aidan, who just as easily blocked the power ball, as well sending his own back with a quickness which made Marcus move quickly out of the way.

Aidan then fired three back, along with Aiah, who was extremely fast, much faster than Marcus and Ra'id. Aiah kept sending power zap after power zap as Rory and Aidan fired from above. Ra'id and Marcus were not prepared for how fast these guys were.

They knew something was coming; Marcus knew a problem would sooner or later arise. He was one of the only witches with access to the full truth. Ra'id had just been informed of Mikayla that night, but never had he any clue of what he was up against or how much. He knew the witch from the Light Council, Eden, had no knowledge of Mikayla's existence. It was only Mikayla's birth father, Amadeus, Marcus's father, Gabriel, Rowan's father, Cato, and her mother, Sunrise, and Mikayla's parents, Santino and Maria, as well as Lazzaro and Dominick, and a female ancient witch, Brynja, who was one of the three elders of the council, aside from Marcus.

The group was kept small for fear of what people would do if they found out. Many would try and utilize her for her powers, and others would try and kill her for them. Some would be dark forces trying to rid the power from existence, or use her powers, and others would be good forces, thinking of it as a necessary evil for fear of what it could mean if she got into the wrong hands. The small group decided it was best kept quiet and they would try and keep her hidden under the radar until she came into her full powers and they were able to explain to her what was going on and how best to use them, all the while still trying to protect her identity. But it was obvious someone had a clue of what was going on, but it was also clear they weren't aware of Mikayla. It was only a matter of time though before they were. Even the best of people could fall into their fear of her power.

Marcus was bred from birth to be a part of the council, and was seventeen years old when he was told of his mission which would take place two years later. He was a couple of years older than Mikayla, but would pose as a senior in her high school for that year to try and gage her powers and to see if anything strange was surrounding her that year. It seemed as if nothing was, and she wasn't showing any powers she knew of yet. He was supposed to stay through the summer, but was called away due to him getting way too close. He had fallen in love with her and his father, Gabriel, and her father frowned upon it. It wasn't that they weren't a good match which had them frowning, essentially they were perfect for one another, but there were bigger issues at stake and him getting so involved clouded his judgment. They felt it made it more dangerous for her. Dominick was told about her much earlier than he was supposed to have been.

Dominick shouldn't have been told about her until his last initiation ceremony into full werewolf, Alpha. This caused Dominick to take on more responsibility than his overly hormonal changing wolf could really handle. Marcus felt bad at how the task Dominick wasn't supposed to have had affected him. Neither Mikayla nor Dominick had ever truly moved on. This hurt him for many reasons. One being he feared because of the situation he created, they would end up together and he would never have a shot with her again, and the other he feared they wouldn't move forward as a couple or as partners to others having been trapped from Marcus' love and fear for Mikayla.

He was much too close to her. He loved her and thought about her every day, but if he ever had hope of being around her again he needed to obey what the elders were telling him to do. He was called up for training, which was why he was supposed to leave at the end of the summer anyways. His father made him leave earlier, telling him anything can happen in the future but this couldn't happen between him and Mikayla, now. Marcus argued for the summer, but lost. Ultimately he knew he could not carry on with her, and instead continued to train for his spot on the council. He was a young warrior; part of the Dark Knights of the Light Council and the Council would have access to more of himself than the average witch. It wasn't a risk they could take if they had remained a couple and her secret could be let out, which could end up being disastrous. Marcus hated it, but knew in his heart it was the right thing to do, but not a day went by he didn't think of her. He was still in love with her and just held on to the fact one day they may be able to be together again.

The zaps were coming so fast, neither Ra'id nor Marcus were able to conjure anything up because they were too busy blocking shot after shot.

"Fuck, they are fast," Marcus said to Ra'id, who was trying his best to keep up the pace with the energy balls being thrown his way as Marcus was busily doing the same.

"Get behind me and put up a block so we can start throwing," Marcus said, trying to get them in a position of being able to fight back and not sit around only being able to defend themselves.

Ra'id stepped behind Marcus and as quickly as he could conjured up the wind to make a tight block, using it as a force field pushing against the power balls being thrown at them at machine gun pace. Ra'id held the force field up as Marcus started aiming for Aiah. But Aiah was faster and was dodging and zapping everything Marcus was throwing. Marcus's didn't want to throw up top because Layla was there and things were going too fast now for him to ensure her safety.

All of a sudden, Aiah grabbed his shoulder. He was hit but the shot didn't come from Marcus. Trying to gage the situation, Marcus scanned the area to see who and what was now trying to join the party when he noticed a hotheaded Ajay running up, throwing everything he had, unprotected. Rory threw one back at him, which hit him in the gut and sent him sailing back.

"No, Ajay!" Ra'id screamed, still holding his force field strong.

"I'm fine, just get her down," Ajay called back, dodging a few more power balls as he made his way into the force field.

Ajay, now safe in the force field, started throwing with Marcus. Ajay threw another shot, which hit Aiah in the back as he was trying to make his way up the wall. This enraged Aidan and he gave a large blast to the force field, which pushed all three witches back, and then he grabbed Layla and dangled her over the side of the building.

"I will fucking drop her right now!" Aidan said.

All three boys stopped. "Just let her go and we will let you go," Ra'id called up to Aidan.

"First allow my brother to scale the wall unharmed and maybe I will give you the girl back," he called down.

"How about an even exchange, we do it at the same time," Ra'id tried to plead, not wanting to give them an advantage in taking her with them.

"I don't make deals with witches! Allow my brother to make it up the wall first, or there is no deal at all!" Aidan ordered as his canines grew long and his eyes burned red.

"Alright," Ra'id said, feeling like he was caught between a rock and a hard place.

Aiah scaled the wall as quick as he could despite his injuries. As he got to the top, Aidan looked at Rory and nodded. Rory started to zap the power boxes around the alley, which immediately began to flame, lighting the buildings that created the alley on fire.

Marcus could feel the heat coming from the fires as they waited below for them to send down Layla. He expected some sort of distraction, so he wasn't surprised at all by the fire, but he was now curious as to just how they intended on getting Layla to them. Just moments later his curiosity was answered as Aidan tossed her into the air, letting her free fall.

"Shit!" Ajay said as they all instinctively conjured up the wind to slow her fall and catch her as it made a net for her to safely land in. Sure enough it worked and she was just inches from the ground, passed out and bleeding.

"What the fuck! I'm gonna kill those fuckers!" Ajay shouted.

"Why did they do this?" Ra'id said to Marcus, looking for answers.

"They have figured out how to get an angel to revel it's wings," Marcus said, staring at the puncture marks and cut on her arm. He didn't need to look up to know the three vampire/warlocks had fled the scene; it was a set-up, throwing her into the air like that to use as a smoke screen.

"What do you mean?" Ra'id said, still trying to figure out this whole thing and now seeing how his family fit into the mix.

"Anyone given Angel's Breath will have some sort of mark upon their skin when bloodletting or tears fall. It was a mark designed for truth telling. A mark is placed as a symbol to other angels to help keep track of them. Their energy is completely off the radar when they jump into a body like that and they needed a way to be able to find them, I guess in case of emergency," Marcus said, tying a part of his t-shirt he ripped around her arm, which was bleeding badly, not fully understanding it himself.

Ra'id said nothing back, only taking in the information as his concern for his sister grew.

"Um, what are you two nerds talking about?" Ajay said, completely out of the loop.

Marcus just looked down and shook his head. He felt he was screwing things up again, now one more person knew. "I will let your brother explain things to you on the way to the council .I will be taking her with me to Michigan." Marcus said as Ra'id shook his head in agreement.

"The fuck you are!" Ajay said, pushing Marcus away from Layla. "She's not going anywhere with you and I am not leaving her. Tell him Ra'id!" Ajay screamed.

The fire was getting hotter and Marcus felt like he was a hamburger on a grill.

"Ajay, this is what we must do. You have to trust me for once," Ra'id said calmly to his little brother.

"Fuck you, Ra'id. You're so stupid. She is not going with him and you can't pay me enough to step foot into the chamber of the council. Fuck that shit!" Ajay said and grabbed Layla, but Marcus kept his hold on her as well.

"Well, wherever you guys go, I will be coming." Marcus said, conjuring up a bond between his hand and her wrist.

"Get the fuck off of her before I kill you, man. I don't want to, but I will." Ajay said with a look in his eyes which said he meant just that. At the moment Ajay's voice sounded more beast then man.

"AJAY!" Ra'id snapped. Ajay turned his head towards his brother and zapped him hard enough for Ra'id to fall on his ass. Ajay's jaw slightly contorted as the wolf within him became restless.

"Stop it! I will make you a deal. She comes with me, that's non-negotiable, and you can, too. I will explain everything to you once we get there if you promise not to be a wild card when we get there. If you even get out of line one time, then I will have to bind your powers as you will be in contempt of the Council of Light." Marcus said, really not wanting him to come along but feeling this loose cannon wouldn't stop until he found his sister, so it appeared to be the better of the two options.

Ajay laughed. "You cannot bind my powers!" He said triumphantly.

"Actually Ajay, he can. It's part of the power one is granted when he is accepted into the Dark Knights, no one really knows were the power comes from but it is there. You should really have paid better attention during your training," Ra'id said, disappointed in his little brother.

Ajay stepped back to think it over for a moment. His jaw loosened a bit. "Fine then, I will go with you and Layla but any funny stuff and I will kill you before you have a chance to even think about binding my powers." Ajay threatened. "Just to make it clear, I don't live by the rules of the council! That's your guys deal, not mine!" Ajay added, defiantly.

Ra'id stood back and just shook his head. He and his brother were so different and he worried about the choices his brother made. Ajay was a free spirit, but he was also a loose cannon and that scared Ra'id and kept them from being close.

Marcus looked towards Ra'id. *It's the only way, if I take her he will not stay with you. He will tear up city after city trying to find her, which could add problems. I have no other solution, I am sorry.* Marcus thought only to Ra'id.

Ra'id nodded his head in agreement.

"Alright then, we have a deal." Marcus said to Ajay, holding out his hand to shake it, but Ajay shoved it aside as he carefully checked over his little sister. Ra'id said nothing; he just orbed right out of the alley.

"We need to get out of here, the flames are getting to warm. Let's orb her back to her house and let her recover before we make it to Michigan." Marcus said.

"Let's do it then," Ajay said with a little less of a hostile tone now he felt better about being able to be by his little sister's side. Together they held on to Layla and orbed back into Ajay and Layla's apartment to heal her wounds before they made their way to Rowan and Mikayla.

Marcus knew they would be next. He needed to get a hold of Dominick, but Dominick was at his last cycle of initiations and couldn't easily be reached.

43

Two full weeks had passed as the boys lived day in and day out in wolf form. They made their way across the Mackinaw Bridge late at night undetected to explore some of the Upper Peninsula. Normally it wasn't their territory, but they had the OK to do so because Lucio's sister was to be married to an alpha of the Upper Peninsula. It was Saturday as they found themselves in love with the forest in the Upper Peninsula. They weren't very far into the U.P., staying close to the boarder so they could make it across later that night and make their way back down.

Dominick was turning out to be a strong leader, backed by a strong right hand from Mario and a pack of fierce hearts. They were unified as a pack and didn't miss a beat. Dominick ran a tight ship. It was early Saturday morning, the sun was just starting to peak its head above the horizon. It was also time to forage some food. They began their morning hunt. First they would sniff out the area to detect what was there.

They worked as a tight pack, going only so far away from the meeting point searching for food. Something in the air was off. Dominick came across a strange smell. Mario came across the same scent, as well as the boys. It wasn't a smell that should be in these woods. It was a scent only Dominick recognized, but decided he couldn't be sure until he tracked it down.

After each one had picked up the scent, each almost a half a mile or so away, Dominick ordered them to follow the scent so they could stand together. He feared what he knew in his heart was true. The scent was that of hyenas. If he had not been so close to Naki, he wasn't sure he himself could have specifically placed the smell. Instinctually they knew it didn't belong there and would have followed the smell either way.

Dominick reached the area first. He saw other creatures had already begun digging up the sight of the bodies and feeding off of them, but one thing was familiar, the outline of what was left over of their carcasses. Dominick saw that was distinct, three dead hyenas partially decayed and partially eaten lay partially uncovered in the middle of the forest, packed away in a thick area of brush and trees.

At first he wasn't sure if it was Naki and her three noblemen ,but it looked as if these creatures were all male. Naki had warned them of the three hyenas who had lost their way, making their way to the states, having landed in Maine. It was plausible they would make it to the Upper Penisula at some point if they had headed this way, which by the looks of it Dominick thought they did.

Briefly he thought of Mikayla and wondered if they were after her. He knew it didn't make any sense but it seemed almost too coincidental to him.

Mario made it towards him first, checking out the carcasses. *What the hell? Are those...* he trailed off as Dominick interrupted him, knowing what he was thinking.

I don't think so, I think it might have been the three renegade hyenas that they were in search of, Dominick answered as the other wolves made their way towards the carcasses.

What the hell could have killed three hyenas in these woods? Lucio asked, dumbfounded.

Perhaps a hunter got'em, Tony blurted.

If a hunter had shot them, then why didn't he take the bodies? Mikey jumped in.

Dominick said nothing, he only tried to check out the scene. He first checked for any signs of shots, but knew it was unlikely, agreeing in his own head with Mikey. Plus, if they had been shot and then made their way far from the hunter to die, it seemed highly unlikely they would have all stacked themselves up side by side to die.

The smell of the carcasses was strong and hideous, a couple of the other wolves gagged at the smell. It truly was the worst smell they had ever encountered. They weren't normal creatures; they were creatures of immortals, which made their carcasses' decaying scent stronger and more powerful than a mortal creature.

Dominick, however, strong and brave, ignored the smell as he explored. Mario, just as brave, helped.

No shots anywhere... Dominick said, stepping back for a moment to catch some fresher air.

Mario did the same as he shook his head he didn't find anything like that, either.

Lucio noticed something about the carcass in back, his neck looked strange and he moved forward to explore as Dominick and Mario took a break, still trying to take in some fresh air. He couldn't be sure without ripping a hole in the dead hyenas neck to expose the bones. Knowing it needed to be done, he took a deep breath in and in one sharp, clean move he tore the flesh away from the bone. The taste in his mouth was acidic. Absolutely the worst thing he had ever encountered, he thought as he gagged. A couple of the other wolves chuckled at the sight. He shot them a quick glare then looked back down at the carcass.

This one has a broken neck. It was snapped clean, Lucio said as he stepped away from the carcass so he could get some fresh air.

Without another word, Dominick and Mario each took the other two carcasses and did the same thing.

Yup, clean break, Mario said.

This one has been snapped, as well, Dominick said with a worried look on his face. He knew in these woods, besides themselves, there wasn't anything natural that could do something like that.

Alright, let's make a circle and see if we can pick up any other clues, Dominick ordered.

Man, can't we eat first? Ricky said grumpily as his stomach made grumbling noises despite the hideous smell which plagued the air.

No one said anything, they just gave him a look that questioned whether or not he was out of his mind.

Dominick didn't want to dismiss his hungry pack member. *After we make the circle we will find some food.* He directed his eyes to Ricky.

Ricky said nothing, he just looked down realizing he had over spoke his bounds. Dominick nodded towards the group to have them search the area.

The sun was still making its way up into the peak of the sky. The forest was better lit as they individually searched the grounds in a circular formation so they wouldn't miss any area within the immediate area.

Mario was searching northeast of the carcasses when he came across tire tracks. He wasn't sure whether or not it had anything to do with the hyenas, so he checked for evidence bodies had been dragged along the ground. There was nothing he could see that indicated this was done, but something still didn't settle right with him.

Hey, I found some tire tracks, but I don't see any evidence that they could have been dragged, and it would have taken the strength of four men to move just one body, and the sight seems too far away for anyone to have done so in one clean sweep. I'm gonna retrace my steps back towards the carcasses to see if I missed something. I didn't notice anything on the way here, but I will look again. Mario sent a telepathic message to Dominick, who was also north but a little further west.

It's probably nothing, Dominick said as he continued to search his own area.

Yeah, that's what I am thinking, but something is pulling at my gut, Mario explained.

Dominick lifted his head towards the sky, realizing Mario was tapping into his sixth sense. Now Dominick's instincts were telling him he better help Mario. If it turned out to be nothing, he would go back with Mario to the area he himself was checking out and they could double time it in order to save time.

Hold on, I will meet you at the tracks, Dominick ordered. *The rest of you guys keep looking around, I'm going to check on something that Mario found,* he informed the rest of the wolf pack.

All right, Mario said as he tried to decipher the tracks. He knew it had to be a truck or SUV of some sort by the size of the tires. Mario also noticed a couple of leftover footprints. Unless the rest of the footprints had washed away, which was likely, it looked as if there may have only been two people in the car.

Lucio had already searched his part and came back to center before anyone. He decided to take the additional time to check the immediate area, although they had already done a sweep earlier. As much as he hated to go by the rotting corpses, he thought there may be a clue buried by them. He took a deep breath in before poking in around the corpses.

With his sharp teeth, he sank his teeth into the left over scruff of the first hyena and pulled it a few feet from the pile. Then he went to the next one and did the same, only he pulled it in a different direction as he tried to create a clearing he could search through. Lastly, he took the third corpse, and again pulled it away from the area and began to search through the leaves and twigs and dirt.

At first nothing seemed out of the ordinary. Lucio couldn't find as much as a footprint. He turned to sit on the edge of the clearing he had made. The sun was even higher in the sky, warming up the already unseasonably warm air. Lucio thought about how warm it was, even for the U.P.

The air around him smelled of rotting hyena and was getting worse as the sun made its way higher. He was hungry and hot. A gentle breeze through the trees was appreciated as Lucio tilted his head towards the sky, grateful for the coolness as the wind passed through the forest fanning him.

He was hungry and tired, but glad to have a moment to sit and enjoy the breeze. The wind was picking up as a few more cycles of air made their way through the leaves. Lucio yawned before refocusing his attention back on the clearing. All looked as it did, besides a few leaves which had been shifted from the breeze.

Scanning the area, he watched as another leaf started to vibrate from the wind and, as the wind picked up, the weightless leaf danced gently into the air as the other leaves around it began to stir, uncovering what at first appeared to be a single piece of trash with a glossy sheen to it.

Lucio got up and walked over towards the glossy item on the ground. At first he thought his mind was playing tricks on him because what he was looking at didn't make any sense to him. He blinked his eyes a few times and refocused his eyes, but the picture was still the same. Immediately he grabbed hold of it in his mouth and with unearthly quickness made his way towards Dominick and Mario.

Here are the tracks, Mario pointed with his head towards the ground. *Truck or SUV could indicate hunters, but it makes no sense that they would just leave the carcasses in the woods*, he added.

It doesn't make sense at all, Dominick agreed.

They made their way slowly retracing Mario's steps and searching in reasonable proximity around the path.

After a while of not finding any resting place, Dominick's gut was telling him something wasn't right. *I can't find anything. It just doesn't make sense. It doesn't seem possible that any man or men could have enough strength or stamina to carry three carcasses, one right after the other, without some sort of break. Perhaps the other footprints did wash away because I can tell you for a fact no two men could have done this on their own.* Dominick said, trying to figure out what kind of men could have done this but came up without any good explanation.

Unless it wasn't men at all. Immortals could have easily done this, Mario chimed in as if a bell went off.

No bite marks were found, so I doubt it's a vampire, and wouldn't a witch just orb the bodies away? Why the truck? It isn't even the work of witches, anyways. Perhaps we have some warlocks wondering around? Still though, whoever it was made sure that they used as little of their powers as they could, Dominick calculated.

Why would they do that? Mario asked, confused.

So they wouldn't be detected, that's why, Dominick answered.

The two looked at each other, trying to piece together another clue when they heard footprints quickly coming towards them. Dominick was the first to spot Lucio running as fast as he could with something hanging out of his mouth.

You need to see this! Lucio called after, spotting them as he made his way as fast as he could towards Dominick and Mario.

Slowly Dominick made his way towards Lucio as Mario followed. Everything in his gut told him whatever it was Lucio was carrying wasn't good. If it had been just a regular clue, Dominick knew Lucio would have just told him telepathically. But he hadn't, instead he chose to take the evidence directly to him.

Lucio finally reached them and quickly spit out the picture he held in his mouth. Dominick looked down and saw the picture laying in front of him. His heart started to pound fast and hard as he stared down at the picture in frightened disbelief.

Why is there a picture of Mikayla? Mario asked, completely confused and not quite yet grasping the connection. *Mikayla...* he then whispered softly as he trailed off, trying to figure out why a picture of his sister would be out in the woods after realizing none of them had any pockets in their fur to be carrying around pictures and such.

We have to go, Dominick said as calmly as he could.

The sun is up, how are we supposed to make our way across the bridge now? Lucio hated to question his alpha, but it was a legitimate question. They were in wolf form and they were almost twice as large as a regular, full grown wolf. If they ran across the bridge they would not go unnoticed, but if they transformed back into human form they would be naked and slow and doubtfully would make it across the bridge without being stopped by authorities.

Dominick knew Lucio had a point. He also knew they had been in wolf form long enough to take another week out during the next full moon to complete the full transformation, but now they needed to get home. Struggling for an idea, he looked towards Mario.

It's too risky, Mario said, shaking his head, knowing if they made it across as wolves they would expose themselves.

Dominick thought for a moment, he was the alpha and supposed to lead. It wasn't a good thing for them to leave for the last week, but he didn't see any other way. Besides, once Mikayla's dad found out he would rush back as fast as he could. Santino loved his daughter and would fight to the death.

Alright, we don't have any money on us so we can't get across anyways, even if we could get a hold of some clothes at a camp site. If we walked back it would take too long. I will have our fathers come pick us up. We need clothes and we need to get home fast, Dominick finally came up with the most logical solution, one he couldn't think of at first because he was taught to solve problems without the help of the fathers, it was part of becoming a pack, but this was different. Truly this was an emergency and this is what had to be done.

Dom, you know something, don't you? Mario asked point blank.

I'll wait and fill you in when our fathers come pick us up. We'll ride back together, but your father should be around when I tell you this, Dominick admitted, but made it clear he wasn't taking the conversation any further until Mario's father was around.

Mario was worried but nodded in agreement as he felt his stomach turn in knots from worry. However, for the moment, there wasn't anything he could do but sit patiently and hope that everything was alright with his sister.

Dominick knew it would take their fathers a good couple of hours to make it back to the cars, and another couple of hours just to pick them up across the bridge. The next few hours they were stuck. Dominick let out a stressful, loud growl into the morning sun, sounding as if he were in pain. Then he took hold of himself and tried to make contact with his father. The further away you were from each other the harder the connection. It would be almost impossible for them to make the connection with the women back home. He had just hoped his father had stuck around close enough to the bridge for him to hear his call.

Luckily, he had.

44

With a sudden jerk of her body Mikayla opened her eyes. Her heart was beating fast as she lay still, trying to grasp where she was. A familiar light was shining in her face. She blinked a few times and realized it was her window filled with morning sunshine. Quickly she scanned the rest of her room to find everything was normal. *What a horrible dream...* she said to herself as her heartbeat began to slow itself down.

The dream was awful and she wasn't entirely sure what it had meant, but she was pretty sure it was caused from the love spell she had tried to perform the night before. She thought to herself it was probably a symbol of letting Dominick go and her fear her family would not accept Caleb. The Marcus thing she decided had to be from the recent letter sent to her. She couldn't understand the blonde women or the child, though, so she chalked it up to the crazy things that just seemed to happen in dreams. Whatever it was, the dream was intense and left her feeling a little overwhelmed. She decided it was best to wash all the feelings out with a hot shower before Rowan came to pick her up.

Mikayla had just finished eating breakfast when her phone rang. She didn't recognize the number and let it go to voicemail. Rowan was on her way over to pick her up. They were going to spend the afternoon on the lake getting some color before the night came. Instead of going to the lake house, where a bunch of the women were gathering, they decided to go to Mikayla's secret spot with lawn chairs so Mikayla could freely fill her in. The last thing she needed was for her mother to overhear her and worry. Not only that, she feared if her father called she would then tell him, who in turn would only tell the boys, making them return home early to try and ruin her life.

They left everything locked in the car but their lawn chairs, towels, and sunscreen. The day went by slowly as Mikayla filled Rowan in with story after story.

"So far I think I like this guy!" Rowan said, excited for her friend.

"So far I KNOW I do!" Mikayla said back with a carefree smile.

"Mmmm….Perhaps you love him?" Rowan teased.

"Perhaps…" Mikayla said, looking up into the sun with a wicked smile on her face.

Rowan sat up with excitement. "You do! Oh my God, Kali, you're in love! Does he…" Rowan was about to ask a question which Mikayla had cut her off, already knowing the question and supplying the answer.

"He does. It's not just that he says so, I can see it in his eyes and feel it in his touch. It's magnetic. The best way I can explain it is it feels somehow like we were made for each other," Mikayla admitted.

"I know exactly what you mean. You think I am crazy for dating your brother, but it is the same for us. Even if I thought it was the worst idea in the world I wouldn't be able to keep myself away from him." Rowan said, having understood perfectly what Mikayla had just explained.

"Well, I suppose I have a little more understanding of you and Mario now." Mikayla offered her best friend some support, rather than the usual eye roll she performed when Rowan talked too gushy about Mario.

"Tonight he's gonna get grilled by me, though!" Rowan laughed.

"Oh yeah, Row, you are so tough! I am sure he will be shaking at the very sight of you!" Mikayla laughed back.

As the sun soaked its rays into their skin, they became hot once again. They headed for the water, running off the dock and making themselves into tight little cannon balls. Despite their tiny frames, the duo's splashes were impressive. They both came up for air laughing as boats passed by honking their horns. Then they noticed one heading over towards them.

The boat looked familiar and before they knew it, Lucio's younger brother Johnny had made his way over.

"What are you guys doing over here? Everyone's at the lake house!" Johnny asked with a confused look on his face. He and a few others from the different families stared at them in wonder.

Mikayla looked at Johnny, who was now seventeen and almost finished with his junior year of high school. She noticed somehow he was starting a growth spurt and she hadn't even noticed until seeing him in his swim trunks. Her eyes began to shift to the other boys as she noticed they too were hitting a growth spurt. She couldn't believe just a month ago they looked like juniors in high schoo.l but now they could easily pass for college kids.

Rowan said nothing back, waiting for Mikayla to answer.

"Hello, are you to deaf?" Johnny asked with an odd look on his face.

"Sorry, you look older somehow and I was taken back..." Mikayla couldn't help but blurt out what she had been thinking in her head.

"Well ,if your done with Dominick I can take over where he left off," Johnny said raising his eyebrows and looking dangerous. Mikayla had seen that same look in Dominick's eyes around the same age.

"Me and Dominick are not a couple, we haven't been in years!" Mikayla said, frustrated by his comment and even more frustrated by the look she had once saw that marked the beginning of the end for her and Dominick. "We came here so we could have a girls BFF day out. Is that a crime?" Mikayla added.

"Not a crime, I just was wondering why the hell you would hang out in no man's land instead of at the house were everyone is at, that's all. But you guys do your girlie thing!" Johnny said and smiled down mischievously at Mikayla.

Mikayla wanted to grab for a towel, she didn't like the way he was looking at her or how any of them were looking at her. It was strange, but they were doing it to Rowan, too. Unfortunately they were in the water and there were no towels to be grabbed.

"I'm going to offer you guys a ride back one more time," Johnny said as he started to slowly back up the boat.

"Thanks, but we need to finish our girls day out," Mikayla said and managed to smile despite the weird energy the boys were just giving off.

Johnny backed the boat up further and once he was in position floored it towards the sand bar on the other side of the lake, leaving behind waves that hit Mikayla and Rowan in the face.

"Ok, creepy!" Rowan said.

"What the hell was that?" Mikayla added.

"Reminds me of Mario and Dom at that age," Rowan observed.

"It's strange though, don't you think?" Mikayla said as her intuition was tapping at her brain.

"I don't know, I think it's hormones," Rowan said, seemingly less concerned than Mikayla.

Mikayla felt in her gut something was up but she didn't know what and decided she wasn't about to ruin her day over it. She decided for now she would shake it off, but once Dominick was home she and him were going to have a serious talk.

They splashed around in the water a few times and let themselves dry off before making their way back towards the car.

It was already five o'clock by the time they got back into the car. Rowan reached for her phone to check her messages, but her phone had died.

"Shit!" She said as she looked around her car.

"What?" Mikayla asked puzzled.

"I wanted to check my messages but my frick'in' phone died and I forgot I lent my Mom my charger because hers wasn't working yesterday and she had to have a charger because she went to pick up herbs a couple of hours away from here." Rowan explained. "Kali can I please check my messages from your phone."

Mikayla reached for her purse. She put her hand inside and tried to feel around for it but felt nothing there. As if it would appear by shaking, she took hold of the bag and gently shook it and then peaked in, but still it wasn't there.

"I must have forgotten it..." Mikayla said, still trying to locate it.

"You seem to forget your phone a lot these days!" Rowan grinned. "Oh well, no biggy, it is unlikely that I would hear from Mario anyways. I knew he said they wouldn't be able to call much, if at all. Well, it is what it is, so I will take it as a sign that it's a day for just me and you. How about we get some burgers on the way back to your house?"

"A big, fat cheeseburger sounds good to me!" Mikayla said as she put her purse back on the floor. "After we eat let's get ready at my house. My Mom will still be out at the lake house by then so we can dodge any questioning," Mikayla then added.

Rowan agreed and started towards the little diner they frequented in the summer to grab a quick dinner.

Mikayla had let Rowan take the first shower. She wanted to lay down for a minute before getting ready anyways. Tonight is going to be special, she thought to herself as she realized she needed to pick out the perfect outfit. She started thinking about what she had in her closet, picturing herself in each one as she pictured what Caleb would see. Somehow it didn't seem like a jeans kind of night. After mulling it over in her mind for a while, she decided on her floor length cotton blend black sundress with charcoal grey tribal patterns lightly woven in every five or so inches spanning lengthwise. If you were far away from the dress, you would miss the patterns. It made the delicate cut of the dress dark and hardened. The top was tight across her chest, which made her bust look larger than it was. It was empress cut, but somehow gently hugged her silhouette, showing how fit she was. The dress was sexy and dark, but at the same time innocent and light. Mikayla thought it was perfect for the evening. She would make it casual by wearing a pair of black flip flops on her feet and silver studs in her ears. Her hair would definitely be worn down and smoothed bone straight with her flat iron. She wanted her eyes to stand out, so she planned on a little heavier eye makeup, without being too heavy, and a lightly tinted lip gloss to make her lips look naturally kissable. Mikayla didn't like the feeling of lipstick, but she always had lip gloss with a tint on her at all times. So, it was decided. She figured out the perfect outfit for what Mikayla had hoped would be the perfect night. As she thought more about the night, she started to doze off, but was quickly awaken by Rowan as she opened the door to the bathroom, asking Mikayla if she could borrow her white dress.

"Of course. It's in the closet, hanging." Mikayla answered as she stretched her body on her bed. "Did you leave me any hot water?" She joked, laughing as she sat herself up on the bed.

"Nope, you will just have to freeze!" Rowan said as she walked with a towel wrapped around her body towards the closet to grab the dress.

"Perfect! I love cold showers!" Mikayla played along as she finally made her way towards the bathroom. She quickly turned on the shower and jumped in.

The water was still hot as Mikayla put her head under the head of the shower and felt its steady, even, warm pellets saturate her hair. She closed her eyes as she lathered her hair with shampoo and thought about Caleb. As if she couldn't help herself she smiled. She was so excited to see him even though it had only been since early in the morning she had been with him last.

As she was rinsing her hair, a voice came into her head. *Mikayla...* was all she heard, but she knew the voice all too well, even after all of these years. Her body froze momentarily and then she heard the voice call again. *Mikayla, where are you? Answer me...* she then heard. Her face flushed at the voice. It sounded the way it did when Rowan had first tapped into her telepathically. The voice startled her at first, and then anger followed.

She was sure hearing Marcus's voice had something to do with her falling in love again. Trying to ignore the incident, she began to massage conditioner through her long locks. She thought of her psychology class and decided she was probably just manifesting fears about leaving herself open to falling in love again. Once more Marcus's voice entered her head. *I know you are hearing me Mikayla...* she tensed up, it sounded so real. Frightened by the intensity of the voice, she stiffened briefly before a surge of anger washed over her. You're not ruining this for me, she thought to herself and concentrated on blocking out the voice. She waited a couple of minutes for the conditioner to soften as she filled her head with thoughts of only Caleb. The voice had quieted. In that instant she felt she became even stronger. No longer would anyone who had once tried to control her surroundings ever have a say over her again. The past couple of weeks she had proven to herself she was a lot stronger than any of them ever gave her credit for. Not only did she block his voice from her head, she had blocked him from her head.

The bathroom was filled with hot steam from Rowan's shower and then her own. She had been thinking of Caleb and what it was going to be like later that night when she told him she loved him also. She wondered when she had become a woman. Just a few weeks ago she was still a child under strict supervision and all of a sudden, out of nowhere, she had become a young woman. She wiped the steam off the mirror, curious to see if somehow her face had changed as well. It wasn't that she was looking expecting to see a different person, but she was curious to see if there happened to be any subtle changes.

As she stood in front of the mirror looking through the spot she had just cleared with her hand she noticed somehow she did look different, but it wasn't her looks that had changed, it was something behind her dark blue eyes. She studied herself for a moment and realized it was happiness, then she looked a bit further and she realized she also saw the confidence of someone who would do great things. A smile swept across her face as she put a hand to her mouth to contain the bubble of excitement about to burst out.

After she finished with lotion and deodorant, she blew dry her hair and then, after brushing her teeth, applied her makeup. Wearing an oversized t-shirt, she finally came out of the bathroom and headed towards her closet to grab her black dress.

"What's this! You never opened it?" Rowan said, shocked with a smile.

"What?" Mikayla said caught off guard.

"The letter Marcus sent you."

"I forgot all about that letter, I didn't realize it was still in the trash. I have no need to open that letter." Mikayla sounded a bit defensive.

"But aren't you kind of curious as to what it is he had to say?"

"No, I don't care."

"You mean to tell me you aren't the least bit curious?"

"Not really," Mikayla said as she made her way into her closet.

"Alright then how about you open it for my curiosity? I am dying to know what it says!" Rowan said, holding the letter as she followed Mikayla into the closet.

Mikayla stared at Rowan for a moment with an annoyed look. "Do what you want," she said as she took off her t-shirt and slipped into the sundress.

"Kali, it has been like four years… I can't believe you wouldn't be brave enough by now, especially with Caleb in the picture, to at least see what it was he wanted to say." Rowan said, trying to understand why she was being so stubborn.

Mikayla let out a deep breath as she tried to choose her words. "Look I waited for him for way too long. I waited four years for an explanation and I finally get one that can't be more than a page. It makes me feel stupid for ever having fallen in love with him in the first place. Rowan, it's a pity letter for sure, but I don't need pity and I find it funny that I end up with that letter the same week I meet Caleb. Well, let me tell you, the letter won't make any difference to me. I don't really care what it says. Marcus is part of my past and a short part, at that. I don't want to live in the past. I'm already forward and I feel like opening that letter somehow gives it power. I am in love with Caleb and I don't have any interest in what some so called ex-boyfriend has to say four years later." Mikayla explained.

"Well, I guess that makes sense… but I can't take the suspense so I'm opening it!" Rowan laughed as she ran out of the closet, holding on tightly to the letter.

Mikayla ran after her and tackled her on the bed, trying to grab for the letter as Rowan was trying to keep it away. They were laughing hysterically as they wrestled for the un-opened letter. Rowan was doing a good job keeping it away, but the envelope was beginning to get crumbled as the wrestling continued.

All of a sudden a loud rip stopped the giggling for a moment. The letter was now ripped in half. They both quietly stared at it for a moment before Rowan quickly grabbed the letter out of her half of the ripped envelope. Mikayla didn't stop her, the letter was now unsealed and so would be the information.

Rowan read the half of her letter in a matter of seconds with an odd look on her face. Without a word she took the other half of the letter out of Mikayla's hand and put the two torn pieces side by side. Again it took only a matter of seconds and then she was finished.

"Well?" Mikayla said quietly.

"All it says is: Mikayla I am so sorry for everything I put you through. In a short time I will explain everything to you in person. For now, please do me a favor while Dominick is away. Stay close to home and don't go out alone. Be very careful and use your instincts. I will see you soon. Love, Marcus," Rowan read.

"Whatever," Mikayla said as she shrugged her shoulders and got up off the bed to put some silver studs in her ears and a few silver rings on her fingers.

Rowan wasn't so sure she should have pushed opening the letter. Her own curiosity got the best of her and right now she couldn't read Mikayla's feelings about it. She seemed cool and uncaring, but that wasn't much like her. Rowan knew Mikayla was saying she was in love with Caleb, but despite she felt her friend should be able to give some sort of reaction.

"Sorry, I shouldn't have pushed." Rowan offered.

"Don't be, I would have done the same thing," Mikayla said and smiled at her friend.

"Ok what gives?" Rowan asked, confused by Mikayla's indifference.

"What do you mean?"

"You're being way to cool about this. Are you alright?" Rowan asked.

"I told you, it no longer matters. Plus, the letter just proved a point in my head. It is my past and in my past I allowed people to have a hold over me. The letter didn't tell me anything other than what to do," she said as she slipped on her last ring.

"I guess I can see your point. I was so curious myself as to where he went and what happened I couldn't help but want to know. Again, I am sorry for pushing it. But I am glad that you are all right with it." Rowan said, giving Mikayla innocent puppy dog eyes.

Mikayla laughed. "It's fine, I promise," she assured.

"Good! Then I say we put it in the trash and get ourselves to Caleb!" Rowan said, sounding upbeat.

"Can you believe in the letter that he actually assumed that I would see him? What nerve!" Mikayla said, referring back to the letter.

"That was pretty ballsy of him. I guess I never realized how sure of himself he is. He didn't even ask if you have a boyfriend. It's like he knew you didn't. Well, I guess now you do, but when you got that letter you didn't. It almost sounded as if he thought somehow you were still waiting for him. The letter is kind of weird. Besides, what the hell are you supposed to be so careful of, anyways? It's like he's trying to prevent you from going out and meeting people. Weird." Rowan replied, starting to understand how Mikayla saw the letter.

"Exactly. I thought back then that he was so much different than Dominick, but I see now that he is not, and at least Dominick is always present. But none of it matters now. These past weeks have changed me. Caleb has changed me. Not from myself but into myself. He treats me as an equal, yet he still has a protective side, but a side that protects a woman he sees as his partner, not his woman. That's the difference," Mikayla explained.

"I get it." Rowan said as she crumpled up the note and tossed it into the basket as if she were on a basketball team and had just made the winning basket.

"Nice shot!"

"Thanks!" Rowan smiled.

"You ready or what?" Mikayla then asked.

"I am ready! Let's do this!" Rowan replied,

They made their way down the stairs and out the door. Once they were in Rowan's car she remembered her phone was still dead. "Shit!" She shouted as she picked up her phone. "Hey, can I borrow your car charger?" She asked. "I'll get it back to you later. Not like you'll use it, you never have your phone on you these days!" Rowan added, giving Mikayla an accusing smile.

"Sure, let me just grab it out of my car." Mikayla said as she made her way out of Rowan's car and to her own to grab the charger.

She handed Rowan the charger and immediately she plugged it in and set it down as she backed out of the driveway. Mikayla checked to see if she had remembered to put her phone in her purse and noticed that she had. She picked up the phone to see if she had any messages waiting from Caleb, but she didn't. The only phone calls and text messages she had were from some strange number she didn't recognize, her mother, and Dominick. She was not in the mood to read or listen to the messages. Nobody was going to ruin this night for her, she thought to herself as she stopped checking all of the missed calls. Thinking about the letter, and now bombarded with calls and texts from Dominick, her blood began to boil. No, she was definitely not going to let either one of them ruin her perfect night. She rolled her eyes as she shut her phone off and smiled at the satisfaction it gave to her and then slipped it to the bottom of her purse.

That ought to shut them up for the night, she thought to herself as she reached for the volume of Rowan's stereo to turn the music up loud as one of her favorite songs came on. Rowan and her sang at the top their lungs and continued the whole way until they reached the parking lot.

Mikayla popped in a piece of spearmint gum and applied some lip gloss to make her lips shine softly. Rowan grabbed her purse and then her phone.

"Oh my God, Mario and Dominick have called me so many frickin' times! What the hell do you think they want?" Rowan said, getting ready to push send to Mario's number.

"Wait, don't!" Mikayla begged. "Maybe they somehow found out I was hanging out with Caleb. We've been attached at the hip for the past couple of weeks, so it's possible that someone had seen us. It probably got back to them. I know it's asking a lot, but Rowan could you please not call until I am not around. Wait until we are in the bar so I don't have to hear anything, and if they ask to talk with me you can honestly say that I am not available. Please, Rowan," Mikayla begged.

"Of course, that's probably exactly what it is. Had it been an emergency I'm sure we would have heard from your mom by now. I will call him from the restroom after a drink. I don't want Caleb to think I am rude!" Rowan said being understanding. "It's really not fair how you have been sheltered and treated, and right now you deserve to have some peace," she then added to make sure her best friend really knew she did understand and agree with her request.

"Thank you, Row," Mikayla said softly and then smiled a sad and lonely smile.

"Always," Rowan replied.

Warm air surrounded them as they finally made their way towards the bar.

45

Frustrated by another call he made being put to voicemail, Marcus shut his phone off and threw it against the couch in Layla's apartment. Mikayla was not answering her phone and he was worried. He tried to call to her telepathically, but she had shut him out and blocked it. It took him several times to try and tap into her, and once he finally made a connection she blocked it. He was sure it was because she had no clue he was actually trying to get a hold of her, at least that's what he had been trying to tell himself.

The truth was he had always been able to sense her energy. He knew the love was still there, and he was still in love with her, but something had happened over the last two weeks. He was no longer able to sense her, but from the message he received from Dominick, he knew she was alright. It was something he couldn't wrap his head around, his fear was she had fallen back in love with Dominick. But knowing Dominick, he would have made it more than clear, of course unless Dominick didn't know, he thought to himself.

That's how these things worked. In order to speak telepathically as witches, you had to be either a part of a coven, close enough to someone to tap into their energy, or in love. Once either was broken the energy line was cut. He feared his line was severed. There was no use in trying Rowan, but he had attempted anyways with no such luck. He would have rushed right to her but his duty kept him with Layla.

Marcus had a knot in the pit of his stomach which began to tighten as he thought about Dominick. He knew that Dominick wasn't able to be reached at the moment because he was at his last initiation before full wolf transformation.

Despite the obvious outcome, he tried one time to call Dominick. The call went straight to voicemail. Marcus picked his phone up one more time to try Mikayla again and again he got no answer.

Marcus threw his head up towards the ceiling in defeat before leaning forward as he heard footsteps coming towards him.

"Well, what's the next step?" Ajay came into the living room where Marcus was now sitting with his head down as his hands cupped the back of his skull and rested his elbows on his knees.

"We have to go to Michigan. I am not supposed to leave your sister, so you guys will have to go with me," Marcus replied.

"I don't want my sister in any more danger!" Ajay shouted quietly through his teeth so Layla wouldn't be woken.

"She's probably already out of danger and besides, if she's not, this is the last place she should be. They know where you are now," Marcus informed him.

"I still don't entirely understand what the hell is going on. My mom told us everything she knew, but I don't understand why the girls from this age group were all killed off except for two." Ajay said, scratching the back of his neck, which was itching from stress.

"Three," Marcus said as he looked at the ground, wrapping his hands around the back of his head in frustration.

"Three?" Ajay questioned.

"Yes, three. There weren't two survivors, there were three, and I am not supposed to relinquish that information to anyone. I mean it, you have to keep that to yourself. Only a small, select group knows. I've already told one person who I wasn't supposed to, but knew I could trust, now I have broken my vow twice." Marcus said as he looked up at Ajay, who was standing up across from him, looking down.

As their eyes met, Ajay knew whatever Marcus knew was major. "What's going on?" He asked pointblank. He had little room for patience since it involved his sister.

Marcus sat quietly for a moment. He had already said too much, as he had been given strict instructions not to and knew he was about to break every one of them. The more he thought about it, the more he realized the few members on the council who knew didn't know this attack was coming and had they known, it was likely the information would have been revealed to Layla.

"Have you ever heard of a seer?" Marcus started.

"Yeah, but they don't exist anymore because both sides felt they were much too dangerous and somehow over the years they had died out," Ajay said following.

"No. I mean you have most of it right, but there isn't none, there is still one we fear and whatever it was that he saw involved a female witch born the same year as your sister. It obviously had to do with the shifting of power towards good, at least that much we think to be true, but afterwards things quieted down. Most who don't know the truth think whoever was to shift the powers had, in fact, been killed but something else happened that, again, most people don't know about. Not even the council, except for those few I mentioned." Marcus explained and paused to make sure Ajay was following.

"So, what happened and why are they after my sister now if the one they were after died?" Ajay questioned, still not understanding what was going on.

"That's just it Ajay, she didn't die. This is why seers are so dangerous. They only get a glimpse into the future and things can change or be made even worse if that is indeed what happened, which again, we are pretty sure did. You see, if they would have never killed off the baby girl witches, then the prophecy would never have become true. By doing what it is they did, they created it and now it seems as if they have figured out that the one still lives. The strange thing is that they didn't just kill Layla, which means there is something else going on. I suspect they don't want to kill her anymore and aren't worried about the shift of powers, I think they want to hoist her powers." Marcus explained.

"Whose powers?" Ajay asked, still confused.

"Mikayla's," Marcus said quietly.

"Alright you lost me, who is Mikayla?"

"The third witch," Marcus spilled.

"So, there really is three and you all must have known that she was the one in danger, so you hid her and used my sister and I assume the other witch as decoys?" Ajay said as his anger started to rise.

"Not exactly, they knew that your sister and Rowan had escaped, but they didn't know about the third one because she did die. Well, at least briefly. What happened next was what changed the prophecy." Marcus said, calmly trying to get Ajay to calm down as he noticed his hands were balled into fists.

"She died and came back to life you're saying? How?" Ajay asked, trying to remain in control.

"How familiar are you with the council?" Marcus asked.

"I don't pay much attention, obviously that is Ra'ad's thing not mine." Ajay admitted.

"Well we are part of the Dark Council, which means we are warriors who are in training to become possible candidates as future members of the Seven Points Council, which is a step below the Elders, of which three of the seven of us will eventually have potential of being an Elder in our life time. Of the ones of us who actually make it to elder, one then will become a member of the Council of Light. Your father was on the Chair of Seven, as well as my father. The girl Mikayla's father is Amadeus, the First Light of the Seven Chairs, which means that he holds the greatest chance of becoming an Elder. He leads the chair and is first speaker to the Elders during meetings. This man is the one who mentors your brother. My father is actually one of the three Elders," Marcus began, but was interrupted by Ajay.

"Get to the point!" Ajay said, becoming frustrated.

"I'm trying. You see, Amedeus is Mikayla's birth father. She doesn't know. Amedeus has one of his dearest friends raising her as his own. A werewolf named Santino, who is the right hand to one of the heads of the Assembly of the Moon. The reason he is raising her is because an Angel named Arella, who was close to Amedeus' wife, Mariella, stepped in and stayed by her side as the killings were happening to help and protect her, but something went wrong and they were ambushed when Amedeus got called out. They fought them off the best they could, but in the end Mariella was killed, as well as the baby. As Amedeus felt her life slip away from afar, he orbed back in to find Arella standing over her lifeless body. Arella took one look at Amedeus and told him his child would live and that she would be special and her powers limitless and within one quick move had jumped into the fetus inside. Amedeus then had to deliver the baby from his slain wife's body. Mikayla is that baby. This is who they are , and others could be too if they found out what she was and the kind of powers she possessed," Marcus said, almost feeling relieved to get it off of his chest.

"So, you protect her and leave my sister and the other girl unprotected?"

"No, you all have been watched by the Dark Knights all along. Your brother has been in transition over the past week so things have been more scattered than usual. A witch is missing and presumed dead, which means a spot opened up. Your brother was hand chosen to be moved up from the apprentice council of the Dark Knights." Marcus said, feeling a bit responsible. "We hadn't known anything was coming so soon," he added.

"All right then, what's next?" Ajay said.

"We need to get to Mikayla, soon. More than them will be after her. We need to figure out what it is that she is capable of. That will help us figure out what they want from her or why they want her dead," Marcus said. "As soon as Layla is healed, we move," he then added.

"Are you all talking about me?" Layla stood at the door of her room looking as if she had just had a rough night, because in fact she did have a rough night.

"Layla!" Ajay ran towards his sister and gave her a hug. "I am so sorry I didn't get there sooner," he whispered as tears filled his eyes.

"You got there and that is all that matters," she whispered back.

She then turned towards Marcus and made her way to him. She took a seat next to him on the couch and let out a deep breath. "I assume you will fill me in?" She asked, knowing there was a lot more going on than she was told.

"Yes," Marcus answered.

"I suppose I should clean myself up so we can get going then?" She asked, although she already knew the answer.

"If you are healed, then we need to go," Marcus said.

"I'm healed," she said as she placed her hand on his knee to comfort him, then stood up and made her way towards the bathroom to take a shower.

Marcus turned towards Ajay. "Remember, no matter whom it is, whether they are part of the Light Council or Council of Light, you must not tell anyone, even if it seems that they know. The people who I told you of know and that is it. No matter what, Ajay, or things could turn more dangerous," Marcus said firmly.

Ajay nodded in understanding. He couldn't say much because he was still trying to take it all in. His anger was boiling as he thought of his father, who unnecessarily died. He wanted to blame them all, but he knew he couldn't. The best thing he could do was stick with his sister and Marcus, nothing else mattered at the moment.

46

Dominick had been able to reach Lazzaro after several attempts. Without hesitation, all the father wolves made their way as fast as they could back to the car. Despite running at full speeds it took them a good couple of hours to reach the car. Once they had reached the car and changed back into human form, they all reached for their cell phones and began to dial.

They finally managed to get a hold of their wives, who were having a day at the lake house once they got to their cars. Santino's heart dropped when he heard the girls were not with them. They tried calling the house, and both Mikayla's and Rowan's cell phones. Rowan's parents couldn't be reached either. They were in the middle of something important, which they closed down the shop for the day. Santino knew it was a slim possibility he could reach them because Rowan's mother had talked to Mikayla's mother and let her know they wouldn't be joining them and why.

Mikayla's mom, Careena, made calls to home with no answer from her cell phone as she made it out the door and hurried home. It took her a half an hour before she was home. There was no sign of Mikayla. She waited around for quite a while for a phone call, or for her to show up, but there were still no signs she was coming home.

Her gut instinct told her Mikayla was alright. She knew for a fact she would be able to feel if something terrible had happened, but that wasn't the feeling she was getting. It was mid-afternoon and her morning sickness had finally settled in. She decided to make some mint tea as she waited for Mikayla to return home, or give her a call, having left messages for Rowan as well.

The longer she sat, the more her mind played tricks on her. Fear set in as she did what no self-respecting wolf mother would ever do, she snooped through Mikayla's room to try and find a clue to where she was heading that day. Her car was there, so she safely assumed Rowan had picked her up. Mikayla's room was tidy, as usual, and her mother couldn't see anything that would lead her to any conclusions. It was in Mikayla's bathroom where she found the clues.

Mikayla had left her sunscreen open, it was the first thing Careena had noticed. Normally Mikayla was a neat freak and would have cleaned the top off, closed it, and put it away, but the top was off and the lotion still hanging out around the top waiting to be used was still wet. Careena flew out of the bathroom and headed towards Mikayla's swim drawer. She tried to remember which suits Mikayla owned to see if any were missing. Perhaps someone without the memory of a wolf couldn't be sure of what someone owned, but Careena remembered and noticed Mikayla's new one was missing.

Quickly she made her way towards the hall closet. She had just finished laundry earlier that morning and wanted to see if a beach towel was also missing. Sure enough, there was a towel missing from the morning stack of fresh and soft, oversized yellow and white beach towels. Careena was now more nervous, as she realized Mikayla had never made it to the lake house. She quickly reached for her phone to call back to the lake house to see if she did in fact show up.

It was Lucio's mother who picked up the phone.

"Annabelle, has Mikayla shown up there?" Careena's voice was frantic.

"Not yet. Is Mikayla on her way? You got a hold of her?" Annabelle replied.

Careena could hear all of the voices in the background at the lake house. She then heard what she thought sounded like Johnny say Mikayla's name, but couldn't make out what he was saying.

"Who is that? Is that Johnny?" Careena said, even more frantic.

"Hold on Careena, Johnny saw Mikayla," Annabelle said as she put the phone to her shoulder and had a quick conversation with her son. "Careena, are you still there?" She came back to the phone.

"Yes, what is it? Did he see Mikayla?" Careena said anxiously.

"He did, just a little bit ago. Rowan and Mikayla were at another part of the lake and said they were having a girls day," Annabelle relayed.

"Thank god!" Careena said, grabbing her purse and heading back out the door to her car. "I am on my way out there," she added as she reached her car.

Careena started her car as she called Santino to tell him the seemingly good news.

"They are alright! They are just having a girls day at another part of the lake. Probably just needed some time to feel like young women is all!" Careena said as tears poured out of her eyes.

"I love you," Santino said.

Careena was too upset to reply. She knew Mikayla should have been told the truth years ago but was ordered not to. Careena felt if Mikayla did know the truth, her powers would be greater and she would have a better chance at fighting off anything coming at her. She also knew her daughter was extremely smart and thought if she knew the truth her judgement would be sound. Right now Careena blamed all of them, and the only thing that would make her feel whole was her daughter. She had had enough. Careena was going to do what she should have done years before, tell Mikayla the whole truth.

"It's alright. Don't cry, my love. I will be home soon," Santino said, his voice quivering a bit at the sound of his wife's tears and the fact Mikayla had in fact been accounted for.

"Johnny will take me to where he saw her. I will keep her close until you can get home," she said, sniffling while driving as fast as she could back towards the lake.

"Take your time. I don't know what I would do if anything happened to you," Santino said, trying to protect her from a far.

"Nothing will happen to me. I just want to find my little girl," she said, agitated that in a time like this someone would tell her to slow down. Even though she knew Mikayla was alright, she couldn't get to her fast enough if for nothing more than to wrap her arms around her beautiful daughter. She may not have birthed her, but loved her no less than if she had birthed Mikayla herself. It was her little girl and she meant the world to her. She was having another boy and this would be the last child she would have. Mikayla being her only girl was special to her.

As soon as Dominick had jumped into the car he tried Mikayla with no such luck. Immediately after he hung up on Mikayla's voicemail he placed a call to Marcus.

"Dom? What happened? Is Mikayla ok?" Marcus said without saying hello. He knew only an emergency would have pulled Dominick out of the woods.

"I'm not sure… we think we know where she is ,but something strange is going on," Dominick started but was interrupted by Marcus.

"Something is going on. Last night the third witch was attacked. Best I can tell is that these were vampires that had some sort of powers. I think they must have been warlocks that had been turned into vampires. They were strong and it seemed obvious that they are on to Mikayla. I don't think they know yet that she exists. Most likely they will be coming after Rowan next. She is in danger. Mikayla is in danger. We are coming there in a little while. I just have to wait for Layla to heal before her powers are up so we can orb," he said, seemingly all in one breath with the quickness of words spoken.

"I think we have an even bigger problem. I think that someone knows about Mikayla. We found a group of three renegade hyenas up north…" Dominick started, but again was interrupted by Marcus, who was dealing with a lack of sleep.

"Hyenas? What the hell are they doing in Michigan?" Marcus was trying to make sense out of the relevance.

"Just listen would you!" Dominick yelled.

Marcus quickly shut his mouth and waited for Dominick to finish.

"Anyways, they are dead. We didn't kill them, someone else did, but that's not all. We found a picture of Mikayla by the bodies. It was in the Upper Penisula, Marcus. There is no other explanation for her picture to be there other than someone had gotten a hold of a picture of her somehow and gave it to them so they would know what to look for. That's the best we could come up with. Whatever is going on, one thing is for sure, she is in danger. We will be home in a few hours. Meet me at my house when you can. If something changes I will call you," Dominick finally finished.

"Why were the hyenas there in the first place? Were they just hired guns or what? Perhaps they were there to grab her? It doesn't make sense…no one knows about her but a select few," Marcus started to dissect the problem.

"I know a little more and I will fill you in on the rest tonight when I am not driving a hundred miles per hour," Dominick said.

"See you in a while." Marcus understood Dominick needed both hands to drive.

Dominick said nothing back. Instead, he turned off his phone, threw it on the dash, and proceeded to drive as fast as he could while the others braced themselves for the ride of their lives.

Mario watched the phone make its way onto the dash. He was still not filled in on all the details. He was trying to be patient and knew whatever it was he was about to hear required some explanations from Dominick, Lazzaro, and his own father. Mario watched as Dominick looked at his father, and watched as Lazzaro then turned to look at Santino. An unspoken language was being spoken, Mario realized, as he watched his father nod in understanding. Santino then turned towards Mario and he knew right then he was about to be filled in.

"Son, there are a few things that you need to know," Santino began.

"I know," Mario replied, bracing himself for whatever it was he was about to hear.

Santino began to tell him about Mikayla. He started from the beginning and worked his way towards the present as Dominick jumped in from time to time. As the words came out, Mario began to feel dizzy. Then Rowan was brought into the conversation and the dizzy feeling started to become fuzzy. Everything he thought to be true wasn't, yet the way he felt was still the same. He needed a while to digest the information and remained quiet as they filled him in. Mario had nothing to say after they finished talking. Instead, he opted to look out the window quiet and lost in thought. They knew he needed a minute and gave him the mental space to do so as Dominick continued to speed down the highway.

The car ride back towards Ann Arbor was beginning to feel like the longest ride of Dominick's life. Everyone was quiet and no one could seem to get Mikayla or Rowan on the phone. His heart was racing faster than he could make the car move. The seven sons and seven fathers packed themselves into four cars and headed back home. It was disruptive for them to leave a week earlier, but for what could be at stake it was just a minor inconvenience that would lead them to follow up during the next full moon. For now the most important thing was for them to get home.

"Dominick, you can slow down. She is at the lake and getting there twenty minutes earlier isn't going to help if we crash on the way," Lazzaro said.

"They aren't with her yet," Dominick said as he continued to floor the jeep.

"Son…" Lazzaro began, but was cut off by the look Dominick gave him.

Lazzaro was proud of his son and knew in that moment Dominick would make a fine Alpha. Without instating his true Alpha position, Lazzaro quieted and let his son continue to do what he felt he needed to do.

"They had a picture of her…whether it was the hyenas or whoever killed the hyenas, someone was looking for her," Dominick said for what Mario thought was probably the hundredth time.

Mario's stomach was in knots. He just found out his twin sister was actually not even his twin. Despite the news, she still was his sister and he loved her no less, and the thought there were people out there who wanted to hurt her made him angry inside. Then he kept thinking of Rowan and how she, too, could be in danger. The thought of anyone as much as thinking about laying a hand on her made his eyes glaze over to solid black. His predatory side was being pulled out.

"Son, keep it together," Santino quietly whispered to Mario as he noticed the whites of his eyes were non-existent.

"I'm trying," was all Mario could manage back. He was lost somewhere between shock from the truth and preparing to fight anyone and anything who came near his family and his girl.

Mario was furious he didn't have the truth when Dominick had. Dominick explained to him he wasn't supposed to have the information either, but right before their prom years back Marcus had told him. He also said he made a promise not to reveal the information and Dominick's word was solid. Now he had to tell because the direct threat of danger was around and, out of the greater good, Dominick had to spill the truth. Mario tried to remain calm and told himself Dominick was doing what was right. He did understand, but he was feeling helpless, stuck in the car without any contact from Rowan. With the thought of her beautiful face, he dialed her number again to find it was still going straight to voicemail.

"Still going straight to voicemail," Mario said looking out of the window. He had a gut feeling she was still alright. He felt he would know if something had happened to her, but he wouldn't sit comfortable until he heard her voice. Somehow wolves could sense things about those they loved. It was thought this was true because of how connected to spirit they actually were.

"Let's not think too much about this. Johnny said they were at the lake together just having some girl time. Nobody else was with them. I am sure everything will be fine. As soon as I know that they are accounted for I will go to the council," Lazzaro said.

Santino nodded in agreement. He too was still worried, but felt what Lazzaro had just said was the truth. Santino watched out the window like Mario. The trees passed by fast. They looked like a blur at the speed they were going, yet the sky seemed to stand still. It only made him think of just how small they really were down on earth, even with their immortal powers.

The ride seemed to turn into a blur as minutes passed to hours and they were now just an hour away from being home. Mario opened his phone to try Rowan one more time. This time he didn't get the voicemail, this time he actually heard the phone ringing.

"It's ringing!" He shouted, then quickly listened for Rowan to pick up.

He listened to the first few rings. Every ring without her picking up made his stomach tighten just a little bit more. Mario felt out of control. It wasn't until the fifth ring she picked up.

"Hey you!" Rowan said from the other end with loud rock music playing in the background, as well as the confusion of many people competing with the music for conversations. Mario even heard a couple of drunk "woos" coming from the crowd.

He knew she was at a bar. He knew she was alright and, while she was out having the time of her life, he had been stuck in the car imagining God only knows what could be happening to her. Immediately his eyes glazed over to all black again as he lost his cool.

"Where the hell have you been?" Mario demanded loudly as his voice started to change over to more beast than man. Rowan could barely hear what he had just said, but noticed something wasn't right in his tone.

47

"I can barely hear you! Are you sick?" Rowan asked as she tried to make out what he was saying. It wasn't just the background noise making it hard for her to understand him, his phone was cutting in and out. She figured he was in a bad reception area.

"I said where the hell have you been, Rowan! I have been trying you all day!" He tried again.

Rowan could make out where and you, as well as her name, and all day. She figured he asked where she was earlier in the day. "I was at the lake with Mikayla. Girls day out. Now we are listening to some band at the Backroom in Ypsilanti. We just got here. Your voice sounds funny. I can barely hear you. Are you sick?" She tried to fit it all in, knowing with the reception her conversation would be a long one.

"I am pissed! You need to go home now, Rowan. I am coming home," he barked his order like he was in the military talking to the lowest grunt in the unit.

"I really can't hear you, you're breaking up! Sounds like you are coming home. Are you sick?" She asked for the third time, still unable to make out the rest, but trying as she made her way towards the restrooms where it was more quiet.

"No. Rowan, listen to me, You need to meet me at my house. You and Mikayla both," Mario yelled.

"Mario, I can't hear you. You're breaking up. Call me when you get back into town," Rowan said, struggling to try and make sense out of what he was saying.

"I want you to leave the bar now, Rowan. Do you hear me?" Mario yelled one more time, trying to get his point across. Rowan finally heard him.

"I am not leaving just because you say to leave. You know what; this shit has got to stop. You guys are always trying to boss Mikayla around and I am not about to let you start in on me. I don't know what your problem is, but enough is enough Mario," Rowan said firmly, wondering if he caught everything \she said.

"I am not playing around Rowan. I can't explain right this minute. Just listen to what I am asking and do it," he said, trying to sound a little more calm but failing at his attempt.

"No, I am out with Kali and it is an important night. I will see you later," she said when she heard him start yelling. Rowan had enough. She saw her best friend being happy for the first time in a long time and she wasn't about to let the boys come in and ruin it, so she decided to hang up the phone.

Mario stared at his phone in disbelief. "What the fuck is happening?" He asked out loud to himself.

"What?" Dominick asked.

"She fucking hung up on me," Mario sat frozen with his eyes wide open from the shock.

Normally Dominick would have had a smart comment for him such as, "it's about time," or, "she finally came to her senses," but right now the only thought in his head was to drive faster.

Rowan stared down at her phone for a moment. She couldn't believe she had just hung up on him and felt for a moment she wasn't being fair and desperately wanted to call him back. She looked over at the table where Mikayla and Caleb were. Caleb was looking at Mikayla the way a man looks at a woman when he truly is in love. She looked back at him the same way. Rowan noticed the glow around the two of them and knew tonight it was about Mikayla. One thing she was sure of is her and Mario would be just fine, even if this had started a small argument between them. Tonight she was going to do the right thing for Mikayla's sake. Mikayla deserved her happiness, as well. Rowan made her decision and quickly shut off the phone and made her way back to the table.

"Hey, sorry about that," Rowan apologized for walking away and talking on her phone.

"Was that Mario?" Mikayla asked.

"No, I thought it was but it was just my mom checking up on me," Rowan lied, not wanting to get Mikayla worked up.

"Oh, that's cool. I thought it seemed strange if Mario was calling. Usually they never call home on these camping trips of theirs," Mikayla said, looking at Rowan.

Rowan felt awful about lying and she would later tell her friend the truth, but right now she wasn't about to let anything interfere with Mikayla's night.

"Yeah, that's what I thought," she said as she picked up her beer to take a sip. "So, Caleb, when is your friend's band supposed to start playing?" She added, trying to change the subject.

"In a little bit. I think they are supposed to start playing between nine and ten. So, pretty soon," Caleb answered as he looked down at his watch.

Mikayla was glad to see the conversation between Rowan and Caleb seemed so natural. They had been there for about an hour and Caleb and Rowan had made fast friends. Caleb's friends were a bit more distant, although they were nice, and Jamahl especially had a good sense of humor. They had already met, so it made things easier, but Jamahl seemed busy with his girlfriend and Ali was more of the serious type. Mikayla felt he almost looked on edge, as if he really didn't want to be there but had to and was just waiting for something to happen. What Mikayla had no idea, but she had spent enough time around Ali to know while he was nice he was also the quiet, serious type. Mikayla decided he was the one who balanced Caleb and Jamahl's wilder ways.

The bar was fairly large and dimly lit. It wasn't quite the show bar Dominick owned, instead it was more simplistic. Wood floors and tables with beat up bar stools for seating. The dance floor was much smaller, but the stage was larger. It was a great place for bands to play. Along the walls were random pictures of bands who had played there throughout the years, along with some random knick knacks, giving it an eclectic vibe. The bartenders and wait staff wore blue jeans and t-shirts, making it feel laid back.

Mikayla couldn't help but stare at Caleb. He was one of the most handsome guys she had ever laid eyes on, and tonight she thought he looked especially cute. It wasn't that he was dressed up, he wore dark jeans with some fade marks along with a white fitted tee-shirt and flip flops, but the black baseball cap he wore made him look carefree. Mikayla liked that.

Caleb was just as smitten with Mikayla. He loved the black sundress, she too looked laid back in the simplistic cotton blend sundress. It reminded him of being somewhere tropical and he knew one day he would take her somewhere like that. Maybe they would live their life in paradise under the sun somewhere were the palm trees grew and the sun never left. The thought made him smile as he looked towards Mikayla.

Mikayla could see the look behind his eyes. She didn't know what it was he was thinking, but every bone in her body said it was something about her, something good. She blushed a little and gave a big smile. She felt stupid, but she couldn't help herself.

Caleb noticed she was squirming a little and laughed at her big smile towards him. She looked so cute. Mikayla quickly turned her head, embarrassed. He reached over and gently grabbed her face and planted a soft kiss on her cheek. Holding it there for a moment, he thought with his whole heart how he loved her. Mikayla smiled again.

"Well ,I don't want to interrupt this love fest so I think I will grab us another pitcher of beer!" Rowan said as she got up off her stool and made her way towards the bar, leaving Caleb and Mikayla behind laughing.

"So, I am glad to see that you get along with Rowan. She will be a good ally in the weeks to come when the boys come back," she said without thinking about it.

The look on Caleb's face changed to a look of worry. Mikayla got nervous, she thought perhaps she spoke to soon. Maybe he didn't really want there to be more weeks to come. She quickly tried to change the subject.

"I mean, she could be if we still are hanging out," she tried to say casually.

Caleb realized the look on his face had thrown her off. That wasn't his intent. He had every intention on being with her in the future, he was thinking about forever. But when she said Rowan could be an ally he realized the plan tonight was for Jamahl and Ali to check her out and that wasn't going to be a pretty scene. Caleb wondered how he was going to explain that one. They planned on trying to do it in a way in which she wouldn't remember it was them, but you never knew with these things. Everything came with a risk. He also really did like Rowan and was hoping with all his heart Rowan turned out to be nothing more than a witch.

"Mikayla, I hope she will be a good ally because I plan on being with you for a very long time," He said and quickly smiled as he grabbed her hand.

Mikayla was relieved. She decided he was probably just worried thinking about how things would change when the boys came home. Mikayla worried about the same thing. She looked at him and gave a gentle smile.

"So how long is a long time?" She asked.

"Forever works for me," he said.

The answer sent chills throughout her whole body and she knew in that moment without a doubt tonight she would tell him how she felt and they would be connected in a way which would bond them forever.

"I was hoping you would say that," she said honestly.

"Hoping he would say what?" Rowan interrupted as she came back to the table with another pitcher of beer and began to fill peoples' empty glasses.

"You don't want to know," Ali said, having come back to the table in the middle of their conversation.

Caleb gave him a look that said to watch it.

Ali picked up the message. "I am just saying some things should be left between a couple," Ali tried to show his brother a little more support.

"A couple? Are you guys officially a couple then?" Rowan asked as she finished pouring the last beer to herself.

Mikayla didn't answer, she didn't have to because Caleb answered for her.

"Yes we are," he said and winked at Rowan.

Rowan smiled back and looked at Mikayla. Mikayla couldn't help but beam. It felt too good to be true, so she was sure something fucked up would happen, but she wasn't going to let it ruin the moment. She still had a whole other week with Caleb before the trouble makers came home and she was going to make sure to connect with him as much as she could to solidify the relationship.

The lights went a little dimmer as the lights of the stage came on. Jackson's band was on stage. He was the singer of the band. They wasted no time and dove right in to a heavy metal rift. They played only instrumentals for the first few minutes and the sound began to change into more of a screamo style as Jackson started singing. Mikayla and Rowan were more than impressed.

"Holy shit, these guys are really good!" Mikayla said.

"Yeah, I know. I was surprised when I first heard them myself," Caleb agreed.

"Wow, they are good. Are all their songs that good?" Rowan asked, not taking her eyes from the stage.

"They are," Ali said, also agreeing Jackson's band truly had talent.

They weren't singing any cover songs. It was all original music, most of which Jackson wrote. His voice was amazing. It was clear and on point. His range was wide and he was utilizing every part of his voice.

It wasn't just Mikayla, Caleb, and Ali who thought the band was good, they seemed to have a band of groupies which swarmed the dance floor, Rowan noticed.

Caleb was starting to feel a little nervous. He wondered if he was really going to go through with his next plan. The problem was, he wasn't sure just when Jackson was going to call him up. He started to fidget a little. Uncomfortable by another new feeling, he finished off his beer and poured himself another glass as Ali watched with one lifted brow.

"Shut up," Caleb said before Ali had a chance to comment. Caleb downed half of another glass of beer.

"Thirsty?" Mikayla asked, wondering why all of a sudden Caleb was drinking like a fish.

Your boyfriend is either nervous or an alcoholic, Rowan thought to Mikayla.

Mikayla gave Rowan a smile as she wrinkled her nose. *You're going to make me laugh, stop!* She said back, not wanting to laugh seemingly for no reason. She decided it just might make her seem crazy.

Caleb, in the meantime, proceeded to finish off the rest of the newly poured beer and poured himself another. Ali shook his head. *Seriously, don't start*, he thought to Ali.

You just remember what we need to do. I suggest if you don't want your girlfriend finding out, that you need to remain as coherent as possible. Wait, I get it. You're really going through with it? Ali remembered what Caleb had planned.

Shut up, was all Caleb said back as he threw down another sip.

The band was about four songs in when Jackson started to talk between songs as the band quieted. "A friend of mine wrote a song with us, and I would like it if you gave him a big hand as he comes up to sing it," Jackson said, pointing over to the table they were sitting at.

Mikayla looked confused. Caleb looked nervous. Ali looked annoyed. Rowan looked amused, she understood exactly what was going on. She looked to Caleb and smiled.

"Correct me if I am wrong, but I do believe he is referring to you!" Rowan then took a sip of her beer.

Caleb said nothing. Instead, he finished another sip of beer and hopped off the bar stool. Mikayla watched in shock as he made his way towards the stage. She knew his voice was great, he had played around many times singing to her, but it was never serious. Mikayla was wondering if now he would be serious. She watched with anticipation.

Caleb climbed onto the stage and stood next to the microphone as Jackson took another microphone without a stand. Caleb was glad Jackson had let him have the security of the microphone stand. Normally Caleb would not be nervous, but Mikayla was about to watch him sing a song he wrote about her. The things in the song were true, but his reasoning for writing and performing it in front of her was not of pure intentions. He had hoped if something went wrong later, she would remember this moment. Caleb knew it was selfish, but it was part of his nature when it came to the things he wanted and she was all he wanted now.

Caleb said nothing as he took hold of the microphone. He pulled his baseball cap a little bit lower, covering his eyes a bit. Then with few words he introduced the title. "This is called Mikayla," he said and glanced at Mikayla.

Mikayla felt like she couldn't get a breath. She felt fuzzy all over. Rowan smiled at her in approval.

The music started. It was a slower song with a metal riff along with a hint of a reggae undertone. Jackson was doing background vocals. The words were beautiful, yet very dark. There were parts where Caleb's beautiful singing changed into a deep screaming voice with some cookie monster vocals. When he did that Mikayla's whole body tingled. She wanted him even more than she had before. He was laying it all out for her with an amazing song he took the time to write and the nerve to perform. Something which could have been so cheesy ended up being totally sexy.

She couldn't get all the words throughout the song the first time through, but there was a part which struck her as being very dark. It was almost like a warning:

Under the moon, I watch over you as you sleep.
You dream of me I can hear it when you weep.
I walk in the daylight holding your hand,
trying to pretend I am just a normal man.
One day I will tell you all
when you succeed in breaking down the final wall.
Through the blackness I grew drawn to your light
from first sight it was only you I saw.
One day you'll be bled by choice
I'll let it be a decision from your voice.

Mikayla wondered what it all meant. Parts she thought she understood, little did she know she understood none of them.

The chorus was easier to understand:

Dear Mikayla, Mikayla I fell in love with ya,
I got something I wanna say
something I hope will make forever for us stay.
You might not understand it all now but time will reveal
that love is what I feel.
Love always, Caleb.

Mikayla thought it was so cleaver the chorus was like a love letter. She especially loved the last part when he screamed, "Love always, Caleb!" The other part of the chorus was beautifully done, and then became very dark at the end. It sent chills down her spine.

The song was over and the whole bar seemed to take notice the song was great. Mikayla even noticed quite a few girls going a little overboard trying to block him as he exited off the stage. He gave zero notice to them as he made his way to Mikayla, looking only at her. As he approached the table he didn't even ask if she liked the song, instead he grabbed her and kissed her, not caring who was around. To him, at that moment it was only her and him in the bar. She felt the same.

Jackson's band already began to sing another one of their songs. This time they picked a faster song. It was the song Caleb had exited the stage with and heard in the background as he made his way towards Mikayla.

They were lip locked for what seemed like forever to Ali and Rowan. Rowan looked at Ali and playfully rolled her eyes. Ali thought it was much deserved and held his beer up towards Rowan. Rowan giggled and tapped her glass against his. Ali then managed a smile back. He was trying to keep himself a little distanced because he knew if he didn't he would end up feeling too much guilt when he was checking the status of whether or not she was the one they were looking for.

Caleb took a seat next to Mikayla after they had stopped kissing. Mikayla blushed a little. She wasn't into PDA and neither was Caleb, but the moment called for it and neither one of them seemed to be able to help themselves.

Jamahl and Mary finally made their way back towards the table to join the rest of the party as Jackson's band played perfectly in the background. Everyone was having a goodtime. Rowan felt hopeful for Mikayla and decided making new friends was a good thing. Tonight she was not going to think about Mario. Tonight was about Mikayla and her making new friends.

48

Coreena was sitting on the porch of their house with both the cordless phone and her cell phone sitting right next to her when the boys pulled in. Santino jumped out of the car before it had come to a complete stop. Mario did the same from the other side of the car.

"Any word?" Coreena said with tears in her eyes.

"She and Rowan are at a bar in Ypsilanti. We are going to get her," Mario spoke before his father had a chance.

"Thank God! I searched all over the lake and couldn't find them. When I came back to the house, I noticed that they had been here but they left no note informing me of their whereabouts," Coreena said as the tears poured down her face.

"I am going with you," Santino said just as Dominick made his way up to the porch with his father following behind him.

"No, I don't think you should. I think you should stay here and make sure your home is safe. Once we get her we need to make sure that our houses are secure. There is more going on here than what we thought. We just can't all be in the same place," Dominick said.

"I agree. I will be going to the council. Santino, you stay here and wait for the boys to bring the girls home. I need to try and get a hold of Xavier Munoz so he knows what is happening first," Lazarro said, trying to organize the situation as fast and tightly as he could.

Santino just shook his head in understanding as he closed his eyes tightly, worried for his little girl.

"Do you want me to call Amedeus?" Lazarro asked Santino.

"Wait until you get to the council. The boys can handle this end. She's not in immediate danger, at least not that we know of and we don't need to heighten the area. For all we know the two incidents are separate," Santino said without thinking about what he had just said in front of Coreena.

"What two incidents are you talking about?" She demanded having been a nervous wreck all day.

"I will tell you when the boys leave," he said.

Coreena was usually patient, but tonight she had anything but patience. "No, I will not wait! You better tell me what is going on! Now, Santino!" She said as tears started streaming down her face even faster, flooding her cheeks.

"You boys better get going," Santino said as he made his way into the house after Coreena, who had stormed into the house, slamming the inside door open.

Mario nodded and followed Dominick and Lazarro back to the car. They dropped off Lazarro at his house before they made it out of the neighborhood and sped back to their condo to meet the others and Marcus.

They had pulled in just about the same time as Lucio and Mikey. The others pulled in just shortly after. They all made it upstairs to their condos. Lucio and Mikey shared the condo on the right next to Dominick and Mario. Ricky, Tony and Vince shared the three bedroom condo on the end and to the left of Dominick and Mario. All the boys went in for a quick change of clothes and were to meet back at Dominick and Mario's in ten minutes.

Dominick fumbled with the keys for a minute before sticking it into the lock. His senses told him someone was already in his home. He looked at Mario and his senses were telling him the same thing. "Probably Marcus," Dominick said. Mario nodded as Dominick carefully opened the door, but was startled to find the face he saw was not Marcus'.

Without thinking Dominick moved quickly in as his eyes changed to black and grabbed the stranger by the throat and threw him up against the wall. The stranger zapped him, but at the moment the energy barely phased him. "Who are you?" He growled in an inhuman voice.

"Whoa! Dominick, let him down!" Marcus called as he made his way from the kitchen with a glass of water and a bag of unknown herbs.

Dominick took his hand off of Ajay's throat and looked at Marcus. "Sorry I didn't realize that you came in pairs," he then said.

Mario said nothing and made his way towards his bedroom to change, he couldn't get to Rowan or his sister quick enough.

"I will be ready in five," Dominick then added as he quickly made it to his bedroom where he noticed the door opened.

"Dominick, there is something else..." Marcus started to say before being cut off by Dominick.

"What the fuck?" Dominick said as he noticed one of the most beautiful girls he had ever seen laying asleep in his bed. Her hair was long and dark and her skin a golden olive. She was slender and cut. Her lips were full and her nose was petite, yet interesting, and sat amongst high cheek bones. In a way she reminded him of how both Mikayla and Rowan were both so pretty. The three of them could pass as sisters. He looked down at her and thought how peaceful she looked. It somehow made him feel peaceful. Lost in thought he couldn't help but stare until he was snapped into reality when Marcus came into his room.

"That's what I was trying to tell you. That's Layla. She's the third witch. It was her who was attacked last night. I didn't think you would mind if I let her take a nap to rest up while we were waiting for you," Marcus said, still holding the glass of water and bag of herbs in his hand.

"Huh?" Dominick said. "I mean I don't mind. I was just taken by surprise," he quickly recovered, still staring at Layla.

"Sorry man, she was better this afternoon but I think orbing this far away took a lot out of her. I have some herbs here that will help her feel better. I was just getting ready to wake her and give this to her," Marcus said as he walked over to the bed with Ajay walking in behind.

"Could you guys please quit staring at my sister while she is sleeping," Ajay said, annoyed two men were having a conversation about her and over her as she slept.

Marcus ignored Ajay, as did Dominick. They weren't doing anything wrong, so they continued their conversation as if Ajay wasn't even in the room.

"Will she be safe here while we go get the girls?" Marcus asked.

"She should be," Dominick answered.

"What's this should be shit?" Ajay butted his way into the discussion.

"Who the hell is this guy?" Dominick again ignored Ajay and directed his question towards Marcus.

"Layla's younger brother," Marcus answered, but gave no more power to him than that. He had about had it with Ajay's attitude and now understood first hand why Ra'ad was always so annoyed with him.

"That's right, I am, and I will decide what is best for her," Ajay puffed himself up.

"Anyways, we will come here afterwards; it shouldn't take us too long to grab the girls." Dominick said. "Marcus…I don't know how to say this, but I think you might need to wait outside of the bar and keep an eye open out there. I have a feeling if Mikayla sees you then it might be impossible to get her to go willingly. You know how stubborn she gets when she is mad," Dominick added, loving the small jab he got to take at Marcus.

Over the past four years Dominick and Marcus had formed a bond and a sort of friendship over the secret they shared about Mikayla, but nonetheless, they were still plagued by having been in love with the same girl. The girl which neither one could call their own any longer.

Marcus mulled over what Dominick had said. He knew he was right, but not because he knew Mikayla could be stubborn. Somehow he had missed that part about her. Maybe it was because he hadn't stayed around long enough to find out. The thought made him feel farther apart from her, which only made him want to see her more. This was the first time in four years he had been even remotely close to where she was. The pit of his stomach was doing turns. He had a lot to explain to her and he hoped she would understand everything and forgive him. Even if it was a long shot, somewhere in his mind the scene played out with him telling her the truth and her throwing her arms around him, telling him she still loved him and they could pick up where they left off. It never occurred to him he would have any competition other than Dominick.

"You might be right," Marcus said, using his head rather than his heart.

Dominick headed into the closet to grab a change of clothes. He then made his way into his bathroom to freshen up and closed the door behind him. Marcus sat on the bed next to Layla and tapped her lightly on the shoulder to wake her as Ajay hovered over him.

"Layla," Marcus said softly.

"Hmm…" Layla mumbled with her eyes still closed.

"I need you to wake up and take some herbs. It'll make you feel better."

Layla opened her eyes to find herself in a strange room. She blinked, trying to remember how she had gotten there. "Oh," she said as it dawned upon her where she was at. She sat up and took the glass of water and herbs from Marcus and proceeded to take them.

"Thanks," she said after she had finished the last sip of water. The water tasted so good, she didn't realize she had been that dehydrated. She was sure she was a bit low in iron too after having been bled. Nothing sounded better than a huge steak at the moment.

"You will be safe here and your brother will stay with you. I won't be gone long," Marcus explained.

"You're not leaving without me," Layla said, handing him back the glass of water.

"Your brother will be here to protect you and within a few minutes you will be stronger. They aren't looking for you so I think this is the safest place for you," Marcus tried to reason with her.

"I am not scared of that. I want to help. I don't want them to do to Rowan or Mikayla what they did to me. I am only worried for them and I may be of some help," Layla said, putting her foot down.

"No, I can't have you put in any more danger," Marcus said.

"Yeah, Layla. Let them do whatever it is they do. We are no longer a part of this mess," Ajay said, agreeing with Marcus. Marcus was glad he was backing his decision.

"Ajay, you are not my boss. You will respect whatever decision that I make. Neither of you can stop me, so you might as well just quit trying. I am coming with you," she said firmly. "We are coming with you," She added as she stared at Ajay.

Ajay bowed his head in understanding. He knew his sister and could see the battle was already lost.

"Layla, please just listen…" Marcus started, but was cut off as Dominick opened the bathroom door ready to go.

"Let's do this," Dominick said as he made his way out of the bathroom, interrupting Marcus who was speaking.

All three looked at Dominick as he came out the door. Layla's heart sped up as she looked at his face. She blushed as he came through the door.

"Hi," was all she could think to say.

Dominick looked at her and noticed her eyes were as black as night. She was so exotic looking and looked so fragile in his oversized bed. He didn't say hi back, all he could manage was an acknowledging head nod.

Layla wanted to kick herself for managing nothing more than a wimpy hello. Ajay picked up on it and looked from her to him. He hoped it wasn't what he thought it was, not with a werewolf who had too much testosterone, being the alpha. Thinking about it further, he wasn't sure who exactly he felt sorry for and shook his head at the thought. Layla noticed and glared at him.

Before Layla could think of something more cleaver to say, voices piled into the living room.

"The pack is here. We have to go," Dominick said, making his way towards the bedroom door.

"Hold on, I am coming," Layla said as she swung her legs out of the covers and planted her bare feet on the floor. She was wearing a pair of tight blue jeans and a tight white tank top with her long hair tied loosely half back as she let the natural waves flow freely. Layla wasn't going for style, but somehow she still looked stylish.

Dominick couldn't help but stare at her. He quickly cursed himself, wondering what the hell was wrong with him noticing another girl in a time like this. Chalking it up to being in wolf form for two weeks, he quickly shook it off.

"You're staying here," he said, looking at her from the doorway.

"We already played that game and I won so you might as well save your breath so we can get there. You never know when you could use a witch. They had three and so shall we," Layla said, standing up and slipping her flip flops back on.

"We will have three witches. Marcus, Mikayla, and Rowan," Dominick said as he made it out of the bedroom.

Layla was annoyed by that, but before she could zing him back he was already out of the door. She noticed her spirit wolf leap out in front of her and pause in the doorway as the spirit wolf looked back at her. The spirit wolf threw its head to the sky to give a silent howl to the moon only Layla could hear. Then as quickly as the spirit wolf leaped out of her body, it leaped back in.

Marcus looked confused, like he had just missed something, but he wasn't sure what it exactly was and looked to Ajay for clarification. Ajay just shook his head in a gesture that told Marcus not to ask.

"Alright, here's how it's going to go. The pack comes in with me, minus Vince who will stay outside with Marcus to keep an eye on the front," Dominick said.

"What about me?" Layla said, staring him down with her arms crossed. Her heart was doing flip flops and she knew without a doubt. She wondered why it had to be with someone so full of testosterone.

"Nope. Next question?" Dominick dismissed her and then asked if anyone else had any questions.

Layla was furious. "I am going with you, so you might as well just tell me where I should be or I will have to decide for myself!" She screamed.

All eyes opened wide and stared at her. Mario smiled for a moment. He had to appreciate a girl who could bark louder than Dominick.

Dominick was now annoyed. He couldn't explain what it was, but he knew he didn't want this girl in harm's way. She was being stubborn, and if she wasn't a witch he would lock her in his room to keep her safe, but he could tell it wasn't an option. He had no more time to argue with her.

"Alright then, perhaps we could use a witch on the inside. Ajay you're coming in with us," Dominick said, making the change as he stared at Layla.

No one quite understood what it was that was going on, but they could all tell something was in the air. Layla smiled in satisfaction.

"Why am I getting dragged into this?" Ajay whined.

"Shut up, Ajay," Layla said, having also had it with his attitude. Normally they were the best of friends, but all day his attitude had been bad. She knew it was because it was bringing up the death of their father. This whole thing tied into it, but now was not the time to let that get in the way of saving Rowan and Mikayla. That was the only important factor at the moment. Once they were safe then they could figure out the rest. She felt tied to these girls from having similar things happen. Also, she felt tied to them because they were the only three female witches that survived that year. Three was a powerful number and she knew that. She grabbed Ajay's hand and looked at him, sending him calming thoughts. Ajay's tense shoulders relaxed a little.

They headed out the door, piling into three cars. Layla, Ajay, and Marcus rode with Dominick and Mario. The ride to the bar was quiet. No one made a sound and the radio was turned off. It had only taken them about fifteen minutes until they pulled into a parking lot in front of the bar.

"Alright, you guys stay out front. Layla, do that mind talk thingy that you guys do to Ajay if you see anything that we should know about, ok?" Dominick said as he looked at Layla.

She nodded in understanding as she opened the door and got out. Ajay and Marcus followed. Mario and Dominick also got out and waited as the rest of the pack made their way out of the cars and towards them.

"Let's go," Dominick ordered and the pack, minus Vince and now containing Ajay, made their way into the bar.

Marcus let out a deep breath. He could hardly stand it. She was so close he could feel her despite the fact she had blocked him out.

"Are you alright?" Layla asked, observantly.

"I'm fine," he said without looking at her. "Alright, Vince you take the left, I will take the right, and Layla you will take the center. There is less likely to be traffic from the center," he then added, trying to make a plan to help secure the front perimeter while shaking off the feeling of wanting to rush inside to Mikayla. He was a soldier and a soldier takes care of his duty first. Tonight was the first time in a long time he actually had to remind himself.

49

Mikayla had just finished her second beer. "I think it is time to break the seal!" She said to Rowan.

"You want me to go with you?" Rowan asked.

"I can walk with you to the bathroom. I have to go too," Caleb said, not really having to use the restroom but he wanted a chance to be alone with her, even if it was for just a few minutes.

Mikayla looked at Rowan, wanting to make sure she was fine to be left alone at the table with Caleb's friends.

"I will be fine, I need to nurse the rest of this beer!" She said, understanding Caleb was trying to steal a private moment. Besides, she was having a great time talking with Mary and Jamahl. They were so funny and friendly. Ali was finally starting to loosen up, as well. She needed to get to know these people to help merge their groups together so everybody could be friends. Although she worried what Dominick's reaction might be.

Mikayla and Caleb headed all the way towards the back of the bar to where the bathrooms were located. The hall to the bathrooms was long and dark. Caleb thought it was the perfect spot to steal a few kisses from Mikayla. As soon as they turned the corner and were in the darkened hall, he threw her up against the wall and kissed her fiercely. She melted into him, kissing him back.

Mikayla pulled back for a moment. "I really do have to pee," she said.

Caleb smiled, staring at her for a few minutes before letting her go and walking her the rest of the way to the ladies room. He decided he might as well try to go as well while he waited for her.

There were only four stalls in the ladies restroom, which Mikayla thought was ridiculous considering the size of the bar, and one was out of order while the other three were occupied. She automatically was at the back of the line coming into the bathroom. She counted only three girls in front of her and hoped they were all fast.

Rowan was back at the table, nursing the end of her third beer and enjoying the buzz. It helped her to not think of Mario barking at her earlier. She had enough of the boys' controlling ways, as well. Mario was everything to her, but he needed to understand people didn't want to live a life of imprisonment. She blamed herself for always being so easy going. This night marked a start of something new. Mikayla and her would have to put their feet down as a united front to the boys. They needed to back off just a little to give them some breathing room. She could see how much Mikayla had benefited from them being absent the past couple of weeks, which only made her realize the importance of independence. Rowan was officially angry with Mario and knew it was time they had a serious talk.

Jamahl was telling a funny story while Rowan had been lost in thought. Everyone at the table laughed in unison at the end of the story. Rowan didn't want to seem rude, so she began to laugh along with them. Pretty soon she was back into the conversation, laughing and having a good time.

Rowan finished off the rest of her third beer and watched as Mary poured her another glass. She really like Mary, and was defiantly going to exchange numbers with her. Mary was smart, funny, and kind. She really knew how to make you feel at ease. Mikayla suspected she had the gift of reading people with the way she interacted with others. Whatever it was, there was definitely something about Mary which drew people to her and made everyone around feel at ease.

"Thanks!" Rowan said, grabbing hold of the now full beer.

"No problem, I am a professional! Just remember, I work for tips!" Mary joked.

"Hey, I got a tip for you! Never eat yellow snow!" Jamahl said, straight faced.

Ali's eyes squinted and he turned towards Jamahl. "Seriously?" He said, straight faced.

"What?" Jamahl said, with a grin still on his face.

"That's the best you could come up with, "Never eat yellow snow.' What are you in kindergarten now?" Ali said as he mimicked Jamahl's voice.

"Man I got your kindergarden right here!" Jamahl said as he grabbed Ali in a headlock as he laughed.

Ali couldn't help but laugh as his usual seriousness faded. Rowan noticed Ali somehow looked like a little boy at the moment, innocent and free. At the look of enjoyment on Ali's face, Rowan started to giggle first. Then everyone started to laugh.

Rowan was laughing when she all of a sudden felt the breeze from the front door against her back. She wondered just how many people had come in at once for the door to be open that long. She spit a little of her beer out when she saw Mario, Dominick, and the rest of the boys walking through the doors.

"Oh my god," Rowan said without thinking. Jamahl and Ali shifted their eyes to the door.

Caleb, we have trouble...the wolf pack is here. Something is going on, Jamahl thought to Caleb.

I am taking Mikayla out of here, Caleb thought back.

Caleb, we are here for Rowan, not for Mikayla! We need you now, Caleb! Ali said sounding stressed out. He wanted his brother to be happy, and he tried to remain unattached, as they usually were, but this whole trip both Caleb and Jamahl had fallen into some sort of trap and become attached to women. Ali was starting to feel the same way. He couldn't help but like Mary, and the more he was around Rowan he couldn't help but like her, too. Even Mikayla was great, but he felt a little resentful knowing his brother's feelings for her could end up costing them.

Ali, we can use her as a bargaining tool, Caleb answered back, lying through his teeth.

Ali knew he was lying and would have to take matters into his own hands. Caleb was his brother and he loved him, he loved both him and Jamahl more than his own life. Things were changing and he needed to figure out what it meant, but for now he still needed to get the job done. He would let his brother off the hook and take care of it himself, with or without the help of Jamahl. *Good idea*, Ali said giving his brother his approval to leave out the back.

Mikayla, if you want to finish your date then you need to find a back way out! I am not kidding. Mario and Dominick are here. They haven't seen me yet. Go ahead and leave, I will cover this end, Rowan thought to Mikayla, who was currently in an empty stall.

Are you fucking kidding me! That is it. I am going to tell them off as soon as I get back to the table! Mikayla was furious.

Kali don't! I am serious. You deserve to finish your date. This night is important to you. Don't let them ruin it. Just take him out the back door and tell him you want to spend some alone time together. Tell him that you texted me to let me know, Rowan made it sound more like an order.

You're right! This night is important to me. Tonight I am not getting into it with the boys. Will you be alright? Mikayla wanted to make sure it really was alright to leave Rowan holding the bag.

Yes, I am, but I am pretty sure I will be fighting with your brother for the rest of the night for hanging up on him, Rowan said, sounding pumped up and prepared to do so.

Ouch! I am so sorry, Mikayla offered. She hadn't realized Rowan had now reached her boiling point as well.

We will be fine. Now get because they have just spotted me and it will only take them a few seconds until Dominick figures out where you are and who you are with! Rowan said.

Mario spotted Rowan and made a bee-line towards her as the boys followed. Dominick could see Mikayla wasn't at the table and started looking all over the large, dimly lit bar to see if he could spot her.

"Brace yourselves," Rowan said to Mary and her friend as she watched Jamahl and Ali rise up from their stools.

"Where the fuck is Mikayla?" Dominick shouted before he even reached the table.

"She's not here, man," Jamahl said, trying to remain calm but preparing for a fight.

"The fuck she's not! I wasn't talking to you, anyways, so shut the hell up!" Dominick barked.

Mario was furious and grabbed Rowan by the arm.

"Ouch! Mario!" She said and backed away.

"I didn't mean to grab you that hard. You need to come home with me, now," Mario said, trying to resist the urge to grab her and throw her over his shoulder and take her out of the bar. He was so angry to find her at the table with a bunch of strangers in such a dangerous time. Mario tried to remember she had no clue what was really going on.

"Well you did! I don't know what the emergency is, but I have had enough of you guys bullying us around! Don't ruin us by this!" She screamed as she got up from the table.

Everyone stood around glaring at each other, not saying a word after Rowan had yelled. The bouncers stood up from the stools to look over and assess the situation. Dominick observed this and knew nothing good was about to come out of the situation. Ajay rolled his eyes, feeling caught in the middle of a soap opera full of people he didn't know or care about; however, he did noticed Mary and gave her a smile. Jamahl caught sight of it and became angry.

"Want to take a picture, bro?" Jamahl said, giving a warning.

"I'm not your brother, man," Ajay mouthed off back.

"Enough!" Dominick said. "We need to split up, Lucio take that side with Ajay, Mario and I will take the restroom area and the rest of you take the center," he ordered.

"I need to use the restroom!" Rowan said suddenly and headed to the bathroom. Mario started to go after her before Dominick stopped him.

"Wait for a second, she needs to cool off or we won't ever get them out of here. Mikayla is probably back there with that jackass," he said, holding Mario back.

They watched as she made it back towards the darkened hallway.

Mikayla quickly finished peeing and rinsed her hands. She bolted out of the bathroom so fast to see a worried look on Caleb's face. "Rowan just texted me. The boys are here. They are going to try and ruin this date and I have something important I wanted to tell you tonight. Let's sneak out of the back," she said, looking into his eyes. Feeling bad for lying about how she got the information she put her head down.

Caleb said nothing. Instead he grabbed her by the hand and led her towards the kitchen where there was a back door. They quickly made their way through as a waitress yelled at them they were not allowed back there. Caleb quickly found the door and without acknowledging the waitress made his way through.

I hope you found a way out the back because big and bigger are on their way towards the bathroom. I am in front of them heading the same way, Rowan thought to Mikayla, trying to give her a heads up as she made her way down the dim, long hallway that led to the restrooms.

We just walked out the back door, Mikayla thought back. *Thanks, Rowan! You truly are my very best friend,* she added.

Caleb had rode his motorcycle to the bar, hoping to have time alone with Mikayla after the bar. He parked his bike in the back of the parking lot located next to the right side of the bar. Going out of the back door actually put them closer to his bike. They quietly made their way towards Caleb's bike, each lost in thought and each trying to be quiet, as if the boys could hear them inside of the bar.

50

Dominick and Mario finally made their way back to the hallway with Rowan still in their sights. They watched as she turned the corner and quickly sped up, also turning the corner to catch the door of the women's restroom closing as she went through it.

"I bet Mikayla's in there. Perhaps that means Caleb is in the men's restroom. I will check. Wait here in case they come out," Dominick said as he swung open the men's bathroom door.

There appeared to only be one other drunken frat boy on his way out. Dominick decided to check the two stalls. Quietly he knelt down to see if he could see any feet. There wasn't any. He then quietly pushed open the first stall. It was empty. He thought for sure the second stall would have Caleb hiding in a crouched position on top of the toilet. This time he kicked open the door, leaving his hands free for a fight just in case. There was something about that guy he didn't trust, but he couldn't put his finger on it. He didn't smell like anything he was familiar with, but his instincts told him there was more to him than Caleb just being a normal college student.

The door flew open, revealing another empty stall. Dominick was confused, he thought for sure Caleb would be in there, but he wasn't. He stepped back for a moment, trying to figure it out.

Ali got up as soon as he saw the Alpha and his right hand start towards the hallway heading for the bathroom. *Did you make it out?* He asked to Caleb.

Yeah, just made it out the back, Caleb said back as he lead Mikayla away from the back of the building.

I will contact you in a bit. Don't tune out, this is too important, Ali said, making his way towards the coat room which was empty because of the warm weather. *Stay here for a minute, Jamahl. We need things to look fine for a moment, but in about two minutes you need to make your way out. I will let you know where to meet me,* he explained as he snuck into the dark empty coat room.

Quickly he orbed himself into the girls bathroom. He was relieved to have landed in an empty stall. He was glad there was an empty stall. Crouching down he checked to see if there were any other feet in the other three stalls. He saw none and stood up, looking through the crack of the door, waiting for Rowan to come in. Not long after he stood did he see the door swing open. *Oh, this is perfect!* He thought to himself.

Rowan made her way to the sink and starred in the mirror. She wanted to cry, not liking the scene she just made with Mario. Her heart was breaking, she loved him fiercely and didn't want to fight but she had to stand up for what she believed was right. She couldn't figure out why they were so scared of them making new friends. The issue between Dominick and Mikayla was clear, not right, but still clear. It was Mario's issue she didn't quite get. She thought for a few seconds and decided he might just have some jealousy issues. Rowan knew she wouldn't stay in a relationship that was controlling. She needed to have a serious talk with him, but tonight wouldn't be a good time with the height of the issue mixed in with a few drinks. Tonight she needed to get back to her car and drive home. If she could avoid him then she would text him she was going home but they would have to have a talk in the morning, she decided. She needed a little bit of space because she was too upset and angry at the moment to have a productive conversation. Besides, a little space might do him some good, she thought to herself as she blinked back tears. Her face felt flushed and she turned on the sink to splash her face with cool water.

Ali watched as she bent forward with her head close to the sink. It was the perfect chance for him to sneak up on her and hopefully bleed her before she had a chance to see him in the mirror. He still was going to make his best attempt at being undetected for the sake of his brother.

The water was coming out of the sink fast and loud as Ali quietly made his way out of the stall. He snuck up behind her without any indication he was there. With an unearthly quickness he grabbed her by the mouth to keep her from screaming as he kept her head bent down and away from the mirror, holding her arms tight to her body as he wrapped his free arm around her waist and then sunk his teeth into her shoulder, bleeding her until he felt her go limp.

Rowan was startled. For a moment she thought it was just Mario being funny, trying to make things better. The thought made her not want to scream but to laugh, but she realized his cologne wasn't right. It wasn't Mario's but it was familiar. Before she could decipher what was going on, she felt two pricks going into her neck. It was painful at first as she started to scream, but just as quick as the pain came it left, leaving her with a euphoric pleasure. She was stunned and her buzz from the beer heightened the sensation, and within what seemed like forever, but was only a few seconds, she had passed out.

Now would be a good time to get your coat. Meet me at the condo. It will take them awhile to figure out where we live if they can figure it out at all, Ali thought to Jamahl as he grabbed Rowan and threw her over his shoulder and orbed out of the restroom to the condo.

Jamahl looked at Mary. He didn't want this to be the last time he saw her. His first instinct was to take her with him, but under the circumstances he knew she wouldn't understand. A half-truth would be the best thing for the moment until he could figure out the rest. He tapped her on her shoulder, interrupting the conversation she was having with her friend Lauren.

"Hey, things are getting a little out of control for the night. I need to be with my brothers. Will you be alright?" He said, looking into Mary's eyes as he gently held her chin in his hand.

Mary studied him for a moment. She could see that there was pain in his eyes. Right now he needed to be with his family, she knew that and smiled up at him. "Call me tomorrow, we'll have dinner or lunch or whatever," she said, trying to be understanding.

Jamahl bent down and kissed her gently. Mary almost felt it was a goodbye kiss and backed away for a moment to look at his face.

Jamahl knew what she was thinking. "It's not goodbye, not by a long shot. Only goodnight," he smiled. She smiled back up at him and put her arms around him as he bent down for another quick kiss. Then he walked towards the front of the bar and made his way towards the coat closet.

Dominick exited the bathroom, the look on his face was a mix between anger and bewilderment. "Something strange is going on. Caleb isn't in there. Wait for Rowan while I help look for Mikayla. My guess is she isn't in the restroom, but if she is you can grab her. I think her and Caleb are watching us and hiding somewhere in the bar," Dominick said to Mario as he started walking backwards, making his way to the hall, not wanting to waste any more time.

Mario nodded and leaned against the wall outside of the bathroom with his arms crossed. He had a knot in the pit of his stomach. Rowan seemed really angry at him and he wasn't entirely sure why but something was going on with her. There was no way he was going to lose her, she was the air he breathed and he would do whatever it took to keep her.

Dominick quickly turned himself around as he made his way down the hall. He was half way down the hall when he saw Jamahl heading towards the front door. That worried him and he began to walk faster as he watched Jamahl jump into the coat closet. He was at the end of the hall now and glanced over at the table to find both of Caleb's friends were gone, leaving behind the two girls who were at the table. Not wanting to get the run around from the girls, he made his way swiftly to the coat closet he saw Jamahl step into. When he finally reached the closet it was dark and empty. His vision at night was perfect, but right now he wasn't seeing anything. As if in a brief denial he turned on the light switch. The closet lit up only to show it was still, in fact, empty.

"Mother fucker!" Dominick said and punched a hole in the wall before rushing back towards Mario, who was still outside of the bathroom waiting for Rowan. As he turned the corner he found Mario leaning against the wall with his head tilted towards the ceiling. He looked exhausted.

"I knew there was something shady about those mother fuckers! The tall one just walked into an empty closet and disappeared into thin air!" Dominick made no point of being quiet.

"Witches?" Mario questioned.

"I don't know, and we don't have time to figure it out. You need to go in there and grab her," Dominick said, looking towards the bathroom door. "What the hell is she doing in there?" He added, noticing she had been in there for quite a while.

"She knows I am out here. I think she's punishing me. Or maybe Mikayla is in there," Mario said, peeling himself from his spot on the wall.

He reached the door and looked behind him to make sure no one was coming before opening the door. The bathroom appeared empty. His heart sank into the pit of his stomach as he entered in disbelief. He quickly bent down and assessed the bottom of each stall. His heart started to pound so loud he could feel the vibrations in his throat. One by one he opened each door and still the stalls were empty. He sped out of the bathroom.

"She's gone! She is fucking gone!" Mario shouted as he exited the bathroom.

"Fuck fuck fuck!" Dominick said, trying to figure out what to do next. "We need Marcus to tell us who the hell those guys are," he decided and started to rush down the dark hallway towards the front of the building as he called for the wolfpack.

Caleb and Mikayla had reached his motorcycle. He had two helmets and handed one to Mikayla. Caleb put his helmet on and climbed on the back of the bike and opened the face cover of his helmet.

"Where to?" he asked.

"How about your house?" She suggested.

He smiled, wanting nothing more than to take her back to his house and hold her. Things were coming to a head and he wanted to keep her all to himself and never let her go, but he knew the pack would find his house within a matter of an hour. It wasn't safe.

"You know they will find us there," he said.

"Rowan's not going to tell them where you live," she defended the loyalty of her friend.

"It's not Rowan. I know guys like that and they are resourceful, believe me. It will only be a matter of time, so I think we need to pick another place," he replied.

Mikayla thought for a moment while fumbling with her helmet. All of a sudden she heard her name being called from the right front side of the bar.

"Mikayla!" Marcus shouted, having spotted her. His heart skipped a thousand beats as he watched her fumbling with a helmet. Layla ran towards Marcus.

Mikayla was in shock. She couldn't believe what she was looking at. Caleb tried to snap her out of it by calling her name, but she was briefly frozen until she saw one of the most beautiful girls she had ever seen run up next to Marcus.

Marcus didn't want to make any sudden moves. He wasn't sure who the guy on the bike was or what he was capable of, if anything at all.

As soon as the girl ran up to Marcus the spell was broken and she quickly put on her helmet and jumped on the back of the bike. "Go!" She commanded.

Caleb felt confused by what had just transpired, but he knew whatever it was couldn't be good and revved up his bike. He knew he needed to take her some place that would be hard for the pack to find. The image of the lake where they almost made love came into his mind and he knew it was the perfect place.

The only problem would be there was only one exit to the parking lot, which would give the couple in front of the bar a view of his license plate. He hoped that wouldn't occur to them as he sped through the parking lot, keeping an eye on the couple who now seemed to be quickly running towards them. He finally came to the exit and made a left when he felt a pull on his bike that made it start to slow down.

"What the fuck?" he shouted and looked into his review mirror to find the guy who had called Mikayla's name had an invisible pull on the bike. In that instant, Caleb knew what he was and things were about to get ugly.

As Dominick and Mario approached the front of the bar, the others had already reconvened by the doors, waiting faithfully for their alpha.

"She's not here, but I gave her description to a few people and they said that she had been here," Lucio said. The rest of the pack and Ajay nodded they also had come up with the same answers.

Dominick said nothing as he made his way out of the door. The pack and Ajay followed.

Caleb had to think on his feet as he watched in the review mirror. Quickly he reached his hand back and zapped the cord, putting up a wall behind him. The girl then started in, trying to drill a hole through the invisible wall he had just put up. She conjured up wind and made it start to turn in a tightly packed funnel until it was spinning fast and sharp. The funnel broke the barrier. He started to speed up to try and get away as he still kept an eye on the review mirror, watching as the two witches tried to break the wall. Then he saw Dominick and Mario storm out of the bar. The whole pack and a few witches stood in the middle of the street, facing the back of them.

"Mother Fucker!" Caleb shouted.

Mikayla shut her eyes, trying not to look at Marcus as Caleb was driving. She was completely unaware of anything going on. Marcus was plaguing her mind.

Marcus orbed in front of the motorcycle.

Caleb shouted back to Mikayla. "Keep your eyes shut, baby. Promise me just keep your eyes closed."

Mikayla said nothing. Her eyes were already closed.

Caleb sped towards Marcus while trying to draw from all the energy he had within. His body started to vibrate and with all of his mite he grabbed hold of Mikayla's arms with one free hand to make sure she would make the transfer even if the bike didn't and orbed them to a street one over. He was amazed orbing the bike worked. Caleb didn't think it was possible, but somehow he pulled it off. The only down side was they were only a street over and it would only be a matter of minutes before the witches figured out they weren't far.

51

Aidan, Rory, and Aiah had been tailing the boys since they arrived in the evening. It wasn't easy for them to dodge the evening sun coming out of the airport. They were dressed in all black with sunglasses and baseball caps to try and avoid the sun as much as possible so they wouldn't burst into flames. Rory was the only one who was affected on the way into the rental car; part of the sun caught the side of his exposed cheeks and started to smoke as they tried to hurry into their rental car. Once they were safely in the car with tinted windows, Rory let out a scream from the flame as he put it out. Quickly the wound healed itself. It hadn't been enough to spread throughout his body. Aiah's hand did the same thing when a women in front of them on the plane opened the shade to her window. He grabbed the shade and shut it as he told the lady he had an allergy to the sun and to please keep it shut. The woman starred in bewilderment but didn't open it again for the rest of the flight.

Aiden felt even more desperate at that moment to get his hands on the right girl. They took a big chance by moving in the daylight, even the plane had been a chore. It was direct sunlight that would kill them; however, it wasn't as quick as legends would have it told. In order for a vampire to be killed in sunlight, it had to be direct, and the vampire needed to be in it for a few minutes. It was kind of like the lighting of a new candle's wick. It took a few minutes for the flame to take hold. By no means was it ever an exact science, which is why vampires seldom took the chance, but right now it was their only chance of being able to turn that around. This was a chance worth taking, and luckily for them they had made it with little damage.

It wasn't long before Caleb left on his motorcycle, followed by Jamahl and Ali in a jeep, and they were headed in the same direction. From the place where they were staying, only the three of them came out of the house. They were not with any girls yet, but most likely were on their way to meet them. Aidan had no clue what the witch looked like, but figured they would be able to decipher who she was by following them.

It was around seven when the motorcycle followed by the jeep led them to a parking lot outside of a bar. Ali and Jamahl found a spot next to Caleb. Aidan drove around the block once before entering the parking lot. They knew it would be unlikely for them to be seen, having tinted windows on their car rental along with the fact Caleb, Jamahl, and Ali weren't expecting them. For all they knew they were still in Italy. Tonight was the night Aidan felt he was getting his hands on the other witch at all costs.

After one lap around the block, they pulled into the parking lot. They chose a spot far enough away from Caleb, Jamahl, and Ali, yet in a position where he could see the front entrance of the bar. Aidan, Rory, and Aiah watched as the three brothers made their way into the bar. They were alone.

Aidan was frustrated by that, but knew it was too risky to go in the bar. Instead they decided to stay parked until they came out. More than likely they would be leaving with the witch, or at least talking to her after the bar. Aidan looked at his watch and realized it could be hours before there was any sign of them. In the meantime, they watched as people filled into the bar. They studied each group of girls going into the bar, wondering one by one which one was the witch.

The evening started to become interesting when they saw a couple cars pull in. Seven large muscled boys jumped quickly out of the car, followed by three of the witches they had just faced the other night. Aidan smiled in satisfaction.

"Well, well, well, it looks like we found the right spot," Aidan had said, watching as part of the group entered the bar and part of them stayed outside. Aidan had smiled at watching them play "look out" in the front of the bar when all along the people they were watching for were watching them.

"What do we do now?" Rory had asked.

"We wait," Aidan said back.

To the boys' surprise, however, the night was finally cut short when they witnessed Caleb sneaking out of the back with a beautiful girl. "Ah ha…" Aidan said quietly as if he could be heard. Rory and Aiah made no noise as they watched Caleb hand the girl a helmet before putting on a helmet himself.

"So, this must be the girl," Aidan said, still watching.

"What if it isn't?" Aiah asked, worried they might be about to follow the wrong girl and blow their plans.

"It has to be her. The seer said he would be drawn to her, therefore I conclude that it would have been him who had made contact with her. Also, those witches got here quick and they seem to have a pack of wolves with them. She is about to be hard to get to. I think we need to take the chance and use our heads. Why else would he leave out the back?" Aidan replied.

"I guess so. Maybe, just in case we should wait to see who the witches come out of the bar with. Obviously they are looking for the other witch, and if she is in there then it should only take a few minutes until they come out. If they are empty handed, then we know for almost certain she is the one. We can use the finding potion the wizard gave us to catch up with Caleb," Rory said. Aidan and Ahiah just looked at him. Again he came out with something that made a perfect plan.

"Sounds like we wait, then," Aidan said, grinning. Aiah and Rory shared the same sneer on their faces.

They were so focused on the quiet activity by the bike, they almost forgot about the two witches and one werewolf standing in front of the bar until the girl suddenly looked over toward the entrance. The male witch was definitely calling for her and she didn't look happy. =They watched as the three lookouts ran towards the entrance of the parking lot, trying to get to the bike. Then they witnessed as the witches tried to stop Caleb, but Caleb couldn't be stopped. The battle was quickly lost when Caleb had orbed him, the girl, and the entire bike out of the direct area. That's when they saw the rest of the pack and the other witch run out of the bar.

"I believe we have our witch," Aidan said with a grin across his face.

"We should go now," Aiah said.

"No, we shouldn't. We need to hang back until they leave. We have the finding potion the wizard made for us, and while we don't know enough about the girl to find her with it, we can find Caleb," Aidan said as he put his hands behind his head and watched as the witches tried to erase the memory from the few people who had witnessed the scene in the street.

"What a waste of fucking time!" Aiah said, watching the same thing, annoyed by the display of immortals cow tailing to mere humans yet again. Aiah bought all of Cyrus's propaganda and this display of hiding in front of the mortals truly disgusted him.

"Fuck! Why didn't you stop them, you stupid piece of shit!" Dominick yelled as he shoved Marcus hard enough for Marcus to fall to the ground. Something which never happened to him before.

Marcus jumped quickly to his feet. "Getting mad at me right now isn't going to save her. Besides weren't you supposed to be watching her?" Marcus snapped back.

"You both shut up, you are wasting time!" Layla yelled as she commanded everyone's attention.

Dominick's pride and anger got in the way, forcing him to start to speak, but was quickly shushed but Layla.

"Alright, we need to split into groups. I will go with Mario. Layla you will go with Dominick and Ajay with Lucio. The rest of you go as a pack," Marcus gave out the orders.

"You're not the leader here, this is my town!" Dominick yelled. He then stared long and hard at Marcus. He saw Layla roll her eyes in the background and something about that made him let up. "Alright, Ajay will go with Lucio, Mario and you, and I will take Layla with me. The rest of the pack will run together," he then said, repeating what Marcus had just said. Everyone just looked around at each other, trying to see if anyone else caught that. They all had, but everyone else was too scared of Dominick to call him on it, except for Marcus.

"That's what I just…" Marcus started, but was cut off as Layla grabbed him firmly by the hand in a gesture which reminded him now was not the time to be correcting an over-sized, angry wolf. "I mean, that sounds like a good idea," Marcus finished.

"First, we need to see if we can get a read on her energy," Layla said. Marcus and Ajay just looked at her. She was a natural leader. "Well, what did you guys think we were going to do, wing it? They could be going anywhere and it could change, it's best if we try and follow the trail of her energy," Layla added.

Marcus felt a mess. He should have known that and he did, but he was so scattered at the moment he was just going to run out looking for her blind, throwing out finding spells which probably wouldn't work until it was too late. Layla was right and he was now glad she was there.

The three witches formed a circle, holding hands, as the wolves hung back and watched. Layla and Marcus began to chant in a language the wolves didn't understand. Ajay wasn't chanting, causing Layla to open one eye to look at him. She realized he didn't know the chant at all.

She slowed it down to try and get Ajay to pick it up. At first he didn't try, but she squeezed his hand in encouragement, making him start to try. It took a good few minutes for him to get the words and another few minutes for him to get the rhythm. Pretty soon they were chanting in unison in the parking lot by the bar, surrounded by wolves who were becoming impatient.

The chanting went on and on for another few minutes. Dominick couldn't help but stare at Layla. Something about her he was drawn to. This only made him feel guilty and he looked away, but as if he couldn't help himself, he turned his eyes back on her and watched as the three witches chanted. All of a sudden he witnessed a dim light shine from in the circle. Then he watched in amazement as the light split into four small balls of soft yellow, which were glowing energy sources. All the wolves were awed in its beauty and simplicity.

One by one, Layla handed each one a ball, taking the last one for herself and Dominick. He watched her in amazement.

Mario watched as the groups gathered. Marcus came to stand by him. "Wait a minute. What about Rowan?" he asked with anger in his eyes.

"We will find her after we get Mikayla. They will see that she is not who they are looking for and may end up putting two and two together if they already haven't. They didn't kill Layla, so I think she will be alright for now," Marcus said.

Mario started to get agitated and lost it. "No fucking way! You guys find Mikayla, I am going after Rowan!" He shouted.

"It could be disastrous to the greater good if we lose Mikayla!" Marcus tried to explain.

"Fuck you, Marcus! You act as if I don't want to find my sister! I do, but we have enough people here to look for both, and so help me God, if something happens to Rowan because we didn't go and find her. With or without your help, I will find her!" Mario clenched his fists tight to his sides.

"Mario, I don't think you understand the bigger implications," Marcus started to explain, but was interrupted by Mario stepping into his face.

"I'm going after Rowan," he said firmly as his eyes flashed to all black and his voice to more beast than man.

"Mario, back down. That's an order," Dominick intervened. "Can you guys get a ball of energy for Rowan?" He asked.

Layla looked at Marcus. "They didn't kill me because you guys came, there is no telling who has her or what they will do, Marcus. Mario needs to find her," she said.

Marcus gave in and nodded his head in agreement.

"Yes, we can. Marcus you take Lucio with you and Ajay can go with Mario," Layla said.

Dominick was getting a kick out of her strong personality.

"Fine," Marcus said, wanting to argue but knowing it was no use.

Again the three witches stood in the circle and began a slightly different chant. Ajay had to quickly learn that chant, as well. Within a few minutes, they were in unison again. All of a sudden another dimly lit yellow light shined and formed into a little ball. Layla took hold of the ball and handed it to Mario.

"Ajay, you remember how to let the light guide you?" She asked her brother. Ajay nodded his head.

"Alright, you guys get going. I will explain to the rest of the pack how to use theirs. Get going, but make sure you leave your channels open, Ajay. Oh, and Ajay, don't give Mario any shit!" Layla said. "We are essentially working for the same thing. Remember that," she then added.

Mario and Ajay quickly made it to one of the two cars the group had come in and left.

"We need another couple of cars," Marcus said, looking at the single car left in the parking lot. "Layla are you strong enough to carry Dominick through an orbing?" He said as he turned towards Layla.

"I think so," she said, sizing up Dominick's massive side.

This made Dominick feel a little weird, having a girl size him up to carry him. Dominick wondered if Marcus had put it that way just to take a cheap shot and decided it was probably so. Right now he wouldn't get into it with him. Now wasn't the time.

"Alright, let's get a couple of cars. Dom, you want to direct the rest of your pack or should I?" Marcus asked.

Dominick said nothing, but gave Marcus a look of caution before turning to the rest of his pack. "Alright you guys, go as one group. Layla will explain how to use the energy source," Dominick then looked at Layla, giving her the floor.

Layla stepped to them and took the ball in her hand. "You need to concentrate on her face and her name and then try to focus in on her heart. Once you have tapped into her energy, the ball will glow a little brighter. As the ball glows bright, you let go of it and slowly it will move in her direction. Just follow it. But if the light dims, you need to start it over.]It's not perfect, and it works slower than you would want, but it will be much quicker than trying to look for her blind," she said, handing the ball back to Mikey.

The wolves tried to get a read on her energy. It took a few minutes, but sure enough the ball started to glow brighter. Mikey let it go and it started to travel west. Quickly they jumped in the car and followed it's light.

Marcus then grabbed Lucio and orbed back to the condos.

Layla then took hold of Dominick. She couldn't help herself shivering from the goosebumps which flooded her skin when she touched him. His body was strong and warm. She noticed his body, as warm as it felt, was also flooded with goosebumps. She grabbed a hold of him tight and orbed them back to the condos, following Marcus and Lucio just a couple of seconds behind.

52

Ali and Jamahl were back at the house with Rowan, who was passed out. They put a blind fold over her eyes, just in case she came to. Quietly they motioned on what each was to do, not wanting to talk so she wouldn't be able to identify their voices. Jamahl motioned for Ali to follow him out of Ali's bedroom for a moment.

"Man, I don't know what is wrong with me, but I don't feel good about this," Jamahl said. "What if she is the one? Do we really hand her over to Cyrus?" He added.

"I can't help it, but I don't feel great about it either. This was our job to do, and I am not sure we should cross Cyrus. Let's just hope it's not her," Ali said, thinking of Caleb.

"Will we hurt her?" Jamahl asked, concerned.

"No, I don't think so. I think a small cut will do. I don't think we need both tears and blood," Ali said, checking the blade of the small knife to make sure it was clean.

"Well, let's just get it over with," Jamahl said, having his heart grow heavier with an unexpected feeling of guilt.

The two went back into the room. Rowan was still passed out. Ali stepped towards her with the blade in his hand. As if he were being pulled back, he couldn't manage to make the small cut on her hand. He mouthed the words, "fucking shit," before attempting again. Jamhal stood by, watching. Finally, Ali steadied his hand and placed it on her forearm and cut in. Rowan made a noise as she came to. The blade cut deeper and she screamed. Jamahl quickly got behind her to bleed her some more and soon she was out again, leaving behind a few tears, making wet marks on the blind fold.

Jamahl was amazed at the energy which flowed through his veins. It was much more powerful than human blood, and he was left with a slight buzz from Rowan's blood. It was enough for his guilt to be temporary lifted as his predatory side took over. Right now he was just a vampire feeding.

"At least we now have both," Ali carefully whispered cynically.

Rowan's arm began to bleed. Jamahl and Ali's canines sharpened at the sight, both already having tasted her blood. Ali tried to get a hold of himself and motioned for Jamahl to now follow him out of the room.

"We need to get a hold over ourselves," Ali said with rapid breathing.

"I am trying," Jamahl said, trying to fight the feeding urge.

Blood was like a drug to them and her's was especially addictive. The surge of power that went into their veins was overwhelming. If she had not been somewhat of a friend and a risk to Caleb, they might not have been able to control themselves.

Together they started taking deep breaths in and out until their canines retracted. Ali nodded towards Jamahl in a gesture that told him he was now fine.

"I think I'm good, too," Jamahl said back as the leftover ache in his jaw began to fade.

They walked into the room, where a small amount of blood was dripping from Rowan's forearm down to her hand, they noticed a small drip was still making its way down her index finger. Both boys tried to hold in their breathes as they went towards her to start checking for any ancient symbols appearing in flesh tones on her body.

First they checked her face, briefly uncovering her eyes. They found nothing and proceeded to find nothing as they checked the rest of her face and neck area. Still they found nothing. Next they checked all of her limbs to come up empty handed. But again there weren't any marks.

Jamahl shook his head. He knew what was next and this one made him even more uncomfortable. Ali waved for him to turn his head, realizing to look further under her clothing only took one. It was Ali who was the best pick, since his brain was more scientifical then Jamahl's, and he could do this without making it a sexual thing. Carefully Ali uncovered body part by body part, only exposing a tiny bit at a time, trying to keep the central pieces covered as he tried to be careful of where he placed his hands. He felt bad, but tried to do it objectively. It was like being a doctor, he told himself as he tried to respectfully check over his patient. In the end he found no marks.

Ali shook his head before tapping Jamahl out of relief. He was glad this witch was not the one and his brother wouldn't have to worry about losing the girl he so quickly fell for. The seer had seen he would be drawn to her, but never specified if it was the witch. For whatever reason, Caleb was bonded to Mikayla.

Ali had Rowan completely put together again before tapping Jamahl on the shoulder. Jamahl turned around with fear in his eyes. Ali just shook his head. Jamahl's fear turned into a big smile plastered on his face. Again Ali motioned for Jamahl to go outside of the room with him.

"I think our best bet is to go back to the bar. We can put her in a stall and have Mary go check on her. She can wake her up. It should feel like she just zoned out for a moment," Ali said.

Jamahl liked that idea. Mostly he liked the idea because it would get him back to Mary. "You take Rowan and I will go back to the front of the bar and re-enter," Jamahl said.

Ali nodded as they made it back into the bedroom. Jamahl orbed first. Ali, holding tightly onto Rowan, orbed just seconds after.

Mario and Ajay followed the brightly lit glowing ball. It was telling them to head West, back towards Ann Arbor. It was taking them a little South, as well. Mario was getting frustrated at all the red street lights which seemed to be in between him and Rowan. He was ready to kill whoever had her. Mario didn't care about any consequences at the moment, he only cared about getting the love of his life back. Images of her flew through his mind. When she was safe he would make sure that she was never in harm's way again. He was going to go out the next day and buy her a ring. The faster he married her the faster she could move in with him and then he could always keep her safe.

"Red light, red light!" Ajay shouted as he watched Mario blow through a red light and a truck came to a screeching halt, missing them by only a matter of inches.

"Oops," Mario said dryly.

"Oops! Oops isn't going to help us find your girl, man! If we get killed in the process there won't be anyone to help find her!" Ajay said.

Mario took what he said into consideration but said nothing. He only considered the thought in his own head.

The ball all of a sudden took a quick right and then a quick left.

"What the fuck is it doing?" Mario asked, unsure of which way he was supposed to turn.

"I don't know?" Ajay said, just as confused as he watched the glowing ball go from left to right and right to left before going all the way up to the roof of the car with a quickness which cracked the ball, turning out its light.

"Fuck! What does that mean?" Mario said with horror in his voice. "WHAT THE FUCK DOES THAT MEAN!" He then shouted as Ajay picked up the yellow cracked ball now absent of light.

"Pull over for a second. We need to try and get this lit again," Ajay said, hoping he could mend the crack and, while Mario wasn't a witch, hoped his connection with Rowan would be enough for him to get it restarted. Ajay alone wouldn't be able to because he didn't know her, so he wouldn't be able to tap into her energy.

Mario pulled the car over and came to a screeching halt. Quickly they both jumped out of the car. Ajay had the ball in his hand, trying to figure out how he would mend the crack without losing the property of the magic of three. Alone he couldn't make the energy ball happen.

Ajay started to talk to himself.

"What? What are you saying, man?" Mario asked, frantically.

"Just shut up for a second," Ajay said, still concentrating on the ball.

After a few minutes, Ajay had an idea. He was going to treat it like metal. This would allow him to mold the ball back together without adding to the ball. The properties in the energy globe would be the same, he thought.

He rubbed his hands together until the heat from them was as hot as fire. Mario watched in amazement as he could actually see a few low flames coming from his palms. Ajay took the globe into his hands and held it until the two sides of the cracks started to drip. He quickly rolled the ball between his hands until it was smooth again. The ball felt like silk in his palms. No longer could he feel the crack, so he opened his hands to check. Sure enough the crack was gone, leaving behind a smooth, unlit energy source. It was still hot so he cooled it down by blowing on it.

"Alright, we need to start over," Ajay instructed.

"Is it fixed?" Mario asked.

"We are about to find out. Let's not waste time," Ajay said.

Mario understood. The two came together in deep concentration. A few minutes went by but the globe didn't budge. Neither Mario or Ajay was willing to give up, they only concentrated harder. Finally, after ten minutes, the ball started to glow dimly. They now had some hope and concentrated even more. Pretty soon the globe was glowing brightly. They didn't hesitate for a minute and jumped back into the car, letting the globe guide the way.

The globe was making a hard right. Mario followed it until he and Ajay realized the car was now turned around in the opposite direction.

"I think that fucking thing is broke, it's pointing back to where we came from," Mario said in defeat. He actually wanted to get out of the car and beat the shit out of it until the car was nothing more than scrap metal, and then he wanted to cry.

"Well, at this point it's the best we got. Let's just see where it takes us," Ajay said, having a little more faith in the globe than Mario had.

Mario didn't have a better idea. He started heading back in the direction they had just come from. Letting out a big sigh, he hoped with every ounce of his being the ball wasn't broken and it was in fact leading them in the right direction.

53

Caleb was only driving as fast as he thought he could get away with without being pulled over. He knew after the display of witches coming after him it may only be a matter of time before they caught up with him. He didn't have Rowan, so he wasn't sure why they were concentrated on him rather than on Rowan. He speculated Dominick was behind it. Caleb thought it was strange, still, the way Mikayla had responded to the male witch's voice, and he didn't like it. But right now that wasn't his focus, now he had to try and tell Mikayla some version of the truth if he hoped to keep her. He wouldn't be able to tell her everything, but he didn't have a lot of time. If he wanted her to have any faith in him then he needed to tell her something.

It had only taken him a couple of minutes to reach the highway. Flooring his bike, it sped up to a hundred miles per hour. Mikayla could feel the speed of the bike and hung on to Caleb for dear life with her eyes still closed.

Quickly the exit Caleb needed to take came up and he proceeded to get on the off ramp. Looking back to see if there were any cars behind him, he tried to focus his energy even more than he had back at the bar and grabbed tight onto one of Mikayla's arms. Once he was certain they couldn't be seen, he released his energy and orbed.

This time he made it even further. He was actually only a few miles from the park. Keeping the bike steady, he kept the bike at a hundred miles per hour on the darkened road. Within just a couple of minutes, they were in the parking area.

It was much too risky to park in the lot, Caleb decided. Instead he pulled into the woods a bit before stopping the bike. He left it still running as he instructed

Mikayla to get off of the bike. She hoped off without a question and began laughing as she watched him pull his bike into some bushes.

"You're going to scratch up your bike!" She said, laughing.

"I don't care if it means I get to be with you without your brother and friends finding us!" He said as he turned the bike off and tucked the helmets back in further. He then looked up at her and smiled as he threw his keys into his pocket.

"Um, they are good but I don't think that they are that good!" Mikayla said, still laughing at the ridiculousness of Caleb trying to hide a whole motorcycle and a couple of helmets.

He grabbed her hand and they walked through the path, trying to find the cozy space they had been before. As they walked, Caleb started thinking about the witches at the bar. He was almost certain they were there for Rowan, but nonetheless they were witches and were trying to stop him going off alone with Mikayla. Although he wasn't formally trained by a witch on how to utilize his powers, he had a pretty good idea of the things you could do. He remembered the location spell and was nervous they would being using it to track them. They had a good lead on them, but if indeed they were using the spell, then within less than an hour they would catch up. Caleb decided to try something that would by them another hour or more.

He knew he couldn't shut off the energy source, but he could take some of her energy and spread it around a ten mile range to confuse the energy globe. He read about this, only never having tried it. *Think Cale,b think!* He thought to himself, trying to organize his thoughts.

"You're awfully quiet," Mikayla said as she squeezed his hand.

"Sorry, I was just thinking," Caleb said honestly.

"About what?" Mikayla said, thinking it might have something to do with Dominick and her brother at the bar.

"Just you and me," he said.

"Look, they will eventually chill out…please, just be patient… I just found you and I am not ready to let you go," Mikayla said as if she felt she were answering an unasked question.

Caleb, not wanting her to follow up on the conversation any further, bent down to kiss her gently on her forehead as if to reassure her she had indeed answered his question and everything was going to be alright.

Mikayla sighed in relief. Caleb continued to think of ways to throw them off of their trail. They walked a little more in silence, holding hands as they made their way down the path.

Finally, after a couple of seconds, it came to him, but he would need live energy sources to help him. He decided to turn it into a game with Mikayla, he had no other choice. If he didn't tell her something she would have freaked out.

"Want to see something I learned in the boy scouts?" He lied through his teeth, finally breaking his silence.

"Sure!" She said and giggled at the question, finding it to be adorable and felt relieved to hear him talking again.

Caleb held her hand, trying to pull out some of her chi. She thought it was odd, but she could feel a pull from within her go through her hand and into Caleb's. Knowing it was a weird sensation she was having, she opted to not let him in on that little secret. Caleb then turned his head up towards the sky and, with his free hand, made a creepy sounding call into the night sky which sent chills down Mikayla's back.

They both stood silently, as did the forest around them. All of a sudden Mikayla's hand started to become hotter and hotter until it felt like it was on fire, yet at the same time she couldn't seem to let go of Caleb's hand. She hoped Caleb would not notice the warmth of her hand and run away from her freaked out.

The moon was no longer full, and the forest was darker this time, and as the stillness of the forest started to frighten Mikayla, she heard a sound she didn't recognize in the background. Caleb could feel her tense up and squeezed her hand with reassurance he wouldn't let anything happen to her.

The sound started getting louder.

"What is that?" She whispered.

"You'll see," Caleb said, looking down at her face.

Mikayla looked up to see Caleb smiling down at her. She decided it was more of a mischievous grin. The look should have made her more frightened, but it didn't because she could see the love in his eyes and she knew he wouldn't let anything happen to her.

They waited as the sound got closer. Mikayla couldn't see what it was, but she could see a few black masses coming their way from three different directions. As the masses grew even closer, she noticed the masses were actually individual tiny masses which added up to the bigger masses. She squinted her eyes as she thought she recognized exactly what they were.

"Are those bats?" She said, still whispering.

"Yup," Caleb answered as he squared his shoulders and lifted one hand towards the sky.

"How did you do that?" She asked as the bats fluttered all around them. It should have been a scene straight out of a nightmare, but Mikayla found the swarm of bats quite beautiful.

"Boy scouts," he said and smiled down at her.

"Come on! Really, how did you know how to do that?" She asked again as she watched in amazement.

Caleb didn't answer, instead he needed some of her energy without her knowledge. He bent down and kissed her and as she kissed him back, he breathed as much of her in as he could. Just before he released her from his kiss, he reached up to the sky with his free hand, which had already been hanging high in the air and grabbed a bat. Quickly he brought it down to his mouth and breathed into the bats face. Then he put a seal on it ,which Mikayla couldn't see. The seal wouldn't last more than a couple of hours, but it would be enough time to throw anyone off for a little while until he could figure out what else to do.

He repeated this a few more times sending out five bats carrying some of her energy. She wasn't sure what he was doing, but she loved all of the kisses he was planting on her and just let him do his thing. It made her forget she had just seen Marcus for the first time in four years.

After Caleb released the last bat, he grabbed and hugged her tightly. Then he ran his hands from the top of her head to her feet. She laughed, wondering what the hell he was doing.

"What the hell are you doing now?" She asked between giggles.

"Just checking to make sure it's you. It's really dark out here," he said, trying to play it off as if he were just trying to make her laugh. What he was really doing was putting a seal on her so her energy would be harder to read. Again, this wouldn't last long but he was just trying to buy some time.

That was the thing with magic, there was always a yin and a yang. For a finding spell there were ways to hide things, but ultimately one's own energy was always stronger and would be the source for all magic.

"I can assure you, it is me," she said as he stood up to face her. "And what the hell were you doing with those bats?" She asked as he took her hand and started walking further into the woods.

"Giving them some of your energy," he said honestly, not having come up with a better lie, but at this point she thought what he was doing was joking around, so he figured it would fly.

"You are truly a strange one, Caleb!" She said as she held his hand and followed behind him, letting him lead the way. She could barely see and was glad to have him go ahead of her first and guide her.

They finally reached the spot where they had been just a few weeks before and took a seat by the water. It wasn't as bright as it had been that night, but the light was much better by the water than in the forest.

Quietly they sat and listened to the sounds of the forest. Mikayla was still feeling a little dizzy from her three glasses of beer. Caleb was stone cold sober now, and he couldn't stop thinking about the male witch who had tried to stop them.

"So, who was that back at the bar?" He asked flatly, not knowing a better way to phrase the question.

Mikayla sat quietly for a moment. She had hoped he hadn't noticed, but reality was he couldn't have missed it. "Marcus," was all she said.

"Well, who is Marcus and why did he look so upset?" He probed.

Thoughts of Marcus flooded her brain at the question. It was like she saw everything they ever were together in a matter of seconds. Tears filled her eyes at the old pain. Tears fell from her face at the thought of the forces which seemed to be trying to come between her and Caleb. She was in love with him, and he was her freedom.

She sniffed once and Caleb knew she was crying. The pit of his stomach started to ache out of fear for what she was about to say. He couldn't look at her, instead he kept his eyes on the water.

Aidan, Rory, and Aiah drove around for a little bit, trying to see if they could find Caleb so they could tail him. Even though they had a finding potion, they weren't sure it would work. They weren't wizards and weren't sure they even had the right energy to make it work. Also they only had one. After twenty minutes of driving around with no such luck, they had to make the call.

"We have to try it, it's only a matter of time before the pack and witches catch up to them and we need to get there first," Aidan said.

"What if it doesn't work?" Aiah said.

"Then we go to plan B, which will actually be much harder," Aidan said.

"Yeah, I can't imagine being able to take her from Cyrus. He may just kill her and then we have nothing. This is our one chance to walk amongst the day and get out from under Cyrus," Rory added.

"Exactly, but if we can't find her ourselves we won't have a choice but to try," Aidan said, taking out the potion and handing it to Aiah, who was sitting in the front passenger seat. "What's first?" he asked Aiah

"I think I just need to concentrate on Caleb while I ingest the potion, and then I am supposed to be drawn to where he is at," Aiah said, interpreting the notes made by the wizard on the scrap piece of paper.

"Alright, but make sure you really try to feel Caleb before you take it. This is possibly our one chance. I hope this really is the witch we are looking for," Aidan said, coming up to a stop light.

Aiah closed his eyes and pictured Caleb. Slowly he drew in more and more about Caleb as he concentrated on the picture in his mind of him. After a few minutes, with his eyes still closed, he ingested the whole contents of the potion, making sure to get every last drop.

"Anything?" Aidan asked too soon.

Aiah said nothing as his eyes were still closed. He could feel the liquid move through his throat and into his stomach. He then felt it start to branch out from his center like roots growing through his body and spread throughout the rest of his body. It felt warm at first, but quickly cooled off for a brief moment before turning red hot. Aiah's forehead began to sweat as Rory and Aidan looked at him in wonder. They weren't sure if he was alright or not. He still hadn't answered Aidan.

The heat started to cool off again to a nice warm feeling, and just then Aiah felt a click in the back of his head and then he felt pulled. "Go straight through the next two lights, then make a left," he said.

Aidan smiled and floored it.

It took them only thirty minutes having floored it through the back roads until they finally came to a parking lot on a darken road. It looked like a park on the water. Aidan decided not to pull into the parking lot for fear of being noticed. Instead he pulled a little further down the road and turned the car around and parked on the side of a road perpendicular to the main road.

Quickly after they parked they ran down as Aiah led the way. They made it into the parking lot and scanned for Caleb's bike, but didn't see it. Aidan motioned for them to use caution. If Caleb saw them coming it would blow their chance. Quietly Aiah moved towards the entrance of the forest. They were vampires and could move quick and quietly.

Aidan spotted Caleb and the girl first, grabbing onto Aiah's arm and pointed. They were sitting down by the water, looking ahead. Slowly they made their way closer to a cluster of trees. Quietly they each scaled up a massive old tree with thick, sturdy branches to get a bird's eye view. It was pretty certain she was the one, but they had to make certain. Then, once they were sure it was her, they would have to wait for the right opportunity and then they would strike.

Caleb thought he had heard something that didn't belong and quickly turned his head, a predatory instinct. He squinted both of his eyes to see if he could see anything behind them in the forest, but he saw nothing was there. It never occurred to him to look into the trees. The ones who were after them would be on foot and it was too soon for anyone to have found them yet, so he chalked it up as a small animal of some kind.

Mikayla didn't hear anything and as the tears still streamed down her cheeks, she started to wipe away the tears. She wanted to get the image of

Marcus and Dominick out of her mind and the best way for her to do that was to tell Caleb the truth so he wouldn't misunderstand why she seemed so affected by seeing Marcus.

"Alright, I will tell you, but I need you to hear me out before you say anything," she started.

Caleb's stomach tightened just a little bit more as he turned his head back towards the water, trying not to look at her.

"I loved Dominick my whole life. Then when we were seventeen, just before our senior year, he cheated on me. Several times. All the boys had gotten really weird towards the end of our junior year in high school, I suppose it was their hormones. Anyways, I broke up with him. My senior year a new kid came to school, Marcus, the guy from back there. We had every class together and became fast friends. Then we started dating. I was in love with him. I thought he was in love with me, only to find that the night of our senior prom he didn't show up to take me, Dominick did. Marcus just up and left, with a note saying that he would explain everything soon but I never heard from him again until about a week or so ago when he sent me a letter. But that's the shortened version. The point is that my heart was still broken after that for years," she said as tears streamed down her face like she was in a confession, allowing her feelings to be shared.

Caleb felt like he was going to puke. He wondered now if she was still in love with this guy by the way she was crying. Seeing Marcus had affected her and Caleb didn't like it. He was ready to crush something.

"So, you're still in love with him, I take it," he said through his teeth, trying to sound rational.

"I said not to interrupt me!" She snapped. "Sorry, it's just I need to tell you everything," she corrected herself.

"No, I am sorry," Caleb said, trying to remain calm. He wanted to reach for her and pull her in close, but now wasn't the right moment so instead he sat quietly as she began to finish.

"My whole life people have sheltered me and treated me like I am a baby. You never did. When I am with you I feel free. You feel like my future and I love how bright that looks. The night you told me you loved me, I felt it. But what you didn't know was that I knew I loved you too, but I was afraid." She said, pausing as Caleb grabbed the back of her neck and pulled her forehead to his as he felt his heart begin to soften. "I was afraid that I would be hurt again, but I realize that with you it is different. You're not trying to own me, you just let me be me. You have no idea how much that means to me. I love you, Caleb, with all my heart and I don't know how long you have here, but I want to spend that time with you. I love you so much that the thought of you leaving kills my heart. I am yours, Caleb, and tonight when I saw Marcus all I felt was anger; anger that all the boys in my past were trying to step in my way of freedom and of being happy. You are all I'll ever need, Caleb." She said as the tears streamed down her cheeks.

Caleb rubbed the back of her neck as his forehead gently rested against hers. His eyes were closed, but he could feel the tears dropping from her eyes. She was finished talking and had told him what she needed to. He leaned his mouth towards her and kissed her. Caleb wasn't going to tell her he loved her, the moment called for him to show her. He put all of his energy into one soft kiss on the lips and held it there as he thought about how much he loved her. She kissed him back with just as much conviction.

Caleb backed off of her for a moment and cupped her face in his hands, looking deeply into her eyes. He knew he needed to start to tell her some things, which may change her mind about him, but he also knew tonight was now not going to be the right time. Instead he studied the lines of her face as the mascara from her eyes bled down her cheeks.

Gently he started to rub away the streaks the mascara had left behind. She felt so loved as he wiped away the tears. The mascara was almost gone as he continued to clear her face. He studied her as he did so with love. The last of the mascara was just under her right eye. He wet his finger with his mouth and began to wipe the last of it away. All though the night sky was dark, his vampire vision allowed him the ability to see clearly. His gentle smile quickly faded. Underneath the last of the mascara he noticed something new. His eyes widened in disbelief at what he was looking at.

"What is it?" She said, having noticed the sudden change in his face.

Caleb said nothing, as so many different emotions and thoughts flooded his brain. He couldn't believe what he was seeing. Just below her right eye he saw two perfect dots on either side of an ancient looking symbol that looked roughly like a single feather. It was small in size and the color was only a couple of shades darker then her actual skin tone with a slightly burnt orange tint. The lines were perfect and unmistakable.

All this time and it was her, he thought to himself. He knew right then nothing would ever be the same. The deal was off, and he knew it would only be a matter of time until Cyrus came after him. He didn't know what would happen to his brothers, but he was confident they would stay by his side. One thing he knew for sure was no one was going to take her away from him, no matter what. She had been so sheltered and was unprepared what the world was going to do with her. He became angered at the thought. She knew nothing, not even of herself. It would be a hard road, but he would have to tell her the truth of everything, but that would take time and tonight wasn't the right time to start.

"Caleb! What is it?" She repeated, worried by the look on his face.

"Nothing. I love you, Mikayla, and for the rest of my life I will protect you," he said, looking down at her.

"I love you so much, Caleb. I can't help myself," she said, hugging him tight.

Caleb grabbed hold of her, wrapping his hands around her back and pulled her into him. He looked down at her and stared for a moment as she stared back. She tilted her head up towards him and they began kissing slowly.

The slow kisses started coming faster. Caleb's brain began to race. He was on high alert and somehow felt even closer to her than he had before, and even more protective over her than he ever thought possible.

Mikayla let out a sigh as the kissing became deeper. Again she found her body tingling. It was aching for him to be close. Caleb became hungry for her as she sighed. He lifted her up and she automatically wrapped her legs around his waist.

Holding her up, the kissing turned from soft and loving pecks into passion filled kisses. Caleb wanted her badly. He grabbed the back of her hair and pulled her head back as he began to kiss her neck. Tonight he wanted to bite her, but not to feed, only to feel closer to her and to taste her so he could always know where she was. Mikayla moaned, which only made Caleb break out into goose bumps.

Mikayla started to tongue his ear gently. He could hear her tiny breaths, which sent chills down his spine. She then began to kiss his neck. That only brought forth his inner beast, and within a second she was laying down on the ground with him on top.

She looked up at him and removed his shirt as he helped. He then reached down to the top of her dress and pulled the front down, exposing her before him. She arched her back in want. He started to kiss them as she unbuttoned his pants, using her foot to help pull them down around his knees. He then found her mouth again and began kissing her as he hiked her dress up.

Once her dress was up, he slid her underwear to the side and went down on her. She moaned with pleasure as she felt all the muscles in her body tense up and then suddenly release. Quickly Caleb found her mouth again.

"I want you Caleb," she softly whispered.

He wanted to restrain himself so her first time would be in a bed, but he was having a hard time telling that to his selfish side which wanted her now, and he wanted to make her his now. The selfish side took over as he pulled himself out of his boxers and pulled her underwear off. He wasn't going to go all the way, he told himself. He was only going to break the barrier to make it easier for later. Over and over he kept telling himself that, but right now he had never wanted anything more.

He watched her face as he gently slid a little ways into her. It was a little painful for her, he could see by the look on her face as he came to the thin piece of skin inside. He backed out and paused, unsure of whether it would be best to push slowly or give one hard push. One thing he knew for sure was he didn't like to see her in pain. The less she felt the better. First he tried slowly, but the look on her face was a mix between wanting and pain.

"Are you sure?" He asked, looking into her eyes.

"I've never been more sure of anything," she said, looking up at him. But truly she was scared. This was her first time and she had just seen Marcus and was feeling furious about it. He shouldn't be in her head at all, but was. She remembered how he had made her feel and how hard it was for her to get over. It wouldn't be like that with Caleb, she knew. He was different and there was something about him that told her he would always be there for her. She closed her eyes and took a deep breath. Her fear lifted a little as she was now only thinking of Caleb.

He could feel her legs trembling underneath him. He finally decided the slow way was more torturous indeed, and he backed out one more time, staring down at her. Mikayla's legs were still shaking a little. He knew, he needed to get the worst part over with. Looking at her face, he quickly thrust himself into her, feeling a snap almost half way in and he knew the hymen had broken.

The pleasure was almost overwhelming for Caleb. She was now his and he knew the connection between them would be impossible to break.

Mikayla, on the other hand, screamed briefly in pain as tears streamed her face. She felt sad and loved all at the same time. Her love for Caleb grew even more in that single moment. Caleb stopped inside of her and held her for a moment while placing gentle kisses on her face, waiting for her to direct the next move.

"I'm ok, just go slow," she said, sounding really innocent as her voice trembled as the shaking in her legs moved into her voice, it almost broke Caleb's heart.

He nodded and kissed her. He slowly began to move in and out as he gently kissed her along the way, stroking her face and making sure she was all right. Loving her and knowing he was going to spend the rest of his life with her, he gently smiled, looking down at her as she looked back up at him with trusting eyes.

"I'm going to marry you…" he said, slowly stroking her.

She let out a moan of pure pleasure, causing Caleb to move a bit faster. The faster he pushed the louder her moaning became, suddenly the pain on her face became that of pleasure.

54

Jamahl spotted Mary and her friend. They were still at the table drinking beer and listening to the band. He came up behind her and put his hands over her eyes.

"Listen here you mother…" she started to swear, but was cut off when she heard Jamahl start to laugh. "You're back!" She said and threw her arms around him.

He reached down and hugged her. "Yeah, me and Ali came back. Looks like the trouble left." He said, still holding on to her. "I'm going to need a beer," he then said.

Mary's friend was on it and poured him a fresh beer and pushed it over towards him. He thanked her as he still was holding on to Mary.

Ali had made a perfect landing into an empty stall with Rowan. She was still out, but he knew he only had a few more minutes until she would come to. He rubbed his hand over her neck to quickly heal the marks from where he had bit her and then tried to do the same with the cut on her arm. The cut on her arm didn't work as well, but he thought it would have to do. He peaked out of the crack in the stall to make sure there wasn't anyone else in the bathroom. Ali decided the night was his lucky night, having come into the girls small restroom twice now to find an empty room.

Quickly he pulled her out of the stall and gently sat her down, propping her back up against the wall. He was hoping she would just think she had passed out. He was counting on it.

Suddenly he heard girls voices coming from outside of the bathroom. As fast as he had appeared he disappeared, orbing himself into the empty coat closet.

He walked over to the table where Jamahl sat sipping on a beer.

"Where are Mary and her friend?" Ali asked as he approached the table.

"I told them to go and check on her because she had been gone a long time. They just thought she had left with her boyfriend, but I informed them that he had left without her," Jamahl smiled, taking another sip of his beer.

Ali wasn't much of a drinker, but the stress of the night had made him reach for the beer automatically. He poured himself a glass and slammed it, and then he poured himself another as he motioned for the waitress to come over so he could order something harder. Jamahl just laughed, continuing to sip on his beer and wait for Mary.

Rowan was passed out when Mary and Lauren entered the bathroom.

"Oh my God! Rowan!" Mary shouted and ran over to her. She knelt beside Rowan and started to shake her. "Get me a wet paper towel," she ordered Lauren. Lauren quickly was on it, grabbing towels from the dispenser and wetting them with water from the sink.

"Rowan, can you hear me?" Mary said as she patted her face down with the cool, wet paper towel Lauren had given to her.

Rowan started to mumble a little as Mary kept wiping her face down with the soaked towel.

"Rowan, can you hear me?" She asked as Rowan started to stir. "Rowan, wake up. Wake up, Rowan," she added as Rowan began to move her head and mumble louder.

"What the hell?" Rowan mumbled as she started to open her eyes. "Where are we?" Rowan said, having come to but feeling confused.

"In the bathroom. I think you have been in here for a while! I thought you left, but Jamahl said he never saw you leave so I came back here to check on you and, well, here you are!" Mary said still working the wet towel. "What happened to you?" She then asked.

Rowan sat for a moment thinking about it. She tried to remember, but all she could remember was washing her hands before feeling an intense pain followed by an intense pleasure, from what she didn't know, and then it was all just a blank.

"I don't know, but one minute I am washing my hands, the next minute I felt a pain of some sort. It was a sharp pain and then I felt intense pleasure. That's all I remember," Rowan said rubbing her head.

"You must have slipped and hit your head or something," Mary said, confused by the end part of the pleasure, but then had a thought. "Maybe the intense pleasure was from whatever dream you were having while you were passed out," Mary offered.

"That sounds possible, knowing me. What I can't remember is why I passed out. I don't feel any pain on my head and really I hadn't drank that much," she said as she strained to remember anything after washing her hands, but she couldn't remember any of it other than the sensations.

"I don't know either, perhaps the stress from your boyfriend? I don't know, but you did seem mad. Did you two fight back here?" Mary asked, trying to help put the pieces together.

"No, I didn't even see him. Where is he?" Rowan asked as she struggled to get herself up. "Strange, but I feel like I just gave blood. I think my sugar is low," she said, now standing but feeling weak.

"Your boyfriend left a while ago. I will take you home and grab something for you to eat on the way," Mary offered.

"No, Mary. You don't need to ruin the rest of your night because of me. I think I can get myself home," Rowan said, washing her hands but still feeling weak.

"I won't hear anything more. I am taking you home and that is final, missy!" Mary insisted with a smile on her face.

Rowan hated for her to have to leave, but she did think it was a good idea. She really wasn't feeling well. "Ok. Thanks Mary, that is really great. I will owe you big," Rowan said, deciding to take her up on it. She didn't want to pass out on the road and hurt someone else or herself.

"No problem! That is what friends are for!" Mary said, sounding not at all put out.

Rowan really liked the sound of that, 'friends,' she thought to herself. Mary was great, there was just something about the girl you couldn't help but like. She was edgy but seemed to have the kindest heart.

Mario and Ajay were following the energy globe. They were headed back towards the bar. It seemed as if it was broken, but they had nothing else to go on. They were back in the parking lot of the bar again. Ajay gave Mario a questioning look. Mario shrugged his shoulders and quickly made it out of the car and headed towards the bar while Ajay followed after him.

They entered back into the bar. The bouncers gave them a questioning look. "I don't want you two causing any trouble in here. If I even suspect you two are up to no good then you are out. We can't have people popping in and out of the bar like this. So just keep it in check," the bouncer said before letting them pass.

"We don't want any problems," Mario said. The bouncers felt a bit of relief, they knew who Mario was and it was one family no one wanted to mess with since they were rumored mafia.

Ajay had something else he wanted to say, but couldn't, knowing if he opened his mouth they wouldn't get through the doors.

The bouncer stepped aside and let them in.

Mario scanned the area and was surprised to find Jamahl and Ali back at the table drinking beer. Dominick could have sworn Jamahl disappeared into the closet. But if that were true, then why did he come back. Mikayla was gone, he thought to himself, confused by what he was seeing. He headed straight towards the table.

"Where is she?" Mario tried not to sound too confrontational.

"I thought she left with you, man?" Jamahl said, lying through his teeth.

"Yeah, I bet. Better yet, who the fuck are you?" Mario asked as his fists balled up.

"What do you mean?" Jamahl asked.

Mario's eyes flashed. Jamahl could see the wolf was about to lose his shit. He didn't want to fight him, but he would if it came down to it. This was Mikayla's brother, and it would do Caleb much harm to make enemies with him.

Just then, as if saved by the bell, Ali chimed in.

"That's funny, she is right over there with Mary and Lauren. Huh, I could have sworn that she left with you," Ali said, pointing to the hall where Mary and Lauren seemed to be helping Rowan down the hall.

Mario ran over to her. "What happened?" He shouted as he practically knocked over Mary and Lauren grabbing hold of Rowan.

"I don't know what happened, but we found her on the floor of the bathroom. She must have passed out. I was just about to take her home. She doesn't feel well and I think she needs something to eat," Mary said, trying to be helpful.

Mario didn't know how to take Mary. He wasn't sure if she could be trusted, but something about her tone made him so he dropped the protective behavior and thanked her. He swooped Rowan into his arms.

"I am so sorry, Rowan, are you ok?" Mario said softly.

"I am fine, just feel weak and hungry," she assured him back. Even though she had been mad at him, she was so glad he was there. Their fight no longer mattered. She was in his arms and she felt safe and loved.

"Can we go home now?" She asked.

"Yeah, we can. You're coming to my house tonight," Mario said. There was no way he was going to tell her what was going on. Something had happened to her, he didn't know what, but for now she was safe and right now that was all that mattered to him.

"Good," she said.

"Ajay!" Mario called to Ajay, who was standing a few feet away. "I need you to drive my car while I drive Rowan's back to the condo," he said, throwing his keys to Ajay.

"What about my sister?" Ajay said, realizing the task with Rowan was done.

"Don't you have a way to get to her?" Mario said, not wanting to shout the way across the bar.

Ajay nodded.

"As soon as we get back you can go," Mario said.

They headed out towards the bar. First Ajay, followed by Mario, who was carrying out Rowan. Mary and Lauren just stood there, not quite sure what to say.

"Mary!" Rowan tried to shout.

Mary looked to her.

"Thanks so much. I will talk to you soon," Rowan smiled. Mary smiled back, glad to see Rowan didn't hold her responsible.

"I hope you feel better! And go get something to eat. You will feel better!" Mary said, waving.

Mario said nothing as he kept moving towards the bar, stopping only briefly at the table where Jamahl and Ali were still sipping on beer, acting as if they weren't watching them, but Mario knew they were. He could feel it.

"You two motherfuckers better stay away from my girl and my family, or so help me God I will remove your spinal cords with my hands," Mario said, sounding rather calm for someone who was threatening to kill someone.

"Mario! Stop it!" Rowan tried to yell, but couldn't. "I am sorry, you guys. Thank you, it was fun and I will see you later," she said as Mario carried her off towards the door.

"Not happening," Mario said back.

Jamahl and Ali just ignored him and instead waved at Rowan as Mary and Lauren came back up to the table.

Ajay and Mario, carrying Rowan, made it out of the door.

"I don't think that guy likes you guys," Mary said with a confused look on her face.

Jamahl didn't want her to feel bad, so he put his arm around her and kissed the top of her head. She was so sweet and it was the first time he had ever fallen for a mere human. But she wasn't just human, she was something more, Jamahl decided. She was truly unique.

55

The groups had all followed their energy globes out west of town and found themselves on a darkened road. They had to take the cars so they could follow the energy globes. Unfortunately, even magic had its limits and there was no way to use an energy globe while orbing, and there was no way to orb to another person. You could only orb from place to place. It had to be places grounded by earth.

The road seemed to have water that followed behind a forest to the right of them. Dominick could smell the water. "There is a river about a half mile away from the forest over there," he said to Layla as he pointed out of the window towards the right side of the car. Layla didn't look, instead she kept her eyes steady on the globe.

The globe started to get brighter as it started to slowly pull towards the right. "We are here! Pull over!" Layla said, already taking her seatbelt off before Dominick had a chance to pull over.

He admired how committed she was to finding Mikayla, someone she didn't even know. She was definitely a tough cookie, he thought to himself, smiling at the use of referring to her as a cookie. But that was the best word he could come up with.

Lucio was in the car behind them with Marcus. The energy globe in Marcus's hand also started to glow, but it was pulling towards the left. Lucio followed and pulled over to the right side of the road, parking behind Dominick.

Marcus hopped out of the car and ran across the street with the globe at hands length, not wanting to waste one more second.

"Where the fuck are you going?" Dominick called as Layla carefully walked backwards to the right of the cars, watching Marcus running across the street.

"The globe is pulling this way!" Marcus said without turning back.

"No it's not! Ours is pulling this way!" Layla shouted as Marcus and Lucio made their way across the street.

Marcus stopped in his tracks and turned around.

"Where is the rest of the pack?" He asked as he looked down the street where they had just come from.

Dominick, Lucio, and Layla all looked down the street as well. It was dark and they couldn't see anything. Quickly Marcus threw a ball of light down the street ,lighting up the sky briefly.

As the sky lit up like the fourth of July, for a brief second they spotted the other car. The pack was already out of the car and heading in the opposite direction. Marcus, without explaining what he was about to do, quickly orbed to the pack, leaving the globe with Lucio.

"What the hell? Where are you guys going?" He asked, hoping they just didn't get what it was the energy globe was telling them, and then he saw it for himself.

Vince held up the globe and it was headed in the opposite direction as his globe.

"Fuck!" Marcus yelled. "Alright, go. Just follow it," Marcus instructed and orbed back.

Before he said anything, he rechecked his globe, and sure enough it was pointing to the forest across the street.

"All the globes are pointing to different directions!" Marcus said.

"Ah, so I am pretty sure that with what we saw back at the bar, and now this, that guy is a witch and has put a filter on our search globes somehow," Layla said matter of fact.

"Fuck, who is he? I don't get it. I am supposed to have access. And how does a witch know about her? Something here doesn't make sense at all," Marcus thought out loud.

"I have zero answer to that question right now. All we can do is each follow the path of the globes and the pack can listen for sounds in the forest,"

Layla said, taking over realizing, the usually so strong and perfect Marcus was starting to unravel for some reason. Something she thought she would never see. The dark knights were tough guys who were cool and calm and seemingly emotionless at times.

"Call me if you see her," Marcus instructed, crossing the street again as Lucio followed.

Layla didn't bother to comment. Instead she headed into the forest opposite with Dominick. The globe was leading them forward towards the water. They had entered through the pathless part of the forest, making their own entrance. Layla knew somewhere nearby had to be a parking lot, but the search globes didn't lead them to a parking lot, it lead them there.

They came to the water where the light from the moon shined a little brighter.

"So what does that mean?" Dominick asked as he watched Layla follow the globe, not taking her eyes off of it.

"What does what mean?" She asked ,only half listening.

"What you said back there. That he must have put a filter on her. How does that work?" He asked.

"That's tough to answer simply. See there is always a yin for a yang with magic. If he suspected, which by the looks of it he did, that we had formed a search globe, then he could have taken some of her energy and transferred it to other places, but one thing is for certain, they are in here somewhere. The filter doesn't last very long and her energy has to be within range for it to keep. The key is sneaking up on them before he orbs her out of here. Or worse yet…" Layla trailed off, realizing she was about to sound insensitive and she didn't mean it that way, she was only thinking of possibilities.

Dominick knew where she was going with it, but also realized it wasn't her intent to frighten him, instead he just nodded his head that he understood.

"I don't understand, it seems like you should be able to conjure up a spell and go straight to her?" Dominick asked, quietly following Layla and the globe.

"Well, actually we can. But spells take time and also takes elements from the earth, neither of which we had time to do. So this was our best bet. Don't worry, Dominick, we will find her," Layla explained, still not taking her eyes off of the globe.

Dominick felt frantic inside. He was almost afraid to find her, afraid she may be dead. It was the first time in his life he had ever felt scared. He didn't know Layla, but there was something about her that made him feel a little bit better. Looking at the side of her face and how concentrated she was, he couldn't help but appreciate her determination to save someone she didn't even know.

The globe started to dim. Layla stopped and Dominick, walking so close behind her, ran into her and knocked her over.

"Shit, I am so sorry!" Dominick said on the ground next to her, having tripped over her body. "Usually I am never this clumsy. I don't know what is wrong with me," he added, jumping to his feet and extending a hand to help Layla up.

"I get it, believe me if my girlfriend had been kidnapped I would feel the same way," she said, reaching up to take his hand, not really needing one but respecting his efforts by pretending.

Dominick pulled a little too hard and Layla was yanked forward heading for another fall. Quickly Dominick caught her before she finished her face plant. Her body was pressed up against his. She couldn't help but like being in his arms.

"Ex," he said, steadying her.

"Huh?" She said, trying to focus back on the globe.

"Mikayla is my ex, but she is still my friend and my family," he said.

"And you still love her," Layla added, watching to see if the globe would brighten again so she could let it go and follow.

Dominick said nothing and Layla knew it was because he did. The feeling hurt but she knew it wasn't rational. All of a sudden she was snapped out of her irrational thoughts by the globe relighting itself, burning brightly. She let it go and it started to work its way back the opposite way.

"Fuck!" Layla said.

"Fuck. What do you mean fuck?" Dominick said, following Layla as she followed the globe.

"Didn't you notice that we have now turned around?" Layla asked.

"Yeah," Dominick said, trying to remain calm.

"Well, we are being toyed with," she said.

"I have an idea. You say she is here somewhere, right? So why don't I go wolf and we can track her using the globe as a guide. If the light goes out, we will know to put our search elsewhere." Dominick said, taking control over the situation.

"Good idea," she said, admiring how he came in with a smart, solid plan.

"There is just one thing, I need a favor from you," he said, not feeling embarrassed at all. After all his body was large and well defined.

"What's that?" She asked, but already had an idea.

"My clothes, can you hold them?" he asked, already taking of his shirt with the quickness.

Layla blushed. "No problem," she said, trying to sound indifferent. But as soon as he handed her his shirt, his pants were off and she hadn't had time to look away. She was glad it was so dark at the moment or she might have really been embarrassed.

Layla looked down at the pile of pants, shirt, socks, and shoes she thought had to be a fourteen and shook her head. She then grabbed a leaf and centered herself to tap into her center. As her eyes were closed she started to shove the leaf into the left palm which was balled into a fist. One by one she added leaves into her palm. Then she chanted something under her breath and tapped the side of her hand, thumb side, three times. Then, with one hand like a Las Vega small time magician, shook her left fist once, opening her palm. Dominick watched in amazement as a bag came out of her hand.

Layla picked up Dominick's things and placed them in the bag as she tried hard not to look at him. "You better transform," she said, worrying about the time.

Dominick said nothing and looked up to the moon as he focused on the two rhythms of his heart beat. One slow and human, the other werewolf fast and hard. Tuning in, his body began to change shape a bit as his body increased in size and hair. His canines grew an inch as his forehead expanded. He no longer could talk. Instead he sat quietly for a moment, listening to the forest and sniffing for Mikayla.

As he tried to pick up on Mikayla, he heard a scream from the forest. It was apparent to Dominick Layla hadn't heard it. So he opened his ears wider. Then the scream came again. This time it was louder and Layla too had heard that one. She looked down at Dominick and they began to run towards the scream, jumping over fallen logs and dodging the prickers from bushes.

The screams stopped, Layla could no longer hear anything and neither could Dominick. But they still ran as fast as their legs could take them. Layla was quite a ways behind, but still putting every bit of energy towards catching up.

Dominick smelled something familiar in the air, a mixture of orange and vanilla swirled between the heavy smell of green from the forest. It was Mikayla and she was close by.

The forest came to a paved opening. It was the parking lot Layla knew had to be around and here it was. Dominick quickly scanned the lot for the motorcycle, as did Layla. There was no sign of the bike and they moved forward, across the empty parking lot and into the forest. Now they were on an actual path, which made running towards the scream easier as they no longer had to jump over moss covered logs while dodging thick brush.

As Dominick led the way, without all the obstacles in his way he became even faster. Layla could barely see him when he jumped back into the forest ,heading towards the water. Quickly she made her way into the same tiny opening, trying to keep an eye on him. Knowing he was so much further ahead of him, she conjured up her spirit wolf and sent it forward to follow Dominick. As if her feet suddenly sprouted wings, she became faster as she was tied to her spirit wolf. Finally she could see him a little bit better. She watched as he started to change form, back into a man. She assumed the last thing he wanted was for Mikayla to be horrified. Mikayla had no clue what Dominick was. Layla quickly reached in the bag, taking out Dominick's pants and called to him.

"Dom!" She whispered as loud as she could without giving away her position.

Dominick stopped and turned around, wanting to make sure Layla was alright only to have a pair of pants flying at him. He went to reach for the pants, but the pants flew through his hands and disappeared. Confused, he looked down to find Layla used some magic to put the pants on him, saving time. He had no time to say thank you, instead he gave a smile and turned back around and broke out in a full blown sprint.

The water was only a few feet away. Dominick scanned the area. First he saw nothing, until something on the ground caught his eyes. It was Caleb, lying face down on something. He looked around for Mikayla until it registered Caleb was actually on top of her. Dominick was enraged. He ran even faster before coming to the water and over to where Caleb was over Mikayla.

Dominick couldn't look down at Mikayla for fear she was dead. He only heard a couple of screams and then nothing. He swept in with the speed of light and grabbed Caleb by the back of the neck before Caleb had the chance to see him coming.

With the strength of ten men, Dominick tossed Caleb across the small opening, landing him hard against a tree. He gave out a beastly growl and his eyes were solid black as his mouth showed his wolf teeth.

Mikayla looked up and was horrified. It didn't register at first what was happening, only that some wild beast was attacking. As she looked up she recognized Dominick, but was frightened by the solid black of his eyes and his mouth which was slightly contorted with fangs the size of a lions. As he let out a beastly growl, Mikayla screamed again. She was in the middle of a nightmare. Quickly she pulled up her top as she scooted back, trying to get a read on the situation.

56

Lucio and Mario were making their way fast through the forest on the opposite side of the road with Mario leading the way holding the globe.

Suddenly, Lucio stopped when he thought he heard a scream. Mario felt Lucio behind him pause and turned around. Again the scream was piercing and followed by a few horrific beastly growls. It was faint, but nonetheless Lucio recognized it as a scream of horror, as someone was witnessing two unearthly creatures with unimaginable strength in the middle of an attack. Marcus heard nothing, but knew something was going on by the way Lucio's face looked.

"Mikayla," he said softly and turned around to run in the direction. Marcus didn't question, he only followed fast behind.

Caleb had hit his head hard. He knew they would be coming, but they arrived faster than he thought. Ready for a fight, he got to his feet. He was going to try and refrain from using magic. Mikayla wasn't ready for all of this yet, and he wanted to protect her until he could tell her the truth in a nonhostile environment.

Dominick was relieved when Mikayla screamed, she was still alive. It took him only a minute before he realized what it was they were doing. As if a sword had entered his heart, his chest sunk in. A pain unlike any other had washed over him. She had fallen in love with, Marcus but she had not given herself to him, and with that Dominick always held on to the chance they would one day be together again. He always assumed it would be he who would take her virginity, but he always assumed it would be on their wedding night. At that moment, he realized that would never be. Dizziness washed over him as rage filled throughout every inch of his body.

"Dominick?" Mikayla whispered as tears filled her eyes, knowing the pain he felt, ignoring the beast she had witnessed come out of him. It was the same pain she had once felt when he had started sleeping with any girl who threw herself at him.

Quickly Caleb pulled his pants up and stood to his feet, readying himself for a fight.

"I don't want any trouble," Caleb said, trying to reason with the half man half beast.

Dominick said nothing, he let out a loud howl into the sky. Caleb knew it was him calling the rest of his pack. Dominick then lunged forward, picking Caleb up by the neck and tossing him against another tree.

Caleb's left shoulder hit the tree first and before he had a chance to steady himself, Dominick was right back at him, throwing massive, heavy fisted punches to his face. Despite how strong Caleb was, and how much pain he himself could withstand, he felt every one of Dominick's hard blows. In the background he could hear the horror in Mikayla's voice as she tried to call the fight off.

Suddenly, Mikayla's voice was louder and Caleb knew she was close. He didn't want her to get caught in the fight. She was scared, he could hear it in her voice, but nonetheless she was trying to help him. He became angry and began to throw some really hard punches himself. Dominick stumbled back slightly with a look of shock on his face. He had never encountered anyone strong enough to move him before. Quickly he steadied himself when he felt a tiny, soft hand grab his arm.

"Mikayla step back," he said with his voice still distorted. "This guy has been messing with your head!" He then added.

"No, Dominick, stop! He loves me, he would never hurt me! Please, I am begging you to stop!" Mikayla cried and only held on tighter as Caleb saw his opportunity to throw another blow to the side of his head. Mikayla watched in horror as his head snapped backwards.

Dominick, trying to remove her from the danger, pushed her back. She stumbled backwards and hit the ground, only infuriating Caleb more.

Caleb watched as Mikayla tried to get back up again, determined to stop the fight.

"Mikayla, step back. Please I am begging you!" Caleb yelled as Dominick landed a punch to his throat. For a brief moment Caleb's air was cut and he gasped.

"You guys stop it!" Mikayla screamed, running back over towards them.

They were throwing blow for blow, violent and inhuman, but still Mikayla made her way in the middle, catching Dominick's elbow to her head. She fell down to her knees and the world around her started to go black. Mikayla tried not to pass out, but the blow was hard, and despite trying to keep her eyes open they closed, causing her to drift into a sea of blackness. She was out cold.

Dominick turned in concern and knelt by her side. "Kali?" He called her name and then put his ear to her chest. She was still breathing. Before he could let out a sigh of relief, Caleb was on top of him.

"Get the fuck off of her!" Caleb shouted as his canines came out.

Dominick was in shock, he had seen Caleb in the sunlight and he hadn't given off any scent a vampire would. What he witnessed from Caleb went against everything he was taught. "What the fuck!" Dominick said as he grabbed Caleb by his shoulders and threw him to the ground so hard the dirt beneath them caved slightly inward. In turn, Caleb held on to Dominick, flipping him over his head just before he had hit the ground. Another patch of dirt was left with an indent.

Dominick and Caleb wrestled around on the ground, using massive strength to try and take each other out. Finally Dominick threw him against another tree. Caleb hit his head again and before he even opened his eyes, Dominick delivered a punch so hard one of Caleb's eyes swelled shut.

Caleb, using one eye, tried to defend himself, but Dominick was too strong and he was going to kill him, this he knew. Caleb looked at the ground to Mikayla, who was still passed out, and realizing she was now no longer a witness, he reached within himself, his heart on fire. The energy built in his hand, supplied from his heart as he tried to disengage himself from the punches being delivered to his body. Once he felt the energy full of power in his hand, he unleased it close range to Dominick's heart.

Dominick felt the burning of fire entering his chest and he let out an awful, beastly scream. Caleb used the opportunity to hit him again, letting his anger take over. With Dominick distracted by pain, Caleb used quick, hard and fast blows. Dominick almost couldn't feel the blows coming from Caleb, the fire in his chest was the only thing he could concentrate on. Again, Caleb zapped him one more time in the chest, burning him even further. Dominick screamed again in agony, in a voice neither beast nor man but somewhere in between and fell to his knees.

The scream was so loud that it awoke Mikayla. Her head was fuzzy, and for a moment she had forgotten where she was. It was night time and she could smell a creek nearby. Looking around it finally dawned upon her exactly where she was and what was happening. Her head hurt badly, it felt as if someone had driven a car right through her brain. Still dizzy, she watched in confusion as she saw Caleb standing over Dominick, who was on his knees with his head bent forward while his body swayed, holding some sort of round, white light in his hand. The light looked eerily familiar as she watched Caleb release the ball of energy into Dominick's chest.

"No!" She cried out, trying to get to Dominick, who was still attached to the stream of light coming from Caleb's hand. Dominick was no longer screaming in agony, his body looked as if it's soul had left ,leaving his body nothing more than a puppet.

"Stop it Caleb! CALEB STOP!" She shouted with a voice louder than she herself even recognized. Quickly she jumped to her feet, despite the pain shooting through her head.

Running towards Dominick, Mikayla noticed something about the look in Caleb's eyes. The color had changed, and just like Dominick, his canines seemed to have lengthened, however his face was slightly distorted as well. It was something about the skin underneath his eyes, it seemed to grow pale and veiny. She didn't have time to figure out what was really going on at that moment; instead she put the thoughts aside and focused only on getting to Dominick.

Caleb saw her and shamefully released Dominick. Mikayla made it over to Dominick just as his body hit the ground. "What did you do?" She screamed as she tried to asses Dominick's condition.

Before Caleb could manage to say anything, he felt a force of energy zap his chest. He looked up to find the girl from the street shooting energy balls at him from both of her hands faster than he had ever seen done before as she moved forward. Caleb was knocked backwards, she zapped him one more time. Now it was Caleb who was losing consciousness and he fell to the ground exhausted and feeling defeated as if he were ready to die.

Layla wanted to make sure he was down and held. She was getting ready to put a holding spell on him, just in case he came to before the rest of the pack and Marcus caught up, when she felt a burning blow to her back. She didn't have time to scream before hitting the ground with her eye's closed.

Mikayla looked around in horror. Caleb, Dominick, and some stranger she didn't know all laid around her with their eyes closed. She had no idea what to do first, but she knew she should call 911 and reached for her purse, but before she could even get to her purse to find she had again forgot her phone, she heard clapping. She was startled and looked up to see where it was coming from through the flood of tears drowning her eyes.

Out of nowhere three figures dropped from a really large tree not too far away. Mikayla swallowed in fear. She had a bad feeling in the pit of her stomach as she saw the three figures coming towards her.

"Nice show," the pale figure with dark hair wearing all black said as he came forward.

Mikayla knew now was not the time to speak.

The pale figure looked over at Dominick and closed his eyes as he took a long sniff of air in. When he opened them, Mikayla could see that like Caleb his canines had grown long and sharp as the skin underneath his eyes became pale, showing dark blue veins in an uneven pattern traveling downwards. Every hair on the back of her neck stood.

"Ah, the smell of death," he said, looking down at Dominick. Mikayla quickly turned her head to look down at Dominick. She could see his chest was still rising up and down, but it was very shallow.

"He's still breathing," Mikayla whispered in relief. Aidan heard her.

"Not for long. I can hear his heart beat and the blood in his body is starting to slow down. It's only a matter of an hour or less and you're friend here will be dead," Aidan said smiling.

Mikayla looked down at Dominick. The tears in her eyes flooded even more, spilling over onto her cheeks.

"Oh don't cry…I can help you," Aidan said with a grin.

"How?" Mikayla said, trying to steady her voice through a sob.

"Well let's just say you need to do something for me first," Aidan said.

"Help him, please!" Mikayla cried, not really wanting to play the game.

"I will, but you have to do as I say," Aidan said, no longer smiling.

"Anything, just help him," Mikayla said, sobbing and not caring what she would have to do as long as Dominick would live.

Aidan, Aiah, and Rory walked over to Mikayla, who was leaning over Dominick. Aidan knew it was only a matter of time before the others showed up. He didn't have much time to waste.

"You have certain abilities, this I know. Don't ask how I know, there isn't any time. But I need for you to reach into your center. Tap into your energy and give me the powers of a witch and then lift the curse off of me, giving me protection to walk amongst the daylight," Aidan said.

"You're crazy, I don't know how to do that!" She screamed, frustrated.

"His heart is slowing down… I don't even think he has an hour to live," Aidan said.

Mikayla was confused at how he knew that about her. She wanted to save Dominick, so she left that question out. "How do I do this?" She said, trying to steady her voice.

"Just as I said. Let the energy build up within you, when it feels full then from your heart you grant me the powers to walk amongst the daylight and the powers to manipulate the elements."

Mikayla thought it all sounded crazy, but she had no other option if Dominick was dying. She was willing to try anything, no matter how far-fetched it seemed. She closed her eyes and felt the energy swell inside of herself, and just as he had said it would, and as she did when she unlocked Dominick's bedroom door, she released the energy at the stranger, granting him what he wished for.

The energy was moving, slowly twisting and turning. Mikayla was shocked by the soft blue light that looked like fog traveling over towards the stranger.

Aidan watched as the blue fog traveled towards him. He gasped as the fog entered in through his nostrils, forcing his mouth to open. The slow moving fog changed pace and form. It was now a fast moving liquid stream flooding into Aidan's mouth. For a moment he lost his breath. The look of it was horrifying as Aiden's head was tilted up towards the sky and his arms pressed out to his sides as if he were standing in hurricane force winds. When the liquid was done moving through him he grinned, feeling the power shift within and quickly turned towards Rory, lifting him in the air without touching him. Aidan smiled. He knew there was no more time left to change Rory and Aiah. He knew he had to guide her through healing the wolf, that way she would be indebted. Little did she know she had the power without him, and he was going to use it as a means to trick her.

First he sealed off the area with his new powers, creating a forcefield around them. He began to laugh an evil snicker in excitement. Then he kneeled behind her, brushing her hair away from her neck. "You're going to have to trust me. I need to bleed you while you do this or it won't work," Aidan said, lying through his teeth.

Mikayla looked down at Dominick. His breathing became even shallower. Everything she had witnessed when she wasn't out cold had been overwhelming. She was completely confused at what was going on, but whatever it was, one thing was for sure; Dominick was quickly dying in her arms.

"If he dies then you won't be able to save him. You don't have much time to decide," Aidan said, grinning. It was the truth, she couldn't resurrect the dead, but she was the only one on the earth who had the power to stop the process of death. Nothing else would save Dominick. That part was true. Bleeding her was the lie. He just needed to drain her powers so she couldn't take back the powers she had given him.

Aiah and Rory were displeased they weren't yet granted their powers, but they knew Aidan wouldn't let them down. He would make sure they were turned as well, so they stood quietly behind.

Mikayla closed her eyes. "Fine," she said. "What do I do," she then asked with tears still streaming down her face.

"As soon as you feel me bite your neck, I want you to do the same thing with finding your energy, concentrating on life force. Once you feel it, you'll need to place your hands over his heart, releasing the energy into him slowly," he said as he tried to sound helpful.

Mikayla knew there was something wrong with this picture, but right now she had to do it for Dominick. She had to at least try, even if it meant she might be about to die in the process. Mikayla would gladly give her life for his. She could see Dominick was starting to fade fast. She tilted her head to the side, helping to expose her neck. At that moment, she was frightened and started to shake a little as she tried to center the energy which slept within.

Aidan leaned forward, admiring her neck and the way she smelled. He brushed her hair to the side again and held it there as he sank his teeth into the pulsating vein. The taste of her was amazing and filled him with an energy he had never experienced before. It was euphoric, forcing him to have to concentrate on not bleeding her entirely. He didn't know what would happen to his powers if she was killed, and he wasn't willing to take the chance if she died so would his powers.

Mikayla let out a painful whimper as his teeth broke her skin. It was painful at first, causing more tears to fill her eyes, but soon the pain subsided, flooding her with pleasure. She had to concentrate much harder on the energy within. Mikayla tried to focus on the pleasure as she tried to use it to help conjure up enough energy to release into Dominick. As the energy became full, it swelled within her and she knew she had enough of it to give to Dominick. Then she did as he had told her and placed her hands over his heart and let the energy release slowly.

Caleb started to stir. His head felt swollen and dizzy. He was confused by what had hit him. He slowly looked to the right of him and saw the girl from the street face down with her eyes closed, not too far from him. Then he remembered. Mikayla must have helped me, he thought to himself, momentarily happy she was still on his side. He sat up to see where she was at. A look of horror swept over his face as he saw where she was and who she was with and what he was doing. Caleb's teeth came out and before he was even up he threw an energy ball at Aidan, but it bounced off an invisible forcefield. Caleb was confused for a split second, until he realized how the shield must have been put up. "NO!" he shouted and jumped to his feet and moved quickly towards them.

"Mikayla, don't! Let the shield down, now! Even if it was him who put it up! Look at me! You have to get away from him," he yelled, approaching the force field, trying to break it down with energy zaps one right after the other.

Rory started laughing.

"Very clever, Caleb, she didn't put the shield up, Aidan did," Aiah said smugly, trying to taunt Caleb.

Caleb was horrified. He knew it almost as soon as his power ball had ricocheted off of it. It seemed as if Aidan had his own agenda and, at that moment, he understood without a doubt what it was. It was bad enough he was going to have to protect her from his own father, but this put a new twist on the situation. Caleb knew things were bad.

Mikayla could hear Caleb start to talk, but her energy was drained from healing Dominick and being bled. She wanted to tell him she had to save Dominick but she couldn't. Instead she collapsed forward on to Dominick as the last of the energy made its way into him.

Caleb watched as she dropped forward. "MIKAYLA!" He shouted as loud as he could. Looking up at Aidan, who had streams of Mikayla's blood dripping down the sides of his mouth, he tried to think quickly at something to bargain with to make Aiden release her. Aiden smiled at him as he licked the sides of his mouth and let out an "mmm..." letting Caleb know just how tasty she was.

"You should be so lucky that it is us who have her, Caleb, and not handing her over to the man who killed your parents," Aidan said, planting a seed he hoped would get Cyrus killed.

"What do you mean, who killed my parents?" Caleb shouted as his gut tightened as an image of Cyrus shot through his brain.

"Think about it, Caleb," Aidan said, further planting the seed as Mikayla's blood dripped off his chin, dropping on her back as she lay sprawled over Dominick's body.

"By the way, Caleb. Good job, we saw everything... I really think that she enjoyed it! That's great because now she will have something to compare me to..." Aiden smiled, trying to enrage Caleb further, hoping Caleb would use this anger to take care of Cyrus.

Caleb could smell Mikayla's blood. He let out an unearthly growl meant to kill as he loaded his energy full, now even more enraged, and started shooting faster, with even more force at the wall between him and Mikayla. Finally a hole was made in the shield.

Aidan looked up at Caleb a little worried and a bit amazed Caleb was able to put a hole in the invisible wall so soon. Aidan was afraid he would get in. Caleb just kept at it. Nothing was going to stop him from getting behind that barrier.

"Aiah, Rory, hang on to me!" Aidan said.

Rory and Aiah quickly moved and grabbed hold of Aidan, who was holding Mikayla. Aiden taunted Caleb one more time and licked the side of Mikayla's neck slowly, and then smiled looking Caleb in the eye. He then reached within himself and orbed all four of them out of there.

Caleb quickly tried to reach through the hole to grab Mikayla, but she was gone before he even had his hand inside. He screamed Mikayla's name as she disappeared before his eyes.

57

"NO! NO! Fuck! Shit!" He then said as he pounded his fists against the wall until it finally dissipated. Without the wall to hold up his fists, he fell forward onto his knees.

Lucio and Marcus could hear Caleb call out Mikayla's name as they came into the clearing. Lucio saw Dominick down and ran over towards him. Marcus saw Layla on the ground and ran towards her. He leaned down to listen to her heart beat. He found one and sighed with relief. Without saying a word he looked to Lucio. Lucio nodded to him Dominick also had a heartbeat.

Marcus got up and tackled Caleb, who was just getting up off of the ground.

"Where is she!" Marcus yelled as he gripped Caleb by the throat, holding him into the air, forcing Caleb's canines to come out. Marcus quickly let go. "What the fuck are you?" He then asked, stepping back.

Caleb was exhausted. He needed to find Mikayla and currently didn't have a clue of how to do that. "I'm…a…halfbreed…" Caleb said, exhaustedly.

"Who turned you?" Marcus asked, trying to figure out who he was associated with.

"I wasn't…turned. I told you…I am a half breed… I was born this way," Caleb said relaying the information easily due to his mind trying to figure out what just happened and what he needed to do.

Caleb was barely paying attention to the present scene ,or the people in it. All he could do was try to think about where Aiden would take her so he could orb there and get her back, but not before killing all three of them violently. His head was spinning and he felt hot all over as he tried to think.

Immediately Marcus understood what he was. He was completely uninformed of his existence. "Where the fuck is she?" Marcus repeated, deciding his other questions could wait until after Mikayla was safe.

"I don't know," Caleb said, trying to catch his breath and think.

Marcus came back in, grabbing him by the throat. "Where motherfucker?" He shouted.

Caleb zapped his hands to get Marcus to let go, but Marcus was on a mission and ignored the pain, only gripping tighter.

"I don't know! They took her!" Caleb shouted, still feeling exhausted, as if he didn't have any fight left. "I have to find her…" Caleb trailed off.

"Who are they?" Marcus, still gripping his throat, asked.

"Three warlocks that were made into vampires a really long time ago… Pure evil…" Caleb answered, exhausted and struggling for air.

"Who made them?" Marcus asked.

"Fuck you," Caleb said as he tried to find the will to move, now getting annoyed at this Dark Knights questioning. Caleb struggled for a moment to find his center. Quickly he let the energy build within and zapped Marcus again. This time he sent Marcus backwards, releasing the grip he had over Caleb's throat. Caleb knew he needed to orb out of there. Just as he started to orb, Marcus jumped at Caleb and grabbed hold of him, pulling his self into the orb.

"Mother fucker!" Caleb shouted as they hit the ground somewhere else in the forest. Marcus attaching himself in mid orb had thrown Caleb off, tossing them out of the orb and on to a mossy patch in the forest.

They wrestled around for a brief moment. "Stop! You need to get the fuck off me so I can find her!" Caleb then shouted.

Marcus backed off for a moment and looked at him, hoping he was ready to tell him where Mikayla was. "Are you ready to tell me then, you piece of shit?" Marcus said as he pulled himself up off the ground and onto his feet.

"Look man, you don't understand, I was trying to protect her. It isn't what you think," Caleb said, truthfully.

"Protect her? If you were trying to protect her then where is she?" Marcus shouted at him with anger fueling his voice.

"I don't know what happened. Something went wrong. You need to back off so I can find her. The more time I waste dicking around with you the less chance I will have at finding her alive," Caleb began to shout back in frustration.

"You're going to find her? I find that hard to believe. I am giving you one more chance to tell me!" Marcus warned him.

"Man, I told you. I am not the bad guy! I love her and I will spend the rest of eternity searching for her if that's what it takes. You are putting her in jeopardy right now, not me. If you want her dead then you are doing a great job at having a hand in it! Now fucking stop following me!" Caleb was starting to become angry.

Marcus had nothing left to say. He saw Caleb was sincere when he said he loved her, which only infuriated him further, and without warning shot a fast ball of energy towards Caleb, using both hands. Caleb quickly blocked the shots, sending them back towards Marcus. Marcus dove to the ground to avoid the fast fire coming his way. He rolled a couple of times, trying to keep his eyes fixed on Caleb.

Caleb took it as his opportunity to get away from Marcus so he could find Mikayla. Marcus looked at Caleb, ready to throw back another ball of energy as he stopped rolling, but with a blink of an eye, he was gone.

Marcus got to his knees, looked up into the sky, and screamed a sound so horrible the bats hiding within the trees all around fled from fear into the night sky.

The pack finally reached Lucio. Vince, Mikey, and Ricky helped Lucio pick Dominick up to take him back to the car. Tony picked up the very light Layla to follow them out of the forest. Marcus wasn't anywhere to be seen.

Mario, Ajay, and Rowan made it back to the condo. Ajay kept calling to Rowan, but she wasn't answering back. He had a bad feeling. He also tried to call to Marcus, but he was blocked. Ajay had a bad feeling.

Ajay followed them back into the condo. Mario took Rowan right into the bedroom. She had been half asleep on the way home and was still that way. He quickly undressed her, putting one of his t-shirts on her for pajamas. Rowan just mumbled a few things, she was feeling very drained. Mario just kept telling her to sleep. Once she was in bed, he pulled the covers over her and kissed her forehead and told her he loved her. Rowan said nothing, she was asleep as soon as her head had hit the pillow.

Mario came out of the bedroom to find Ajay sitting on the couch with a worried look on his face.

"What's the matter? I thought you were gonna meet up with your sister and Dom to help find my sister?" Mario asked, trying to read the look on Ajay's face.

"I can't reach her. I can't reach Marcus, either. I don't have a good feeling, man," Ajay said, having absolutely zero ideas at this point.

Mario's throat closed a bit and his stomach twisted. Please let my sister be all right, he said to himself as he closed his eyes. Please let everyone be all right, he added to his silent prayer.

"Well, you're the witch. What do we do now?" Mario asked, wanting to do something to help find his sister now Rowan was accounted for.

"We wait…" Ajay said, looking out of the French glass doors and into the darkened night time sky. He took a deep breath in and focused on the moon. "We wait…"